Electric Barracuda

Electric Barracuda

Tim Dorsey

An Imprint of HarperCollins*Publishers*

ELECTRIC BARRACUDA. Copyright © 2011 by Tim Dorsey. All rights reserved. Printed in the United States of America. No part of this book may be used or reproduced in any manner whatsoever without written permission except in the case of brief quotations embodied in critical articles and reviews. For information address HarperCollins Publishers, 10 East 53rd Street, New York, NY 10022.

HarperCollins books may be purchased for educational, business, or sales promotional use. For information please write: Special Markets Department, HarperCollins Publishers, 10 East 53rd Street, New York, NY 10022.

FIRST HARPERLUXE EDITION

HarperLuxe™ is a trademark of HarperCollins Publishers

Library of Congress Cataloging-in-Publication Data is available upon request.

ISBN: 978-0-06-201776-5

11 12 13 14 ID/OPM 10 9 8 7 6 5 4 3 2 1

For Nat

People are just as happy as they make
up their minds to be.

—ABRAHAM LINCOLN

Prologue

PRESENT

Orlando.

Tourism on steroids. Florida's mutant chromosome with mouse ears.

One of the newer attractions is an air-conditioned dome over a sprawling, man-made replica of the state's natural landscape.

They bulldozed nature to build it.

Outside the dome, a dragnet tightened.

An endless string of harsh, red brake lights stretched to the horizon. Evening traffic snarled on Interstate 4 through theme park country. An unmarked Crown Vic with police antennae whipped into the breakdown lane and sped past crawling minivans and station wagons. Its passenger-side tires slipped off the shoulder, kicking up a cloud.

A cell phone rang.

"Agent White here."

"We got him!" said Agent Lowe. "We finally got him!"

"Serge?"

"That's the man."

"Don't mess with me."

"I can't believe it either. After all this time."

"I'm more amazed he hadn't been nailed earlier. How many years? How many murders?"

"Dozens."

"Years or murders?"

"Take your pick."

"I still don't see how it's possible he could remain so active for so long, with nearly every agency in the state after him."

"It's Florida. He blended in—and had a lot of luck. But now it's finally run out."

"Who broke the case?"

"Agent Mahoney."

"Mahoney? That nut job?"

"Apparently he got better. How far away are you?"

"Twenty minutes. I'll be there in ten."

My name's Serge.

The LSD just kicked in.

I can tell because my legs are walking away. *Come back here!* Legs don't listen for crap.

This isn't my first trip. And I don't even do drugs.

My name's Serge.

Last time I accidentally got dosed by Lenny. This time Coleman.

And what am I doing in handcuffs? Have I been arrested? Dear God, they're taking me to jail! . . . Or maybe it's just this drug—fight the hallucination.

My name's Serge.

Damn you, Coleman! That boob must have gotten it in the onion dip again. And I can't resist potato chips. Ruffles. Wise. Lay's. Cheetos, Fritos, Doritos. Aren't snacks fucked up? . . . *Snack, snack, snack, snack* . . . What an unnegotiably aggressive sound. The Roman Empire invented snacks, right after the aqueducts. Irrigation flowed, food plentiful, people munching between meals in the city-states. They ate these little, sun-dried meaty things, highly distasteful and falling out of favor until olive oil. I just made all that up. The key to life is making shit up. Everyone does it or society would unravel, like, Gee, your hair looks great! Or: God told me you're wrong . . . Here come my legs—I'll try to grab them. Rats, too fast. Why do we even need snacks? More important, why do we need anything else? Do they make Bugles anymore? Bugles were *really* fucked up. When I was six, I'd bite the tips off and play "Taps," like I'm doing now, except I just have my fingers in front of my mouth with a tiny invisible bugle . . .

. . . People are staring. Act normal.

That's how I know it's LSD. People tend to stare. They also stare at me the rest of the time, and I've become humbly accustomed to the limelight. But currently they're staring from a picture in the newspaper on my lap. Some kind of country fair holding prize pig races to celebrate the local yam harvest. Now they're running around, yelling and pointing at me. They've got a bunch of torches and pitchforks! They're charging! Right off the page, right at my face! Here comes the first pitchfork in my eyes! Hold freak-out! Quick, close the newspaper! . . . Speaking of politics, what's happening to America? All vital signs spell collapse: unemployment, environment, national security, energy dependence, world respect, violent riots escalating into town hall meetings—our entire population completely polarized, half the country ready to kill the other half. And over what? For a week it was the Dixie Chicks. Things sure have changed. FDR tried to calm us: "Nothing to fear but fear itself." Now politicians encourage the jitters. Panic is the new patriotism. "Today's Threat Level: Duck!" But you don't even want to think of fear on an acid trip. *Fear, fear, fear, FEAR!* My body is decaying! I can feel it! I can hear it! I can smell it! And it smells like . . . liver treats. Who would have thought? I need gum. It's in that pocket and . . . Wait, what's this plastic tube? An empty prescription bottle? And it has my name on it.

My name is Serge.

The medication on the label is some serious stuff. That's weird. But what does this Byzantine puzzle mean? The Byzantines liked snacks, to go with their puzzles . . . It's slowly starting to come back— . . . Of course! Lenny didn't drug me back then—and Coleman didn't this time. I'm just out of pills. My brain must have finally rid itself of their mind-blunting effects. This rampaging, all-over-the-road psychotic nightmare is just my normal thought-party. Excellent.

I'm looking out a window. We're moving fast. Florida nightscape whizzing by. Lights blink at an intersection. A screaming comes across the sky. It's some kind of loud horn. We're going to crash! Flames soon lapping my flesh! . . . Another illusion. Resist. Close your eyes, think positive thoughts . . . A song. It's pretty, I'm smiling and singing along in my head: "What's so funny about peace, love and understanding?" Exactly: I'm totally re-dedicating my life to getting along with everyone. But who wrote that marvelous tune? Elvis Costello? I hate that fuck . . .

Ouch.

What's this hurting my wrist? A handcuff again? Sure looks real. Wait, it *is* real. But where did it come from? Maybe this guy sitting next to me knows . . . Excuse me, sir . . . Holy cripes, it's Agent Mahoney! Now I get it—I've finally been captured. And that horn is a train whistle. Mahoney's taking me somewhere on a choo-choo, probably the Big House, just like in *The Fugitive*. I know: I'll use this unfortunate downtime to pretend I'm in that TV show. "Serge A. Storms . . . A man wrongly convicted (wink) . . ." We're coming around a bend. I see lights ahead. Another crossing gate. But what's that idiot in the pickup truck doing on the tracks? The horn's blaring nonstop, steel grinding, sparks showering. We *are* going to crash! Hang on! . . .

. . . How long have I been unconscious? Whoa, my head, my wrist . . . The handcuffs broke! I'm free! The train's on its side, so I'll just climb out the shattered window that's up on the ceiling . . . Therrrrrre we go. Trot along the top of the car, leap off the side, tumble down this ditch—*ow, ooo, ow, ooo, ow*—nothing to it, and that's basically how you escape. Now I just walk to the nearest truck stop, hitch an eighteen-wheeler to Texarkana, reinvent myself as an audience-favorite horseshoe champion who's a committed pacifist yet expert in jujitsu and ragtime piano and is finally pushed too far when the bank forecloses on a sixth-generation dairy farm and hires goons from the traveling midway to menace a soft-spoken widow who is the only person in town unaware of her own smoldering sexuality . . . Oops, spoke too soon. There's a flashlight in the distance. A voice. Someone's coming! Quick! To the bottom of the ditch! Cover yourself with branches and trash!

"Serge!"

A flashlight swept the bottom of a ditch.

"Serge, where are you? Yell if you can hear me."

A head poked up from a pile of ripped-open garbage bags. "Coleman?"

The flashlight beam hit a face. "Serge, what are you doing at the bottom of that ditch with rotten food all over your head?"

"Isn't that what I usually ask you?"

"Everything okay?"

"Couldn't be better." Serge hopped up and brushed himself off. "I just escaped."

"Escaped?"

"It was touch and go, but I slipped Mahoney's grasp again."

"Mahoney?"

Serge pointed. "The big train derailment—...
where'd the wreck go?"

Coleman turned around and looked at the dark side
of a building. "Nothing but our motel."

Serge squinted at his sidekick. "What's going on?"

"Beats me." Coleman clicked off the flashlight. "We
were back in our room watching an old rerun of *The
Fugitive*, and during the train crash in the opening cred-
its, you ran out the door yelling, 'I'm free! I'm free.'"

Serge slowly smiled and nodded with understanding. "I must have gone into a fugue state."

"What's that?"

"Hard to explain." Serge climbed the muddy embankment. "But remember that time you were really ripped on
peyote and passed out in that motel bed where the sheets
were tucked in super tight, and somehow you got turned
around in your sleep so your head was trapped at the foot
of the bed, and you woke up trying to fight your way out,
screaming that bugs had encased you in a cocoon, and
you were turning into a giant winged insect?"

"That wasn't a cocoon?"

"Your variation on the fugue state."

"I get it now."

Serge began walking back to the motel. "Think *The
Fugitive* is still on?"

"Yeah, you've just been gone a few minutes."

"Let's watch the rest. Maybe they'll catch the one-armed man."

They went back inside their room as a convoy of unmarked cars cut their headlights and quietly rolled into the parking lot of the budget motel.

Coleman glanced toward a banging sound from the closet. "What about the guy you're keeping tied up in there?"

"Oh," said Serge, looking up from the TV. "Almost forgot about him."

A Crown Vic with blackwall tires arrived at the motel. Agent White rushed over to Agent Lowe.

"Where's Serge?"

"Get down!" Lowe whispered. "He might see you."

White stared curiously at his colleague, crouched behind a car, dressed completely in black, pulling a black hood over his head.

"What the hell's going on?" asked White. "I thought you said on the phone you had Serge."

"We do." Lowe pointed over the trunk of the car. "He's in that last room."

White's head sagged. "When you say you have someone, that means in custody. Back of a squad car. Maybe even handcuffed."

"Not all the time."

"Yes, all the time."

"He's just as good as in custody." Lowe fitted night-vision goggles over his eyes. "We've got him pinned. See?" He gestured to his left at the black-clothed SWAT team squatting next to him. "Now, will you get down before he sees you?"

White stayed standing with hands on hips, watching his partner apply black face paint. "You're still hung up about not making the SWAT team?"

Lowe's goggles remained fixed on the motel room. "I'll make it the next round of tests. I was *this* close."

"But you still can't do a chin-up. And you collapsed again during the mile run. They had to use a stretcher."

"I've been working out. Huge progress on chin-ups."

"How many?"

"I bought a chin-up bar."

Something nagged at White. "The parking lot . . ." He looked around. ". . . The entire block. Why is it so dark?"

"Had the power company cut all outside lights." Lowe removed the goggles and pulled a black ski mask down over his painted face. "For our ninja strike." He turned to the nearest SWAT member and gave him a spirited thumbs-up. "Ready to rumble?"

"Just stay out of our way, limp-dick, and don't fuck this up."

Lowe smiled at White. "That's how SWAT brothers talk."

Out of the darkness, a human form materialized on the far side of the parking lot, casually walking toward them.

"Jesus!" Lowe whispered. "He's going to ruin everything."

The form took shape, wearing a tweed jacket and rumpled fedora. A toothpick wiggled in his teeth. His necktie had a pattern of vintage Las Vegas casino signs. He walked around behind the car.

White nodded in recognition. "Mahoney."

Mahoney tossed the toothpick over his shoulder. "It's my collar. I peeled the banana."

"No argument," said White. "But how'd you find him?"

"Serge has been slipping for years." Mahoney dramatically fit a fresh toothpick in his mouth and stared back at the last motel room, where the outline of a lampshade glowed behind a moth-worn curtain. "Screwed the pooch and registered under his own moniker."

"So why don't we take him?" said White. "What are we waiting out here for?"

Mahoney glanced down at Lowe. "Ask the Green Hornet."

A series of ripping sounds. Lowe tested various empty Velcro pockets on his tactical jacket designed to hold tactical equipment he wasn't authorized to carry. "We're waiting for the lamp to go out so he'll be more off guard during our lightning breach with flash-bang grenades." He produced a waterproof, spiral-bound book from a zippered pocket. "It's in the manual."

White rolled his eyes.

They waited.

The lamp stayed on.

Next to a lamp sat a snowy TV set. Serge slapped the side. A black-and-white episode of *The Fugitive* came into focus. "This is the one where he's shot by police and takes refuge in an orphanage at a Navajo reservation outside Puma . . ."

Muted screams from next to the bed.

"Do you mind?" said Serge. "I'm trying to watch this."

The desperation grew louder.

Serge sighed. "Everyone wants attention." He got up and walked over. "Okay, you ruined my show. Now what's the issue?"

The bound and gagged hostage looked up from his chair with pleading eyes.

Coleman killed a Schlitz and crumpled the can. "So who is this guy anyway?"

"Ever see the TV show *To Catch a Predator?*"

"Yeah."

"I caught one."

"Where?"

"At the playground. He was lurking in his car with porn."

"What were you doing at the playground?"

"Just driving by this time. I used to love playgrounds, but jeez, I haven't played in one in at least, what? Three months?"

"Why not?"

"If you're an adult without a kid, it draws looks, even if I'm just going for the Guinness record on the monkey bars. And parents hustle their tots away every single time I stand on top of the jungle gym, beating my chest and roaring like a silver-back gorilla, even though I'm only trying to show them how it's done."

"They don't appreciate it?"

"You'd think I was a red-ass baboon."

"What about the teeter-totter?"

"One *is* the loneliest number."

Coleman stubbed out a roach. "Too bad."

"It's all right," said Serge. "We're living in new times. Parents are understandably nervous these days.

I've decided to stay away from the swing sets and not to add to their anxiety over, well, guys like this."

"How'd you catch him?"

"Child's play. He was too engrossed, and I flanked the car on foot—at his driver's window before he knew it. First he thought I was an undercover cop and tried to hide the porn, but I said I was just a concerned citizen and wanted to have a little chat, emphasizing community fabric and maybe direct him to some treatment programs. You know, real polite and reasonable like I usually am."

"You're always caring."

"But sometimes it turns ugly anyway. He's a pretty big dude, as you can see. Jumped out his car and knocked me down. No biggie, I've been knocked down before. I get up and explain he hasn't committed a crime yet—there's still time to get help, but he just knocks me down again."

"And that's when you captured him?"

"No, I thought of what my psychiatrist said and stayed calm, because this wasn't about me; it was for the children. I kept getting up, over and over, doing my best to win the heart and mind, but he'd just slam me to the ground again. After a while, I'm brushing dirt out of my hair and thinking: This really isn't a conversation."

"And that's when you jumped him?"

"Almost there. When he saw he couldn't rattle me, he went for my hot button, pointing back at all the giggling, running kids and . . ."—Serge momentarily closed his eyes— ". . . I can't bear to repeat what he said, but certain threats were made. He yelled that because of me, he was now *definitely* going to do all these horrible things, just out of spite."

"That isn't nice."

"Intimidate me all you want, but when you bring kids into it, a sequence of Serge's pre-determined neighborhood-defense protocols are triggered. The only part I regret is that the families had to see it and fled again."

"Because you were fighting?"

"No, because I stuffed him in my trunk. Even if someone clearly deserves to be locked in my trunk, the general public still gives off this vibe they're a little uncomfortable."

Serge unzipped a small duffel bag on the nightstand. The hostage tried screaming under the duct tape across his face.

Coleman found something on the floor, smelled it and put it in his mouth. "What are you going to do with him?"

Serge turned to the hostage. "Would you like to know, too?"

The Fugitive played on in the background.

Terrified eyes grew wider.

". . . *So, stranger, what brings you to these parts?* . . ."

Serge dumped the duffel's contents on the bed. "You know those frowned-upon CIA interrogation techniques, like waterboarding? Except I don't have a board. But I have plenty of water! They say people start talking almost immediately . . ." He quickly ripped the tape off his captive's mouth.

The man yelled briefly at the sting, then babbled nonstop. "I swear I won't do anything I said! I was just messing with your mind! You have to believe me! I'll change!"

Serge smiled. "I know you will."

The tape went back, and Serge returned to work.

"Yuck," said Coleman, removing the item from his mouth and throwing it in the wastebasket.

Serge ripped cellophane off a spooled package. "What was that?"

"I think a mothball."

"When did you suspect?"

"When I saw it on the floor."

Serge unrolled the package. "And you still put it in your mouth?"

Coleman shrugged. "I could be missing out."

Serge clicked open a box cutter.

Coleman leaned closer. "What's that?"

"Observe." Serge held up a strip of airy gauze, oozing with mucoid slime. He stepped forward and placed the cool, moist ribbon on the captive's forehead. "Very thin, soothing, quite flimsy. A child could tear it apart. No possible way to harm anyone, right? So how can I possibly teach you a lesson with this?"

"How can you?" asked Coleman.

"Know my passion for all things Home Depot?"

"Well established."

Serge began unwinding the roll of wet gauze. "I recently learned something interesting about plumbing repair. Now grab those scissors to cut off his shirt while I fill my squirt pistol . . ."

. . . Outside the room, heavy traffic wasted gas as the car sprinted between red lights at every block. They were in Kissimmee, just below Orlando. Highway 192 to be exact, otherwise known as Irlo Bronson, the budget tourist strip on the east side of Interstate 4 from Disney World, where families who couldn't plunk down three hundred a night at the Grand Floridian commuted to the Magic Kingdom from ten miles of economy motels, where cabaret signs flashed $39.95 and FREE HBO. In between: mini-golf, go-carts, swimsuit outlets, and all-you-can-eat buffet barns filled with people shaped like upside-down lightbulbs.

As the road continued east—and the drive back to Disney lengthened—prices cascaded downhill where the highway took a gooseneck jog south toward Old Town. Bottom-barrel room rates drew an increasing clientele that wasn't tourists, or at least not the species seeking chamber-of-commerce-approved fun: a high-mileage, tumbleweed crowd anchoring the short tail of the left-expectancy bell curve. Serge's World. With their growing, undesirable number, motel deeds changed hands, and the highway began seeing stark buildings that were the recognizable shells of recognizable hospitality chains, which now had unrecognizable names on temporary banners. Parking lots filled with rusty shopping carts, and shirtless guests sat outside rooms on milk crates, drinking malt liquor with purposeful gazes that suggested this was still too much achievement.

Nearby:

No trace of the historic Big Bamboo Lounge, leveled and paved for retail space.

Near that:

A SWAT team monitored a lamp in a window. The parking lot was empty except for a sleek black car at the other end. With all the streetlights off, nobody had noticed it before, but someone was sitting in the driver's seat.

"How long has *he* been there?" asked White.

"Who?"

The agent pointed. "Beemer."

"Not sure," said Lowe. "Car was already there when we arrived. I think."

"Some surveillance work."

Lowe raised his night goggles toward the vehicle. "Looks like he's got some kind of camera with a long lens. Who can he be?"

Mahoney replaced his toothpick with a wooden matchstick. "Smart money's a gumshoe."

"What?"

"Dick, peeper, shamus, sleuth, whore hound, private eye."

The man in the Beemer set his camera on the passenger seat and got out of the car. Tall, trim, brown leather jacket. He took a step toward the last motel room . . .

"Whoa." Lowe lost his squat-balance and banged against a fender.

The Beemer's driver noticed the SWAT team for the first time, then pretended not to. He leaned against his car, lighting a cigarette in a theatrical display of no intentions. Headlights hit his face.

A Cadillac Eldorado pulled into a parking slot five spaces down.

White shook his head. "Now who the hell's *that*?"

Mahoney dabbed humidity off his forehead with a strip-club cocktail napkin. "The Mystery Man."

"Mystery Man?" said White.

"There's always a Mystery Man."

"What's he do?"

"Reveals himself later."

Another car pulled into the lot, this one with headlights already off. It parked halfway between the other vehicles and the SWAT team. A woman behind the wheel of a turquoise T-Bird.

"Lowe," said White. "What did you do, call a convention?"

Without turning her head, the T-Bird woman looked sideways toward the Mystery Man, whose eyes darted between the woman and the private eye, who watched them both and glanced at the SWAT team, which rotated surveillance among all three cars and the lamp in the window . . .

Serge sat at the motel room's desk. Combed hair still wet from a shower. Lightweight tropical shirt with pineapples. Loaded .45 next to the lamp. Coffee mug. The desk had an ashtray under one of its legs to stop a wobble.

Clattering keyboard.

Coleman pulled up a chair. "Typing on your new laptop?"

"Well, not *mine*. But same difference."

"What are you writing?"

"A rap song."

"Why are you writing a rap song?"

"For my new website." *Tap, tap, tap.* "If I want my specialty Florida tours to go global, I'll need the hip-hop vote."

"What kind of new website?"

"Remember the old one I launched after visiting that Lynyrd Skynyrd bar in Jacksonville?"

"Yeah, you had to start your own because the other sites didn't like your reports telling tourists which hookers to trust . . ."

". . . And how to take evasive, controlled-spin maneuvers during bump-and-jump carjackings."

"The people need to know," said Coleman, pointing a joint for emphasis.

Serge tapped keys rapidly. "That's why I'm taking it to the next level."

"But, Serge, how is that even possible?"

"I'm adding theme vacations."

"Like theme parks."

"Except without the parks."

"I don't understand."

"Florida *is* a theme park," said Serge. "And the theme is weirdness."

"So that's what's going on out there."

"My first theme vacation: the 'tourist fugitive.' You come down here and pretend to be on the lam."

"Where'd you get the idea?"

"Schwarzenegger's movie *Total Recall.*" Serge uploaded a digital photo. "Science-fiction thriller in the next century, where Arnold takes a vacation to Mars, and the travel agency gives him the option of just a regular trip or a theme. And the theme he chooses is secret agent."

Painful moans and panting from behind. Coleman turned around. "I think he's unhappy."

"I love chemical reactions." More typing. "Especially counter-intuitive ones. Now pay attention."

Coleman faced the screen again.

"Florida is Fugitive Central," said Serge. "A single crackdown in 2008 called Operation Orange Crush netted two thousand five hundred outlaws, which conservatively extrapolates to at least a hundred thousand more left at large. That's one for every three neighborhood blocks, and I like to drive around, trying to guess which one and question them."

"What do they say?"

"Most just run off, which means I'm guessing right."

"Why do so many fugitives come here?" asked Coleman.

"We've got everything a murderous desperado could want: great weather, cool drinks, a million trailer parks, plus pharmacies and bank branches on every corner. Those qualities also attract retirees, often to the same place, in a naturally occurring sitcom."

The desk wobbled; Serge's foot scooted the ashtray back under the leg.

"What are those pictures?"

Serge scrolled down the laptop screen. "A mug shot rogues' gallery of Florida fugitives. Ma Barker, Bundy, Cunanan, Wuornos and so many lesser maniacs they don't even make the fine print."

"Why not?"

"Florida's the perfect camouflage," said Serge. "Up in Middle America, even one of our low-profile whack jobs would stick out like Pamela Anderson bronco-riding a UFO. A minimum of fifty calls to the cops. But down here we're so over-saturated with hard-core street freaks that everyone energetically ignores them. We don't *want* to notice and report each strangeness flare-up, or we'd totally cease to be able to run errands."

"I saw a guy this morning eating ants," said Coleman. "Big red ones, just squashing them with his thumb on the sidewalk."

Serge coded up a Web link. "The public will never stop thanking me for this vacation."

Coleman pointed. "What's that?"

"Aerial view of the eastern Kissimmee strip. My first fugitive stop."

"But why would regular people want to pretend to be on the run in the first place?"

"Because it's the best way to experience the finest parts of our state, which is the underbelly. They'll naturally resist at first, but once people are forced to taste our underbelly, they won't be able to get enough."

"Underbelly's good?"

"The waiting lines are shorter," said Serge. "Second, it forces you off the tourist-brochure grid and into the woodwork, where all the best shit is. Third, hiding out is a blast—think of all the chuckles we've had in seedy motel rooms."

Coleman looked back at the moaning hostage. "I see what you mean."

"Wish he'd pipe down."

"I don't think he can help it."

"Because he's one of those worrying types: *Oooo, look at me. I'm all tied up. This crazy guy's going to do something bad.* They don't realize how uneasy they make everybody around them with that kind of victim mentality." Serge clicked open some text on his laptop.

"On the other hand, he's the perfect audience to test out my new rap song."

"You finished it?"

"The chorus is two-part harmony, so I'll need your help." Serge pulled up lyrics on the computer screen. Coleman read the song. "Where are my lines?"

"After I sing each verse, we alternate. I marked our respective parts with an *S* and a *C* in parentheses."

"Which am I?"

"*C*, for cogent."

Serge found an audio file in the computer and killed the equalizer on the vocals, creating a karaoke version. The music started.

"What's that?" asked Coleman.

"Flo-Rida."

"Who?"

"Our homegrown favorite-son rap hero. Even has a map of the state tattooed like a beast on his back."

The tempo picked up. Serge cranked the volume. He grinned at the gagged hostage. "I think you'll love this, but give me the honest truth. Don't be swayed by the ropes and duct tape."

Coleman finished reading the lyrics. "I think I'm ready."

Serge cleared his throat. "From the top . . ."

The music blared, and the pair began lunging toward the captive with gang-style hand gestures.

I'm Captain Florida, the state history pimp
Gatherin' more data than a DEA blimp
West Palm, Tampa Bay, Miami-Dade
Cruisin' the coasts till Johnny Vegas gets laid

Developer ho's, and the politician bitches
Smackin' 'em down, while I'm takin' lots of
    pictures
Hurricanes, sinkholes, natural disaster
'Scuse me while I kick back, with my View-Master

(S:) I'm Captain Florida, obscure facts are all legit
(C:) I'm Coleman, the sidekick, with a big bong hit

(S:) I'm Captain Florida, staying literate
(C:) Coleman sees a book and says, "Fuck that shit"

Ain't never been caught, slippin' nooses down
    the Keys
Got more buoyancy than Elián González
Knockin' off the parasites, and takin' all their
    moola
Recruiting my apostles for the Church of Don Shula

I'm an old-school gangster with a psycho ex-wife
   Molly
Packin' Glocks, a shotgun and my 7-Eleven coffee
Trippin' the theme parks, the malls, the time-shares
Bustin' my rhymes through all the red-tide scares

(S:) I'm the surge in the storms, don't believe the
hype
(C:) I'm his stoned number two, where'd I put my
hash pipe?

(S:) Florida, no appointments and a tank of gas
(C:) Tequila, no employment and a bag of grass

Think you've seen it all? I beg to differ
Mosquitoes like bats and a peg-leg stripper
The scammers, the schemers, the real estate liars
Birthday-party clowns in a meth-lab fire

But dig us, don't diss us, pay a visit, don't be late
And statistics always lie, so ignore the murder rate
Beaches, palm trees and golfing is our curse
Our residents won't bite, but a few will shoot first

Everglades, orange groves, alligators, Buffett
Scarface, Hemingway, an Andrew Jackson to suck it

Solarcaine, Rogaine, eight balls of cocaine
See the hall of fame for the criminally insane

Artifacts, folklore, roadside attractions
Crackers, Haitians, Cuban-exile factions
The early-bird specials, drivin' like molasses
Condo-meeting fistfights in cataract glasses

(S:) I'm the native tourist, with the rants that can't
be beat
(C:) Serge, I think I put my shoes on the wrong feet

(S:) A stack of old postcards in another dingy
room
(C:) A cold Bud forty and a magic mushroom

Can't stop, turnpike, keep ridin' like the wind
Gotta make a detour for a souvenir pin
But if you like to litter, you're just liable to get hurt
Do ya like the MAC-10 under my tropical shirt?

I just keep meeting jerks, I'm a human land-filler
But it's totally unfair, this term "serial killer"
The police never rest, always breakin' in my pad
But sunshine is my bling, and I'm hangin' like a
    chad

(S:) Serge has got to roll and drop the mike on this rap . . .

(C:) Coleman's climbin' in the tub, to take a little nap . . .

(S:) . . . Disappearin' in the swamp—and goin' tangent, *tangent, tangent* . . .

(C:) He's goin' tangent, *tangent* . . .

(Fade-out)

(S:) I'm goin' tangent, *tangent* . . .

(C:) Fuck goin' platinum, he's goin' tangent, *tangent* . . .

(S:) . . . Wikipedia all up and down your ass . . .

(C:) Wikity-Wikity-Wikity . . .

In a dark motel parking lot, a T-Bird's convertible roof began to retract. The SWAT team's surveillance rotation stopped, all night goggles on the sports car.

"Good Jesus," said one of the commandos. "I'm in love."

The rag-top finished tucking itself behind the backseat, providing an unobstructed view of a smokin'-hot babe with curly, fiery red hair. She looked up in her mirror, sensually applying equally red lipstick.

"I could watch her do that all day," said Lowe.

"Pardon me," said White. "The room?"

"Right." Lowe turned. "Hey look, the lamp just went out."

"So we move now?"

"No." Lowe tapped a page in the spiral-bound manual. "Have to wait for him to get drowsy." He stowed the book in a black tote bag with countless pockets and clasps and snap rings.

"What's that?" asked White.

"My SWAT team bag."

"You're not on the team."

"Got it at a police supply store."

"The ones that sell stuff to people who aren't police?"

"Here's where my Taser will go, and scrambled telephone, gas mask, parachute flares, bio-warfare antidote syringes, non-electrostatic knee pads for bomb defusing, flexible under-the-door fiber-optic video cam . . ."

"Why are you lugging it around if you don't have that stuff yet?"

Lowe pulled out a sandwich. "Lunch."

The SWAT team signaled it was go-time. They choreographed a series of silent hand signals, raised black entry shields and moved out with invisible stealth.

Suddenly a pounding noise from up the street. Growing louder.

"What the hell's that?" said White.

"Sounds like Kiss."

A giant semi-tractor-trailer raced toward the motel, its roof fringed with blaring megaphones.

"... I ... want to rock-and-roll all night! ..."

The truck whipped into the parking lot, followed by an air-conditioned tour bus.

White clenched his eyes and smacked his forehead. "Not him!"

Spotlights along the semi's side illuminated a mural of a gigantic, snarling canine above a list of network air times.

The truck screeched to a halt in front of the last motel room. People from the motor coach jumped out with shoulder-mounted cameras, others flooded the parking lot with TV lights.

In quick succession, rock-concert flash pots exploded from the semi's roof, its rear doors flew open and a gleaming motorcycle sailed out the back, flying fifty feet with special tubes shooting fire from the mufflers. It landed with a jarring bounce, made a skidding U-turn and stopped. The bike was a massive chopper with extended chrome forks and a snarling logo on its teardrop gas tank that matched the semi's mural. Lying far back in the saddle was a muscle-rippled, rawhide-faced man with long, peroxide blond hair that fell down across an open leather vest and hairy chest. From his shoulders flapped a giant, American-flag super-hero cape. Standing on each side were rows of buxom babes in star-spangled bikinis, combat boots and dog collars. The cycle remained stationary, its rider gunning the engine for the cameras.

A SWAT member stood up in what was now practically daylight. "Look! It's the Doberman!"

Another stood. "I love his show!"

A third pointed at the dog-collar women. "And he brought the Litter!"

White leaned against the side of the Crown Vic and folded his arms. "Change of plans. Let's see how the element of surprise works."

"... I ... want to rock-and-roll all night! ..."

And with a salute into the cameras, the celebrity bounty hunter opened his throttle wide, popped a wheelie and squealed across the parking lot.

"Now that's a real man," said Lowe.

The Doberman raced even faster, still balanced on his back tire, preparing to crash through the motel door. Except he misjudged by a half foot and hit the wall. The bike flipped, catapulting him into the bushes. Cameras and lights raced toward thick shrubbery with nothing but cowboy boots sticking out the top.

The dog-collar women pulled him from the hedge and steadied him on woozy legs.

"Where am I?"

A woman on each side raised his fists high in the air like a winning prizefighter. The rest of the Litter hopped up and down and clapped. "The Doberman lives! He was willing to lay down his life for American justice! . . ."

Agent White lowered his head again and took another deep breath. Then he nonchalantly walked across the parking lot toward the last motel room.

Coleman ran to the window. "What the hell is all that noise?"

Serge continued typing. "See anything?"

"Looks like they're filming *The Doberman*," said Coleman, firing up a joint. "That show rocks, especially the Litter!"

"What are they doing?"

"I don't know, but there's like a million people right outside . . ."

RIGHT OUTSIDE . . .

Agent White stepped over a broken piece of motorcycle and knocked on the last motel room.

The door opened. "Yes? . . ."

The SWAT team pounced.

Coleman slid the curtains wider. "Serge! Come quick! Across the street! They're arresting our wino friend, Snapper-Head Willie!"

Serge joined Coleman at the window. "I don't see him."

"That big pile of SWAT guys," said Coleman. "I'd hate to be on the bottom."

"I'm shocked," said Serge. "A pile that big means Snapper-Head was into some serious shit. If I'd have known, I never would have let him stay in our other motel room. But I figured since we weren't using it, why not give back to the community?"

"Why *do* we have another motel room?" asked Coleman.

"Just posted the reason on my new website," said Serge. "Fugitive Rule Number One: Always have an 'Out.'"

"What's an 'Out'?"

"What our government never has: exit strategy." Serge watched the SWAT team begin to unpile. "A fugitive should never go anywhere unless he knows a back way out. And it doesn't have to be literal, like a door. It can be a diversionary tactic, psychological ruse, political unrest, crowd-mystifying card tricks or big-tent sale extravaganza."

"What's our 'Out' this time?"

"I registered a decoy room across the street in my own name. Then I got this other room over here with false ID, so I'd have full view for advance warning in case heat's on the way."

"You mean the people over there are actually after us?"

"Not a chance," said Serge. "I just got the decoy motel for authenticity in my website report. Otherwise this is all a bunch of fucking around. And I'm sure we're not the real target because I've taken every precaution, covering my tracks by zigzagging across Florida on a variety of roads and mental states."

"Then what's going on out there?"

"A character flaw in Snapper-Head. Probably chopped someone up and distributed the pieces in trash cans around the Norway pavilion at Epcot."

They watched the SWAT team lift handcuffed Willie to his feet.

Coleman shook with the heebie-jeebies. "It's scary to think we were talking to someone so unstable."

"That's the thing about Florida," said Serge, standing in front of his whimpering hostage. "You never know when the guy next to you is a ticking bomb."

Agent White stuck a tiny key in the handcuffs and popped them open. "Sorry about that."

Snapper-Head rubbed his wrists. "Jesus, was it absolutely necessary for all of you to pile on top of me like that?"

Lowe held up the spiral-bound manual.

Behind them at a strip mall, Mahoney dialed an ever-dwindling number of pay phones.

White opened his wallet and handed Willie a ten-spot. "Get something to eat."

"Beverage?"

White gave him a lawsuit-conscious glance and pulled out another five.

Mahoney returned. "Just mumbled on the blower. Our mark had a decoy room."

"Gee, you think?" said White.

Mahoney opened a matchbook from a billiard hall that ran a crooked sports parlor. "Scored fresh digits on the flop twenty."

"What?"

"Got the location and number of Serge's real motel room."

"You sure about that?"

"Bet your pecker."

"Nicely put." White turned to the SWAT team, milling and eating fast food in the parking lot. "Okay, everyone, listen up. We just got the address of the real motel room. Let's roll."

Half-drunk milk shakes hit the ground. Sedans peeled out and raced east on Highway 192, followed by a tactical van, convertible T-Bird, yellow Cadillac Eldorado, black Beemer and a music-blaring semi-trailer.

Across the street, two people watched the departing motorcade from a slit in motel curtains.

"Look at all those people," said Coleman.

"They got a whole dime novel." Serge loaded his pistol. "Coppers, bounty hunter, private eye, femme fatale and the Mystery Man."

"Who's that other guy?" asked Coleman.

"Which one?"

"The dude yelling at the sky, swinging a *Star Wars* lightsaber and peeing on the sidewalk."

"Just a normal person. He's not involved."

The Fugitive ended.

Horrible sounds of anguish and thrashing from the hostage chair.

". . . *A Quinn Martin Production* . . ."

Serge closed the laptop. "Our new friend's going to be a distraction from here on out." He stood and tucked the computer under his arm. "Plus, this is the point where he probably wants his privacy. We'll continue our summit in the bar."

"Bar? Now you're talking."

"Grab whatever you need because we're not coming back."

"Why?" asked Coleman.

"I just decided a second ago," said Serge. "Fugitive Rule Number Two: Always suddenly depart when nobody expects it, especially yourself. To prevent establishing patterns for police to track, we must behave deliberately erratic and question the prevailing wisdom on planetary physics, papal infallibility and sleep-boners. Keeps the mind sharp."

It wasn't a lengthy packing process. Serge had proclaimed that for this leg of the tour, luggage needed to be light and versatile since they'd be hopping modes of transportation. "Fugitive Tip Number Seven: Match your personality with the ideal backpack for outstanding warrants."

Serge's bag was a high-capacity, K2 base-camp mountain-climbing combo with compression bands and slots for ice hammers. Coleman's was much smaller with a teddy bear's head on top.

Once the bags were full, they slipped arms through padded straps and walked up the street to another motel.

Serge strolled through the lobby.

He pulled up short in the lounge entrance. Coleman crashed into him from behind.

"Ow"—rubbing his nose—"why'd you do that?"

"Dig!" said Serge.

"I already dig. You had me at 'bar.'"

"No, I mean dig, it's the Nu Bamboo! I have to stop and marvel each time I enter, because when history is lost, it's usually forever. But not at the Nu Bamboo!"

Serge marched to his regular stool at the bar, where a bottle of water appeared without asking.

"Thanks, Patty." He set his backpack on the floor and opened the laptop on the counter.

Coleman hopped on the next stool and raised a finger: "Bourbon." He glanced around with an odd feeling. "This joint looks familiar, but I can't quite place it."

"Because it used to be across the street."

"They moved the building?"

"Just the majesty. Remember the Big Bamboo Lounge, where we went after my grandfather's funeral?"

"Definitely." Coleman's drink arrived. "That tiny, dark place with all kinds of shit tacked up like a souvenir cave."

"Heaven on earth." Serge took a long pull of water. "Back in the early days, the original Bamboo was the only place for miles, this little hut back in the weeds surrounded by cow pastures to the horizon in all directions. Disney wasn't operating yet, just under construction, and after a day of drywalling Cinderella's Castle, workers descended on the watering hole, beginning the tradition of plastering the place with name tags and other theme park keepsakes. Then the Magic Kingdom opened and the torch was passed to other employees who needed a stiff drink after wearing Pluto and Bashful costumes all day. Locals affectionately called her 'The Boo.' "

Coleman knocked back his whiskey. "Like if Disney World had a dive?"

"I wish." Serge opened a brimming computer file of previously taken photos. "The Bamboo's founder died, and its future became a question mark. Then it closed—at least temporarily—while the faithful launched a campaign to save the landmark. But before they could, she was gutted by fire, which officials suspect was accidentally set by homeless squatters."

"That always sucks." Coleman's finger wiggled at the bartender.

"Wasn't a surprise to me. Shortly after closing, a friend mentioned he'd stopped by the place, hoping against hope. Looked abandoned, but he tried the door anyway and it opened. Totally dark inside, and these two guys popped up from behind the bar and asked if he wanted a drink, five dollars. He said he didn't think so. They said, 'Okay, two dollars.' He said he was leaving and they asked him for a ride somewhere. Soon after, the fire."

Coleman looked around again. "So if it all went up in smoke, how'd the stuff get here?"

"Farsighted patrons salvaged what they could beforehand and stored it. Then this place opened." He looked toward the bartender. "Hey Patty, fill him in."

She strolled over and wiped the counter. "Just after we went in business, all these people came in, about fifteen of 'em, carrying boxes. The owner never heard of the Boo and was understandably skeptical, but they made such a passionate case." She swept an arm around the memento-cluttered interior. "That cushy chair over there is from the office of Walt Disney himself. And the red vinyl stool at the end of the bar is Ralph Kent's, located in the same position it occupied at the original Bamboo. His widow gave it to us."

"Ralph Kent?" asked Coleman.

Serge got up and led Coleman across the room. "Legendary Disney artist and fixture at the old haunt." He pointed at a framed drawing on the wall. "Original Mickey Mouse." Then down at the historic stool. "To those in the know, there's the trademark duct tape over a rip in the vinyl, which is how you know it's Ralph's . . ."

Patrons came and went, including a short, bearded man with an aviator's scarf, dark gloves and flying goggles propped on top of his head. He took a seat in the Walt Disney chair, remaining still and quiet. Staring at the back of Serge's head.

Agent White stood in a parking lot with negative amusement. "Wrong guy again. I think you can get off him now."

The tactical unit unpiled.

A TV crew uprighted a crashed motorcycle.

White pulled out his handcuff key as another bum got up with skinned palms.

The SWAT team headed back to their van in a bitter haze of frustration.

Lowe raised a hand in the air and called over: "Great job, fellas. An honor working with you."

One of them kicked Lowe's SWAT bag into the road, and a bus ran over it.

Lowe raised his hand again. "Thank you."

White opened his wallet and began counting out cash for the whiskered man. "Sorry for the misunderstanding."

Lowe came over with a shredded black bag. "That doesn't look like Serge."

White glared.

"You think it's another decoy room?"

"Don't talk to me for a while."

Mahoney ran over from a pay phone with another scribbled-on matchbook. "New address."

The convoy raced back up the strip, toward the Nu Bamboo.

Coleman squinted at a drawing on the wall. "Mickey Mouse is shooting a bird at Iran."

"From 1980," said Serge. "During the hostage crisis. I believe that one's unauthorized."

Coleman pointed in another direction. "Check out the sign: THIS IS A BAR, NOT A REST AREA, NOW GET THE FUCK OUT! That's classy."

"The spirit of the Boo lives." Serge looked down at Coleman's drink in a mason jar, then back at the bartender. "No toilet-paper coasters?"

"Some of the newer customers aren't ready."

Another bourbon arrived in front of Coleman. "But, Serge, how'd you find this place? I never would have thought there was a bar way back here."

"Me neither." Serge kept typing on his laptop. "It's virtually impossible to locate without word of mouth. The only hint is that tiny, easily missed sign by the highway, 'Nu Bamboo Lounge,' actually *written* in bamboo, but half the letters have fallen off. Then it's a treasure hunt, wandering around until you find it stashed behind the lobby of this inn."

"So why aren't we staying at this motel instead of our dump?"

"Because this isn't a dump. The Fugitive Tour must have integrity." More typing. "And I needed a place closer to the original Boo's site for spiritual closure."

Patty brought over another water. "You wouldn't know where we could find the old ambulance?"

Serge shook his head. "Been looking."

"Ambulance?" said Coleman.

"Broken-down *M*A*S*H*-style thing by the highway. The original Bamboo was pretty hidden, too, back in tall brush, and that landmark ambulance is how people spotted it." Serge turned his head and noticed the bearded man in the pilot's scarf. The bearded man noticed him. They both looked away.

A crowd of fans gathered on the sidewalk of a sub-economy motel. Disposable cameras flashed. Autograph requests. A TV crew collected mangled motorcycle parts. A roadie yelled inside the semi: "Get the backup chopper."

White paid off another Sterno bum and turned to Mahoney. "Thought you said you finally had the right motel."

Mahoney spit out a matchstick and nodded with reluctant admiration. "Serge has his game back."

"It's not a game to me."

Lowe walked over and whistled. "Another decoy."

White looked down at the destroyed SWAT bag in Lowe's hand. "Aren't you going to throw that away?"

The agent shook his head. "It's seen battle."

White sighed again and stared off. "How many motels can Serge be registered in?"

"Five," said Serge, tapping a keyboard.

"Five motels?" said Coleman. "Why so many?"

"A question of ethics." *Tap, tap, tap.* "I can't just phone this in or I'm a fraud to the blogosphere. So I'm Method-acting, personally experiencing all the things I post to my website."

"But isn't it costing a lot?"

"Actually it's free. Our surprise guest from the playground had a lot of cash on him."

The evening wore on. Customers ran out the front door of the Nu Bamboo and back in. Then back out again. A pounding, heavy-metal bass thundered by on the street, rattling mason jars along the bar. The noise trailed off and the glasses became still.

Patty poured a beer for one of the regulars who'd just dashed back in. "What the heck's happening?"

"Don't know. All these unmarked cars keep speeding back and forth past this place. And the Doberman's truck is with them."

"*The Doberman?*" said a man in a Bucs baseball cap. "I love that show, especially the one where he tried climbing down from a roof, but the rain gutter broke off the building."

Serge furtively glanced at the bearded man, who hadn't budged from the Disney chair. The man glanced back. They both quickly looked up at the ceiling.

A half hour later, more hard rock thumped up the road toward the bar. Except the noise didn't fade off into the distance like the other times. Just blared nonstop. All the customers raced outside.

The dragnet pulled into a nearby parking lot.

Coleman stood in front of the lobby and drained a mason jar. "That's a pretty cool Cadillac."

"I've always wanted a yellow El Dorado," said Serge.

Bringing up the rear was a turquoise T-Bird with the top down.

Serge squinted and rubbed his eyes. "No, it . . . can't be. I'm seeing things."

"Look." Coleman gestured with his empty jar. "Isn't that our motel? The SWAT team's surrounding our room."

"Probably have the wrong address," said Serge. "There's no way they could have figured out my alias. Unless . . ."

A bearded man with a pilot's scarf stepped up next to Serge. They didn't acknowledge each other.

Several customers pointed at once. "And here comes the Doberman!"

A new motorcycle flew out the back of a semi and wiped out in a row of garbage cans.

The bearded man, from the corner of his mouth: "It's time."

Serge nodded slightly. He tugged Coleman by the arm, and the trio slipped into the darkness behind the Nu Bamboo.

Evidence techs combed the room.

Mahoney stood in the motel doorway.

White looked down at the registration card in the agent's hand. "What alias did he use?"

Mahoney glanced at the name. "Dr. Richard Kimble."

White rubbed his chin. "Kimble, Kimble . . . why does that name sound so familiar?"

"David Janssen's character in *The Fugitive*."

"Why would he do that?"

"It's personal," said Mahoney. "He's taunting me."

White looked across the room as someone from the medical examiner's office photographed the head-slumped body tied to a chair in a large puddle of water. Eyes permanently open. "You sure that's Serge's work?"

"Solid MO." Mahoney opened a manila folder. "Vic's ID: one Arthur Franklin Kostlerman the Third, registered sex offender, decade stretch in Raiford; nothing since but a series of flatfoot rousts for hinky hoofing near schools and parks. Vehicle orphaned at playground Tuesday." He turned a page: "Eyewitnesses bumped gums about some sap getting a trunk tour." The agent looked up and nodded as a camera flashed. "Hands-down Serge. Trademark joker-deck snuff scene."

"But what am I looking at?" said White. "In all my years I've never seen anything so sick, except I have no idea what I'm seeing."

"M.E.'s still stumped," said Lowe.

"Got this one," said Mahoney. "Serge rides the home-improvement pony."

"Come again?"

Mahoney walked over and knocked on the deceased's chest like it was a door. He looked back at White. "Nobody home."

"That sounded hard as a rock."

"Gibraltar."

"But what is that damn thing around his chest?"

"Plumbing aisle. Pressure line repair." Mahoney picked up an excess roll of tape from the bed. "Like gauze you'd dress a wound with, except it's been spiked. Serge wrapped his chest with a few hundred feet of the stuff."

"How'd that kill him?"

"Didn't." Mahoney pulled a fountain pen from his pocket, leaned down and stuck it through a trigger guard so as not to smudge any latent prints. He held up a small plastic squirt pistol. "This did."

"What was in it? Poison? Acid?"

"Tap water." Mahoney raised it to the light. "Gem, too. Vintage early fifties, shaped like an alien ray gun."

"Jesus! A man is dead!"

"The big snooze. Water activates slime on the film, which contracts and dries to form a concrete-hard fitting around a plumbing leak. Except a sex offender is no match for a lead pipe, and the death squeeze continues like an iron maiden. My guess? Serge explained the science to the perp, that his ribs would start cracking like a slow Buddy Guy drumroll, puncturing internal organs—but if it was his lucky day, his lungs would have trouble expanding and he'd pass out first. Maybe. Then Serge took it slow, real slow, standing back and squirting him with the pistol. This one was particularly heinous."

"Why?"

Mahoney held up the water gun again. "He had to reload."

White stared off. "What kind of demented bastard?"

"But you gotta give him points for style."

"How's that?"

"Molester killed with a child's toy."

"I'm not laughing."

"You're also not paddling."

"What do you mean?"

Mahoney placed a hand on the victim's chest. "Chemical reaction creates heat transfer. This just happened." He turned back around. "Serge is slipping the net."

"Shit." White summoned nearby uniforms. "Top priority. Standard roadblock matrix. Get Serge's photo out . . ."

Cops dispersed.

"That dog won't hunt," said Mahoney.

"Just watch," said White. "This is my town. Looks like a busy city and an easy place to escape, but they built the theme parks to the south, surrounded by agricultural land. Just a few major arteries to seal— International Drive, Orange Blossom Trail, Interstate 417, firewall Orlando to the north and points south. Then all we have to worry about is the airport and Amtrak station."

The motel manager came in with a portable office phone. "There an Agent Mahoney?"

"Depends," said Mahoney. "Alimony come up?"

The manager shrugged and held out the phone. "I just know you got a call."

Mahoney placed it to his head. "Mahoney here, jaw to me . . . uh-huh . . . I see, I see . . . Don't you mean the *Big* Bamboo? . . . Really? . . . Okay, thanks Scratchy. I owe you." He tossed the phone back to the manager.

"Who was that?" asked White.

"Snitch who ratted this flop." Mahoney reached in his pocket for a toothpick. "There a joint near here called the Nu Bamboo?"

"Yeah, opened a year ago. Why?"

"Serge eyeballed at the bar. Might still be there . . ."

Sedans screeched into the parking lot of the next motel. Agents poured through the lobby. White was first in the bar. He lunged at the counter and held a mug shot to Patty. "Seen this guy."

Patty barely had to look. "Yeah, Serge. He's right over . . ." She set a mason jar in front of a customer and looked around. "He was just in here."

"When was the last time you saw him?"

"A few minutes ago. We were all standing out front watching these cops race around."

Lowe raised his hand. "That was us. We're under deep cover."

"Shut up," said White, then back to Patty. "Any idea where he went?"

"Nope," said the bartender, setting empty glass jars in the sink. "If you know Serge, one second he's here talking a mile a minute about how he could stay forever, then he gets bored and poof."

"Thanks for your help." The detective handed her a business card. "If you think of anything else—"

"White!" Mahoney yelled from the far end of the bar. "Come quick! I think I found something!"

The agent raced over. "What is it?"

Mahoney pointed down at a stool. "I'd know that duct tape anywhere."

"Yeah?" said White, leaning forward in tense anticipation. "And?"

"It's Ralph Kent's."

"I don't understand your methods, Mahoney, but this puts us on Serge's trail, right?"

"No, I'm just jazzed."

White's thoughts drifted to strangulation.

"*Look!*" yelled one of the customers.

Everyone turned.

"*It's the Doberman!*"

"*And he's got the Litter!*"

The bounty hunter entered the bar with blood-matted hair and left arm in a makeshift sling. Patrons swarmed for more autographs.

"*You're my hero! . . .*"

"*Are you on the hunt? . . .*"

"*Remember when you ran over yourself with your own dune buggy? . . .*"

White grabbed Lowe. "Come on. We've got real work to do."

The detectives sped west in an unmarked Crown Vic.

"Roger," White said in the police radio. He hung the mike on the dash. "Everyone's in roadblock position."

Lowe flipped through his manual. "You really think we've cut off all escape routes?"

"Tighter than Fort Knox," said White, scanning both sidewalks. "Called in the Orange County sheriff. Got deputies checking everyone on even the most obscure back roads."

A short drive up the Kissimmee strip: more bottom-shelf amusement. Bungee towers, video arcades, rock-climbing walls. Farther off the highway, a long, dark grassy field.

Serge and Coleman climbed from a golf cart. Then up a ladder.

They were sitting in front.

Something roared to life with a tremendous, shuddering noise.

Coleman sipped a flask and looked back at the bearded man in a scarf. The man saluted. Coleman turned and yelled in Serge's ear: "Who is that guy?"

"Rickenbacker. I called in a favor."

"What kind of favor?"

"Help me with the Fugitive Tour," shouted Serge. "This is our 'Out' for Kissimmee."

"And yet nobody's chasing us?"

"Not a soul," said Serge. "My audience deserves nothing but the finest fake chaos."

"Why?"

"You still don't get the conceit of this tour?"

"What?"

Serge threw up his arms in exuberance. "It's hot out of the mold of that uniquely American genre: the Great Chase Movie!"

The grass field began moving beneath them. Slowly at first, then picking up speed, then slowing again.

Coleman looked around. "Is this thing safe?"

"Rick's the best. Couldn't be in better hands."

Velocity increased again. They reached the middle of the field. Then slowed again.

A loud bang.

The flask flew from Coleman's hand. "What the hell was that?"

"Just a backfire," said Serge.

A shout from Rick in the rear seat: "Better hang on."

Serge and Coleman bounced up and down, clutching a horizontal metal bar.

They reached the middle of the field, which was connected back to the road by a winding cart path. The path ended at a slapped-together wooden ticket booth facing the highway. A tattered orange wind sock hung flaccid. The booth was unstaffed and padlocked. But during the day, tourists could see an old bearded man inside. And a sign: HISTORIC BIPLANE RIDES, $50.

Another hard bounce, and threadbare tires left the ground. They touched down again.

Bang.

The wheels lifted off for good this time, and the restored two-winger gained altitude. Sort of.

The wind sock suddenly inflated and threatened to tear loose.

Coleman clutched Serge's shoulder and pointed with a quivering arm. "Power lines!"

"Relax. Rick's done this a million times."

"Has he ever hit the power lines?"

"Never . . . Okay, a few times, but just skimmed with the wheels. Not his fault—he had a tailwind."

"A few times!"

"But the tires are rubber, so they're insulated from electricity. In theory."

"Do we have a tailwind now?"

"Hell yeah. Strong one."

The plane slowly rose toward the brightness of the Kissimmee strip.

Coleman covered his eyes. "I can't look."

Rick gave it the throttle and up she went, twin bursts of sparks as wheels clipped high-tension lines.

Coleman peeked through his fingers. "We made it. We didn't die."

"Told you." Serge stuck his face over the side as they flew above the highway. "Hey, there's all those police cars again, and the SWAT team."

"I can see the Haunted Mansion," said Coleman. "And Space Mountain."

"What are all those highway flares?"

"Where?"

"Interstate entrance ramp."

"Some kind of wreck?"

"Don't think so," said Serge. "Looks more like a roadblock."

"I see more flares over there . . . and more that way."

"Another bunch by the tollbooths."

"They must be after someone really frightening," said Coleman.

"Good thing we left town when we did."

Higher and higher they went into the chilly night air. Over MGM and Universal and Pirates of the Caribbean. Soon, they left city lights behind. Sparse countryside. Farms and forests. It became quite peaceful as the moon's reflection tracked across the countless lakes of Lake County.

"This is actually kind of nice," said Coleman.

"I love my job," said Serge.

"So where are we going now?"

"Fugitive Tour Stop Number Two. They'll be raving for years about this make-believe chase."

Rickenbacker banked his wings and the plane came around hard to the left. The pilot locked on a course straight into the giant full moon sitting low on the western horizon, perfectly silhouetting the two heads in the seat in front of him.

PART I

A Month Ago

Chapter One

MORNING

FDLE, otherwise known as the Florida Department of Law Enforcement, is the state's version of the FBI.

Furniture was rearranged in the Orlando bureau. Workers carried two desks into a private office meant for one.

A task force had been formed.

Agent White sprayed disinfectant and scrubbed the top of his scratched-up metal government desk, of which he was the forty-seventh steward. Same procedure for his beige phone. Then he meticulously set family photos around a scuffed desk blotter with a virgin calendar pad.

Across the tiny office, in front of the window with missing blinds, Agent Lowe dumped out his collection of SWAT team shoulder patches from across the U.S.

and Canada. He arranged them in rows on the top of his desk and held the formation in place with a large rectangle of tempered glass.

Agent White was black. Thirty-eight years old, new school. Everything by the book. Seamlessly responsible. Never late on a house payment, changed his oil every three thousand miles and recycled. He hit the gym Monday, Wednesday, Friday, so he could chase suspects. Despite White's age, his hairline had prematurely receded, and he was concerned it might affect advancement. So five years ago he shaved the works, giving him a vague resemblance to Michael Jordan.

Promotions followed.

White maintained an impeccable record, which led to his appointment as commander of the task force.

"What are those?" asked White.

Lowe placed decorative items around the edge of his desk. "Model police cars and helicopters and boats. The lights and sirens work."

"We need to stay focused," said White. "This is a very important assignment. It'll take every edge—"

Woo-woo-woo-woo-woo . . .

"Turn off the Adam-12 car," said White.

The task force was what they call on TV a cold case unit. Ostensibly designed to reopen dead-end homicides. In reality, it was a bone-toss to the press. And it had one particular suspect in its crosshairs.

The media embarrassment had been seismic. A series of unsolved, high-profile murders. All gruesome, all very public. Charred body splattered poolside after falling off a motel balcony, another unrecognizable corpse from a sabotaged amusement ride, plus a home-brew guillotine and two bodies hanging forty stories up from a construction crane. The handiwork of a single hand.

Not unusual for Florida. But they all took place in the middle of spring break, generating extensive coverage in northern markets, meaning tourism.

Off the record, law enforcement couldn't have cared less. The homicides closed dozens of cases against violent, organized criminals who'd remained just out of reach. But headlines were headlines, and they always rolled downhill. A series of telephone calls wound its way through the bureaucracy from Tallahassee to Orlando, until Agent White was called in.

"You can count on me," said White. "How many people do I get?"

"Lowe."

"What? A low number?"

"Agent Lowe. There's a budget crisis."

They picked White because he was good on camera. They gave him Lowe because he was useless half the time. The other half, he did damage.

Lowe: short, skinny, ultra-pale, thick glasses that barely passed the medical, and the curse of genes that grew wild, comical hair. White may have resembled Jordan, but Lowe *was* Woody Allen. Couldn't develop muscles to save his life. In the police weight room, bench-press spotters constantly grabbed barbells before they crushed Lowe's larynx. But nothing crushed his spirit. Lowe never wanted to be anything other than a cop. Since childhood. He graduated at the bottom of his academy class and proudly hung the diploma on the wall of his new office, next to a photo of him with a SWAT team during career day. Since then, his career had stalled from chronic short-term disability leaves. But unlike malingerers, all his injuries were overly legitimate. Contusions, concussions, fractures and lacerations. Lowe was hyper-eager to prove himself, and never hesitated to sacrifice his body. Dependability became Lowe's trademark. During every felon chase, he could be counted on to leave by ambulance. They ordered him to stop jumping on the hoods of getaway cars and being flung. His reports had the best handwriting. He always wanted to get a dog, but never did.

Thus the birth of a reluctant alliance. The two-man Untouchables squad rolled up their sleeves.

Of course, the top brass never expected them to apprehend anyone. They understood media attention span—and their own money woes. "See? We're doing something about those spring break murders." Then a war of attrition, out-waiting the reporters until the next shiny case hit CNN.

But they hadn't counted on White.

And he hadn't counted on Lowe.

"Lowe, what on earth are you doing?"

Lowe looked up from his desk. "Shaving my arms to decrease drag in case Serge tries to make a water escape."

"Why don't we just start with the files," said White.

"You got it, chief." Lowe stood and turned sideways to squeeze between the desks, finally reaching a dozen cardboard storage boxes stacked against the wall. "Where should I begin?"

"Whatever's on top."

Lowe removed an armload of folders and handed half to his supervisor.

And so began the tedium that never makes the TV shows.

"Look at all these morgue pictures," said Lowe. "I can't believe this guy's never been caught."

"It's Florida, fugitive heaven." White rifled through his own autopsy shots. "We've got over a hundred thousand outstanding warrants, making our state the perfect place to fall off the radar."

Lowe grabbed another folder. "Chief, this one's got his name spelled wrong. It says 'Sergio.' "

White flipped through his own folder. "What year?"

Lowe looked puzzled. "Says 1964. But Serge was just a kid. Why would he have a jacket back then?"

"Sergio was his grandfather." White jotted notes from an ancient arrest report. "Belonged to this old Miami Beach gang that ran a small-time gambling and fence operation. Apparently Serge spent a lot of time with his granddad, kind of like the crew's mascot."

Lowe whistled in awe at the next page. "Was Sergio really mixed up in the 'Murph the Surf' gem heist?"

"So they say."

"Look at the names of these known associates," said Lowe. "Chi-Chi, Coltrane, Moondog, Greek Tommy . . ."

"The gang that couldn't shoot straight," said White. He stopped and studied one of the last-known photos of Serge. "This picture's five years old. Got anything newer over there?"

Lowe grabbed a folder from the bottom of the pile he'd just completed. "Here's one. Six feet tall, trim, Latin features, short black hair with a dusting of gray on the sides, tropical shirt. You can't see it from the photo, but the dossier describes penetrating ice blue eyes."

"Say 'file' instead of 'dossier.' "

"Also mentions a longtime accomplice, Seymour Bunsen, aka Coleman. Looks like a slob in this booking mug, stains on his Big Johnson T-shirt, five seven, moon face, beer gut, hair like he just got out of bed. Says he's an omni-substance abuser."

White laid out overlapping documents. "These guys are all across the state, sometimes in the same week. That's not cheap." He opened another folder. "Let's try to follow the money trail."

Lowe grabbed another folder. "But how do they make their money? . . ."

"Time to make some money!" said Serge.

He drove across Tampa to a sterile office building in the industrial sector just east of the airport, and parked beside a VW microbus.

"The first day at our new job!" Serge bounded joyfully up the front steps. "I always love the first day! Because it's often the last."

Coleman followed at a hangover-regulated pace. "Why do we have to work anyway?"

"Because it's good for the soul." Serge opened a glass door. "I can't believe they hired us."

"I can't believe how little they're paying us."

"Because this is a job that requires a high level of education and compassion for your fellow man," said

Serge. "It's like teachers. They know they're decent folk who are going to do it anyway. And when people are that virtuous, there's only one thing to do under our system: shit on 'em each paycheck."

"But we're not qualified."

"That's why I had to lie," said Serge. "I hate to lie, but gave myself a pass this time because we're actually over-qualified. Just no fancy diplomas to prove it."

"Except the ones you printed up?"

"I've always wanted to be a doctor."

Serge headed down a hall.

"Why can't we just keep stealing stuff?" asked Coleman.

"We're going to," said Serge. "But an honest day's work will cleanse the palate so we can appreciate it more."

They entered an office. The most crowded they'd ever seen. Phone banks along each wall; more people gabbing in cubicles.

Serge smiled at the receptionist.

"Can I help you?"

"Serge and Coleman! Your newest valuable hires!"

She picked up a phone.

The door to a side office opened, and a nebbish, gangly man greeted them. Short-sleeved dress shirt, brown clip-on tie, ponytail, counter-culture goatee. He looked at both. "Serge?"

"That's me."

They shook hands. "And you must be Coleman . . . Glad to have you on board." He led them across the room to a pair of empty chairs at a long, continuous desk. "Here's where you'll work. Those red buttons activate your phones. By your résumés, I'm guessing you've done this a thousand times."

"At least," said Serge.

"Groovy. Then I'll just get out of your way and let you go to it."

Serge and Coleman sat and pressed red buttons. One of the phones rang instantly.

"Suicide hotline. My name is Serge. How may I save your life tonight? . . ."

The other phone rang.

"Suicide hotline. This is Coleman. I got a question. Do you know what day we get paid? . . ."

". . . Because life is magnificent," said Serge. "The problem is our wussy culture . . . stop crying . . . you're conditioned to be weak and sniveling . . . you really have to stop crying . . . because it's icky . . . So like on TV last night, I saw a commercial for 'guilt-free dog treats.' What the fuck? No wonder you're screwed up . . . Hey, I'm screwed up, too, except you don't see me calling a complete stranger on some hotline, droning on and on about how there's no point anymore . . . When I said stop crying, I didn't mean start screaming . . . You going to have to stop screaming . . . Jennifer? Who's that? . . . Well, no wonder she dumped you . . . Great, more screaming. Now I understand why I'm the only person you can talk to—"

Click.

"Hello? . . ." said Serge. "*Helllllloooo?* Anyone there? . . . Shit, disconnected."

He hung up.

Rrrrrrring!

"Suicide hotline. Coleman speaking . . . How much did you take? . . . When? . . . What color were the microdots . . . Oooo, purple, not good . . . Do you have a trip chaperone? . . . No? That's still cool. I'll walk you through it . . . First, nothing's melting. Yes, I'm sure. Believe me, I've been there . . . Right, and whatever you do, don't look in any mirrors . . . Because you might start pulling your face off. Any CDs around? . . . Great, do you have *The White Album?* . . ."

Rrrrrrring!

"Suicide hotline. Serge is on the case. Have you done anything crazy yet? . . . Ha! You call that crazy? . . . Yes, I *can* top that . . ."

". . . You're doing fine," said Coleman. "Now open the CD booklet . . . That's right, the Beatles are with you . . . It really is an excellent tune . . . Okay, this next part is very important: Make sure you skip over 'Helter Skelter' . . ."

". . . Stop!" said Serge. "Life is a fabulous gift from the universe that we don't deserve, and you're talking about just throwing it all away? You must be a fun-riot on long plane flights—"

Bang.

"Hello? . . ." said Serge. "*Helllllloooo?* You still there? . . . Good, because I'm beginning to think there's something wrong with my phone. What was the loud noise? . . . You're shitting me . . . Because that's the most retarded thing anyone's ever said . . . Yes it is. Whoever heard of a warning shot during a suicide? . . ."

Chapter Two

ORLANDO

Two agents pored over dusty case files.

"Unbelievable," said White. "Almost all these victims were wanted, violent criminals . . . And the causes of death . . . MRI machine?"

Lowe jumped up. "I think I've got something."

"What is it?"

"This agent. With the FDLE, too. Name's Mahoney."

"So?"

"He's a profiler who's had at least four near misses with Serge."

"Where is he?"

"Indefinite medical leave. Had some kind of mental breakdown tracking our guy."

"Let me see that." White quickly flipped through the file and handed it back. "Find him immediately. Set up a meeting . . . But go gentle."

ST. PETERSBURG

The downtown core was in transition. A toss-up which way it would land.

Chic, new sidewalk cafés and piano bars with eighteen-dollar martinis—next to barfly joints, un-mopped package stores and park benches with hobos passing brown paper bags.

Serge was pulling for the latter.

Downtown always had held promise. Stunning back in its prime, then urban flight and decades of that desolate, post-Armageddon street-emptiness, which kept the developers' wrecking balls at bay, preserving an exquisite mix of early-1900s Florida architecture. The Coliseum, wrought-iron balconies, clay tile, Art Deco, manual elevators with accordion cages. Most of the old hotels were still there, curved canvas awnings extending over sidewalks. Some became retirement homes. Others flophouses.

One such building sat beneath the clamor of the elevated interstate. Paint long since weathered down to bleached wood. A man in a tweed jacket stepped over broken wine bottles in a weed-filled yard and ascended creaking porch steps.

"What's the word on the street, Gums?"

A toothless man looked up from a tin of cat food. "Mahoney!"

Mahoney tipped his fedora and climbed a rickety staircase to the second floor. A feral cat, all ribs, ran down the other way. The agent entered the last unit at the end of the hall and threw his hat on the bed.

The room was spare. A closet of tweed jackets and bowling shirts. Hot plate on the dresser, rows of soup cans, Brylcreem, Burma-Shave, Zippo flints, Philco tube radio. A small desk with a manual Underwood typewriter and stacks of dog-eared paperbacks from bargain bins with the original price—10¢—dames, trench coats, snub-nosed pistols, stiletto heels, switch-blades.

Mahoney's mouth was grim, but his mood couldn't have been more chipper. He celebrated by chewing two matchsticks. The reason was the envelope in his hand. He'd received it a half hour earlier at a nearby doctor's office with burglar bars.

Mahoney had been working toward that letter for months. The biggest sham he'd ever pulled.

The agent fished a nearly full prescription bottle from his pocket and jump-shotted it into the wastebasket.

"Good riddance."

The bottle was mostly full because Mahoney only popped the pills on the days of his appointments. Still, it was a struggle, like earlier that morning:

A pen tapped. It was in the hand of a psychiatrist. There was a couch. A man lay on it in a Brooks Brothers suit and silk tie that made him fight the urge to scratch all over. Manicured nails, haircut like a loan officer, washed and clean-shaven, providing a rare glimpse of his ruggedly handsome Irish features, like Mickey Rourke.

"Nice clothes," said the doctor. "What happened to your old stuff?"

"Probably at the city dump by now," said Mahoney. "I looked like a fool."

The doctor smiled and made a positive notation in his patient file. He looked back up. "What are you thinking about right now?"

Truth: a desperate hankerin' for the toothpicks outside in his '62 Cutlass. "This movie I just saw, *Marley & Me*."

"Really?" the doctor said with genuine surprise. "That's an interesting choice for you."

Because he'd actually seen *Chinatown* on a late-night UHF channel. "Very uplifting. Highly recommend it. Too much anger in the world."

Another positive comment in the folder.

"Are you taking the medication as scheduled?"

"On the hour."

"What year is it?" asked the doctor.

Mahoney got the right answer.

"You don't feel like you're still in the 1940s?"

The agent grimaced. "That was embarrassing. I'd rather forget the whole business."

"So all these delusions of noir? Humphrey Bogart, Raymond Chandler, Mickey Spillane?"

"Looking back, I feel so silly."

"Impressive." More unreadable doctor scribbling. "Last question: What about Serge?"

"That loser?" said Mahoney. "Life's too short."

"You aren't obsessed in the least?"

"Only think about him when you mention his name in this room."

"I don't know what to say." The doctor made a final note and closed the file. "Have to admit when you first came in here I wasn't optimistic, but that's fifteen excellent sessions now without a single slip of slang. Never seen such rapid progress."

"What are you getting at?" asked Mahoney.

"Can't see the point of meeting anymore." The doctor got up and headed for the door. "I'll have my secretary type up the letter. You can wait for it in the lobby if you'd like."

"Appreciate it."

Twenty minutes later, the envelope was in his hand. He cordially waved when the doctor opened the lobby door to call in the next patient. "Take care." And as soon as Mahoney was outside: "Goofball-pushing head cracker needs his ticket punched on a Harlem sunset."

Mahoney didn't even wait to leave the parking lot before ripping the suit off right in his car, throwing on his old threads like he was fighting to come up for air.

And now he stood in his flophouse flat, opening the envelope. A letter on physician stationery unfolded. The last line: "Cleared for active duty."

The page fell next to the typewriter. He opened a drawer. Gold shield and a Smith & Wesson. He grabbed a third toothpick.

A black rotary phone sat on the desk.

It rang.

TEN BLOCKS AWAY

A '68 Ford Gran Torino sped south on Fourth Street.

". . . Recalculating, drive point-two miles and make a U-turn . . . Recalculating, drive point-three miles and make a left . . . Recalulating . . ."

Coleman stubbed out a joint. "Where's that woman's voice coming from?"

"My new Garmin GPS. You know how I love gadgets. And I love my new Garmin!"

". . . Recalculating, drive . . ."

"Does it ever stop talking?"

"That's the only problem." Serge cut down an alley. "I know every shortcut in Florida like the back of my hand, but that chick in the machine thinks she's smarter. Women are always telling you how to drive and getting on your last nerve. Why did I buy this fucking thing?"

"If you know the state so well, why *did* you buy it?"

"Because sometimes I get distracted taking pictures and daydreaming about all the super powers I'd like to have, but not delusional super powers that crazy people scream about on the street. I dial it down to just stuff that's possible, like X-ray vision that sees through only *thin* walls, or a heightened ability to detect bad milk, and then I've missed my destination by fifty miles, so the GPS reminds me, saving precious time and extending my life expectancy."

". . . *Recalculating. Drive point-four miles . . .*"

"What's her weird accent?"

"I switched the Garmin to British in the language settings. Kind of a turn-on."

". . . *Make a left, then make a right . . . Recalculating . . .*"

Serge pounded the dashboard. "Shut up! . . . Shut the fuck up!"

"Why don't you just switch it off?"

"Because it's a gadget."

Cars streamed off the highway into downtown St. Petersburg.

The Gran Torino headed from Central Avenue to Third. Orange cones in the road, police directing traffic. Noon.

". . . Recalculating . . ."

Serge drove by parking lots that had already begun to fill. "I can't believe that hotline let us go after one day."

"They wanted to keep me," said Coleman.

Serge shook his head. "I wouldn't do that to my buddy. Can't leave you at the mercy of any outfit that treated me so shabbily."

"They said they listened to the tapes from your last phone conversation."

"That was tough love," said Serge. "Sometimes you have to scream back and call their bluff."

"At least the paramedics arrived in time."

"You get one bluff wrong, and everybody's emotional."

They waited through two cycles of a red light. Coleman cracked as many beers. "Look at all these cars."

"Nothing compared to what we'll see in an hour."

"How'd you get this other job so fast?"

"Connections."

They continued past more lots. People climbed from vehicles and joined a growing human river flowing east. Others unfolded chairs and opened coolers.

Serge turned left. "Here we are." They stopped at the driveway of one of the only empty parking lots in sight. Serge got out and undid the chain across the entrance, then motored inside.

"Don't forget this." Serge handed Coleman a bag on the seat between them. "It shows you're official."

They went to the trunk for the rest of their supplies.

Almost immediately, the first car arrived.

"Enjoy the game," said Serge, handing the driver a ticket. He tucked fifteen dollars in a zippered pouch attached to his waist.

"Get wrecked," said Coleman, handing the next driver a stub.

Then they picked up their cardboard signs again and stood on the side of the road in yellow safety vests.

Other cars approached to consider the lot, then booed and cursed the pair. Someone shot a bird.

Serge just smiled and waved.

"What's that all about?" asked Coleman.

"Home-field advantage," said Serge, waving at someone else who spat in their direction. "Just keep that sign up so everyone can see it."

Coleman raised the cardboard: PARKING $20.

Serge raised his: TAMPA BAY HOSPITALITY SPECIAL: ANYONE WEARING VISITING TEAM HAT OR SHIRT, $5 OFF.

Cars continued pouring into their lot. Even more shunned it and jeered. Zippered waist pouches became fat.

"Serge, look at all this money. I hope they're paying us better than that last place."

"They are."

More bills went in Coleman's pouch. "I like jobs where you get to touch lots of cash."

"Me, too," said Serge. "Except we'll only have this gig one day."

"How do you know they're going to get rid of us?"

"They're not. We're quitting." Serge tore off a ticket. "Enjoy the game! . . ."

Another carload of people in pinstripes and New York caps parked in their lot and headed toward the stadium.

"Go Yankees!" said Serge.

"But you're a Rays fan," said Coleman.

"The biggest. That's why I took this job."

"Yet we're quitting?"

"Promptly." Serge motioned for the next car. "We need venture capital for the next phase of my life."

"Which is?"

"Relaunching our travel website, under new management."

"But it isn't under new management."

"That's right. Meet the new boss, same as the old boss . . . I always get a kick when I see an UNDER NEW MANAGEMENT sign. Translation: This place used to blow, but we got rid of those assholes." He dispensed a ticket. "Enjoy the game! . . . My revolutionary new twist will turn all other websites into weeping piles of Twittering mush."

"The Fugitive Tour?"

"Got to thinking: How have I found so many cool Florida destinations? I knew a bunch of them before, but the lion's share came after I was on the run, police sirens blaring, crashing barricades, hails of gunfire, knife fights, pistol whippings, hand-to-hand combat with angel-dust fiends trying to bite your ears off. Why should I have all the fun?"

Coleman exchanged another ticket for money. "I don't think they'll get a kick out of that as much as you do."

"Not the brushes with death," said Serge. "They'll just pretend those parts. The real payoff is all the most remote, offbeat locations I've personally vetted. That's the key to my business model: I've spent years crisscrossing Florida on the lam, and now I'll pass the savings on to them."

"You're always thinking of others."

"Because my company runs on love. And at the same time I get to work on my Secret Master Plan."

"What's the Secret Master Plan?"

"A secret."

Coleman stood with a ticket in his hand. "There must be a hundred cars in the lot."

"At least."

"But why aren't they coming in as fast as before?"

"Because the game's about to start."

"Then what do we do?"

"Get the folding chairs out of our car and sit in the shade doing nothing."

"And you want to quit a job like that?"

"There's a catch."

MEANWHILE . . .

Mahoney stood in his flophouse and stared at a black rotary phone.

Fifth ring.

Mahoney liked to let phones ring. Once he picked them up, mundaneness. But until then, hope. Wide-open horizons of intrigue: the boozy broad in a tight sweater with a sob story and trouble uptown . . . a caller with a handkerchief over his mouth who says to check out some freshly poured cement in the bowery . . . the grudgingly respectful police captain telling him to stay away from their latest case or he can't help him this time . . . some Joe spilling his guts over a body in the lake but stops mid-sentence because of the knife in his back . . . His mother who thinks the neighbors are deliberately blowing leaves into her yard . . . Mahoney dared to let himself dream: *The Maltese Falcon?* . . .

Ninth ring.

He snatched the receiver.

"Mahoney. Start yapping."

"Mahoney? This is Agent Lowe."

"To what do I owe the inconvenience?"

"I've just been put on a task force."

"Goody gumdrops."

"We're after Serge."

Silence.

"You still there?"

"All ears."

"We've been going through old files and your name came up. Quite a few times, in fact."

Mahoney thinking: Serge is mine, you diaper jockey. "How can I jibe?"

"That's why I'm calling. I'd like to pick your brain about the way this guy operates. Any ideas where we should start looking?"

"Spit your digits," said Mahoney.

Lowe gave him his phone number. "When I can I expect to hear back from you?"

"I'll yank my flogger and spread cabbage in the clip joints."

"What?"

Mahoney hung up.

He scooped his badge and gun and ran downstairs for the Cutlass. Gravel flew as it fishtailed onto the street. He was forced to do something he couldn't have dreaded more: go to the library and get on a computer.

Serge stood at the edge of a parking lot in a yellow vest. He checked his watch. "First pitch should be any minute."

"I'll get the lawn chairs," said Coleman.

A few more late-arriving Yankee fans and then nothing. Coleman sat under a tree, fanning himself with his sign and pressing an ice-cold beer can to his forehead. "I could get used to this."

"Don't."

"I know. Your website."

"But first we have to call Mooch."

"Mooch?"

"Our boss." Serge opened his cell phone. "Told you I had connections."

Fifteen minutes later, Serge pointed up the street. "Here he comes."

Coleman stood and unzipped his cash pouch with a sulk. "Guess I have to give him all my money now."

"No, we get to keep that."

"Serge, you're babbling."

A vehicle pulled up.

"Mooch!"

"Serge!" He looked around the lot. "Looks like you did a tidy bit of commerce today."

"Bumper business, excuse the pun."

Mooch opened his wallet and handed Serge a thousand dollars.

"Ahem! . . . . I got overhead. Cardboard ain't free."

"*Alllllllll* right," said Mooch. "Here's another five hundred. Let me know when you want to work together again."

Several trucks arrived and idled just outside the lot. Serge walked over to a signpost where he'd hung a parking poster.

Mooch stuck two fingers in his mouth and whistled at the drivers. "Let's go, boys! We got a lot of work to do."

Serge pulled down the poster, revealing the permanent sign underneath: NO PARKING. TOW-AWAY ZONE.

Six tow trucks pulled into the lot, and Serge pulled out.

"Now I get it," said Coleman. "I was wondering why you had to use bolt cutters on the chain at the entrance."

"But the essential ingredient to the scam is the yellow vests. They possess mystical powers."

"Like your clipboard?"

Serge nodded. "People see your vests and automatically bow to authority as if there's no way I could have bought them at Home Depot. But occasionally you get a safety-vest skeptic, so . . ."—he pointed in the backseat—". . . the orange cones crush all doubt . . . Ready?"

"The Fugitive Tour?"

"Let's rock!"

The Gran Torino sped away.

"*. . . Recalculating . . .*"

Chapter Three

FORT LAUDERDALE

The hospital room was somber and smelled funky.

Unfortunately, an attorney had to be there, but that couldn't be helped. Who knew how much longer, and documents needed to be signed and witnessed.

Luckily, no shortage of witnesses.

The patient in the bed was one of the last of the old gang.

And what a gang it was. Not like today. Old school, discipline, living by a code. It was the roaring sixties in Miami Beach, just before the Beatles came ashore, and the gang ruled the strip, making rounds in straw hats and guayaberas. If you were staying at one of the swank hotels back then, you could get a wager down on anything as fast as you could find a doorman or the concierge, who passed it along to the gang. It wasn't even really a crime. At least that's how every-one thought back then, including the police who took their cut. They were just giving the people what they wanted, like providing a public service. It was mainly bookmaking, but they nibbled a variety of other vices with mixed results. The call girls became more of a nuisance than anything, but they kept the hook-ers on for appearances. The gang didn't have a name, until much later when they were called the No Name Gang. There was Greek Tommy, Chi-Chi, Moondog, Coltrane, Mort from the delicatessen, Roy the Pawn King and, of course, Sergio.

Sergio was the craziest, and thought dead for a number of years, until he showed back up in time to die. He was the first to go, when the march of time began thinning the herd. Then Greek Tommy passed, and Mort, and Moondog. Now it looked like Chi-Chi's turn.

Chairs were pulled from the walls and surrounded the hospital bed. There was good ol' Coltrane and Roy the Pawn King, getting up there themselves; and the next generations, Greek Tommy *Junior*, with his ne'er-do-well biker sons, Skid Marks and Bacon Strips. They scooted chairs closer.

Chi-Chi rested comfortably on three pillows.

A cough.

"Just take it easy," said Roy. "You're going to outlive us all."

An effort to smile. "Roy, you're a douche bag."

"See, everyone? He's getting better."

Another cough.

They did their best to conceal true thoughts.

"Excuse me . . ."

Coltrane turned. "Can't it wait?"

"I'm sorry," said the lawyer, "but it's my advice that we get these signed while, well . . . I'm sorry."

"You already said that."

"It's okay," said Chi-Chi. "He's got a job to do. Earn that pound of flesh . . . Where do I put my Hancock?"

"By the little taped arrows."

"Jesus, he can't even hold a pen," said Roy.

"If you could help, we'll get it over with as quickly as possible," said the attorney.

Roy held the pen in Chi-Chi's hand while the lawyer slid the paper, making a straight line of ink.

"Is that really a signature?" asked Tommy Junior.

The attorney stood back up with the documents. "Good enough as long as it's witnessed. If you could just sign on the last page."

"Now?"

"It's okay, Pops," said Skid Marks. "Me and Bacon Strips will sign."

"Tommy?" said Chi-Chi.

"I'm right here."

A smile. "Remember our old runs on the Loop Road? And the Gator Hook?"

"You must be thinking of my father."

Chi-Chi stared toward the foot of the bed, then nodded. "That's right. How is he?"

Tommy Junior looked with concern at the others.

"Chi-Chi," said Roy the Pawn King. "Greek Tommy passed away last year."

Another nod. "That's right," said Chi-Chi. "But what a driver. Never could match him on the old Loop Road, even though I did my best. That's why I was better driving the blocking car."

"You more than held your own," said Tommy Junior. "Dad was always saying that."

"But your *grand*dad," said Chi-Chi, barely managing a faint whistle. "Now, *he* was a driver. And one crazy bastard."

The attorney slid next to Roy the Pawn King. "What are they talking about?"

"Glory days," said Roy. "Running moonshine. Tommy's grandfather actually worked for Capone."

"Chicago?"

"No, Florida," said Roy. "Most people don't realize it, but Al had an operation in the Everglades. Poachers fed him from a network of stills."

"Seriously? . . ." The lawyer neared the bed and stuck an ear in the conversation.

"Those were the best times of our lives," said Chi-Chi.

"The high-water mark," said Tommy Junior.

"Your dad and I were so young," said Chi-Chi. "The world ahead of us . . . Whatever happened to that map?"

"Think he gave it to Sergio," said Tommy. "He was always interested in that history stuff."

"What map?" asked Roy.

"Supposedly my grandfather handed it down to my dad. I never actually saw it, so it might not even exist," said Tommy. "I just heard him and Sergio talking about it one night in the Gator Hook." A chuckle. "Crazy meets crazy."

"Again, what map?"

"You know my granddad was nuttier than hell—always claimed there was something buried out behind the old Capone place in the glades."

"Bodies?"

"No doubt," said Tommy. "But Granddad was talking about something else. Legend has it that just before the Valentine's massacre, Scarface cleared out his Chicago vault . . ."

"The empty one Geraldo opened on live TV?"

Tommy nodded. "After Rivera only found cobwebs, the rumors really took off. As the story goes, Al knew there'd be heat from his hit on the Moran gang, so in advance he divided up the safe's contents and stashed it at various places around the country, including the Everglades. Dad drew a map from memory. But like I said, 'as the story goes.'"

"How'd he even know to draw a map."

"Claims one night he was at the wrong place at the wrong time—saw something he shouldn't have."

Chi-Chi grinned. "As soon as I get out of this joint, let's go dig it up!"

Tommy smiled back. "Deal."

A white coat and stethoscope appeared in the doorway. "Excuse me?" The doctor looked at Roy. "Can we talk?"

Roy stepped into the hallway, bracing for the worst.

The attending physician opened a patient file. "He can go home."

"What?" Roy's head jerked back. "He's getting better?"

"No." The doctor put a hand on his shoulder. "He's got a month, maybe two. But he's stable, and we feel they often do better at home, surrounded by family . . ."

Back inside the room, Chi-Chi had nodded-off, and everyone headed for the door. The attorney slid the witnessed documents into a large envelope and tried to be nonchalant. "So, Tommy, you think your granddad's map was for real?"

"*He* swore it was." Tommy stopped and turned around in the hall. "Except you'd have to know him. Personally, I think Geraldo found more on his show."

SOMEWHERE IN CYBERSPACE

Serge's Blog. Star Date 584.948.

Hey gang! Welcome to the first installment of Serge's Florida (Fugitive) Experience!

Nowhere else will you find the best way to enjoy my fine state! That's right, as a fugitive!

I know what you're thinking: "But, Serge, I'm not a fugitive."

Who says? Society brainwashes us into thinking you have to be chased in order to flee. But anyone can just make a break for it whenever they want. So here's what you do: After work on Friday, screech out of the parking lot and race around the state in a paranoid stupor, glancing over your shoulders, peeking through blinds of dicey motels, darting down alleys and diving in Dumpsters whenever you spot a patrol car, tipping bartenders extra and whispering: "You never saw me." But how many law-abiding citizens have the imagination to experience the magic?

I already hear your next question: "What if the cops get suspicious and stop me?"

Proudly declare you're a fugitive on the run! Then they radio it in, and dispatch comes back with a clean record. And the cop says, "Are you actually wanted for anything?" And you say, "Not even a parking ticket," and he says, "Then how are you a fugitive?" You say, "It's a lifestyle choice. We have an image awards dinner coming up."

First, you'll be staying in a lot of motels. Stick with the most sketchy. I recently tried mixing my routine with a reservation at an upscale chain. You know, the one with those ads where that woman is swinging around the room on red curtains? I'm here to tell you, those things rip right the fuck down. And the rods take chunks out of the wall. Then you go to the front desk to complain, and they look at all the plaster dust and bundle of torn fabric in your arms and say, "What the hell were you doing swinging from the curtains?" I say, "Isn't that how all business people relax?"

Second, disguises. It's your call. I prefer a professional disguise kit; Coleman gets drunk and cuts his own hair.

Third, getaway driving. You know how you sometimes need to change lanes to make a turn? And you
hit your blinker, but in the Sunshine State that's the
official signal for the jack-off behind you in the next
lane to speed up and close the gap so you can't get over?
Not actually a fugitive tip. Just burns my ass.

P.S. Next week, "Al Capone: The Florida
Connection!"

P.P.S. Next fugitive stop . . .

MIAMI BEACH

Restored Art Deco treasures lined Collins Avenue.
Restaurants, apartments, shops. And hotels.

In a $300-a-night suite on the fourteenth floor, with
a sweeping view of the Atlantic, an unconscious man
on the bed regained consciousness.

"Where am I?"

Blood and bruises.

He sat up and grabbed his pounding head. "What
the heck happened?"

Memory seeped back. The *woman*. Like him, a
rough-sex freak. She had indeed kept her promise to
blow his mind with a night to top all others.

Across the room, sitting at a desk with her back to
him, were those curves and fabulous head of fiery red

hair that had first caught his attention in the techno-dance club.

The man jumped from the bed and into his pants. "You're fucking crazy!" He ran out the door without his shirt.

No reaction from the woman. She was on her laptop, faithfully monitoring the same website for any updates. It was proverbial feast or famine. A nonstop flood of images and text for weeks. Then nothing for six months.

The faucet had just come back on.

Serge's Florida (Fugitive) Experience.

"Bingo."

At the bottom of the computer screen: *P.P.S. Next fugitive stop: Kissimmee!*

She scribbled something on a hotel notepad, then went to wake the person in the suite's other bedroom.

A half hour later, guests rubber-necked all through the hotel lobby as a jaw-dropping redhead in dark, movie-star sunglasses rolled a single Samsonite out to the curb. She didn't even need her valet ticket. Who could forget?

A turquoise T-Bird rolled up. The valet got a ten for his trouble, and she took off.

Chapter Four

SOUTH OF ORLANDO

A Crown Vic rolled east on Highway 192. Two occupants checked addresses.

Agent White looked over from the driver's seat at his passenger. "I hate to pull rank, but could you wear a shirt and tie?"

Agent Lowe glanced down at his black jumpsuit. "But it's regulation SWAT."

"You're not on the SWAT team."

"I'm projecting."

"Shirt and tie tomorrow?"

"Will you put in a word?"

"If we catch Serge." White returned to checking address numbers on car washes and nail salons. Then a strip mall, where Uncle Sam and the Statue of Liberty stood at the curb, waving signs for speedy tax preparation. "I thought the Orange Bowl was in Miami."

"So did I," said Lowe. "But it's where his e-mail told us to meet."

They continued through Kissimmee, farther from Disney, closer to the old part of town that had grown out of livestock farms and steamboat docks in the late nineteenth century. The main drag slipped from tourist glitter to neighborhood business.

"There it is," said Lowe.

White pulled into the parking lot and looked up at cursive letters down the side of a building frozen in time.

"Now I get it," said Lowe. "The Orange Bowl. A bowling alley."

They went inside.

White tilted his head. "Lane three."

Pins scattered, six-ten split. A man in a tweed coat and rumpled fedora grabbed another ball and addressed the spare. He began running and swung his arm back.

"Mahoney?"

Gutter ball.

He flicked a toothpick behind him. "Who's chimin'?"

"What?" said White.

"Mahoney," said Lowe. "I called you in Saint Pete."

Mahoney formed a cynical smile. "Pokin' the Serge lay-down?"

The partners looked oddly at each other.

They took seats around the scoring table and White leaned earnestly. "When was the last time you saw Serge?"

Mahoney reclined in the molded plastic chair. "Full-moon baker's dozen in J-town, cashed out scraping leather on a midnight twist before the shield flash."

White squinted. "I didn't understand a word you just said."

"He means a year ago in Jacksonville," said Lowe. "Serge eluded police capture and escaped." He turned to Mahoney. "And that's what led to your last, uh, disability leave? This obsession thing?"

Mahoney just crossed his arms.

White leaned again. "What were you doing chasing Serge in Jacksonville? I thought you were under strict orders to stay away from him."

"Not angling Serge," said Mahoney. "James Donald Woodley."

News flash. White's expression changed. "The cop killer?"

Mahoney straightened the fedora's brim. "Snitch coughed a handle to peg the crib. Dilly switcheroo-ski on the mark drop."

"Do you always talk like this?"

"He means they found out Woodley's alias," said Lowe. "Tracked him down to a motel. Except it turned out to be Serge's room."

"Serge was using the same alias as a cop killer?" said White. "How did that happen?"

Mahoney shrugged.

"And this was the last time you saw him?" asked White.

"No face grab."

"He didn't actually see Serge," said Lowe.

White looked at both of them. "Then how do you know he was there?"

Mahoney stared off across the empty lanes. "It's all coming back to me now . . ."

White looked at Lowe. "What's he doing?"

"I think he's going into a fade-out."

"No!" White snapped at Mahoney. "No fade-outs!"

Mahoney raised his eyes toward the ceiling. "Seems like just yesterday . . ."

. . . **A Plymouth** with bald tires parked in darkness behind a long, graffiti-tagged building with concrete cracks from water seepage.

Doors slammed.

Two men headed for an even darker alley.

"Another thing that pisses me off," said Serge. "Movie titles that are predicates. *Raising Helen, Feeling Minnesota, Regarding Henry* . . . wait, the last one's a preposition. I hate that sentence-diagramming bullshit even more."

Coleman crumpled a beer can. "I say: *Biting Me.*"

Serge stopped. "Coleman. You can conjugate."

"Fuckin'-A."

"You did it again."

Six hours earlier, they had checked into an economy motel on Jacksonville's hardworking west side. Only three cars in the lot. A neon sign with Arabic letters sizzled in the humid heat, someone on a flying carpet. The night manager ate cold chop suey behind bulletproof glass.

And now, after a robust day of souvenir gathering and crime fighting, Serge had returned. It was their first time at the motel, so he employed his patented precautionary tactic of parking a couple blocks south behind a Vietnamese grocery. If the stolen car was made, it couldn't be connected to the room, and if the room was made, he had a stashed getaway vehicle. If neither happened, Serge would make Coleman chase him for fun.

They worked their way toward the motel through multiple alleys.

"Looks like the coast is clear," said Serge. "Ready?"

"But I don't want to chase you."

They turned another corner.

Flashing red and blue lights reflected off the muffler shop next door.

Serge leaped back behind the building.

"What is it?" asked Coleman.

"Cops."

"They found us! Let's get out of here!"

"There's no way they could have found us." Serge peeked around the corner. "I used my backtracking, triple-reverse cloaking fugitive maneuver. Besides, have you seen how busy the police are in this town? Probably some other wanted felon."

Serge slipped into the alley that led to the front of the motel.

"What the hell are you doing?" said Coleman.

"Going to see the takedown." Serge stepped around puddles. "Takedowns crack me up: *I'm not resisting! Stop hitting me with batons! I can't breathe with your knee on my back! Don't do the choke hold! That's the choke hold! Grahhhsfdjgpaojdsg* . . . How can you not laugh at excessive force?"

They slowly crept up the alley and poked their heads around the next corner.

"Holy mother," said Serge. "I've never seen so many patrol cars. Like a thousand cops and . . . why are they surrounding our room?"

"Told you," said Coleman.

"Must be some kind of mistake." Serge pulled back until only one eye was at the edge of the motel.

Bam! Bam! Bam! Crash!

"What was that?" asked Coleman.

"The SWAT team just went in and . . . Uh-oh." Serge began backing up with uncharacteristic fear.

"What'd you see?"

"Mahoney!" Serge quietly turned around. "So they are after us. Let's just creep back to the car."

Coleman began making exaggerated tiptoe steps like he was in a cartoon.

They almost reached the back of the alley, ready to make a dash into the safety of darkness. Serge breathed easier.

Suddenly, from behind, a bath of bright white light.

They spun and shielded their eyes from the headlights of another patrol car that had just pulled up the drive. "Shit!" Serge turned back around. "Walk faster."

Car doors.

"Police! Don't move! Get your hands in the air!"

Serge froze and clenched his eyes shut with a wince.

A different officer's voice: "Now walk backward and keep those hands up!"

The pair complied until they were ten feet from the cops.

"Stop right there! Now turn around very slowly!"

They did.

Two police officers, one aiming a 9mm, the other with a flashlight. Its beam hit their faces. More reflexive squinting.

"You staying at the motel?"

"Yes," said Serge. Then, preemptively: "Room twelve."

The second officer aimed his flashlight down at a mug shot, then looked at his partner. "Neither one of them's him."

"You sure?"

"Not even close."

The first officer looked up at Serge and Coleman. "Seen the guy staying in room seven?"

"Nope, just checked in." Serge felt the brass key to room seven burning red-hot in his pocket. "Why? What did he do?"

"That's not your concern," the cop said as he walked away. "But you might want to stay at another motel."

"Thank you, Officer."

They took off, snaking back through the network of dark alleys for their getaway car. Broken glass broke into smaller pieces under their shoes.

"What just happened?" asked Coleman.

"Divine intervention," said Serge. "We'll know more from the late news."

Two hours later, another twenty-nine-dollars-a-day dump. Peeling wallpaper and soggy stains in the avocado carpet. Serge and Coleman sat propped up in a lumpy bed, sharing a bag of barbecue chips. Their faces glowed from the room's original, flickering Magnavox. The TV newscast ended.

"So that's why there were so many patrol cars," said Serge. "They were after a cop killer."

"But you've never killed a cop."

"And I never will." Serge popped a chip in his mouth. "But Franklin Ignatius Turnville did."

"Who's Franklin Ignatius Turnville? . . ."

. . . **Mahoney blinked** a few times, coming out of his transfixed gaze. He turned back toward the agents. "And that's my last brush with Serge."

Lowe leaned and whispered to his boss. "But how did his fade-out have the perspective of the suspects if he was in front of the motel and never saw them?"

White shook his head not to pursue it.

Bowling pins clacked. The manager sprayed disinfectant in rented shoes. Lowe translated for Mahoney. . . .

White finally sat back in his chair. "So you discovered Serge was there by reviewing tape from the dashboard camera of that cruiser?"

Mahoney nodded.

"That's quite a coincidence," said the agent. "Using the same alias as that cop killer."

Lowe opened a textbook. "Not as much as you'd think. I've been studying false IDs, and it's actually a very common technique—"

"Please," said White, then to Mahoney: "And that's the last you've heard of him?"

A slighter nod. Mahoney conveniently omitted the whole string of spring break murders, when he was supposed to be on medical leave. He'd sworn to take Serge down. And almost did. Even had him at gunpoint in Fort Lauderdale. But they both lived by a mutual code of honor, and Serge had exposed himself to assist police. He wanted Serge more than anything, but not like that.

Mahoney got up from the table, grabbed a heavy black ball that lost its shine in 1962 and rolled another split. He returned and put his hand over the dryer.

"Sure could use your help," said Agent Lowe, opening a file on the table. "We've gone back ten years— every last sighting, victims, motel rooms, ditched cars."

"Goose eggs?" said Mahoney.

"Do you have the slightest lead we might follow?" asked White. "Even the most long-shot detail that might seem irrelevant?"

"Ducats to dice on the heel-cooler shimmy-sham."

"What?"

Mahoney grabbed another ball. "I know his next stop."

"You do?" said Lowe. "Where?"

"Kissimmee."

"*Here?*"

Mahoney picked up the split and marked it on his scorecard.

"But how do you know?" asked White. "We've been poring through ten boxes of reports around the clock."

Another ball popped out of the chute. Mahoney stuck fingers in holes and addressed the fresh set of pins. "Serge has a website."

Chapter Five

MIAMI

A quiet hacienda off Calle Ocho in Little Havana.

Chi-Chi's granddaughter's place. He'd been in assisted living before the hospital stay, but his family wasn't having that now with time short.

Three generations filled the home, taking turns in the bedroom. And of course the old gang.

Coltrane popped his head in the door. "Roy, got a second?"

"What is it?"

"Better we talk out back."

They stepped onto the porch and closed the sliding-glass door. "Got a problem."

"What kind?"

"Money. We were doing a little advance planning, you know, funeral home."

"If his family's short, we can all pitch in," said Roy. "They know that."

"It's a little worse. You might want to go home and check your portfolio."

"I'm not following."

"That attorney of ours, Brad Meltzer?"

"Came highly recommended," said Roy. "Handles all our estates, starting back with Sergio."

"It's gone."

"Yeah, everyone's taken a beating in the market."

"Not the market," said Coltrane. "Brad moved stuff around recently with his accountant. He's got it offshore."

"How do you know?"

"After we saw Chi-Chi's situation, I looked at mine. Then called Tommy Junior . . ." He leaned against a concrete statue on the porch.

"That's the Virgin Mary!"

Coltrane looked down. "Oops." He quickly lifted his arm. "Anyway, we took all our paperwork to another accountant this morning. Guy said it was all completely slimy and totally legitimate. We left a ton of messages, but Brad won't return our calls."

"How could this have happened?" asked Roy.

Coltrane shook his head. "We gave him power of attorney, and he covered himself with a whole pile of Latin bullshit disclaimers."

"Fucker always was having us sign stuff."

"Back in the day, nobody would dare push the gang around like this," said Coltrane. "They knew we'd square things, legal or not."

"But we're old now."

"I know someone who isn't." He began opening the sliding-glass door. "Seven o'clock, the Miami River place."

CYBERSPACE

Serge's Blog. Star Date 374.938.

Florida Fugitive Tip Number 38: When the net really tightens, take disguise to the next level! Hide in plain sight! You know those quasi-employees who stand on the side of the road in costumes, waving signs for businesses in strip malls? Even if there's a full-scale manhunt, cops never check them. Plus, many of those people have dubious routines and chemical hobbies. Which means a bargain for you! This morning Coleman and I bought costumes dirt cheap outside a tax preparation office from two cats who took off for the nearest drug hole. Then we walked all over the place totally concealed in our secret identities. Except I learned you can't just walk all over the place. You sort of need to stay close to the store because the owner will notice and send someone out in a car to get their costumes back, and then Coleman and I were *running* all over the place, which kind of defeated the purpose of keeping a low profile, because regular foot chases are so common in Florida that people pay more attention to the mailman, but apparently they get nosy when Uncle Sam and the Statues of Liberty leap over hoods of cars in heavy traffic.

And I could have easily outrun the guy, except for the flowing green dress and foam crown that kept slipping over my eyes, which is why I crashed into that sidewalk café table, and that's how the guy cornered me, forcing a counter-strike. The unfair thing is I made a deliberate effort to be inconspicuous and not disturb the lunch crowd, using only quick, short jabs with the liberty torch, and then *they're* the ones who made a scene.

Florida Criminal History Lesson Number 61: Chicago's impact on the Sunshine State.

The Lexington Hotel opened in 1892 on the corner of Twenty-second Street and Michigan Avenue. In July of 1928, a man named George Phillips moved into a suite on the fifth floor. His business card said he was a furniture dealer. George also had a winter home, a fourteen-room waterfront mansion at 93 Palm Avenue in Miami.

George was also known as Al Capone, also known as Scarface.

In the winter of 1929, Chicago was not exactly warm. Al stood in his suite at the Lexington, packing for a trip. Capone also kept a vault in the basement. Only the most trusted members of his crew had access. At some point he gave instructions to crate the contents for shipment. Where it went, nobody knows. Or they took it to the grave.

Later that week, Al woke up in Florida. That evening came the news: Back in Chicago, seven members of the rival Bugs Moran gang had been machine-gunned in a garage on Clark Street. The killers wore police uniforms.

It was Valentine's Day.

Al had an alibi. He was meeting with a Miami prosecutor.

In those days, Miami was gangster vacation land. The big bosses left their criminal habits up north, and obeyed the law in the sun. Don't shit where you eat. They became local celebrities, socializing openly at Joe's Stone Crab or Tobacco Road, often with politicians and top police officials at neighboring tables. Everyone was happy. Until Al arrived.

Prohibition-era Miami was not exactly an above-the-table town. Rum coming in at night from Cuba, prostitution, bookmaking. But even by these standards, Al was too high-profile. They tried to run him off. But Capone hadn't done anything wrong, at least nothing in their jurisdiction, and his attorneys successfully fought all comers.

But Al was Al. Just couldn't leave well enough alone. He opened his wallet wide, and construction began on an unusual project in a most unusual Florida location . . .

Next week: foreclosed homes. One person's misfortune is your hiding place!

Serge finished typing his blog entry. He looked up from his laptop at an arm stretched in front of him. The arm was attached to Coleman. Its hand gripped a wheel.

Coleman smiled from the passenger seat. "How's my driving?"

"Excellent," said Serge, stowing the portable computer. "Your faithful service allowed me to make my Web deadline for my tidbit-famished followers. I'll take it from here . . ."

"What are you doing now?"

"Making a note on my clipboard for the next blog," said Serge. "Natural enemy of the fugitive: accidental discovery on the highway. So make sure those tags are up-to-date, blinkers working and definitely no speeding."

"What made you think of that now?"

"See the nose of the black-and-beige sedan sticking out from behind those trees?"

"Not really."

"Way up there, just outside radar range." Serge steered with his knees and jotted on the clipboard. "I pride myself on being able to spot highway patrol before they can ping me."

"Now that you mention it, that's the third cop I've seen along here."

"They're running a wolf pack."

". . . (Recalculating. Make a U-turn) . . ."

Coleman pointed with a joint at the center of the dashboard. "It's that Garmin chick again."

". . . (Recalculating. Make a left) . . ."

Serge glanced at Coleman. "I don't understand a word she's saying. Did you mess with the language setting?"

"Oh, no, no, no. I would never . . . Yes, I did."

". . . (Recalculating. Make a U-turn) . . ."

"Coleman, show me what you hit."

"I think this . . . or this."

Serge leaned toward the Garmin. "Why'd you pick that language?"

"I don't know."

". . . (Recalculating. Turn right) . . ."

"So change it back."

"I'm trying to. It won't let me."

"You locked the screen."

"How do I unlock it?"

"I don't know. I just bought the thing."

Coleman kept trying buttons. "What about the manual?"

"I always throw manuals out. Life's too short."

". . . (Recalculating. Drive point-seven) . . ."

"I can't fix it," said Coleman.

"Son of a bitch." Serge smacked the steering wheel. "All the women in my life, and now I'm taking shit from some chick in Mandarin."

". . . (Recalculating) . . ."

"Shut up! Shut up!"

". . . (Recalculating) . . ."

Serge snatched the GPS out of its cradle and began smashing it to bits on the dashboard.

"Serge, are you okay?"

He threw the last quiet piece on the floor. "Couldn't be better. I finally won an argument with a woman."

"Serge?"

"What?"

"How fast are you going?"

"Only seventy—" He glimpsed the speedometer. "Eighty-five!"

Coleman pointed with his joint again. "There's another cop."

"Fuck! And we're in pinging range. I always knew a woman would bring me down."

"What'll we do?" asked Coleman.

"I wanted to save this for later, but I'm forced to burn one of my 'Outs.'"

"What kind of 'Out' can help us now?"

"Observe the master."

Serge went into the zone of absolute focus. Eyes swept mirrors. Other traffic, lanes, distance vectors.

Coleman trembled in terror. "The trooper's pulling forward! He's going to chase us!"

Serge remained on task. At the precise moment, he reached beside the steering column and threw a lever.

Vehicles behind saw a turn signal come on.

The Corvette in the next lane suddenly accelerated to cut off Serge's lane change and whipped by on the left.

Flashing blue lights. The trooper took off after the sports car.

ORLANDO

The waiting line wound up and down the aisles and backed into the coffee shop.

Agent Lowe stood at the end, peeking around other heads.

At the front was a book-signing table. Stacks of a ghost-written autobiography of a fake life story.

"I'm your biggest fan! Make it out to Ralph."

The Doberman smiled and scribbled, then accepted a book from the next customer.

"I'm your biggest fan! We met six years ago at another signing in Atlanta. Remember me?"

Another book. Another autograph.

"I'm your biggest fan! I'm a writer, too, and I wanted to ask you a question. I'm working on a book right now. I haven't actually started. It's a western. I don't know anything about the West, so I might need to do research. But I hate research, so I was thinking of setting it in the future because who knows what the West will be like, right? And I've never written anything, but everyone always says I should write a book, so I should probably take some kind of class except I don't have the time."

The Doberman smiled and handed the book back. "What's your question?"

"How do I get a publisher?"

The line inched along.

The autobiography's release had been pushed up a month at the insistence of his cable-syndicated TV show.

"We're tanking," said his producer.

"I thought we just added six new markets."

"And lost nine. Nielsen's dropped every week since March."

"What am I supposed to do about it?"

"What you're best at. Headlines. Has to be something absolutely huge."

"Like what?"

"Like that time you went to Mexico to abduct that rapist who fled from Texas, and you got intestinal parasites and had explosive diarrhea in the airport."

"I'd rather do something else."

"But people love that human element, especially the part where you didn't make it to the restroom in time."

"Any other ideas?"

"What would your wife think about having a shitload of kids, which you raise on camera in touching yet nerve-racking everyday circumstance, and then you start banging the nanny?"

"She'd probably shoot me."

"I'll run that by the affiliates . . ." He walked away.

So here the bounty hunter sat in a suburban mall, painfully smiling through compliments. Not because he was ungrateful. Because of his neck brace. He popped a Vicodin.

The afternoon wore on, the line dwindling until only one person was left.

"I'm your biggest fan!" said Agent Lowe, dressed in the SWAT uniform he yearned to officially wear someday. "I've seen every episode. You give us . . . *hope*."

The bounty hunter cordially signed the book. Wheels grinding in his head. Cop fans were the best, the more starry-eyed the better, because they tended to talk out of school. Some of highest-rated episodes came from information he'd mined about classified ongoing investigations, *just between you and me*.

The Doberman handed the book back to Lowe and smiled warmly. "You in a tactical unit?"

"Almost," said the agent. "But I did just get named to this really important task force."

The bounty hunter offered a plastic bottle. "Vicodin?"

"I'm good."

The Doberman shrugged and popped another. "So what's this task force do?"

"It's incredible," said Lowe. "We're after this one-man crime wave who's left bodies all over the state for nearly two decades. His name's Serge A. Storms."

"Never heard of him."

"You kidding?" said Lowe. "Almost every cop in the state has. Nobody can believe he's eluded capture all these years, especially considering how brazenly he disposes of victims. Rewards up to something like two hundred thousand . . . And whoever does capture him will become an instant legend."

The Doberman leaned forward on his elbows. "Please, continue."

"He's totally insane," said Lowe. "Yet crazy like a fox."

"How many people did you say he's killed?"

"We're still finding out," said Lowe. "Like this one time he sucked all the water out of these two guys and laid them out to cure like human jerky."

"Sounds gross," said the Doberman. "I like it. What else?"

Lowe stopped. "I think I may have already said too much."

"Just between you and me."

"Okay," Lowe said enthusiastically. "This other time he set up a motion trigger near Cape Canaveral . . ."

"Why don't we go back to my tour bus for some drinks." The Doberman stood and put an arm around Lowe's shoulders.

"You'd really let me hang out with you?"

"Be my honor," said the hunter, walking him out of the store. "I'm just a TV superstar, but the real heroes are law enforcement like you who hang it all on the line every day."

"We do kind of take risks." He rolled up his right sleeve. "That's where a pencil went in—"

"And I'd love to hear more about this dangerous hombre you're risking your life to catch . . . Have you met the Litter?"

Babes snuggled tight on both sides of the agent.

"Well," said Lowe. "Serge has this website."

The Doberman led him up the trailer's steps. "Let's log on and take a look . . ."

Chapter Six

CYBERSPACE

Serge's Blog. Star Date: Wow!

Yo out there. It's actually me, Coleman. Serge just crashed after staying awake for three days. I'm usually the one that's passed out, but I took some bad acid, so I'll be wide open for a bit, just carrying on with my job, all the little chores that go un-thanked. Serge complains I don't do chores, but I've just spent who knows how long lying flat on the ground, keeping the carpet in place, because it was starting to dome up in the middle, and it goes without saying you can't let it get to the ceiling . . . By bad acid, I don't mean the regular bad, where you're on a mega-freak-out trip like you're both suffocating and having a massive heart attack at the same time and swear to God you're going to die any second. The dying part doesn't make it bad, because if

you're a party warrior, you go: Yes! It's kicking
in! . . . What makes it bad is you do *really* stupid stuff,
like if you go to the mall, and everything's normal—
just weeping and banging your head on a post because
they don't have a Hickory Farms, and a second later
you're covered in cold cream and dragging an inflatable woman, and everyone yells "pervert," but I only
bought the thing so I could drive in car-pool
lanes . . . Good acid's totally different. Took some killer
windowpane last year, and first got pissed because it
wasn't working and I thought I'd been ripped off, and
I'm playing with my zipper, up and down and up
and down, hearing sounds of individual prongs locking
and unlocking in musical scales like a xylophone, and
the mechanism starts blowing my mind and I think:
Hey, a lot of planning went into this motherfucker. So I
took off my pants to get a closer look, zipping up and
down in front of my face. Even more impressive! LSD's
like that, always giving you a new perspective, especially when the pants are over your head, and you're
looking *out* through the zipper: up, down, up, down,
each time giving me a peek through the crotch to the
tune of "Jungle Boogie." And you know how sometimes you just get this paranoid feeling on excellent
drugs that someone's watching you? It was like that
this time, except multiplied by a hundred, probably

because I was in a restaurant. Suddenly all these people began screaming, and I thought maybe some customer had gone berserk, and I crawled under the table. Then suddenly the table went straight up in the air! I'm thinking, holy fuck, what kind crazy McDonald's is this? Turns out some employees had lifted the table and grabbed me and then I was on the sidewalk in my underwear and some pants hit me in the face, and I went back to the motel and kept working the zipper, wondering about the person who invented it, and I finally nod to myself: Yeah, now this guy really had his shit wired tight—he could see the big picture. And I hid under the bed and played with the zipper for the next six hours until the trip wore off. Now, *that's* good acid . . . But this stuff I just took is stale or diluted, so you only get a little high and stay up all night. Which makes it bad *acid*, but great *speed*. The last time I got some I went back for more at five A.M., but the guy refused to hook me up because his wife was yelling crazy in the background: "Does that goddamn idiot know what time it is?" and Serge is shouting from the driveway for me to hurry, and I get back in the car, and Serge says I shouldn't have come at this ungodly hour because the wife sounded like she was on ten periods and I wouldn't be welcome anymore, but I said, no, they're drug dealers—they understand the chemical equation.

He said, what equation? I said, they sold me speed; I woke them up . . . Oh, when I said Serge was zonked from exhaustion, I wasn't kidding. He had a mondo-huge day! We're driving who-knows-where, and he's totally obsessed with his new Fugitive Tour crap, and we pass this field and see all these old tents and people in gray and blue uniforms loading muskets, and Serge makes a wild U-turn and races across a dirt parking lot. I ask what's going on? He says, "A military re-enactment! I've always wanted to be in a military re-enactment!" I said, "What about the Fugitive Tour?" He said, "What?," and jumps out and sprints to the command tent, offering to enlist: "Are you doing the battle of Santa Rosa or St. John's Bluff? Maybe Fort Brooke. Please tell me it's Fort Brooke! You're probably wondering which side I'm on—the side of history!" He sees a campfire that's gone out and an old charred pot on a log. "Is that coffee? I don't care if it's cold. Wait here!" And he chugs half the pot, brown stuff streaming down his neck, and runs back with the thing still in his hand and salutes. "Reporting for duty! Coffee wins wars! Fourscore and seven! Rockets' red glare! Bombs bursting! Bang a gong, get it on!" Before they can say anything, there's a bunch of loud explosions and puffs of smoke from cannons. Serge clapped his hands like patty-cake: "The battle's begun! I'll help you win! Watch this!" Then he dashes onto the field and grabs a rifle from the side of a dead soldier (I think the guy was just faking), and charges from the rear to join the advancing front line of the blue army—"What's wrong with you guys? Show some patriotism! Start yelling!" And he breaks right through the line, still sprinting, waving back at them and shouting, "Follow me! On to fucking victory!" And he ends up all alone in the middle of the field between the two armies, still charging. I guess they were filming some kind of authentic documentary, and Serge is wearing a tropical shirt and sneakers and a wristwatch. So then everyone *does* start yelling, and Serge reaches the line of gray soldiers and clubs one over the head with the stock of his rifle. Man, did that guy go down fast. And this other soldier is like, "What the fuck are you doing?" Serge says, "Preserving the Union!" And then he clubs *him*. Other dudes tried to take the rifle away, but Serge is swinging it like a baseball bat. Now the blue army is really running, and Serge looks over his shoulder: "See how it's done?" But two of the *blue* guys grab him, and Serge says, "What are you doing? I'm on your side! You're going to blow the battle!" But they're just yelling "Asshole!" and "Dick-wad!" So Serge head-butts one and punches the other in the Adam's apple and takes off. I think they canceled the battle because all the blue and gray guys are now running together after Serge. Except Serge is pretty fast, and these dudes are wearing all this heavy, hot clothing. Serge zigzags back and forth across the field, doing loops all over the place. Some of the guys start to faint, and I decide to wait in the car with the beer, and finally I see Serge racing over the top of a hill with a rifle and about a hundred guys behind him. He picked up an American flag from somewhere and jumps in the driver's seat. They're just about to the car, when Serge guns the engine and takes off right at them. Never seen people scatter so fast. I suggest we get out of there, but Serge says that would be desertion and speeds back onto the battlefield, more guys diving out of the way, Serge waving the flag out the window at the documentary crew: "The tide has turned in favor of the Republic!" And he finally reaches the enemy camp and runs over all their tents and back-packs and lawn chairs and shit and says, "Now *this* is a military re-enactment!" And we take a gravel road back to the highway and he tells me the only thing to do after the Civil War is to drive to the airport so he can experience "time shock." We're riding the escala-tors over and over at Orlando International, and Serge is telling everyone about metal stress and the failure rate of different planes and that he thinks pilots secretly have parachutes, and he sees this one guy and almost craps with glee, and I ask, "What is it?" He says that he's been searching airports his whole life, but never actually thought he'd find one, and I say, "One what?" He says, "A Hare Krishna." I say, "I've seen millions in airports." He points and says, "But this one has luggage. He's actually traveling. It could be my finest irony masterpiece!" He runs over to this tourist brochure rack, and then up to the bald dude in a robe, and Serge hands him the pamphlets and asks him for money. The guy gives a dirty look and walks away, but Serge keeps pestering for donations and forcing brochures on him. They're both walking faster and faster until the old guy's in an all-out sprint, and Serge snatches at his robe just before he ducks through security. I tell Serge that I think the guy's upset, and Serge says, "Of all people he should understand: It's karma." Then Serge bought a guitar at Best Buy. Not his original plan, but he was playing Guitar Hero and the song was by the Who, and these kids start laughing, and Serge says, "What's your problem? My high score will fry the program," and one kid says, "You won't even make the top fifty." And Serge says: "The top fifty never saw Townshend in person," and then he smashes the guitar to bits and the store people ask him to get out his wallet. Then we're driving back to this motel, and I think coffee gives you a letdown, because Serge is frowning, and I ask him what's the matter, and he's sitting there with a Civil War rifle, toy-guitar pieces, and shreds of a Hare Krishna robe and says, "Every day it's the same shit."

MIAMI

Just south of the river near Brickell.

Seven o'clock.

Roy the Pawn King, Tommy Junior and Coltrane sat at the bar listening to live, three-chord Chicago blues. Dim red light.

"I still can't believe he did this to us," said Roy.

"Believe it," said Tommy.

"Didn't Capone used to come here?" asked Coltrane.

"Practically a fixture," said Tommy.

Through the doors of Tobacco Road came a pair of bikers in head scarves.

Skid Marks grabbed a stool. "Dad, why'd you want to see us?"

"It's about our attorney," said Tommy.

"That button-down asshole," said Bacon Strips. "What about him?"

Tommy gave them the nine yards.

"Son of a—" said Skid Marks.

"We need your help," said Roy.

Bacon Strips leaped off his stool. "Don't worry. We'll take care of him."

"Sit back down," said Tommy.

They knew when not to argue. And had respect.

"We don't want revenge," said Roy. "We want our money."

"We want revenge, too," said Tommy.

"So you have a plan to get it back?"

"Oh, have we got a plan!" said Coltrane. "But it has to be delicate. Brad sewed this up legally, and the money's offshore. If we just beat the tar out of him, it's gone for good. That's why we're bringing in someone who knows how to fix such things."

"And can be trusted," said Tommy.

"What do you want us to do?" asked Skid Marks.

A harmonica howled from the stage. Roy pulled two envelopes from his jacket. "Brad's not taking our calls, so you need to personally deliver these to his secretary."

The bikers looked at a pair of letters. One was already sealed in an envelope marked CONFIDENTIAL. They read the other.

"I'm confused," said Skid Marks.

"Roy's idea," said Tommy. "That letter you just read instructs our attorney to equally distribute all proceeds among the families' surviving relatives. Brad's to deliver the sealed letter to our authorized agent."

"Proceeds from what?"

"The map mentioned in the open letter."

"Is the map in the sealed envelope?" asked Bacon Strips.

"No," said Tommy. "No map exists."

"Then what's in it?"

"Brad will find out when he opens it."

"But it's marked Confidential."

"That's why he'll open it."

"Now I'm really confused," said Skid Marks.

"Greed is his weakness," said Tommy. "You should have seen him drooling back in that hospital room when we reminisced about the old moonshine days and Capone's place."

"Only one problem," said Bacon Strips. "I don't see how Brad will be able to deliver the sealed letter."

"He won't deliver it."

"I'm lost again," said Skid Marks.

"After he reads it, he'll track down our friend so he can steal the map and recover the treasure for himself."

"The map that doesn't exist?"

"Exactly."

"But how will he find our friend?"

"With your help. You'll secretly meet the friend and bait the trail for our lawyer. Here're extra copies of the letters for yourself."

"What's the rest of the plan?" asked Bacon Strips.

"Don't have it," said Roy.

"Don't need it," added Tommy. "That's our friend's specialty. Once you meet, he'll take it from there."

"I understand now," said Skid Marks, tucking the envelopes in his leather vest and jumping off the stool again. "So where do we find this so-called authorized agent of yours?"

"That . . . gets a little complicated," said Tommy. "You better sit back down."

PART II
The Present

Chapter Seven

SOMEWHERE ABOVE FLORIDA

The sun peeked over the eastern horizon. The first to catch its light was anything in the air. Birds, clouds, wings of a vintage biplane.

The Sopwith Camel made good time as the crow flies, but its airspeed wouldn't get a ticket on I-75. It had taken the rest of the night to reach the coast from their narrow escape in Kissimmee.

Coleman woke up. "Look, the Atlantic Ocean."

"Actually the Gulf of Mexico," said Serge. "The sun's behind us."

"What's that mean?" He bent down, repeatedly flicking a Bic.

Rickenbacker pulled hard on the controls. The plane abruptly tilted down. A buzzing engine roar increased in their steep, noisy descent, like a strafing run.

Coleman abandoned his valiant attempt to light the joint and sat back up. "Where are we going?"

"See the fishing village on that little island just offshore?"

"Barely."

"Our next fugitive stop."

Twenty minutes later, they flew directly above the island.

Coleman looked over the side at a waterfront wharf of rustic wooden buildings. "Serge, this isn't a seaplane."

"Correct."

"I mean, I don't see a place to land."

"That's the fun part."

They left the island behind, heading out into the open gulf. Still descending.

The altimeter's needle followed their sharp drop until they were barely skimming the water. Rick raised the nose and put the plane into another hard back, taking her around 120 degrees.

Due southeast.

They lined up with a second, smaller island, just north of the wharf.

"I see it now," said Coleman. "That tiny runway."

"I love remote runways. Unattended, no authorities. Weeds growing through cracks in the pavement.

Intrigue, *Casablanca*." Serge's right palm shot out. "Camera me!"

Coleman reached for a backpack and slapped a digital in his pal's hand.

Serge raised it. *Click, click, click.* "But here's the cool part. There's just two taxi companies in the area, each independent with only a single car. And besides their regular radios, both have aviation bands. If you're arriving by plane like we are, you can call ahead for a cab ride to the village." *Click, click, click.*

Coleman squinted into the wind. "Things seem different from the air. Way up here, that runway almost looks too short."

"It *is* too short," said Serge. "Only two thousand three hundred and fifty-seven feet, taking up the whole island. Water and treacherous rocks inches from each end. Notorious in aviation circles for planes constantly ending up in the drink. Or worse. Only the best pilots . . ."

"Jesus, Serge. I was just getting over the power lines."

"Get ready to taste life!"

The pilot got on the radio. "Catfish, it's me, Rick. Need a lift for two passengers in five."

Wings wobbled as they swooped over crescent sand shoals and a submerged clam farm in the shallow, emerald green water. Salt filled sinuses. White-capped waves crashed against the end of the elevated runway, approaching quickly at eye level.

"We're too low!" said Coleman.

"Rick's got it."

It wasn't artful, but a quick back-and-forth on the throttle gave the plane a stomach-squeezing burst of lift, popping the plane up over the island's jagged shore and down toward the pavement. Wheels skidded on a giant, sun-faded number five in the middle of the runway, as if there were four others.

The biplane slowed as it reached the end of the runway, then rotated in place. The propeller jerked to a stop. Rick got out and set the ladder against the side again.

Coleman climbed down and threw up.

Rick jumped back from the splash. "Serge, your friend all right?"

"That's just his morning warm-up regimen."

Serge unloaded a couple of backpacks as Rick climbed back into the cockpit, started the engine and threw a scarf over his shoulder.

They exchanged until-we-meet-again salutes, and he was off. The biplane lifted from the runway, veered east and disappeared into the rising sun.

It was quiet again.

Serge hoisted his bag and turned. On the edge of the runway, a short, grinning man leaned against the fender of a checkered cab.

"Catfish!"

"Serge! Long time."

They gave each other the heterosexual, shoulder-slapping guy hug. Serge pointed. "And the man with the teddy bear backpack is my trusty sidekick, Coleman."

"He's not going to throw up in my cab, is he?"

"It's a crapshoot."

They climbed in, and the driver looked over the seat. "Where to first?"

"The cemetery's on the way into town."

Minutes later, they approached a gate and a rusty ship's anchor.

"Serge." Coleman fished a beer from his bag. "How come we always go to cemeteries?"

"First, because they're historic. See?" He gestured at a plaque: EST 1886. "Almost nothing in Florida is that old. The ancient anchor over there was snagged by someone fishing for mullet. And in the early days, they could only hold burials during low tide, because this road was otherwise underwater . . . Catfish, stop here." Serge hopped out with a camera and notebook. *Click, click, click . . .*

Coleman ran up beside him and chugged.

Click, click. Serge lowered his camera. "Coleman, dig. I love Florida cemeteries, especially ones like this: beach sand, fiery azaleas, moss-draped oaks, more anchors, graves surrounded by sea-smoothed boulders and shells and shit around the dead people. So cheerful." *Click, click, click* . . . He stowed the camera, flipped open a notebook and was on the move.

Coleman did his best to keep up. "You said, 'First.' "

Serge uncapped a pen. "What?"

"Cemeteries. You said, 'First, because they're historic.' That usually means a second."

"Second, the Fugitive Tour." Serge accelerated his march, checking headstones. "It's always good to keep a list of tombstone names with birth dates close to yours. Ones who died as infants before they could get Social Security cards. Preferably the same gender."

Coleman stopped and reached for his zipper. "Why?"

"To assume false identities. Everyone does it." He fanned through notebook pages as a visual aid. "I've got dozens of names from every corner of the state . . . Coleman!"

"What?"

"Don't pee on a grave."

"But he's dead."

"There's much we don't know about the afterlife. That guy could be somewhere right now, going 'What the fuck?' How would you like it?"

"I can't cut off the stream."

"Just walk. There's a tree."

Coleman left a drip trail through the sand and peeked around an oak trunk. "But how do you get a new identity?"

"Order a birth certificate from vital statistics, or counterfeit your own with a high-end printer, then score a driver's license. Or just get a library card with a doctored utility bill, and if anyone checks, it's kosher at first blush as long as they don't get too curious . . ."

"Using dead people's names seems creepy," said Coleman.

"What's really creepy is the other major fugitive use of cemeteries. Someone faking his own death by digging up a body, sticking it in his car and setting it ablaze. Fugitive Tip Eighty-eight." Serge continued his quest with growing frustration. "Dang, this cemetery's too old."

"Thought you liked old stuff."

"I do, but for my mission, I need newer headstones, something around 1962 during the Cuban Missile Crisis."

More and more walking, grave after grave, until they finished circling all the way back to the big anchor. "This isn't going to work. I'll just have to make do." Serge stepped into a family plot and opened his notebook again. "Let's see, father, mother and, man, they had a lot of kids . . . five, six, seven . . ."

"This family over here has nine," said Coleman. "And this one twelve. They were really fucking back then."

"Because there was no TV." Serge reached the end of the plot. A small cherub slept atop the headstone. He jotted on a page. "The youngest son's as close as I'll get." He closed the book and headed back for the cab. "From now on, call me Horatio. And I'm one hundred and nineteen years old."

Coleman pulled out another beer. "So is this what we were doing in that spooky cemetery last year in Jacksonville?"

"That's right." Serge reopened his notebook. "My most excellent harvest. Got six names that night within a month of my birthday, including Franklin Ignatius Turnville."

"Turnville?" Coleman scratched his head. "Where have I heard that name?"

"It was the false identity I used to check into the motel where we almost got busted during the hunt for that cop killer."

"The dead guy in the cemetery was a cop killer?"

"Coleman, try to follow: The cop killer did exactly what I did, copying names from graves." Serge stuck the notebook in his pocket. "Fugitive Tip Eighty-eight, Subsection B: Don't use tombstone names for false IDs: You never know who's been there before you."

"Then why are you still collecting them?"

"There's another purpose."

"What's that?"

"Exit strategy," said Serge. "I'm collecting 'Outs.'"

KISSIMMEE

Dawn broke south of Orlando.

The last in a nightlong series of highway flares burned to nubs.

Deputies checked driver's licenses and trunks on the Beachline Expressway toward Cape Canaveral.

Just past them, a Crown Vic sat on the shoulder of a road. Agent White was on the radio, getting a round robin of reports from other checkpoints. "No, I understand. Appreciate your assistance . . ."

Agent Lowe was in the passenger seat, working on a sausage biscuit. "You should try one of these."

Silence.

"Still no luck?"

White stared down the road. "I don't understand it. We covered every escape route . . . And we nearly had him at the Nu Bamboo."

Lowe reached into a paper sack and held a biscuit in front of White's face. "Want one? Smells good."

"Get that thing away from me."

Lowe shrugged. "Don't blame yourself. Whoever heard of four decoy motels?"

White unfolded a road map on the steering wheel. "Must still be lying low somewhere inside our perimeter. It's the only answer."

"Fool's bet," Mahoney said from the middle of the backseat. He sipped black joe from a Moon Hut coffee mug. "Serge couldn't stay planted if he jonesed. Seen him skim the tightest scrape."

"Okay, smart guy," said White. "Then what happened?"

"I'm down on his fade."

"Want to share?"

Mahoney did.

The Crown Vic pulled away from the shoulder of the road, followed by the SWAT van, a yellow Cadillac, black Beemer, convertible T-Bird and bounty hunter tour bus.

Chapter Eight

MEANWHILE . . .

A checkered cab drove toward town, past a small school next to a water tower: CEDAR KEY SHARKS. Over a small bridge with tin-roofed shacks and crab traps. Down by the water on First Street, ibis poked at the muck; flocks of gulls swooped in the stout, onshore wind. *Click, click, click.* Serge lowered his camera. "Coleman, see that rotted, falling-apart stilt house out in the surf that looks like it's about to collapse?"

"Yeah?"

"One of the most recognizable views in the state that nobody recognizes. Nicknamed the Honeymoon Cottage. I'm guessing sarcasm."

"How can it be recognized yet not recognized?"

"Because it's in souvenir stores all across the peninsula, featured on novelty joke postcards—Waterfront

Property for Sale—on the spinning metal racks just above fat-ass ladies on the beach and the totally black cards: Florida at Night."

The taxi reached the middle of the old village.

"Next stop?" asked Catfish.

"Probably get our room." Serge took more shots. *Click, click.*

"What fancies you today?" asked the driver.

"The old Cedar Inn, the Dockside, Cedar Cove and don't forget the Island Hotel, built in 1859 as a general store, which also housed the first post office."

"Which one?"

"All of them."

"What do you mean 'all of them'?" asked Catfish.

"For the Fugitive Tour."

"That's right," said Catfish. "Saw your underbelly website. I'm *definitely* going to have to take that vacation."

Serge smiled at Coleman. "Told you."

They made the rounds, getting rooms at the first three establishments under Serge's real name. Then out to the wharf and the final motel.

"Thanks again, Catfish. We'll take it from here." Serge over-tipped as usual.

"Anytime," said the driver.

Serge pulled a hundred from his wallet. "One more thing. I need a favor."

"Name it."

Serge handed him the C-note and opened his cemetery journal to a page marked *Jacksonville*. "Write this name down . . ." He explained the rest in tedious detail.

"No problem," said Catfish. "When?"

"Wait for my phone call."

"You got it." The cab drove away.

"What was that about?" asked Coleman.

"Part of the Secret Master Plan."

"I know," Coleman said forlornly. "It's a secret."

Serge stood on the sidewalk next to the office door and reverently touched a vintage globe lamp with the establishment's name: DOCKSIDE MOTEL. He went inside and rang a bell on the desk. Coleman rang it five more times.

Serge slapped his hand. "Behave!"

Someone appeared from the back.

"Room four if you got it," said Serge.

"Four's available."

"Excellent. When you find dependable air-conditioning, stick with it, I always say. They haven't changed the air conditioner, have they?"

"Don't know."

"Then I might have to do some rewiring."

"What?"

"The lights may dim briefly but it's nothing to worry about." Serge boldly signed the registration card. *Horatio Farnsworth*. "If I can't fix the a/c, that's the way it goes. People expect guarantees in life, then wonder why the newspaper's wet and the children never call." He received a metal key on a number four plastic fob. "Excellent. No magnetic card. Glad to meet a soldier in the fight."

"What?"

"Hold all calls." Serge ran up the stairwell to the second floor.

Coleman eventually arrived in the room. He fired a joint and rapidly toked to catch up on the day. Serge stood at a wide expanse of windows, surveying the wharf. "Most people hate economic collapse."

"You don't?" Coleman sucked the joint hard and cupped it in his hand.

"Back then, they called them 'panics,' like the Great Panic of 1893 . . . Why are you giggling?"

Coleman chortled as he held his breath, then coughed out smoke. "Panic. All these people in suspenders screaming and running into each other, falling through store windows, knocking over turnip carts, hair catching fire, livestock stampeding, monkeys marching up main street playing cymbals and smoking cigars. I'm really stoned now."

"Doesn't give you an excuse to laugh at others' problems."

"You're the one who said you liked it."

"An exemption for history," said Serge. "Too much collapse and you get a ghost town. But in just the right dose, a local depression can preserve heritage, like Cedar Key. In the 1850s, they built the cross-Florida railroad from Fernandina near Jacksonsville to this very wharf on the west coast. Soon, a bustling shipping port, freighters lining up: turpentine, cedar—naturally—and fresh seafood. They erected a giant sawmill for pencils."

"Pencils were the rage?"

"It was the golden age of lead. Then, in 1886, Henry Plant completed another railroad a hundred miles down the coast to the more convenient port in Tampa, and the ships stopped coming here. Commerce evaporated. That, coupled with the remote geography, froze this island in time, much like you see it today."

"How did they survive?"

"A lot of fishing . . ." Serge aimed his camera up the street at the former Captain's Table restaurant. ". . . Until Florida's fishing net ban. So the state retrained the bitter fishermen to farm clams, which they now cultivate with the latest marine science and profanity."

"I'm bored."

"The fugitive life is boring." *Click, click, click.* "That's what makes it so exciting."

"So we're just going to stay cooped up in this room?"

"No." Serge stowed his camera and began rummaging through the backpack. "We're going to do what all fugitives do between close calls."

"What's that?"

"Shoot pool."

"Pool?"

"Wherever pool's being played, there's guaranteed to be at least one fugitive." Serge pulled his hand out of the backpack.

"Those look like Hot Wheels tracks," said Coleman.

"Because they are."

U.S. HIGHWAY 98

A Crown Vic raced up Florida's west coast. One of those lonely, bygone roads since the interstate went in. Trees and junkyards and more trees. A sign for some restaurant called the Gator Hole, where only the foundation remained. The highway became a straight shot through pine strands, until the first stoplight for miles appeared as a tiny red dot on the horizon.

"Hang a louie up there at Otter Creek," said Mahoney.

They finally reached the light, skidding around the corner at a converted gas station that now advertised live shrimp, worms, cold beer and crickets.

"This is a long drive," said White. "You better be on target with this hunch of yours."

"Like found money." He turned around and looked out the back window as the trailing convoy made the same turn past a traffic sign: CEDAR KEY.

CEDAR KEY

Coleman staggered to the north end of the dock and pushed open a door with a brass porthole. "Serge?"

A wave of an arm. "Over here!" Serge leaned aggressively over the bar. "Excuse me, ma'am? I see the old Captain's Table has been renamed Coconuts."

"I don't know, I just started here."

"You do realize we're way too far above the frost line for coconut palms to survive. Who do I need to speak with?"

"What?"

Serge gathered Hot Wheels tracks off the bar. "I'll be at the pool tables."

Five minutes later, out on the sidewalk. "That was unfair," said Serge.

"They might have had a point," said Coleman.

"Why?" said Serge. "Just because I prefer to use several tables at once? Whole new game, like three-dimensional chess, sending balls between tables with

Hot Wheels ramps. And yet all the signs in billiard halls just say NO GAMBLING, and nothing about Hot Wheels."

Back to the room.

"What now?" asked Coleman.

"Work our way down the Holing Up To-Do List . . . I'll get the spreadsheet."

Serge wound his own mechanical alarm clock and unplugged the room's digital one.

"Why'd you do that?"

"Serge's Fugitive Tip Number Ninety-seven: Immediately unplug all motel clocks. They're susceptible to power failures and assholes."

"Assholes?"

"New trend. You know how in restaurants you always play a practical joke and loosen the tops of salt shakers? And then you forget and fuck up your own food?"

"Why are people like that?"

"Before checking out of motels, a growing movement of pricks are setting alarms for the middle of the night as a wacky joke to wake up the next guest. And some of these newer electronic jobs are pretty complex, and you think you're turning off the alarm when you've just switched from an annoying pulse tone to Heavy Metal Morning Thunder 105.3 FM, the Music Monster! My motto: Life's too important to learn new

clocks, so I unplug them all and get on with the plot."
He sat motionless on the foot of the bed, holing up.

The gears in Serge's alarm clock ticked.

1:00 P.M.:

Coleman drank beer.

Serge opened his laptop.

1:30:

Coleman did shots. "What are you typing?"

UNPLUG ALL CLOCKS. "Coleman, come here. Guess the longest word in the English language that you can spell with just the top row of a keyboard."

"Okay, I'm good at this." He rubbed his palms together and studied the keys. "Uh . . . *pot*. Am I right?"

"Close: *typewriter*."

"*Typewriter?*" Coleman whistled. "That's trippy."

"No shit," said Serge. "Don't tell me there isn't something bigger going on out there in the universe."

2:00:

"Serge, get in here! I need a witness!"

Serge ran into the bathroom. "What is it?"

"I just took the biggest dump in my life."

"Coleman, that's unbelievably disgusting even for you— . . . Holy God! That one's got a couple time zones!"

"It's like a crime scene."

Serge looked closer. "Is that a cuff link?"

2:30:

Coleman changed channels. "Hey Serge." He pointed with the remote. "Geraldo's on."

"The two worst words in the English language." Laptop typing.

"He's about to open some big-ass safe."

3:00:

Coleman was passed out with a leg in a lower dresser drawer.

Serge read Internet headlines. PLUTO PURGED AS A PLANET. "Great, now nobody's safe."

3:30:

Coleman toweled down after a shower.

"How do you feel?" asked Serge.

"Best of both worlds: clean, not sober."

4:00:

Serge watched *No Country for Old Men* on TV. "I need a device like that."

4:30:

Coleman stumbled over to Serge's laptop. "Facebook?"

"I still don't get the concept. Everyone keeps poking me and throwing snowballs."

5:00:

Serge leaped to his feet. "I can't take holing up!" He ran out the door and down the stairs.

Chapter Nine

ROUTE 24

Agent White looked in a rearview mirror full of vehicles. "I really wish they wouldn't do that."

Lowe turned around to face a rumpled fedora in the backseat. "This profiling business is fascinating. You can really predict his movements through psychological probabilities?"

"Muzzle, greenhorn."

"Have you ever been on a SWAT team? . . . . Ow! White, he just hit me in the eye with a toothpick!"

"Both of you! Knock it off!" The supervisor glanced in the mirror. "Like I don't have enough to worry about without babysitting you two . . . And Mahoney, we better not be wasting time out here in the sticks."

"I'm geezed to his shake."

"But of the million places in the state, how can you be so sure he went to Cedar Key?"

"He also posted it on his website."

"Damn it!" said White. "Why didn't you tell me in the first place? I could have sent an advance team." He pushed the gas pedal all the way down.

Someone back at the former gas station stepped outside with a bucket of worms and walked to his Harley. He watched the convoy disappear into the marsh country of Route 24. Then opened a cell phone.

No reception.

He dialed again . . .

CEDAR KEY

"Wait up!" Coleman grabbed a lamppost and panted.

"The Walking Tour doesn't wait," said Serge.

"I don't think I can keep going."

"We're almost to the bar."

"What are we waiting for?"

Serge turned the corner of Second Street and stood in the middle of the road.

"Why are you stopping?"

Serge placed a respectful hand over his heart. "Visitors come out to Cedar Key, and it's all about the seafood restaurants and boutiques on the wharf at Dock Street."

"It did seem crowded out there."

Serge raised his camera. "For me, the island's essence is this view down Second Street, like Key West at the end of the nineteenth century." *Click, click.* "Weathered wooden buildings with peeling paint and rust-streaked metal roofs. Notice how all the canted facades down both sides of the road have post-supported balconies over the sidewalks, creating that narrow, always-welcome feel of a Wild West main street where gunslingers square off while saloon girls and smudged-faced children peek out windows. Not a stoplight on the whole island to puncture this spiritual moment . . ."

Coleman farted.

"Although 'puncture' isn't limited to technology."

They walked again, past the library and post office and a convenience store where the clerk had to carry a cash bag if someone wanted to buy a bottle from the adjoining package place.

Serge stopped in front of the most run-down building on the street and gasped. He sadly ran a palm over gothic letters. "I can't believe it. They closed the L and M. Another sign of the apocalypse."

"What's the L and M?"

"Just one of the most venerable bars in all the state. Pre-dating roadhouses, one of those dubious old fishermen joints that was like drinking on a fog-draped pier in Shanghai." Serge dabbed a tear and pounded the wall. *"Why! Why! Why! . . ."*

It was Coleman's turn to place a hand over his heart. "Please don't tell me this was the bar we were going to."

"Yes."

Coleman pounded the wall. *"Why! Why! Why! . . ."*

A police car rolled to a stop at the sight of two men beating the front of the closed tavern.

". . . Why! Why! Why! . . ."

The officer leaned across his passenger seat. "What are you guys doing?"

Serge turned around. "Pounding a building, asking questions."

"Please don't pound buildings."

"You're right, we're visitors." He grabbed Coleman's arm. "Stop."

The officer watched them warily as he drove off.

"That was close," said Serge. "The natural enemy of the fugitive: a totally random encounter with law enforcement, even when you're behaving completely normal."

"The bar's closed."

"Fear not. I know this island." Serge led Coleman to the end of the block and turned left. They strolled up a walkway.

"What is this place?" asked Coleman. "Looks like someone's home."

"It was, built in 1910, until the Eagles took it over."

"Eagles?"

Serge pointed at a sign as they approached the door.

"The Eagle Club?" said Coleman.

"Good people."

"But the sign says MEMBERS ONLY."

"Just a formality." Serge opened the door.

All heads swiveled around the U-shaped bar. A roar went up.

"The prodigal son returns!"

"Serge is in the house!"

He shook a row of hands until reaching a pair of empty stools.

"Excellent Fugitive Tour," said the bartender. "Been following it on the Net." She placed a bottle of water in front of him. "On us."

"Coleman," said Serge. "Meet Jill. And the other guy back there is Tom."

A man with a full, distinguished head of gray hair waved back.

Coleman signaled for a drink. "He looks like that guy from the Sopranos."

Jill poured a couple extra fingers of Jack for Coleman, then leaned against the bar toward Serge. "I know Cedar Key is a natural for fugitives. God knows how many people out here aren't using real names. Just one teeny problem putting us on your tour."

"You mean because there's only a single, twenty-mile-long road in and out of here?"

She smiled. "Getting cornered sounds like a glitch."

"That's the whole point." Serge smiled back. "What's a vacation without near disaster?"

The Crown Vic's suspension slammed hard against the chassis as the agents sailed over the crest of a small hump bridge to Cedar Key.

"Seal off Route 24!" White yelled into the radio. "I want ten men at that last creek."

The unmarked sedan screeched to a stop at the intersection of Second Street. White's head swung toward the back seat. "Mahoney! Which way? . . ."

Raucous laughter and good times in the Eagle Club. Coleman won a bar bet for how many swizzle sticks he could cram in his mouth.

A cell phone rang. Serge covered his ear and answered. ". . . Uh-huh, uh-huh . . . Good work, Road Rash. I owe ya." He hung up.

Coleman rubbed his face. "For some reason my jaw hurts."

Serge opened his cell again and dialed a local taxi service. "Catfish, you're on."

He hung up and yanked Coleman off his stool. "Time to go to work."

Chapter Ten

CEDAR KEY

Night fell.

Then all hell.

Nobody had seen so much action in Cedar Key since they could remember. Vehicles raced every which way, red and blue flashing lights, radios squawking, black-helmeted commandos knocking down motel doors with truncheons—made all the more dramatic by the tight confines of the town's tiny grid of streets.

And the weather.

Nothing usual. A typical evening of forty-mile-an-hour gusts from the wharf's open gulf exposure, crashing waves high over seawalls and bathing Dock Street in a misty spray. An evening fog rolled off the water, shrouding the island in a ghostly haze.

The street platting was also open exposure, providing full view of the entertainment for Serge and Coleman, casually sitting on a bench in the public park at the east end.

"You sure the island's usually this windy?" asked Coleman.

"It's impossible to keep your hair combed in this town."

Serge's name first popped up at the Island Hotel, and in went the tactical unit. Then out they came.

Heads turned on the park bench as Serge and Coleman watched the brigade charge over to Cedar Cove, then back to the Cedar Inn. The Crown Vic and SWAT van raced past cars going the opposite direction. A yellow Cadillac, black Beemer and turquoise T-Bird nearly traded paint in a mass U-turn, speeding back after the cops.

Another motel.

The SWAT team jogged down the stairs and shook their heads.

"Another decoy." Agent White turned quickly. "What's that noise?"

The Doberman's motorcycle crashed through the end of the wharf and into the Gulf of Mexico.

Lowe ran over with a walkie-talkie. "Think we got something. Manager at the Dockside recognized his mug shot. Registered to one Horatio Farnsworth."

"Move!" yelled White.

The pair on the park bench watched the tide of law enforcement reverse course again across the island.

"Look," said Coleman. "They're hitting our actual motel."

"Perfect."

"How is cops closing in on us perfect?"

"They're not closing in on *us*. It's just another coincidence like Kissimmee," said Serge. "Told you this island is one of the state's ultimate fugitive havens. I'd be more surprised if cops *weren't* busting in places— and disappointed. Was starting to worry that I'd have to pretend police were swarming to test my new Cedar Key 'Out,' but this adds to authenticity." Serge checked his wristwatch and looked at his cell phone. "What's taking Catfish so long?"

He dialed. No answer.

"They pulled the Doberman onto the dock," said Coleman. "They're pumping his chest . . . He's spitting up! He's alive!"

The SWAT team poured back down the stairs of the Dockside.

"Looks like the cops are leaving?" asked Coleman.

Serge watched the unit's departure pattern with concern. "Unfortunately not. This is getting a little too authentic. And Catfish is late."

"Thought you said it was a coincidence?"

"It is, but they could *coincidentally* net us while looking for their actual target."

Serge jumped up. He put his hands in his pockets and hunched his shoulders as if to fight the wind. "Start walking. Fast. And keep your face down. If anyone drives by, don't look at them, but don't look away. And don't run."

Coleman got up. "What's the matter?"

"Island's too small."

"For what?"

"A fugitive. They got more than enough guys for a house-to-house canvass and matrix search of every inch in between. Walk faster."

"But, Serge, it sure looks like they're leaving."

"Except it's an even dispersion. They're heading for assigned pressure points."

"What's that mean?"

"In minutes, someone will be stationed at the end of every street—north, south, east and west—cutting up the island like a checkerboard."

"Why?"

"To keep people confined within every block while the rest conduct the sweep. If anyone crosses a street, they're nailed . . . Damn it, Catfish!"

Sure enough, barely after they safely passed each street, sentries arrived. Serge pulled up his collar and walked as briskly as he could without breaking into a trot. Marked and unmarked cars made rounds in concentric circles, spotlights on buildings and alleys. A yellow Cadillac and black Beemer crisscrossed in front of the L&M.

The sea mist from the crashing waves wasn't confined to the wharf district. It atomized and floated inland like an eerie soup, combining with the fog to give each streetlamp a large globe of its own fuzzy, penumbra light.

Serge watched a convertible T-Bird pass the other way on a parallel street and blinked hard. "Can't be . . ." Now he did break into a trot.

They reached the middle of Second Street again.

But the sentry was already there.

Mist thickened, just an ominous dark form three blocks away, standing on the road's center line.

"Coleman, get against that building."

Serge took up his own position in the middle of the road, facing the shadow.

"What are you doing?" asked Coleman.

"Wild West time," said Serge. "The sentry spotted us crossing the street, so I have to take him out before he can report our movements."

"But you don't hurt cops."

"That's right. I'll just baffle him with disinformation until he realizes we're just harmless tourists on the Fugitive Tour and not the derelicts they're after."

Serge began taking deliberate, individual steps forward, stopping between each. The form at the other end of the street advanced likewise. Serge took another step. Hands hung at the ready by his sides, fingers twitching.

The opposing form mirrored every stride, passing under one of the streetlamps and creating a silhouette. A tweed jacket and rumpled fedora.

"Holy Chesterfields," said Serge. "It's Mahoney!"

Just then, a screaming chorus of police sirens. Flashing lights. Party crashers.

No fewer than thirty squad cars not involved in the original dragnet sailed over the last bridge to Cedar Key. They raced across the street between Serge and Mahoney.

"Catfish! Yes!" Serge dashed back to Coleman and grabbed him by the shirt. "Our 'Out' has arrived. Run!"

They dashed past the old seafood packing house and down toward the bog.

A whisper in the darkness: "Serge? Is that you?"

"Stumpy?"

"Over here."

Serge was able to keep his balance stutter-stepping down a wet bank of weeds, but Coleman chose to somersault.

Stumpy sloshed toward them in rubber boots. "Catfish filled me in. Are you crazy? . . ."

At that moment, on the other side of the island:

"You motherfuckers!"

Police in overwhelming force dragged a handcuffed, shirtless man from a small cottage. Not daintily. They threw him over the hood of the first prowler car, busting his nose.

A Crown Vic skidded up. White jumped out and ran to the police captain in charge. "What's going on?"

"Cop killer from Jacksonville. Been looking for him eight years."

Mahoney strolled over with a wooden matchstick bobbing between his teeth. "Is that James Donald Woodley?"

The captain nodded. "Aka Franklin Ignatius Turnville."

"Shinola," said Mahoney. "Been trying to clear that case forever."

"Consider it cleared."

"Mahoney," said White. "Isn't that the same guy you were after when you nearly caught Serge at that motel last year?"

Mahoney angrily whipped a matchstick to the ground.

White turned back to the captain. "How'd you find him?"

"Lucky tip." The captain nodded across the road, where a uniform was interviewing a local cabdriver.

"What?" said Mahoney. "Some hack pegged his alias, bloodhounded him over here and dropped the dime?"

"No," said the captain. "The driver told us Woodley was an afternoon fare, and after dropping him off, he just had this sensation that he'd seen his face before."

"He knew the guy?" asked White.

The captain shook his head. "Said he remembered it from the newspapers."

"Eight years ago?" said White. "Come on, nobody's memory is that good . . . Mahoney, why are you smiling."

"I recalled a joke. The punch line is, 'Who shit in my tuba?'" Mahoney sauntered jauntily back to the car. As he passed the cabdriver: "Give my regards to Serge."

Lowe stood next to White. "What a crazy day. A serial killer slips from a surefire quarantine zone, and then we solve a cop-killer cold case just a few blocks away."

"Serge hasn't escaped yet," said White. "We've got the only road out of here blockaded in three places."

"So where do you think he is?"

White looked down the fog-choked street. "Who knows?"

A hundred yards away:

"Duck," said Stumpy.

Serge and Coleman squatted down as the clam boat drifted silently under a low bridge full of police cars.

"That was awesome!" said Coleman.

"Will you keep your voice down?" whispered Serge. "They're right up there."

Stumpy was up on the bow, quietly using a pole to push them across the bayou under the cloak of fog and mist. They reached more isolated waters, and he pull-started an Evinrude.

"Where to now?" asked Coleman.

"Flow with the tide."

Serge and Coleman left the flashing police lights of Cedar Key behind and sailed off into the dark gulf.

Chapter Eleven

BACK AT THE EAGLE CLUB

The joint was abuzz with bulletins from across the island.

Locals continued streaming in with the latest rumors.

"They say he killed ten cops! . . ."

"Had a whole arsenal of machine guns and hand grenades! . . ."

"A sex dungeon just up the street . . ."

Others surrounded the Doberman, dripping wet, accepting free drinks and signing autographs.

The door opened again. Three state agents with mug shots of Serge and Coleman.

The room became suspiciously hushed.

"Nope, wasn't in here."

"Who are they, anyway?"

"I'd remember if he came by."

Mahoney sneered. "You'll never win an Academy Award."

At the end of the bar sat a Miami attorney named Brad Meltzer. Legal paperwork spread in front of him. Two letters and a ripped-open envelope marked CONFIDENTIAL.

More than sloshed.

The person on the next stool: "Couldn't help but notice . . ."

Brad turned. "What?"

"That case you're working on. Seems very interesting."

"You an attorney, too?"

"No, but I . . . work in the legal field. What are you drinking?"

"Scotch."

"Bartender, best scotch for my new friend."

Brad realized he shouldn't have left the sensitive files open like that, and began shuffling them back in a folder. Except most went on the floor.

"I got them," said his new drinking buddy, collecting pages from the ground.

Brad abruptly snatched them away.

The person stepped back. "Excuse the hell out of me for helping."

"No, I'm sorry," said the attorney, swaying off balance. "Client confidentiality. My mistake for leaving them out."

Brad went to sit, and misjudged the stool. It scooted out, but he made a nice recovery smacking his chin on the edge of the bar.

"Are you okay?"

"I could use that scotch."

Dewar's arrived.

"Hope you don't take offense," said the new acquaintance. "But I noticed a name in your files. Serge Storms. He's a friend. Seen him?"

Brad wasn't *that* drunk. He did a double take. "Who did you say you were?"

"I didn't. I'm looking for Serge, too."

"Oh," said Brad, nodding. "I get it. You read more of the file than I thought. You want to pump me for information so you can get some of the money from the map. Get lost!"

"Don't be a tool. I knew who you were before I came in here. You think I chose this seat by accident?"

Brad tried to focus his double vision. "Really, who are you?"

"Someone who's not after your precious money." A lie. "In fact I'm here to *give* you money."

"Bullshit."

To Brad's surprise, a brown envelope slid across the bar. He peeked inside.

"That's a thousand to help me locate Serge."

"A bribe?"

"Call it a retainer." The unknown guest got up. "There'll be another envelope five times as thick after you lead me to him."

"But how will I find you?" asked Brad.

"I'll find you."

GULF OF MEXICO

A full moon had just set, leaving a sky of stars most people will never see.

The reason was the coastline. A clam boat hugged it with precision. The pilot knew every rocky shoal. No light pollution from this part of the shore.

Because it wasn't exactly a shore. More like a limbo between land and sea. Mangrove estuaries, marsh grass, mudflats and countless tributaries that left real estate spongy for miles, impossible to develop. The unspoiled Nature Coast from Pasco to the Panhandle.

The type of low-draft boat wasn't meant for open water, but the evening was calm, and there were extenuating circumstances.

"Gee, Serge. It sure is creepy out here."

"What are you, the Beaver? And get rid of that joint. We're running blackout."

"How about I hold it down here?"

"That's the gas tank!"

Serge swatted his hand, and a tiny red ash sizzled out in the black water.

Coleman leaned over the side, trying to reach.

Stumpy swung the till and leaned the other way to compensate. "Serge, your friend's throwing off our keel."

Serge grabbed the back of his belt. "Get back in here."

Coleman excavated a beer from his teddy sack. "Where are we going, anyway?"

"A cruise to nowhere."

"Look, if you don't want to tell me."

"No, that's really what it's call—... just wait and see."

The vessel tacked southeast. Occasional landmarks. The mouth of the Withlacoochee below Yankeetown, Crystal River, fat concrete towers at the nuclear plant, Cooglers Beach. The shore began to glow off Port Richey and Tarpon Springs. Stumpy pulled the till to his stomach, turning the clam boat hard starboard.

"Serge, we're heading away from land. We going straight out to sea."

"To the mother ship."

"You mean like Parliament Funkadelic?"

"No, like dope boats that run parallel to shore just outside territorial limits."

Coleman raised hopeful eyebrows. "Dope?"

"Not this one."

They passed the point of no return. Coast behind them nowhere in sight. Ahead, the abyss.

"Now I'm really scared," said Coleman.

"You should be," said Serge. "We're crazy to ride out this far. And if we don't acquire the mother ship soon—"

"Serge!"

Stumpy extended an arm. "There she is, relative bearing thirty degrees port."

The tiniest twinkling light bobbed above the horizon. Then disappeared below it. Then bobbed up again.

"Looks like a cruise ship," said Coleman.

"Except a lot smaller."

Stumpy got on the VHF. "Mako, this is Clam One, do you copy?"

"Mako here."

"Got two packages."

"Come around stern. But run silent or I'll lose my job."

"Appreciate it."

"What am I going to do? I owe Serge big-time."

CLEARWATER

Camera lights bathed an otherwise dim television studio.

It was a small studio, as they go. Stained concrete floor except for a small patch of blue carpet under a worn Naugahyde couch. An office chair behind a fake, cardboard desk. Three men sat on the sofa. Two wore dark slacks, white shirts, dark ties. The third had a tweed jacket and a fedora.

A cameraman clipped lapel mikes on the guests. Mahoney had brought his own mike, one of those large antique steel jobs used by a night owl jazz DJ in 1947, or an announcer at Ebbets Field.

The show would have no fancy computer-generated intro with exploding graphics. Lowe looked back at the wall behind the couch: a poster with hand-stenciled letters.

FLORIDA'S MOST WANTED.

He turned to White. "We couldn't get on *America's Most Wanted*?"

"They're booked. You take what you can get."

Lowe stuck his finger through a rip in the couch. "How many people actually watch community-access television?"

"We'll soon find out."

"But why'd we drive down here? We could have done this back in Orlando."

"Because Serge is from Tampa Bay," said White. "When fugitives are on the run, they often return to surroundings where they're familiar and comfortable."

Lowe turned the other way. "Mahoney, you really think Serge was responsible for nailing that cop killer named Woodley back in Cedar Key?"

"Like a tit." Mahoney stuck the toothpick back in his mouth. "Had some tight cats rifle files. Remember when Serge was nearly pinched in Jacksonville? Mistaken for the other killer?"

"Yeah?"

"Woodley roped an alias as Franklin Turnville. We got wind and cast the net. He must have felt the weight coming because Turnville fell off the radar. For years, doughnuts."

"What happened?"

"It was like he croaked. Until Turnville suddenly popped up again at that motel. Matching birthday, middle name. Except it was Serge."

"How's that possible?" asked Lowe.

"Standard false ID riff," said Mahoney. "After the miss in Jacksonville, vital statistics found the real Turnville buried in a nearby cemetery. They both obviously got the name off the same tombstone. Problem was, we couldn't find out the new alias Woodley began using after he shed Turnville. That's where Serge came in."

"But if all of us couldn't find out . . ."

"Because Serge thought like him. My gut? When you go tombstone diving, you don't just cuff one name. After Serge got hip to the Turnville coincidence, he correctly guessed Woodley switched to another ID off another nearby headstone—another that Serge had also jotted down. From there it was a simple public records search for Serge to peg which dead guy had come back to life. Probably saving that nugget for when he needed an 'Out' from Cedar Key."

"So it was no accident he led us to that island?"

"Nothing with Serge is an accident." Mahoney reached in his jacket for an unsoggy toothpick. "One thing you need to know about Serge: He always has a Secret Master Plan—"

"*Welcome!*"

The trio on the couch looked up.

The show's host arrived with napkins around his neck to keep stage makeup off his collar. "Thanks for coming! It's going to be a great program!"

"How's this going to work?" asked White.

The host whipped off the napkins and hopped behind the desk. "I go live with a call-in number. Then after the show we keep the phone banks open and wait for all the tips to pour in."

"Live?" said White. "It's midnight. What kind of ratings will we get?"

"Oh, you wouldn't believe. I'm recognized on the street all the time. People always coming up to me."

"What do they say?"

" 'Hey, you're that guy.' Then we'll rerun our segment a bunch more times during normal hours. Just mention me at the press conference when you catch this character."

"How many fugitives have you caught so far?" asked White.

"We're on in ten," said the host. "Everybody ready?"

They nodded.

"Here we go . . ." The host watched the cameraman silently count down on his fingers until a red light came on above the camera and he pointed at the desk.

"Good evening! This is Carson Nooley and welcome to another episode of *Florida's Most Wanted!* With us tonight are three top state agents who are hot on the trail of dangerous serial killer Serge A. Storms. Our live tip hotline is 555-6470." He turned toward the couch. "Detective Green . . ."

"White."

". . . Is it true he once taxidermied his victims alive inside game fish?"

"Yes."

Carson leaned with anticipation. "Did you get to see it?"

"No. But what I wanted to say is that—"

"What about the guy who was torn in half by a drawbridge?"

"What about it?"

"Did you bring any pictures?"

"No."

Nooley leaned back in disappointment. "That number again, 555-6470." He stared at the silent phone on his desk.

White reached in his pocket. "Can we show these mug shots?"

"Don't have the software to put them up."

"How about holding them in front of the camera?"

The host shrugged. "Never done it before."

White stood and held his first photo a foot from the lens. "This is Serge Storms. And this is his accomplice, Coleman. If anyone has any information—"

"We have our first caller!" said Carson.

White ran back to the couch as the host pressed a blinking button and grabbed the receiver. "*Florida's Most Wanted.* You're on the air!"

"I fronted you ten grams, Izzy! Where's my fucking money? . . ."

Carson hung up and grinned. "Sorry, we get that a lot at this hour."

Mahoney whipped a toothpick to the floor and pulled the giant steel microphone to his mouth. "Zotz it, you mumbling haircut. Serge prowls the night jim, packing gat and itching to squirt metal. So iron the sideways, or I'll paste your beezer and we dangle."

"I love this guy!" said Carson. "Switch seats with Green . . . So what are you, undercover as a mental patient?"

Chapter Twelve

GULF OF MEXICO

A hundred flecks of light twirled around the room.

Coleman looked up at the spinning mirrored ball. "I don't get it."

"Disco night," said Serge. "They're doing a seventies theme."

"But how is this a 'cruise to nowhere'?"

"Ship sails out of Tampa Bay, just past the edge of international water so they can legally play slots and blackjack. Then the boat does a bunch of circles in the water before heading back to the original dock. Hence, 'nowhere.' First-timers think it's going to be a jolly evening until they discover they're being held prisoner."

"Prisoner?"

". . . *Shake, shake, shake, shake your booty!* . . ."

"These cruises are brutal marathons. They set out in bright sunlight. And after a few hours of gambling, eating and dancing, they've had a nice time and are ready to head home. But no! They can't escape! Helpless, grabbing the rails in terror, looking for a shore that is nowhere in sight. 'Dear Jesus, will this boat never stop going in circles?'"

Coleman chugged a rumrunner. "But why the seventies?"

"*. . . Stayin' alive! Stayin' alive! Ooo, ooo, ooo . . .*"

"Shrewd business tactic. 'Honey, I forgot how much I love disco. Let's dance!' Then, when it turns gruesome after midnight: 'I forgot how much I hate disco. Please make this hell end!' And the only option is to flee into the casino, drink heavily and blow the mortgage on roulette. Then finally in the wee hours, the boat heads back and serves greasy cheeseburgers and fries to soak up booze, until they reach the dock, where a million cabs are waiting like pelicans for passengers who can no longer remember what kind of car they drive."

"I don't see the problem," said Coleman.

"Because you're a professional. But imagine if an average, upstanding citizen was forced to live like you."

"I see that every New Year's," said Coleman. "They're annoying to be around. Slapping you on the back and laughing for no reason."

"Or suddenly bursting into tears, confiding how they once stuck their dick someplace ridiculous."

"That's always awkward."

"But it's definitely an icebreaker."

Coleman pointed at something Serge had just pulled from his pocket. "Cotton balls?"

"*. . . I'm just a love machine . . .*"

"Fugitive Tip Seventy-eight." He ripped open the plastic Johnson & Johnson package. "Desperadoes always have to stay ahead of science, and the latest threat is facial-recognition programs. First they were just in airports, but now some cities even have cameras up on light poles, panning downtown streets to match against a national crime database. Not to mention nearly every casino, except they're looking for blackballed gambling cheats."

"Does this boat have them?"

"Doubt it," said Serge. "But since it's like a casino, I'll pretend and test my techniques to blog the faithful cyber-audience how to defeat the software."

"With cotton?"

"The public generally thinks computers try to compare your face, when actually they're just looking for five or six specific recognition measurements. Ear length, nose width, distance between eyes and so on. If you can alter at least three points, it won't register a match." Serge gave Coleman a handful of cotton balls. "Just do what I do."

They both crammed cotton balls up their nostrils. Serge pulled a roll of first-aid tape from his pocket and tore off four strips.

Coleman pulled a finger from his nose. "What do we do with that?"

"Tape your ears forward."

"How far?"

"Fold them all the way over like I'm doing . . . Then take this black Magic Marker and color in the top of your forehead so it appears your hairline is two inches lower."

Finally, Serge handed him more cotton. "Now fill both cheeks with as much as you can stand."

They finished.

"*Mdmlakjgd?*" said Coleman.

"*Lfhoahfdi?*" said Serge.

Coleman emptied cotton from his cheeks. "How do I look?"

Serge emptied his. "I can't hear you."

"What?" said Coleman.

They untaped their ears.

"I said, 'How do I look?'"

"Perfect," said Serge. "Now we'll go totally unnoticed."

They replaced the tape and cotton, and went to the lounge.

The bartender had his back to them, switching out empty bottles. He turned around; his natural smile became forced as he assessed his latest customers: cotton hanging out of nostrils, bandaged ears, chipmunk cheeks, colored-in foreheads. Except Coleman had trouble coloring within the lines, and there were several stray marks across his eyelids and lips.

But it was after midnight, and the bartender had seen worse. "What can I get you guys?"

"*Gkjlskdjsd,*" said Coleman.

"What?" said the bartender.

"*Jogjakkd* (What)?" said Coleman.

Serge pointed at a bottle of water. "*Pfddinsdn.*"

Coleman pointed at whiskey. "*Rosnkdslf.*"

They were served. The bartender aimed a remote control at the TV on the wall, turning up the volume on his favorite show. "You guys like *Florida's Most Wanted?*"

"*Sodnjslkjg.*"

"Me, too," said the bartender. "I never miss an episode. The crimes are a scream. This one guy broke into a home, waving a gun and demanding only an eggbeater . . ."

Photos of Serge and Coleman appeared on screen.

"Man, check out those mug shots," said the bartender.

Serge and Coleman glanced nervously at each other.

The barkeep stepped forward for a closer look at the TV. "I'm sure I'd recognize those guys anywhere, especially the fat, ugly one." He turned back around to face a pair of wide-eyed customers. "You fellas okay?"

Serge nodded. *"Hejdfkdls."*

The duo waved and walked off with their drinks. As soon as they were around the corner, out came the cotton and off with the tape.

Coleman grabbed his chest. "That was too close."

"I couldn't be happier," said Serge, scribbling in his notebook. "My trial run went better than I even imagined, holding up under a close-quarters in-person encounter, which is more rigorous than cameras."

"I smell cheeseburgers," said Coleman.

"That means we're close to land."

They retired to the afterdeck with a crowd of staggering gamblers for early-morning drunk food.

The bartender closed up shop and joined his colleagues serving from the grill. Passengers laughed, cried, lay facedown on tables.

Coleman munched onion rings and strolled over to Serge in the chow line. "You wouldn't believe where this guy just told me he put his wiener."

The captain navigated the channel back through Johns Pass and eased toward the dock on the opposite side the waterway.

Serge reached the front of the line. "Cheeseburger, please."

"There you go." It was the bartender. He looked at Serge, then Coleman. He scratched his head.

"Excuse me," said the next customer. "Can I get something to eat?"

"What? Oh, sure thing." He began filling a plate, still watching Serge and Coleman move down the line.

Then it hit.

"Oh my God!"

A plate fell. The bartender ran.

"Hey, my food!"

The ship eased into its berth, and the shore crew secured davit lines. Taxi drivers waited next to a sea of yellow cabs in the parking lot.

The bartender reached the nearest phone and dialed a number he knew by heart.

TEN MILES AWAY IN CLEARWATER

Three state agents and a local-access TV host sat at a table, staring at a bank of non-ringing phones. Ready to throw in the towel.

"We haven't gotten any calls," said White.

"We've gotten a *ton* of calls," said the host.

"But they were all wrecked and laughing at us," said Lowe. "Or wrong numbers for phone sex."

White stood and grabbed his coat. "I'm bagging it."

The phone rang.

"Another call!" exclaimed the host.

"Send us a Western Union," said Mahoney.

Carson grabbed the receiver. "*Florida's Most Wanted* . . . Yeah . . . uh-huh . . . Where? Right now? . . . Hold on."

The agents were almost out the door.

Carson covered the phone. "Come back! We got a real tip! It's my first one!"

White turned with a tired look. "What is it?"

"Gambling ship just came into Johns Pass. Bartender recognized both."

"False alarm," said White. "There's no way they could be on that ship."

Mahoney grinned wryly. "Bunk-a-lamma ding-ding."

"Will you speak English?"

"Only one road out of Cedar Key. How do you think he evaded your roadblocks?"

"I don't know, but he did."

"Cedar Key," said Mahoney. "Farm-raised clam capital of the country. And you know what they have almost as much of as cars on that island?"

"Clam boats. Shit." White ran out the door . . .

A Crown Vic raced down Gulf Boulevard with a red bubble light flashing on the dashboard. White hopped a curb and cut through a parking lot, squealing up to the docks at Johns Pass.

The bartender headed toward them when he saw the police light.

White jumped out. "Where are they?"

The bartender pointed. "Just left."

"Which one are they in?"

"Lost track," said the bartender. "They all look the same."

Three agents watched as a mass migration of identical yellow cabs headed back to the mainland.

Chapter Thirteen

CYBERSPACE

Serge's Blog. Star Date 201.538.

Listen up, gang, because this will be real important later, like foreshadowing.

Florida's population boomed in the 1920s. Both coasts. In fact, Fort Myers on the gulf side was even bigger than Miami. Commerce ready to gush. Except no road to connect the two sides of the state. And a not-so-small hurdle in between.

The Everglades.

"Tamiami" is a contraction of "Tampa to Miami." As in the Tamiami Trail. That's the dream that businessmen had to bridge eighty bad miles across the swamp.

They said it couldn't be done.

But they'd never seen a Walking Dredge.

It crawled across the glades like a mechanical dinosaur, scooping earth from beneath the swamp and building an elevated causeway ahead of it as it went.

The east and west thirds of the Tamiami were agreed upon. The argument lay in the middle. Entrepreneurs envisioned draining the swamp and making a ransom from a bunch of buildings. Whoever's land the trail went through stood to make a killing.

Two parties faced off. Barron Collier proposed a northern route through the county that would later bear his name. The Chevelle Corporation advocated a parallel course to the south, through its holdings in Monroe County. They didn't wait for an official answer—"build it and they will come"—and so they did.

Collier finally won out, and to this day, only the first few paved miles of the Chevelle road spurs off from Forty Mile Bend. The rest of the would-be, twenty-four-mile route is an unmaintained logging road that connects back to the Tamiami at Monroe Station. At best, it's the ultimate washboard. At worst, it's washed out most of the year except the dry season, when rangers from Big Cypress fill gaps where the swamp breached. Thick vegetation hugs the shoulders. Tiny bridges without guardrails, barely as wide as your wheelbase. At better spots, oncoming cars must ride up in the brush to pass. It's literally impossible to turn around. You have to wait for alligators to get out of way, and they aren't in a hurry.

Because of these factors, it's the road of choice when people want to burrow deep off the map.

It's always been outlaw country.

In a 1976 article, a *National Geographic* reporter went down the road and wrote about someone going berserk and shooting randomly at whoever went by. Today only a handful of the state's most private people live out there.

You don't want your car to break down. Especially at night.

It's called the Loop Road.

Al Capone knew it well.

EAST OF TAMPA

Serge looked out the passenger window in the backseat. "Slow down."

The taxi driver let off the gas.

Serge watched an upscale apartment complex going by. "Keep going."

The driver glanced in the mirror. "You don't remember where you live?"

"Looking for a friend."

The cab continued through Hillsborough County in predawn blackness.

"Slow down." Serge appraised another building. "Speed up."

The driver shook his head. "You sure you have enough money? This is a long drive from the casino boat."

"I'm good for it." He flashed a hundred.

The driver smiled. "Where to?"

Three apartments later. Crestwood Villas. "Stop!"

Serge tipped large; the cab sped off.

"What are we doing here?" asked Coleman, hitching his backpack.

"I like this parking lot." Serge kept an eye on the taxi's taillights until they disappeared. Then he set his own backpack on the ground and unzipped a pocket.

Coleman followed his buddy along a line of cars. Some of the sportier new ones had blinking red alarm-system lights. Serge found an older model that didn't. He checked the windshield. "Nope."

More walking.

"What are you looking for?" asked Coleman.

"I hate to pay tolls."

"Huh?"

"Wait and see." Serge stopped again and leaned over another windshield. "Perfect." He slid a flat metal strip down the driver's window and into the door.

Less than a minute later, a beige Impala drove away without headlights.

"Where are we going now?" asked Coleman.

"Hope you like trains."

JUST BEFORE SUNRISE

Three detectives ate eggs.

Mahoney had picked the off-brand pancake house. Reminded him of Mickey's Diner in Hoboken. He looked out the window at a full parking lot. Sedans, Beemer, Eldorado, T-Bird, panel van, syndicated-show motor coach. The cast of drivers sat patiently, no intention of eggs, staring back.

Lowe got off his cell. "Nothing again."

"Keep working down the list," said White.

Lowe looked at the phone book folded open between their plates. He drew a line through a name and called the next. "Didn't know there were so many cab companies that handled the casino ship dock."

White was on his own call—"Are you sure?"— writing quickly in a notepad. "Thanks."

"What is it?" asked Lowe.

"Just caught a break." White held up the notepad. "Driver positively IDs them. Logbook shows the drop at Crestwood Villas."

Mahoney pulled a matchstick from his teeth. "Wise to the spread. Twenty minutes if we beat feet."

White flipped the notebook closed, took a last quick slug of black coffee and threw a pair of tens on the table.

Nineteen minutes later, a Crown Vic reached the eastern side of the county.

Lowe thumbed though the official manual on rappelling from helicopters. "How are we going to handle this?"

"Not by the book," said Mahoney. "When Serge goes down, it won't be like they teach it at the academy."

White glanced in the rearview at the motorcade riding his bumper. "Don't they sleep?"

The Vic took a left into an apartment complex. Lowe leaned forward—two county cruisers already at the brick building. "How'd the sheriff find out so fast?"

Uniformed deputies took witness statements.

White opened his badge. "Who's in charge here?"

"I am," said a corporal.

"Any sign of Serge?"

"Who?"

"Isn't that why you're here?"

The corporal shook his head. "Stolen vehicle report." He looked toward an empty parking slot. "Guy got up to go to work, no Impala."

"Need the full description and tag," said White. "Fast."

"What's going on?"

"No time . . ."

Agent White jumped back in the Crown Vic, typing on the laptop mounted between the front seats.

"So Serge got away in a stolen car?" said Lowe.

"Shhh!" He accessed the Department of Motor Vehicles database. The Impala came up. A few more security-code keystrokes. A page with live streaming data appeared. "Yes!" The detective threw the sedan in gear. "Our luck has definitely changed."

"Why do you say that?" asked Lowe.

"Car had a SunPass unit on the windshield—transponder that automatically pays tolls." Dawn began to break as they sped out of the parking lot. "DOT shows a hit shortly after the cabdriver dropped them off. Toll plaza just south of here."

Coleman lay across vinyl, smiling with eyes closed. Another happy, recurring dream. He had a multi-day ticket at a beer theme park. The smile broadened as he hit the bottom of the log flume and suds splashed over him.

Serge shook his shoulder. "Rise and shine!"

"Wha—?" Coleman sat up in the backseat of an Impala with a riot of uncombed hair.

"It's morning." Serge clapped his hands sharply. "Need to flee again. Ain't this great?"

Coleman looked out the windows. "Is someone about to catch us?"

"No, fleeing's just fun." He chugged a thermos of coffee.

Coleman looked at his wrist and remembered he didn't own a watch. "How much sleep did I get?"

"Maybe an hour." Serge killed the rest of his coffee.

"An hour!" Coleman put his head back down and covered it with his backpack.

"Fugitives aren't allowed to sleep, except for cat naps with one eye open."

"Never?"

"Who knows? Life on the run is all about changing time patterns, and tomorrow's fugitive might have to crash and burn till nightfall."

Coleman pulled an airline miniature of vodka from his backpack. "How long till tomorrow?"

"One day."

"Will you keep track for me?"

Serge wiggled a screwdriver.

"What are you doing now?"

"Buying us some time."

"And we're not being chased?"

"No, but the next time we are, this will put us a few minutes ahead."

Chapter Fourteen

BELOW TAMPA

A Crown Vic raced south through Hillsborough County. Agent White's attention divided between the road and the laptop.

"Damn!"

"What is it?" asked Lowe.

"Another SunPass hit back at the same toll plaza. He double-backed north on us."

The sedan made a skidding U-turn across the highway through an "authorized vehicles only" break in the median. Half the convoy followed; the rest clogged behind a semi that jackknifed and had to make a nine-point turn to get through a tight break in the guardrails.

Forty-five minutes later, the toll plaza came into view. The laptop screen in the Crown Vic updated. "What the hell?"

"Another SunPass hit?"

"He's heading south again." Agent White's head jerked around. "You see an Impala?"

"Nope."

Another U-turn across the median.

Another forty-five minutes.

White punched the dashboard. "Mother—"

Lowe leaned toward the laptop. "He's going north again."

White cut the steering wheel . . .

Ten miles south, Serge and Coleman stood on the side of the road by an Exxon. Waving.

A cab pulled up.

They got in. The driver turned around. "Your call said Clark Road?"

"Correcto-mundo," said Serge.

"You got it."

The taxi pulled away from the dusty shoulder.

A Crown Vic sat next to the toll plaza office, just beyond the overpass with the booths.

The manager sat inside at a video monitor. "Want to see it again?"

"If you don't mind," said White, checking his notebook against the SunPass time records of the Impala, almost exactly forty-five minutes apart.

The manager rolled back the plaza's surveillance tape, and fast-forwarded again, stopping at each clock stamp that matched White's computer records. Each time, no Impala in any lane.

The manager swiveled around in his chair. "Don't know what to tell you."

White pocketed his notebook. "That's odd."

They went outside so White could inspect the plaza layout. "And there's no way anyone can get around the booths and pass through out of camera range?"

"Not a chance." He gestured up at the monitors. "See? Full view of everything."

White scratched his head. He walked to the overpass railing next to the last booth. "How on earth could Serge have—"

He looked down. Then smacked his forehead.

"Are you all right?" asked the manager.

White pointed. "What's that down there?"

The manager looked over the side at a graded route of gravel, stones and steel cutting thirty degrees under the plaza. He looked back up at the detective. "Train tracks?"

"I know. I mean, what line? Who uses it?"

"A lot of people—CSX, Amtrak, phosphate, the museum."

"Museum?"

"Gulf Coast Railroad out of Parrish. They operate old train trips for tourists and history buffs."

"How far?"

"Maybe twenty miles up the road."

"No, I mean how long is the tourist trip the train takes?"

"Through two counties," said the manager. "I rode it once, pretty cool. Round-trip's an hour and a half."

"Or forty-five minutes each way?"

The manager looked south down the tracks. "Speaking of which . . ."

A train whistle blew. White saw a restored army diesel round the bend. He ran to his car.

Another deep blast of the horn.

The agent watched his laptop as vintage passenger cars rumbled beneath. The SunPass screen registered a dollar toll. He grabbed his police radio. ". . . That's right, railroad frequency. I need a train stopped . . ."

A checkered cab wound through southern Manatee County.

"Why'd we ride that train back there anyway?" asked Coleman. "Didn't take us very far."

"But far enough," said Serge. "Remember my fugitive rule of constantly changing transportation modes? Plus I've always wanted to take that train."

"It was pretty cool," said Coleman.

"The coolest." Serge opened a wilderness map. "Forty-four-seat Union Pacific coach built in 1950, not to mention the 1929 Texas and Pacific caboose, number 12070. And there was a bonus reason to ride the train."

"I'm kind of turned around from all the travel," said Coleman. "I have no idea where we are."

"That's normal in a chase movie. Here's the Sarasota line."

"What's in Sarasota?" asked Coleman.

"Myakka."

Meanwhile, thirty miles north. "Found it," said Lowe, climbing down from the coach car. He held out a SunPass unit with torn duct tape. "Stuck on the outside just above a window."

Agent White stood next to the tracks with the engineer. "Where does this train end?"

Chapter Fifteen

SARASOTA COUNTY

The checkered cab continued south. Shopping centers and manicured sprawl. It took the last Sarasota exit.

"Coffee!" said Serge. They hit a 7-Eleven and turned inland. Modern life gave way to cattle country. Egrets pecked cows' backs; blue herons worked the standing water on the sides of Highway 72.

A few miles farther west:

"Pull over there." Serge drained his Styrofoam cup. "Just drop us by the road."

The taxi stopped on one of the highway's few paved turnoffs.

Coleman read a wooden entrance sign. "Myakka River State Park?"

"Fifty-eight square miles of undisturbed Florida majesty," said Serge. *Click, click, click.* "Sloughs, marshes, palm hammocks, and a rockin' treetop suspension footbridge through the canopy."

A ranger parked a pickup just outside the main guard shack.

Serge leaned over from the backseat, paying the cabbie. ". . . And here's a little something extra for yourself because you never saw us. Pay no attention to what I just said. It's only the Fugitive Tour—not like we killed a bunch of people. What's the appropriate tip if we *had* killed a bunch of people? But then I guess at that point you'd be satisfied just getting out alive. Rule Ninety-two: Pump taxi drivers for information generally not available elsewhere. Like if a passenger did kill someone, what's the best way to conceal it from an unwitting getaway taxi driver? Act confident and casually drop 'shallow graves' into the discussion to show you have nothing to hide? By that look on your face, probably talk sports instead. Here's another twenty to forget this whole conversation. I got the super-big coffee. Are we cool?"

Serge and Coleman climbed out.

The taxi sped off.

Just the sound of wind. Three people solemnly appraised each other at a range of twenty yards—Serge and Coleman by the edge of the road, and the ranger at the gate.

Then Serge broke into a smile and a trot. He closed the final distance to the pickup and threw his backpack in the bed. "Coleman, I'd like you to meet a good friend, Jane . . . Jane, this is Coleman."

She shook his hand. "Heard a lot about you . . ." Then, with an irrepressible grin at Serge: "I'd ask what you've been up to, but I don't think I want to know."

"Listen," Serge said in a lowered voice, "you haven't mentioned this to anyone—"

Jane put up a hand. "Stop. I can't be an accessory. You're just another park visitor."

They climbed into the pickup's cab.

Jane drove like a rancher. And cursed like one. Nature Jane. No makeup, brown ponytail halfway down her back. Black-rimmed glasses because she didn't have the guile for contacts. Heavy on the freckles. A tall Sissy Spacek. She and Serge kept glancing at each other. Been five years. Or was it six? They first met when Serge was down by the dam with his camera. It was summer flood stage, and Serge had taken the knee-deep hiking trail in scuba boots. He perched precariously on the slippery spillway.

Jane paddled up in a canoe. "Are you crazy?"

"Crazy about this park!" said Serge.

"There're alligators all around you."

"I understand their habits."

She sighed with contempt. "Get in the boat, you fool."

Jane was never meant to work anywhere other than a park, but rescuing bozos was not in her ambition set. Just wanted to get him back to the airboat launch as fast as possible, less talk the better.

"Let's talk," said Serge. And he was off and running. She formed a determined mouth and paddled faster.

Halfway back, a sea change, drifting with paddles in the bottom of the canoe. Other guys wanted in her pants. Serge wanted the names of flora and fauna. *Click, click, click* . . . Then she noticed those ice blue eyes . . .

". . . And that's a *snowy* egret," said the ranger. "You can tell—"

"That one I know," said Serge. "Colors switched. Yellow feet, black beak . . . Can I ask you something?"

Great, here we go.

"Always wanted to stay in one of your log cabins, but they're always booked. I *love* those cabins."

"Why?"

"Depression-era built by the Civilian Conservation Corps."

"You know that?"

"Who doesn't?"

"I think one might be free. We'll check at the station."

They picked up paddles.

Back on shore: One indeed was available by cancellation. She handed him the key. Who *was* this guy? At first glance Serge represented the cocky masculine type she normally found repulsive, but everything he did made that impossible. She actually caught herself about to smile and say it was a pleasure meeting him.

"It was a pleasure— . . . where'd he go?"

Serge sprinted full speed through the woods, waving a key over his head. "I got my cabin! I finally got my cabin!"

And a great cabin it was. "Cobbled from cabbage-palm trunks and hand-hewn pine, held tight with tar and sawdust." Serge kissed the front door. "Roomy yet cozy, fireplace for rare Florida cold snaps . . ."

Just after midnight, a knock at the door.

Serge looked up from his Audubon Field Guide and got out of bed. "Who can this be? . . ."

. . . Yes, it *was* six years ago. Serge barely aged in all that time. And now he'd finally popped up out of the blue and returned to her park. Jane looked across the pickup's cab and punched Serge in the shoulder.

"Ow."

"Cocksucker! You could have called."

"Swear I must have picked up the phone a hundred times."

"The cabin was empty when I woke up the next morning. Not even a note!"

"I . . . had appointments."

But she wasn't the long-burning emotional kind. "Got the same cabin. Want to go there first or—"

"Deep Hole," said Serge. "Still no check mark on my Life List."

"Should have figured." She quickly cut the wheel. "When you get your little heart set."

The four-by-four truck left the public section of the park and rattled down a bladder-bouncing path through a restricted area accessible only by special permit.

Coleman grabbed the dashboard, but his head kept hitting the ceiling anyway. "So what's Deep Hole?"

"Better wait till we get there," said Serge. "It'll only freak you out."

MIAMI

A small gathering in the back bedroom of a hacienda.

Chi-Chi rested comfortably.

Except when they made him laugh. Old stories from the sixties heyday. Then things ached under his ribs.

"Sorry," said Tommy Junior. "Didn't mean to get you riled."

"No, I'd rather hurt that way," said Chi-Chi, grabbing his left side. "What a memory: the deadbeat asshole in my trunk escaping by popping the hood with the tire jack."

"That was priceless," said Coltrane.

"Yeah, it's funny now," said Chi-Chi. "You didn't get the repair bill." He began coughing.

"Just relax," said Roy the Pawn King. "Guys, no more jokes."

Tommy happened to look toward the doorway. "How long has *she* been there?"

Then they all looked.

A demurely dressed woman in her late sixties. One of Chi-Chi's granddaughters stood next to her: "Says she would like to have a moment."

"What's this about?" asked Roy.

The woman took a respectful step inside. "Sorry to bother at such a time . . ."

"Do you know Chi-Chi?" asked Coltrane.

She nodded. "But I knew Sergio better."

"You knew *Sergio*?" said Roy.

Chi-Chi's head lay sideways on the pillows. "Wait, I recognize you now. But I don't remember where . . . . I'm sorry."

"That's all right." She walked closer. "It was just in passing a number of times."

"Hey," said Coltrane. "I recognize you, too."

"Come to think of it," said Roy, "you *do* look familiar. What's your name?"

"Mabel."

The guys looked at each other.

"Don't know a Mabel," said Coltrane.

"You wouldn't," said the woman. "I've just been sort of keeping track of the gang."

"Keeping track?"

She nodded again. "Since the late sixties."

"Like stalking?" said Tommy.

Roy walked over until they were a foot apart. In a hushed but firm voice: "He's very weak. Let's go outside and you tell me what this is really about."

"It's about Serge."

"You mean Sergio?"

"No, his grandson."

"Roy," said Chi-Chi. "Did I hear her say 'Serge'?"

"You need to rest."

He shook his head. Another cough. "Bring her over here."

Tommy offered a chair. "Thank you."

Chi-Chi turned his head. "Now, what do you have to tell us?"

A long story. She took a deep breath and began . . .

Almost an hour later, she finished. Everyone sat around in silent shock.

"We need to get word to them," said Roy.

"But how?" asked Coltrane.

Chi-Chi raised his head slightly. "Tommy, what about your sons?"

"Uh, they're out of town on business."

"Can't we call them?"

"They hate cells—into this whole freedom-of-the-road thing, like when Peter Fonda threw his watch away at the beginning of *Easy Rider*," said Tommy. "Have to wait for them to call in on a pay phone."

"This won't wait." Roy rubbed his face. "And no offense, Tommy, but this is as sensitive as it gets—maybe not the best fit for your sons. I think I know someone."

"But we can't just—" Tommy began. "I mean it needs to be handled right. We probably should bring all the parties together in one place first or it could be messy. It'll require a specialist."

"Take my word," said Roy. "This is the guy for the job."

"Who?"

A smile. "First name starts with an *M*."

"You don't mean the Undertaker?"

DEEP HOLE

A park ranger truck slid through a sand turn, then accelerated across an open palmetto prairie.

"Come on," said Coleman. "You can tell me."

"Okay," said Serge. "Little-known but infinitely stunning natural Florida feature. Giant sinkhole. Scientists measured as far as a hundred and forty feet down with a remote probe, but who knows the real depth because nobody's going diving."

"Why not?" asked Coleman.

"Because it's got the largest concentration of alligators in the world."

Jane smiled. "Like my own private Jurassic Park. They grow gigantic this far out. We've counted well over a hundred at a time, but that's just the tip of the iceberg—what's on the surface and banks. Who knows how many more below?"

Coleman did a double take at both of them. "There's a big fence around it, right?"

"Coleman, this is real nature," said Serge. "Not a zoo."

"Then we'll be wearing special steel suits?"

"Chill," said Serge. "Unlike gators in the more visited areas of the park, these rarely see humans and have retained their innate fear."

"Wish they had more," said Jane, bounding hard around another turn through sabal palms. "We're getting hit by poachers."

"You're kidding," said Serge. "Way back here?"

"Fuckers come out at night with halogen beams, and the gators don't stand a chance," said Jane. "Still trying to catch 'em."

"How do you know it's poachers?"

"They deliberately leave the evidence in the open, right in our faces." Jane began to steam. "You can tell by the remains."

"Tell what?"

"If the tail's gone along with hide, it's old Florida crackers who are going to eat the meat. I don't like it, but at least I can understand it."

"As opposed to?"

"White-collar weekend-warrior pussies. They just take the heads for trophies and leave the rest of the body to rot," said Jane. "I'm unable to get my brain around that level of cruelty. How can anyone kill another living thing for sport?"

"Well, a lot of reasons," said Serge.

Jane turned and looked oddly at him.

Serge grinned. "I mean, a lot of reasons that are very, very wrong."

A couple miles later, Jane parked on a bluff. "Far as we can take the truck. Have to make the last quarter mile on foot."

They gingerly worked their way down a grassy embankment and began the trek across a vast plateau.

Coleman stared down at the caked, cracked ground. "What are we walking on?"

"Dry lake bed," said Serge. "There's only a tight window each year when you can get out like this. You don't see the sinkhole the rest of the time because it's several feet underwater. And that's why there are so many alligators in Deep Hole." He swept an arm across the pristine panorama. "When dry season hits, all the gators that live in this giant lake are funneled into the sinkhole that's smaller than some motel pools."

Jane stopped and bent down. "Cougar."

"What's she looking at?" asked Coleman.

"Shit, dude."

"Fine, I won't talk to you either."

"No, I mean real shit. She's an expert tracker."

Jane stood back up. "Thought it was boar. We're trying to rid the park because they're exotics."

Serge scanned the earth. "Scat's actually valuable among naturalists to teach species identification."

Jane laughed. "I knew these two rangers who got in a feud because one wouldn't share a panther specimen."

Coleman stopped. "You mean I can make money selling poo?"

"That would be bad etiquette," said Serge. "And most of what you'd find is common. It would have to be an extremely rare sample."

"What if I took some of my own and said I found it?"

"Could lead to a breakthrough," said Serge. "Teams of scientists would extrapolate the profile of a slow-reflexed urban bigfoot with the diet of a mud-fish and the roaming patterns of Axl Rose."

Walking resumed.

"Serge, I see some shit!"

"Easy, Coleman."

Jane nodded. "Now, that's a boar."

"So where's this hole?" asked Coleman.

"Over there," said Serge.

"I don't see it."

"Because right now the water level is even with the ground we're walking on, and it's still too far away."

"You mean *there*?"

"Exactly."

"So it's got a big bank around the edge?"

"That's not a bank."

"What is it?"

"Gators."

"*Those* are the gators? Holy crap, we're still a football field away and they're freakin' huge. And everywhere!" Coleman stopped and stared ahead, then back at the pickup truck up on the bluff, now farther away than the sinkhole. Serge grabbed his shoulders just before he could take off.

"But I don't want to go!"

"It's for your own development," said Serge. "And I promise it's safe. Just watch as we get closer. But walk slow and don't do anything weird."

Sure enough, when they got within a rock's throw, numerous gators got up.

"Fuck me!" said Coleman.

"Reasonable response," said Serge. "First time you see the big ones high-walking up close, it can get a bit hairy. Keep watching . . ."

Gators continued strolling unrushed to the edge of the water, then slipped under the surface. As the trio grew closer, more and more casually went for a swim, until the rest finally splashed in as a group. But there were always a few.

"What about those last three?" asked Coleman.

"Granddaddies," said Jane. "They're not afraid of people as much as the others because they're not afraid of anything. But they'll still go in."

The trio walked closer. A pair of gators got up at a slow, too-cool-for-school pace and disappeared. That left just one.

"He's not going in," said Coleman.

"He will," said Jane.

They walked even closer. "Still not going in."

"That's strange," said the ranger.

A few more steps.

"Jesus Christ!" said Coleman. "Its head's cut off! Look at the blood!"

"Shut up, Coleman!" Then Serge looked toward Jane, who'd carved a little distance from the guys for privacy, her back toward them, staring off at nothing.

Chapter Sixteen

CYBERSPACE

Serge's Blog. Star Date 584.948.

Welcome back, gang! Sharpen those number two pencils! Today's lesson: Fugitive Geography!

Nothing more important than knowing your police jurisdictions . . . and exploiting a weakness.

Look no farther than the Everglades.

It's all about county lines.

The swamp at the bottom of Florida is split down the middle. The eastern half lies in Miami-Dade County; western chunk in Monroe, named for our fifth president. And there's the weakness! Because 99 percent of Monroe lives in the Florida Keys. But the remaining one percent is scattered across the mainland swamp on the gulf side—the *wrong* side—of the state, separated by almost a hundred miles from the rest of the county.

Today, national park rangers and law enforcement from neighboring departments generally handle whatever comes up in mainland Monroe. But back eighty years ago, it was lawless.

Literally.

No police at all. And if cops were needed, the closest officer was nearly three hours away in Key Largo . . . File that thought, because it gets even more exciting!

Now, there's but a single road through the swamp where this jurisdictional glitch really comes into play. Remember our last lesson? That's right, the Loop Road!

Guess who figured this out? Right again: Al Capone!

In the middle of Prohibition, Scarface sent his men just over the Monroe line to build an all-appetite entertainment lodge smack-dab in the middle of the Everglades—speakeasy, brothel, gambling house—at an equally convenient driving distance from both coasts.

Miami police could only stand at their own county line and watch helplessly a few hundred feet away as rambunctious crowds descended each weekend.

But as I've personally experienced, police don't quit that easily, and from time to time cops tried coming up from the Keys for a raid. Except Capone had informants on the payroll to tip him off.

And a plan . . .

THAT NIGHT

Myakka River State Park, cabin number three.

Serge and Jane sat quietly next to each other on the edge of the bed.

Staring at Coleman.

He slammed a beer, got up from his chair on the far side of the room and went to the fridge.

Coleman sat back down and popped another Pabst. He noticed them looking.

"What?"

"Coleman, why don't you go outside."

"That's okay. I like it better in here." He chugged.

"Coleman, Jane and I sort of haven't seen each other in a while."

"No problem." He drained the can and crumpled it. "You can go ahead and talk. I won't interrupt."

"Coleman, you're not—"

"One minute." Another trip to the fridge.

Serge sighed and got off the bed. He intercepted Coleman before he could sit back down.

"What is it?"

Serge whispered in his ear.

"*Ohhhh*, I get it now."

"Thanks."

"But it's scary outside."

"Coleman!"

"Can I just stand in the corner and face the wall?"

"No!" Serge grabbed him by the arm, marched him to the cabin door and opened it.

"Damn," said Coleman. "I've never seen the night so dark." His head jerked. "What was that sound?"

"Just nature." Serge pushed him a step onto the porch. "Get into it."

"But, Serge, I see eyes in those trees! And some more over there!"

"Time to make new friends."

Serge slammed the door.

Knock, knock, knock . . .

Serge closed his eyes and took a deep breath.

Knock, knock . . . "Pssst! Serge, it's me, Coleman."

The door opened. Serge stuck the rest of the six-pack in Coleman's stomach. The door slammed.

Serge turned and smiled at Jane. "Now where were we? . . ."

Outside, Coleman tentatively squatted down on the porch's top step and cracked a beer. His head swung left. "There's that sound again." Hands shook as he lit a joint. "And those eyes . . ." He darted off the porch and ran behind the north end of the cabin. He peeked back around the corner. "Eyes still there." He retreated and took a big hit. When the smoke cleared: "More eyes here, too." He slithered along the side of the cabin, his back pasted against the wall. "The scary sound again . . ."

Inside: Serge and Jane slammed into each other, ripping clothes and tumbling onto the bed.

Serge kicked off his shoes, hitting the fireplace mantel. "Can you leave the ranger shirt on? Unbuttoned, of course."

"Only if I can be on top."

"Tough sell."

They were immediately deep into the act, panting, non-verbal noise. Sliding all over each other from sweat. "Serge?" Not stopping her rhythm.

He caught his breath. "What?"

"I think I just saw Coleman's head go by the window."

"He wouldn't spy."

"I know. It was the back of his head . . . Now he's going by that other window . . ."

"He has his methods."

Jane refocused her attention and accelerated.

"Good God!" Serge's head arched back, eyelids twitching.

She got a mischievous grin. "So you like that?"

"It's near the top of my day."

She rammed down extra hard, enjoying the control as Serge seized fistfuls of the sheets to keep his arms from flopping.

Another violent thrust, and another. "Why are your eyes closed?" she asked with another sly grin. "Are you thinking about other park rangers?"

"No." Serge gritted his teeth. "Other *parks* . . . Bahia Honda, Cape Florida, John Pennekamp, Lignumvitae Key, Alafia River . . . Don't stop! . . . Oscar Sherer, Wekiwa Springs . . ."

A screaming went by the window. Then another window. And another. Then back by the first again.

"What's Coleman doing?" asked Jane.

"Running in circles around the cabin and screaming."

"I realize that."

"Spend enough time with him and you won't even notice. Like living near a busy highway." Serge raised his head. "You're slowing down."

"Sorry . . ."

Halfway through, Serge used a full nelson from Florida State Wrestling and flipped her into a submission hold.

"Give up?" said Serge.

"I'll never give up!"

"Then take *that!* . . ."

Shrieking.

". . . and *that!* . . ."

An octave higher.

She countered with a Dusty Rhodes elbow, and onto the floor they spilled. Screaming from the windows.

Finally, they were done. Spent, shot, wrecked. One of those spectacular, simultaneous finishes that had them both seeing galaxies and nebulae.

Jane lay back on the pillows, pulling wet, matted hair off her face. "I forgot how good you were."

Serge stared at the ceiling from his own pillow. "My compliments to the chef."

Jane raised her head. "Does something seem wrong?"

"Not from over here."

"No, I mean . . . I can't quite nail it down."

"It'll come to you."

She snapped her fingers. "Coleman stopped screaming . . . It's quiet out there."

Serge raised his own head. "Too quiet."

"You think he's all right?"

"That's relative." Serge got up, and Jane followed him to the door. He opened it.

They stared for a baffled moment.

"What in the fuck's going on?" said Jane.

"Coleman!" yelled Serge. "Why are you sucking on that tree?"

Coleman held up a hand for them to wait a moment. Surrounding him were squirrels and birds and bunnies, all watching attentively. Coleman finished sucking, took his mouth off the trunk and exhaled a large cloud at the stars. "I made a bong from this tree."

"You what?"

"I was running around screaming, righteously baked, when it hit me. Just like you said: I needed to get into it." He put his mouth on the tree again. Another exhale. "So I found harmony with mother earth and saw where a woodpecker had already done some work, and I said to myself, 'I know what I can use that for.' Then I got out my pocketknife."

"Unbelievable," said Jane.

"Jane and I are done inside," Serge said from the doorway. "Want to come back in?"

"No, I like it out here." Another toke off the tree. "Nature's cool."

An hour later, Serge silently closed the cabin door and tiptoed down the steps. Coleman was asleep at the base of the tree. A light tapping on his cheeks. "Wake up." Harder tapping.

"Wha—?" Coleman shook the fog from his head. "What is it?"

"Jane's finally asleep." He raised a hand. "I got the keys to her pickup."

"Where are we going?"

Serge led him toward the truck. "First, the twenty-four-hour Walmart."

"I thought you liked Home Depot."

"I do, but they don't have sporting goods."

SARASOTA

Exit 205. Holiday Inn Express.

Three state agents ate Mexican takeout and watched *Forensic Files*.

A cell phone rang.

"Agent Lowe . . . Yes, I remember . . . What! You're kidding! . . . Where? . . ." The other agents stopped eating. ". . . Let me grab a pen . . ."

A minute later, Lowe hung up.

"What is it?" asked White.

"One of the cab companies called back," said Lowe, checking his notes. "Driver had a weird fare. Big tip not to talk."

"From the gambling ship dock?"

"No, train museum."

White jumped up and grabbed his jacket. "Where'd he drop them?"

"Don't know."

White's process of putting his arms through the sleeves slowed. "How can they not know?"

"Some drivers take fares off the meter—and the log-book," said Lowe. "But this guy was so shook he told a colleague in a bar."

"Did they call him?" asked White.

Lowe nodded. "No answer. Apparently pretty drunk in that lounge."

"What about a home address?"

Lowe held up his notes.

White grabbed his keys. "Let's roll."

MIDNIGHT

Coleman grabbed the dashboard of the bouncing pickup as his head kept hitting the ceiling. "I remember this from somewhere."

"Ten hours ago."

"That's right. Deep Hole." His head swung toward Serge. "Wait a minute. We're not going back out there . . . at *night*."

"You've already sucked the tree."

They neared the end of a so-called road. Serge cut the headlights and slowly idled toward the bluff over-looking the lake bed. Another pickup was already there.

"Truck's empty," said Coleman. "But who else would be wandering around here at this hour?"

Serge opened his door. "I have a pretty good idea."

They crept to the edge of the bluff and crouched in weeds. Serge scanned the plateau with goggles.

"Are those real night goggles?" asked Coleman.

Serge kept scanning. "No, they're from a kid's toy spy kit."

"How do they work?"

"They don't. Actually make it darker. I can't see shit." He took them off. "Oh no!" He grabbed Coleman by the hair. "Get down!"

"What is it?"

Serge crawled backward. "I'll explain as we go. But right now we have to get our truck out of sight . . ."

The pair kept their heads low, waiting inside Jane's palmetto-concealed pickup. But not for long.

Soon, a head rose from the other side of the bluff, then the rest of the man as he climbed over the lip and walked toward his truck. A gym bag in one hand. Something else in the other that he set in the back of the pickup.

Suddenly high beams blazed the bluff. The man shielded his eyes.

Serge raced up in the truck and hit the brakes. He killed the engine but left the lights on, and jumped out the driver's door. "Don't move!"

The poacher recognized the park ranger vehicle. "I'm so sorry. I know it was wrong. I don't know why I did it."

"Throw the bag over here."

The man did.

Serge bent down and unzipped it. Carefully opened a towel.

"What is it?" asked Coleman.

"Unfortunately, what I suspected." He zipped it closed. "Gator head." Serge stepped up to the man. "Let me see your hands."

The man held them out.

"Pretty smooth, no calluses, nice nails." Serge looked up. "And that haircut. You work in an office, don't you?"

The man nodded.

"I could have let you off with a warning if you took the tail," said Serge. "Then you're at least feeding your family."

"I just wanted a trophy," said the man. "There were so many of them, I figured, what's the harm?"

Serge stepped closer. "What's the harm in killing something just to kill it?"

"I'll pay a fine. I'll even pay it right now, and extra for your time."

"Some people would call that a bribe, if we were real park rangers."

The poacher stopped in confusion. "You're not park rangers?"

"More like 'society rangers,' " said Serge.

"What about the truck?"

"We 'borrowed' it."

"You mean you stole it," the man said with rebounding confidence. He quickly reached in the bed of his truck and came up with a .357 Magnum. "Now *you* don't move!" The man made a slow, wide circle around the pair until he arrived at the ranger's pickup. He kept the gun on them as he reached through the driver's window and grabbed the keys.

"Are you for fucking real?" the poacher yelled at Serge. "A loser like you threatening someone important like me?" He swung the gun in the general direction of Deep Hole. "I'm going to go back down there and shoot ten of those goddamn things in your honor. But first I'm going to tie you up, and tomorrow they'll find you with the stolen pickup and all the dead alligators and—you can figure out the rest."

Coleman began trembling, then blubbering.

"Shut up!" screamed the poacher. With a backhand delivery, he clocked Coleman upside the head with the butt of his pistol.

Coleman went down, blood streaming, crying full volume.

Serge raised his eyebrows. "Alligators are one thing, but you just attacked a gentle, defenseless animal."

"Gee, I feel terrible."

"I was only going to teach you a lesson," said Serge, "but the curriculum just changed."

"Teach *me* a lesson? Study carefully." He reached down and cracked Coleman again in the jaw.

When the poacher looked up again, the tables had turned.

"Did you hear a bell?" asked Serge, aiming the pistol he'd pulled from under his shirt. "That means school's in session."

Chapter Seventeen

ONE A.M.

A Crown Vic skidded into the parking lot of a low-rent apartment building on Bee Ridge Road. Window a/c units rattled and dripped in the night heat. The doors had frosted jalousie glass.

Three agents ran up stairs to the second floor.

White knocked extra hard. "Police!"

No answer.

More knocking.

More silence.

Lowe took off his jacket and rolled his hand up in one of the sleeves.

"What are you doing?" asked White.

"Busting one of the glass slats to stick my hand in."

"Knock it off." White banged the door again.

This time, glass slats creaked open—on the next apartment's door.

White sidestepped to the neighboring unit. "Excuse me, have you seen the guy who lives here?"

Dilated eyes peeked through a dirty screen between the slats. "What's Carlos done?"

"Nothing. Just need to talk to him," said the agent. "Is he home?"

The man shook his head.

"Know where he is now?"

"Not really." The eyes shifted right. "Likes to tie it on at this bar up 41. Sometimes crashes with friends instead of driving. Said if he wasn't back tonight, he'd be here in the morning."

"Why'd he tell you that?"

"He's the apartment manager. Supposed to snake my toilet."

"Thanks."

The slats cranked shut.

1:10 A.M.

Shadows crossed a dry, moonlit lake bed.

Serge dragged the unconscious poacher on a make-shift litter of palm fronds. Coleman trailed with Walmart shopping bags.

"This is far enough." Serge dropped the litter's handles. "Give me those bags."

"What's the plan for this guy? Throw him in with the gators?"

"Too obvious—and quick." Serge unwrapped a foot-powered inflation pump. He threw one of the bags back to Coleman. "Grab the rope and tent stakes. Hammer it in over there."

Coleman pulled his hands out of the sack. "There are two ropes."

"I'll be taking the other to the far side of Deep Hole." Serge attached a valve and began stomping the air pump.

When inflation reached Serge's required pounds per square inch, he tied off both ropes. "Coleman, your Bic . . ."

Serge finished and tossed the lighter back. "Now grab his wrists."

They unceremoniously dropped him on rubber matting. Then he was dragged again.

After much work and geometric calculation, Serge and Coleman were on opposite sides of Deep Hole.

"Pull tighter!" Serge called across the water. Then he hammered his own tent stakes and walked back around to rejoin his friend.

"Now what?" said Coleman.

"We wake our guest," said Serge. "Boy, is he going to be surprised!"

"But how are we going to wake him at this distance. You conked him pretty good."

Serge reached in another bag and smiled.

"Those things rule!" said Coleman.

Serge stuck a long tube in his mouth.

Seconds later, from the middle of the sinkhole: "Ow! Fuck!" The poacher sprang up into a sitting position and pulled the blow dart from his cheek. Anger quickly changed to other thoughts as he assessed his predicament. "Please!" he yelled to the men on shore. "I'll give you money! Anything! Just get me out of here!"

"I love a quick student," said Serge.

"Hurry!" yelled the poacher. "They're all around!"

"Relax," said Serge. "You don't have anything to worry about—yet. That's the odd thing about gators: You can canoe through hundreds and they'll leave you alone. They're not like Moby-Dick, knocking people out of boats . . ."

"Or life rafts," said Coleman.

"Or life rafts," repeated Serge. "Like the one you're in. Just as long as you stay in the raft, they'll stay where they are . . . Swimming with them on the other hand . . ."—Serge whistled— ". . . Forget it. That's what they live for."

The poacher looked over one side of the raft, then the other, his eyes following lengths of braided nylon rope anchored to opposite shores with tent stakes and holding the raft in the exact center of Deep Hole. He looked up at Serge and grabbed his heart. "Okay, you got me good. I get it now. I'm supposed to untie one of the ropes attached to the raft and reel myself to shore with the other."

"Excellent analysis," said Serge. "And wrong. I used Coleman's lighter to melt the knots. I do my best work in nylon."

"Then what are you going to do to me?"

Serge smiled and raised the tube to his mouth again.

"Ow! Shit!" The poacher pulled a dart from his chest. "What are these things, dipped in poison?"

"Of course not," said Serge. "That would be rude. They're just plain, unadulterated darts."

"Then why are you shooting at me?"

Serge raised the tube again. "Bad aim. You weren't the target." Serge blew. The next dart found its mark.

Hissing.

"You hit the side of my raft! It's leaking!"

"Just pull the dart out and stick your finger over the hole."

The man did. "You're right. It's working."

"Like I don't know my job." Serge walked a quarter way around the sinkhole and fired another dart.

Hisssssssssss . . .

"Your other hand!" yelled Serge.

The man plugged the second leak, arms spread as wide as they could reach across the back of the raft.

Serge continued circling the sinkhole. Another dart.

Hissssssssssss . . .

Serge cupped his hands around his mouth. "Big toe on your right foot."

Another leak plugged.

Serge almost completed circling the hole when the next dart flew.

"Other foot!"

Serge finished the rounds and reunited with his buddy.

"Reminds me of Twister," said Coleman.

"They could sell a lot more of those games if they included a raft."

"Hey!" yelled a voice from the sinkhole. "What am I supposed to do now?"

"My advice?" said Serge. "Don't fall asleep."

"Wait! You're not leaving, are you?"

"Not yet." Serge walked as close to the shore as he could for accuracy. A final dart flew.

"Ow!" The poacher removed his left hand from the side of the raft and pulled the dart from his neck. Then quickly covered the hissing hole again. "I can't plug any more leaks."

"That time I *was* aiming for you," said Serge. "And the dart was tipped."

"With what?" yelled the poacher.

"I ground up some of Coleman's pills and dissolved them in water. Sedative. But don't worry: very slow acting. When certain people are under severe stress, they suffer insomnia. It's not good for your constitution."

"So you just made sure I'll fall asleep?"

"But I guarantee you'll wake up."

"When?"

"Nature has its own alarm clocks."

Serge and Coleman began walking away.

"Come back! Don't go!"

They continued across the lake bed, desperate cries behind them growing softer until they dissipated in the wind.

"Back to the cabin?" said Coleman.

"One more stop for the exit strategy. I need to prepare my Internet audience for tomorrow's 'Out.' Then yes, back to the cabin."

They climbed the bank and got in the ranger's pickup. Another bounding ride through the night. Owls and opossums.

"Glad you turned me on to nature," said Coleman. "I had no idea."

"That's why I like to come out here and mellow."

Chapter Eighteen

THE NEXT MORNING

Banging on the window of a Crown Vic.

Three sleeping agents awoke in grogginess.

More banging.

White sat up in the driver's seat and rubbed his eyes.

Out the windshield was the man they'd met the previous night through a jalousie door.

"He's back." The tenant pointed at a taxi parked nearby.

White jumped out of the car, and the others followed up the stairs.

From back in the parking lot: "Tell him I need my toilet snaked."

Banging again on a second-floor door. "Police."

This time they heard movement inside. A shin banged a coffee table. Cursing. More movement. Glass slats slowly cranked open.

A gold badge appeared. "Agent White. Need to ask you some questions."

The shirtless resident undid the chain and opened the door. Then he plopped in a chair and chased three aspirins with gin-flavored hair of the dog.

"You Carlos? The cabdriver?"

He nodded.

"Heard you had a suspicious fare yesterday."

The driver rubbed his temples. "Please talk quieter."

White stepped forward and pulled a mug shot from his jacket. "This the guy?"

Carlos squinted. "Definitely."

"Where'd you drop him? . . ."

Ranger Jane stood next to her pickup. "What a surprise—you were still here when I woke up."

"You misjudge me by one little incident of disappearing for six years."

She pointed with a thumb over her shoulder. "Have to get to work. But you will call this time?"

"Absolutely," said Serge, hoisting his backpack on the cabin's porch.

"Promise?"

"Why wouldn't I call?" He came down the steps and gave her a quick peck.

She threw her arms around his neck.

The pickup's radio squawked.

"Just a sec." Jane reached in the truck and grabbed the mike.

Coleman stumbled down the porch steps with his own backpack strapped to his stomach.

Serge walked over. "It's supposed to go on the other side."

"I know." Coleman looked down at the teddy bear's head. "I was having some trouble and it just ended up here."

"Let me give you a hand . . ."

Jane jumped in the truck and turned the ignition. "Don't go anywhere before I get back. I still want to talk to you."

"What's going on?" asked Serge.

"Something's come up." She threw the truck in gear. "Didn't get the details, but I've never heard them so excited."

The truck patched out.

"Let's get going," said Serge, heading into the woods. "That was a lucky clean break, no schmaltzy good-byes."

"Didn't she tell you not to leave?"

"Women always say that." Serge pushed through branches. "But they actually *want* you to leave. They love that in a man."

Coleman stepped over a log. "I thought they hated it."

"They say they hate it, but inside they secretly want a rogue."

"Are you a rogue?"

"No, but I play one in books." Serge hacked through more branches. "You show me a guy who does exactly everything a woman wants, and I'll show you the same guy six months later, standing on the sidewalk, wondering why some asshole's toothbrush is in her bathroom where his used to be."

"You know so much about chicks."

"Except shoes."

"Shoes?"

"You can't get away with shoes they don't like. It's the one thing, don't ask me why."

Coleman looked down. "Where are your favorite sneakers?"

"Hid them in my backpack." He splashed through shallow algae puddles. "Knew I was going to see Jane, so I bought these approved hiking boots."

"But you love those sneakers."

"They're like a part of my body after all these years. The toes are starting to wear through, but they're so comfy I just slap on a little duct tape and continue the happiness. But are women happy for you? No. 'You are not wearing duct tape to a five-star restaurant.'"

"We don't tell them what to wear," said Coleman

"Except for the special costumes in bed. But they give us that one victory so we don't stray or use the guest towels."

"Jesus, the guest towels," said Coleman. "Remember when you were married to Molly and I went in the bathroom and didn't know the rule?"

"Been meaning to ask: What the hell did you do to those towels? They looked like evidence a prosecutor holds up at a murder trial."

"Just washin'."

Serge sidestepped. "Pile of shit."

"Thanks," said Coleman. He bent down and held out a hand. "Look what I almost stepped in."

Jane raced toward the guard booth at the main entrance into Myakka River State Park.

A dozen marked and unmarked police cars parked every which way, with more still pouring in from the highway. A tour bus arrived, blaring Kiss.

Nearly every ranger was there, too, clustered in various knots with city police, sheriff's deputies, state agents.

A convertible T-Bird slowed as it approached the entrance. The driver noticed the pandemonium. She stopped on the opposite shoulder and unfolded a road map. A bright red fingernail moved across Sarasota

County. But it wasn't following a road. It traced a squiggly blue line. The driver smiled, re-folded the map and drove off.

Back by the guard booth, a chorus of questions and rumors.

"Everyone quiet down!" yelled White. "Who's in command at the park?"

"That would be me." A rugged outdoorsman in a light green parks department shirt stepped forward.

"You the one I talked to on the phone?"

He nodded.

"Where are the witnesses?"

"Over there." He pointed behind the guard booth at a pair of glowing-pale people in knee-high white socks and the world's largest binoculars hanging from their necks. "Canadian bird-watchers."

The agent walked briskly and held up Serge's mug shot. "Seen this guy?"

"Sure," said the husband. "We were eating breakfast this morning in the hotel lobby and saw one of your American crime shows on the TV. Then we came out here for the pied-billed grebe and semi-palmated plovers . . ."

". . . We weren't even looking for the tufted titmouse," said the wife. "Let alone a boat-tailed grackle. I took some pictures if you'd like—"

"Pardon me," interrupted White. "The suspect?"

"Oh, yeah," said the husband. "Then we were driving back to the interpretive center."

"I always pay attention to the sides of the road," said the wife. "Never know what you'll see. And there they were."

"The suspects?"

"No, yellow-throated warblers."

White pursed his lips. "When did you see the suspects?"

She turned to her husband. "Between the warblers and loons?"

"That's right," he said. "The two were just standing right by the side of the road. Didn't even spook at the sound of our car."

"You're certain?"

"Absolutely. The shapes of their heads, coloring. No way to mistake."

"I got a picture." The wife punched up the gallery on the digital camera preview screen and handed it over.

"It's them!" White looked up quickly. "Where was this?"

The tourists gestured in the direction of the lake. "Outside one of the cabins."

"How long ago?"

"Half hour, tops."

Jane watched from the rear of the crowd, stomach twisting. She began slowly walking backward to her pickup and drove off at a mild speed. Until the truck rounded the first bend. Then she floored it.

"Please, God, let me get there first. I can hide them in the pickup and sneak them out the staff access . . ."

Back at the guard booth: "We got him!" Agent White told the troops. "Only one highway through the park." He turned to the deputies. "Roadblocks at both ends of 72, east- and westbound. Check all trunks." The deputies took off. Then to the city police: "Have rangers show you all other official-use exits and get a helicopter up." Finally, to the ranger in charge: "Which way are the cabins?"

"Follow me."

Hikers and assorted nature buffs scattered from the otherwise quiet road as a convoy of pickups and sedans raced through the winding, oak-canopied drive. Cabins came into sight.

Jane ran around the outside of number three. "Don't tell me they left." She checked inside again. Then back on the porch as a half-dozen vehicles screeched up.

A bolt of panic hit her chest. No way out of this one.

Her boss jumped from the first pickup. "Anyone in there?"

She shook her head.

He turned around. "Check the other cabins."

Unbelievable. They thought she was with them and somehow had gotten there first.

Rangers and detectives soon regrouped. "Sir, all the other cabins are empty or just families."

"Listen up," said White. "We're splitting in two groups. One will work outward from the cabin, and the other in from the park boundaries."

"I can get some people on horseback," said the head ranger.

"Appreciate it," said White, looking up. "We need that helicopter . . ."

Jane felt her heart calming down. But where were they?

Coleman took a branch in the face. "Where are we?"

"Almost to the lake." Serge cleared a last thicket and pushed through tall weeds down to the shore. He ran along the edge as reptilian knotholes in the water watched. "Where is it?"

Coleman ran behind. "You mean the canoe you stole from the rental rack last night?"

"I stashed it right around here before we went to sleep in the cabin." His head swung back and forth. "Damn it! I know every inch of this place."

"But if we're not being chased, why the hurry?"

"If you're going to pretend, then *pretend*. Or get off the make-believe field."

"What's that?"

An aluminum glint. The tip of a canoe sticking out of the weeds.

Serge dragged it from his hiding spot and into the water. "Coleman, jump in and grab a paddle . . ."

The park was quarantined. Nobody in or out. Every police radio peppered with chatter. Not good news.

"Where haven't we checked?" asked White.

"Some of the eastern quadrants," said the head ranger. "And Deep Hole."

"Deep Hole?"

"Remote area generally off-limits."

"Can you get people out there?"

"Already on their way."

White keyed his mike again. "Roadblock one, report."

"Nothing here."

"Roadblock two?"

"Still quiet. Just the Doberman."

The deputy at the second roadblock cradled his mike and stepped into the road, flagging down an oncoming vehicle. The checkpoint was at the east end of the park, set up on a bridge so nobody could run the blockade by racing around the shoulders.

A convertible T-Bird pulled to a stop. "What's going on, officers?"

Every deputy crowded around the knockout red-head, sucking in their stomachs.

"There's a dangerous criminal on the loose."

"My goodness. Am I safe?"

"It's okay, ma'am, we've got it under control. But if you'd like to stay here with us until we catch him . . ."

They all looked up as the police helicopter flew low overhead. And Serge and Coleman paddled under the bridge.

Chapter Nineteen

SARASOTA COUNTY

A silver canoe drifted out of the state park.

Hanging vines, tannic water, lizards changing color.

"Are we there yet?" said Coleman.

"You just asked that."

"What is this we're on?"

"Myakka River, park's namesake."

"It's narrow."

"Current stretch is." He glanced up. "Perfect cover with the trees."

As the canoe approached each bend, alligators slid into the water like thieves.

Coleman looked over the side as one passed the other way. "Good God! It's longer than our boat!" His hands shook so badly he could barely crack another beer, which he chugged in one long guzzle.

"Coleman!" snapped Serge. "I'm counting on you to keep it together until we reach the next fugitive way station. You can't get fucked up as usual."

"This ain't partying." He popped another cold one. "It's nerve medication. You sure about gators not attacking canoes."

"Totally." Serge gazed up again at overhanging branches. "I'd be more worried about the killer swooping turtles."

Coleman spit a spray of Miller High Life over the side. "Killer what?"

"Turtles. Big ones with razor-sharp teeth that wait in overhead trees for unsuspecting canoeists, then swoop and bite their heads off."

Coleman rapidly glanced up and down between the branches and knotholes in the river. Another beer cracked.

"Don't worry." Serge made peaceful strokes in the water. "It's just a goofy myth in these parts. But one that our next stop has gotten a lot of mileage from."

Moments later, the banks diverged and the river opened up. Serge noticed an unintended change of course. "Why are we starting to go in a circle—" He turned around. "Coleman, get that paddle back in the water."

"But I'm tired."

"You're drunk."

"Are we there yet?"

"Yes."

"Where?"

"There."

The canoe skirted a final bend and a dock came into view. Some kind of weathered building, an outdoor pavilion, boat ramp, sounds echoing off the banks: Hank Williams and whooping-it-up beer drinkers.

"Now you're talking," said Coleman. "What is this place?"

"Snook Haven." Serge nosed the canoe onto the ramp, got out and pulled it the rest of the way so Coleman wouldn't make a water landing. "Legendary Florida fish camp overlooking the Myakka east of Venice in the middle of nowhere."

"Look at all those motorcycles."

"Bikers find all the best places in Florida."

They walked around to the entrance, with a large carved snook on the door.

"Serge, there's a sign with a crazy-looking turtle on it."

"Souvenir T-shirts to follow inside." He opened the door. Dark wood. That outback hunting lodge vibe.

"Serge!"

He waved back at two humongous bikers. "Skid Marks! Bacon Strips!"

Big hugs as each lifted Serge off the floor. "Been following your website," said Skid. "Dynamite Fugitive Tour."

Bacon hoisted a mug of draft. "A little too close to reality."

"Nobody would ever find you out here." Skid dabbed a gator nugget in tartar and popped it in his mouth. "When I first saw the tour, I said, Snook Haven has to be coming up next, and sure enough."

Coleman grabbed a stool and signaled for three beers. "So what do your nicknames mean?"

A round of laughs. And so began a prolonged afternoon of river country camaraderie. Live entertainment took the tiny stage.

Banjos.

"They filmed the movie right out there on this river," said Serge.

"Here we go again," chided Skid Marks.

"Early RKO talking film *Prestige*, starring Ann Benning. Takes place at a French penal colony in Indochina that they built on these banks. I'm going there now in my mind . . ."

MYAKKA RIVER STATE PARK

Agent White established a command post down at the lakefront sundries store.

A clearinghouse for fruitless reports.

Until . . .

Lowe rushed in. "Come quick. You're wanted on the radio."

They ran out to his car. "White here."

"We got something down at Deep Hole."

"Serge?"

"No, but you really need to see this."

"Do I hear someone throwing up in the background?"

"Yes."

A late-afternoon sun cast that muted warm, orange glow along a hammock of palm trees. A mixed cast of officials stood solemnly along the edge of the sinkhole. Still taking in a new experience.

Decapitated alligator, shreds of a rubber life raft, tent stakes, nylon rope, and a severed human arm that another gator had been munching and dropped when the first rangers arrived.

"What the heck are we looking at?" said White.

Mahoney took a swig from a sterling hip flask. "Serge."

"Could you be less coy?"

Mahoney flicked a vintage Zippo open and closed. "Seen it a million times."

"*This?*" White gestured at the scene in frustration. "Exactly?"

Mahoney shook his head, still flicking the lighter. It had a blond bombshell from the nose art of a B-17 Flying Fortress. "His milieu."

"You know, you're a very difficult person to talk to."

Mahoney crouched over the arm. "Runs Goldberg long game on sideways jakes to the big snooze."

"Will you please speak the language?"

A police radio went off.

"*Sir, we completed a full sweep. Nothing in the park . . .*"

White stared at Deep Hole. "I don't understand it. We've got even the smallest back road blocked. How did he get out?"

Mahoney gazed across shallow marshland, where a trickle of a river snaked out of sight. A knowing smile crept across his face.

"What is it?" asked White.

"Myakka Midnight Special," said Mahoney. "Canoe Keyhole Squeeze."

"What?"

"I know how he escaped from the park," said Mahoney. "River runs under the bridge and straight down to this fish camp near Venice."

SNOOK HAVEN

Serge returned from the restroom. "Okay, I'm back from Indochina. Everyone ready?"

"Ready for what?" asked Coleman. He raised a finger to the bartender. "Beer."

Serge waved him off. "No beer . . . Coleman, we have to go. We're on a tight schedule. You think this is all just pointless wandering?"

"Back to the canoe?"

Serge shook his head.

Skid Marks and Bacon Strips got off their stools.

"What?" said Coleman, looking around. "You mean you planned all along to meet here? Like another 'Out'?"

Skid Marks just smiled.

"You can ride with me," said Bacon Strips.

VENICE

A Crown Vic raced south on Interstate 75.

"Mahoney, you sure about this hunch of yours?" asked White.

"Does a bear shit in the Vatican?"

"There it is," said Lowe. "Exit 191."

White took the ramp. They sped down River Road, as in the Myakka River . . .

Less than a mile south, two large Harleys roared along a gravel road, through a tight corridor of palms and slash pines. Serge and Coleman on the back of each.

The hogs passed a small dirt access, where a convertible T-Bird sat off at an angle just out of view in the trees. The redhead in the driver's seat watched them go by, then slowly pulled out.

The bikers finally emerged from the woods, back into civilization. Skid Marks rolled up to the intersection with River Road and put his boots on the ground. Over his shoulder: "Which way?"

"South," said Serge.

A couple hundred yards north, the occupants of a Crown Vic just missed two motorcycles turning left onto River Road, followed at a discreet distance by a turquoise T-Bird.

"There's the turn," said Lowe. "That little country road."

White pulled off the highway and stopped by a sign. SNOOK HAVEN, LIVE MUSIC. A cartoon of a green animal wearing a T-shirt: HOME OF THE KILLER TURTLES.

Car doors opened. They gathered on the shoulder.

"Seal this off," said White. "Major felony stop. The rest of you, come with me."

They roared down the gravel road to the riverbank and an old fish camp. White gave snap directions again for another perimeter lockdown. Then he grabbed the handle of a carved-snook door, and three agents went inside.

"Wow," said Lowe. "Look at this cool place."

Mahoney slapped a badge on the bar. He held up a black-and-white photo. "Hey mug, seen this mug?"

The bartender poured foam off a draft. "Sure, just in here."

"When did he blow?"

"I don't know, couldn't have been too long ago."

Same results for the other agents. Everyone had just seen Serge and Coleman, and nobody knew where they went.

"I remember them," said a patron in a fishing vest. "They were talking to these bikers. Seemed like they knew each other."

"Think carefully," said White. "Did they leave together?"

"Might have."

"When?"

Shoulders shrugged.

"White," said Lowe. "Didn't we see a couple motorcycles take off just before we turned onto this road?"

"That's right," said the agent. "And they had passengers, heading south." He ran out the door.

A Crown Vic led the speeding convoy back up the gravel road until they came to the checkpoint. White yelled out his window. "We're looking for four people on two Harleys, southbound. Move!"

PART III

The Past Catches Up

Chapter Twenty

THE TAMIAMI TRAIL

Skid Marks and Bacon Strips rode side by side on glorious machines, lords of the highway, top of the food chain.

It was that kind of day, the open road, wind in their faces, the words "Alive" and "Freedom" written in tall letters across the sky. A sticker on the back of one of the bikes: HONK IF YOU'VE NEVER SEEN A GUN FIRED FROM A MOVING HARLEY.

Serge took pictures. Coleman clung for life.

"Loosen up," Bacon yelled back. "I can't breathe."

"I'm scared."

They took River Road south until picking up the Tamiami Trail in North Port.

"Quarter mile," Serge said over Skid's shoulder. "That's our turn."

The bikers eased off the throttle and swung left in unison like an airplane formation.

A half minute later, a convertible T-Bird slowed and looked down the road the bikers had taken, then sped up again. At the next light, the redhead made a U-turn . . .

Back up the street, two Harleys sat parked outside a ticket pavilion.

Inside: People stared.

It was not a common sight at this particular tourist stop. Serge, Coleman and two hairy, barrel-chested, tattooed bikers stood waist-deep in a pool. Surrounding them were no fewer than a hundred other people, all with at least three decades on the new arrivals. The gawking senior citizens eventually got used to their younger companions and resumed low-impact water aerobics. Some wore out-dated swim caps with stick-on plastic flowers. They spoke German and French and Italian.

It wasn't exactly a regular pool. Actually a large artesian-fed pond. People across Europe believed it had spiritual powers.

"Look at all the old people," said Coleman.

"It's Warm Mineral Springs," said Serge.

"It's warm," said Coleman.

"Constant eighty-seven degrees year-round. They come from across the globe to cure what ails 'em."

"But why are *we* here?"

"First, it's the perfect place to hide out. Low police hassle factor because of the remoteness." Serge waved around at all the octogenarians in the pool. "And these people are generally behaved. Just the occasional dustup with canes and walkers."

"I saw one of those in Boca Raton," said Coleman. "It was a slow fight."

"Second, it's Warm Mineral Springs," said Serge. "Opened 1954, one of the last thriving pre-Disney roadside attractions. A one-and-a-half-acre swimming area over a spring-fed, two-hundred-and-thirty-foot-deep hourglass sinkhole connected to the Floridan aquifer and pumping nine million gallons a day. Then there's my fondness of the weird for which I've become widely known. Remember our walk out here from the admission window?"

"That was freaky."

"Totally surreal, like those near-death experiences you always hear about. The building had this super-long breezeway that creates a dark tunnel with a bright dot of light at the end where you finally emerge at this spring. And along the way, piped-in celestial music."

"That was creepy, too. I've never heard music like that."

"Neither have I. It's like if you took a Muzak song, and made a Muzak version of *that*. Then we came out of the tunnel, and there were all these happy, super-old folks frolicking in this cheerful water park."

"Do you think heaven's like that?"

"Could be worse," said Serge. "You know all those pushy people who keep telling us we're not going to heaven? It could be full of them instead."

Coleman made a face. "But everyone here's so . . . wrinkled."

"Coleman, respect your elders!" said Serge. "I know I do. I see some ninety-year-old dude driving ten miles an hour, clutching the steering wheel to his face. Everyone else impatiently honks, but I say, 'Rock on!' and shoot him a gray-power fist salute. You have to give a guy like that credit, if only for excellent attendance." Serge turned to the group of seniors nearest him and waved. "You're my heroes! I love absolutely everything you're doing with this whole 'not dying' thing!"

They quickly waded away.

"Where was I?" asked Serge.

"Warm Mineral Springs."

"That's right." Serge interlaced his fingers on the pond's surface and made water squirt. "Brochures tout it as the Original Fountain of Youth."

"But Serge," said Coleman. "How can they make such a fantastic claim?"

"That's probably what the people who sell tickets in St. Augustine want to know. I've been expecting a rumble for years, drive-bys in Buicks and Oldsmobiles, raking each other's signs with automatic fire. I even offered my services to this place to put the arm on the competition, walking down the customer line in Saint Aug to correct the historical record. I actually did that, purely on spec."

"How'd it go?"

"I was only trying to explain that the fountain obviously isn't where Ponce de Leon explored, except the older tourists today are jumpy and overreact when I whisper, 'You want to live, don't you?'"

"So you think this place might be for real?"

"The science is behind it. They've got the highest mineral content in the United States. Feel any younger?"

Coleman lay on his back. "I just feel like I'm floating higher."

"Minerals give you more buoyancy."

"Buoyancy is good?"

"In a sinkhole, better than the alternative."

Coleman paddled his arms. "Where do these people get their connection to the Fountain of Youth?"

"That's the funny part." Serge floated on his own back. "They say that after Ponce de Leon got disgusted with Saint Augustine, he brought his search for the fountain to Florida's west coast, making landfall in 1521 at Port Charlotte, just a few miles from here, arguably to find this spring."

"Did he find it?"

"No, Indians killed him with arrows."

"Isn't that like the reverse of the Fountain of Youth?" asked Coleman.

"Doesn't seem to have hurt business."

Skid Marks floated over and blew a small fountain of water in the air. "Serge, imagine my surprise that we would team up again. How long now?"

"Been meaning to keep in touch, but one thing after another."

"Sorry about your granddad."

"Appreciate it."

Coleman wiped a pool booger. "You knew Serge's granddad?"

"Met a few times," said Skid Marks. "My grandfather and his, back in the old days . . ."

"The gang was legendary," said Serge.

Skid Marks smiled. "And talk about trouble."

"Wait," Coleman said to Serge. "You mean *the* gang, like Chi-Chi and Coltrane and Roy the Pawn King that you keep telling me about, running the bookie and fence rackets?"

"That's them," said Serge. "Miami Beach fixtures."

Skid Marks reclined on his back again. "Nobody remembers anymore. No respect."

"Which one was your granddad?" asked Coleman.

"Greek Tommy."

Serge adjusted the inflatable swim fins on his arms. "Tommy expanded the business. One of the best drivers for hire."

"Driver?" said Coleman. "Like getaway?"

"No, moonshine running," said Serge. "In the off-season, when the tourists went home and gambling dried up, they made deliveries from the many stills hidden throughout the Everglades. But it took a lot of talent behind the wheel because cops were usually waiting."

"They all knew about the gang," said Skid Marks. "But they were never able to pin anything."

"Tommy was incredible," said Serge. "Forget what you see in the movies. He knew every back road, every puddle and mud hole and maneuver to get pursuing police stuck. Or take a blind turn and send them sailing into the swamp. Like I said, the best."

"And *your* granddad was the craziest," said Skid Marks. "Lost as many loads as he delivered."

"But never got caught," said Serge.

Skid Marks laughed. "Because the cops were too smart to chase a lunatic like that."

"Those were the glory days."

"And of course the Gator Hook."

"What's a gator hook?" asked Coleman.

"Generally, a hooked pole poachers use to prod alligators out of their holes," said Serge. "But in this case, a landmark lodge in the middle of the Everglades on the Loop Road."

"Remember that night our granddads took us out there?" said Skid Marks.

"Like it was five minutes ago . . ."

EVERGLADES 1964

Two Cadillacs bounced down the Loop Road.

An airboat hopped out of the swamp and came the other way. They parked next to each other in bright gravel outside a plain building with an open door. The floor was bare and so were a lot of the feet.

Wailing bluegrass.

Greek Tommy knew the place well. It was on his regular route, except he didn't make any deliveries there. His "safe spot." The cops all knew his car and he was constantly picking up tails. If Tommy wasn't holding, he'd just drop in at the Gator Hook Lodge.

And when they came to roust him: "I'm just here for the music."

On this particular night in late October, the Miami Beach gang hopped from DeVilles and started toward the door. "Anyone carrying a knife or gun?" asked Tommy.

"No," said Coltrane. "That sign says they're not allowed."

"Why do you think they need that sign?" asked Tommy. "Stay here. I'll go back to the cars and get some."

That kind of place.

They went inside and pulled tables together. Half the customers already stewed. Beer arrived. Someone fell across their tables. He laughed and rolled in saw-dust until friends dragged him outside.

Chi-Chi turned the tables back up. "I'll get more drinks."

Coltrane looked around. "What's going on?"

"What do you mean?" said Tommy.

"It just got a lot quieter."

"Because they're waiting for *him*," said Tommy.

"Him?"

"Ervin Rouse."

"Who's that?"

"Ever heard of 'The Orange Blossom Special'?"

"Who hasn't? Considered the best fiddle song ever written."

"Rouse wrote it back in the 1930s. Got the idea late one night hanging out at the Jacksonville train platform to see the arrival of this fantastic new train everyone was talking about."

"What's that got to do with this place?"

"Ervin lives like a hermit a spit away from here on the Loop Road."

"You had me going." Coltrane laughed. "A world-famous musician living in one of the most remote spots of the Everglades."

"He's not kidding," said Sergio. "I know about this."

"Don't you start, too."

"Here's the coolest part," said Greek Tommy. "On Saturday nights—like tonight—Ervin just strolls up the road with his fiddle, walks into this funky little outback joint and starts playing 'The Orange Blossom Special.'"

"I'll believe it when I see it," said Coltrane.

Greek Tommy picked up his grandson Skid Marks and set the boy on his lap. Except back then he was just called Bobby. The grandfather looked toward a small stage in the corner and whispered something in the child's ear.

Sergio did the same with Little Serge. "See that microphone over there?"

Little Serge nodded enthusiastically.

"Keep watching it," said Sergio. "You'll see something historic you can tell your children about."

Bang.

Coltrane jumped. "That sounded like gunfire."

"It was," said Tommy, eyes remaining on the corner stage. "A tradition. They're shooting off the back porch."

Coltrane looked through the open rear door. "At what?"

"Dynamite."

"Dynamite?"

"Up in the fork of a tree. Winner gets free beer."

Bang.

Tommy pointed. "Here he is."

A grizzled old man walked across the room, wearing a shirt that looked like it was woven by Seminoles. He reached the microphone and raised his fiddle in the air to acknowledge the applause.

Everyone piped down. The old man rested a bow atop the strings—and he was off, playing furiously to an even louder eruption of appreciation.

"*. . . Comin' down that railroad track . . .*"

"I wouldn't have believed it," said Coltrane.

Bang.

"*. . . It's The Orange Blossom Special . . .*"

Bang, bang.

"They're still shooting at dynamite?"

Tommy looked around. "Where's Little Serge?"

"Over there on the back porch with Sergio," said Coltrane. "What's he doing letting him have that gun?"

Bang. BOOM.

"Little Serge just won beer."

"*. . . Goin' down to Florida! . . .*"

Chapter Twenty-one

PRESENT

They all had a good laugh in the tepid waters of Warm Mineral Springs.

"Man, that takes me back," said Skid Marks. "The Gator Hook, 'Orange Blossom,' Granddad . . ."

"Memories," said Serge. "But that isn't even close to the best stories . . ."

A few hundred yards away, outside the ticket booth, a redhead in a T-Bird sat under a coconut palm, keeping her eye on the only two motorcycles in the parking lot.

"Your *great*-granddad," said Serge. "Now, that was the high-water mark."

"Crazy Murphy?" Skid Marks did the backstroke. "Yeah, my granddad told me all about him."

"Not to take anything away from the gang," said Serge. "Moonshine running in the sixties was no piece of cake. But Prohibition—now, that was the real action. What I wouldn't give! . . . I can see it all . . ." Serge stared up at the sky. ". . . Me and Coleman racing through the swamp with a full load of hooch, Eliot Ness on our tail, tommy guns shooting out my tires, but no surrender! Escaping into the glades on foot like chain-gang refugees, just ahead of the bloodhounds, dragging Coleman behind me . . ."

"Serge! Stop dragging me around the water!"

". . . Then we hook up with my trusty Indian guide, Breaking Wind, who makes us invisible to the White Man and we flee by dugout canoe to Chokoloskee Bay . . ."

"Serge," said Skid Marks. "I think you should calm down. Everyone's staring again."

"But I'm invisible to the White Man."

"Serge, please . . ."

"I'm always born too late." He smiled and looked up. "Is it true Crazy Murphy worked for Capone?"

"More like only the occasional delivery," said Skid Marks. "Capone had this wild place just over the Monroe line."

"Damn, I wish I could have seen that," said Serge.

"It was long gone by the time of the Gator Hook, but people still talked about it."

"And now even the Gator Hook's a pile of rubble."

"Greek Tommy would tell me all these insane stories passed down from his dad."

"Like what?"

"Like sometimes he'd be making a drop for Capone and see things he shouldn't. That old spot in the Everglades wasn't just the perfect speakeasy location. If Capone needed to get rid of anyone, well, body disposal almost takes care of itself out there with all the gator holes."

"Except Crazy Murphy actually saw what I heard, right?"

"They didn't call him crazy for nothing. Who knows what he witnessed, the way stories change from generation. But in the versions my granddad tells, at least a couple times he saw guys led off into the swamp at night while Capone stood on the back porch, swatting the air . . ."

"Swatting?"

"He'd catch imaginary flying things and stick them in his pockets. Everyone pretended not to notice. They didn't know it at the time, but his mind was slipping from untreated VD."

"What about the guys who were taken into the swamp?"

"Never seen again, or at least that's what my granddad said. Murphy thought he heard gunfire, but ignored it and kept unloading moonshine."

"Sure sounds true," said Serge. "But you don't believe it?"

Skid Marks shrugged. "There are so many stories, some have to be true, but which ones? Like when Geraldo opened that empty safe at the Lexington on live TV."

"That guy's a toad."

"My granddad said it was empty because Al knew the cops would go ape after that Valentine's Day business. So ahead of time, he had it all crated up and part of the stash made its way to Florida. Supposedly hidden down the Loop Road, somewhere in the swamp behind the old place."

"That's awesome."

"Granddad also told me Jimmy Hoffa's back there."

"He is?"

"No, he's not," said Skid. "That's the point. The more years go by, the thicker the bullshit."

"I hadn't heard about Hoffa."

"One of the three big stories going around," said the biker. "Giants Stadium, a New Jersey incinerator, the Loop Road. Except it's not true."

"But it *is* true that it's a rumor," said Serge. "Excellent!"

"Why?"

"People are talking about Florida," said Serge. "Makes me proud."

A half hour later.

A turquoise T-Bird drove a short distance back to the Tamiami Trail, slowly circling past two parked motorcycles and up an alley behind the Warm Mineral Springs Motel.

Room 21.

Coleman returned from the cooler and tossed frosty cans of beer to the bikers.

"Thanks," said Skid Marks, reclining on a motel sofa under the air conditioner. "That pool was a little too warm for me."

"I wanted to stay longer," said Serge, turning with a glare, "but someone had to do cannonballs."

"Sorry," said Coleman.

Bacon Strips popped his Coors. "So, Serge, where to next?"

"Points south. Got a few options, but the selection has to be absolutely perfect for the Fugitive Tour."

"It's a sacred ride," said Skid Marks. "All my two-wheel brothers have been following it on the Web and raving."

"It's not really a fugitive tour," said Serge. "It's a back-roads tour. I'm trying to get people off the interstates and out of the theme parks to places less traveled."

"Then why are you calling it the Fugitive Tour?" asked Bacon Strips.

"Marketing," said Serge. "You need to make people feel good about themselves."

"What are you doing?" asked Skid Marks.

Serge had the curtains and sliding-glass door open in the back of the room. *Click, click, click.* "Photo documentation of this time capsule."

"The motel?"

"See those angled concrete overhangs? One of the finest surviving examples of 1950s parasol architecture." *Click, click, click.* "And that original neon sign, Warm Mineral Springs Motel? Notice how none of the lights are burned out. You rarely see that." *Click, click.* "It's because of those old people from the pool. They still pump enough money into this place to keep her maintained. And we're far enough between population centers on the Tamiami so there are no eyesores like Old Navy and Linens 'n' Fuck." *Click, click, click.*

"Serge," said Skid Marks, getting off the couch. "Could I have a word?"

They stepped out on the porch and closed the sliding-glass door.

"I saw Brad's Beemer on the way to Snook Haven," said the biker. "I think the plan's working."

"Of course it's working," said Serge. "Just keep phoning him tips where I'm heading, like Kissimmee and Cedar Key. When I first got your message, I was ready to strangle someone. Every time I lower the bar of human expectations, some asshole like Brad comes along and exploits people on their death-beds."

"Here are copies of the two letters," said Skid. "What have you got in mind?"

"Better you not know."

"But the money's offshore."

"The Secret Master Plan is prepared for all contingencies."

Skid Marks looked back in the room. "What about Coleman?"

"Keeping him in the dark," said Serge, opening the sliding glass. "His lifestyle is the one variable that Master Plans have yet to conquer."

They went back inside.

A loud knock on the door across the room.

Serge jumped and grabbed his gun. "Who can that be?"

Skid Marks looked at his watch. "Relax, it's one of ours. Supposed to meet at two." He answered the door.

"Wingnut!"

"Skid Marks!"

The new biker walked into the room. "Serge! Catch!"

A set of keys flew through the air.

"That's the car you ordered," said Wingnut. "Papers in the glove compartment. Clean title, new plate, registration up-to-date."

Serge opened his wallet. "How much I owe you?"

"I owe *you*," said the biker. "Just get it back to me when you're done, and try to go easy on the paint job."

"Thanks, Wingnut."

Coleman opened the cooler again. "You can just order a car? How many people in this state owe you favors?"

"Favors are a new hybrid energy source of the Fugitive Tour," said Serge.

"Ready?" Wingnut said to the other bikers.

"Thanks for the brews." Bacon Strips stood.

"Take care of yourself," said Skid Marks. Both bikers gave Serge and Coleman another round of bear hugs.

"Thanks for the car," said Serge.

"It's the least," said Skid Marks. "For everything you've done—and what you're going to do."

Serge walked them out the door. Then froze at the sight in the parking lot. "Holy cow! An electric blue '69 Barracuda!"

Wingnut climbed on the back of Skid Marks' hog and grinned. "Thought you'd like it."

Serge and Coleman waved as two Harleys sped off down the Tamiami Trail.

They went back inside and closed the door.

A minute later:

Knock, knock, knock . . .

"Back so soon?" said Coleman.

Knock, knock, knock, knock . . .

"Probably forgot something," said Serge. *"Coming! . . ."*

He opened the door.

A drop-dead redhead in a black leather jacket and matching leather pants.

"Uh . . . Molly!" said Serge. "What a surprise! Great to see you!" He looked down. A pistol.

She poked it in his stomach. "Back up."

He did.

She waved the gun toward a wall. "Now get over there with your stupid slob friend!"

They lined up as told.

"Molly," said Serge. "What's the need for the pistol? Don't you remember all the good times?"

"Good times?" said Molly. "A husband doesn't hose out the trunk of the family car at midnight every two weeks, saying you 'hit another animal.'"

"But I did! I swear!"

"Shut up!" Molly widened her shooting stance in the doorway and aimed the Colt .45. "This is payback!"

"Wait!" Serge raised his hands in the air. "I can explain."

Coleman raised his own hands. "I didn't know they were guest towels."

"Serge," said Molly.

"What?"

"I wasn't talking to you."

"Then who were you talking to?" asked Serge.

From outside, a small boy peeked around the edge of the doorframe.

Serge's eyes narrowed. "His name's Serge, too?"

Molly lowered the gun. "You do the math."

"Hold it . . . you're not saying—"

"That's exactly what I'm saying."

"Buy why didn't you tell me in Miami after the hurricane?"

"That's why I came there," said Molly. "But before I could break the news, you clubbed me in the head with an electric guitar and knocked me unconscious."

"Only because you pulled that gun on me."

"You always twist everything the way you want to see it."

"I'm sorry," said Serge. "You're right."

"And don't try your forfeit strategy on me. I'm onto that shit: falsely agreeing just to get out of a fight because you think there's no way to win an argument with a woman."

"Okay, you're wrong."

"Can't you at least once agree with me?"

"You're half right?"

"Go to hell," said Molly. "You and your fucking insane genes." She turned toward the child who was repeatedly kicking a wall. "Kid's like a tornado. I'm at the end of my rope."

"Can't be that bad," said Serge.

"You're about to find out." Molly looked down. "Go over there and say hi to your dad."

"Whoa!" said Serge. "Don't leave. I've never taken care of a child."

"Told you this was payback."

Molly walked out and slammed the door.

Chapter Twenty-two

EVERGLADES 1929

April 25.

The first anniversary of the Tamiami Trail.

Fanfare.

Heralded as an modern engineering marvel, but the bulk of the traffic remained in the future.

Crossing the trail was still a novelty. The bold, the curious. Some just wanted to see alligators. Northerners.

And at night, especially without a moon, it couldn't have been more dark.

That changed toward the end of the year. Happened on weekends. Started around nine or ten each Friday and Saturday. Flowing inland from both coasts, the Everglades night flickered with the headlamps of Studebakers and Model Ts, a strand of glowing beads stretching through the swamp. The lights occasionally caught herons and vultures taking flight.

Those heading west out of Miami made a left turn about forty miles in. Eastbound Fort Myers traffic looked for gas pumps at a two-story clapboard called Monroe Station. They turned right.

The visitors met somewhere in the middle of the Loop Road. Piano music, laughter. They parked where they could outside a building with bright chandeliers, people dancing in the windows. Others staggered off the porch and fell in a decorative, circular fishpond of limestone blocks.

Precisely four hundred yards behind the lodge, a kerosene lantern hung from a branch. The music and revelry were but faint sounds if the wind was blowing right. Distant flickers from the chandeliers.

Two men not dressed for the task jammed shovels into the ground. Frenchy and the Swede. Dress pants and shirts and suspenders. Jackets hung from other branches near the lantern. They would need to buy new shoes.

Another spadeful of dirt flew.

"How big do we have to dig this thing?" asked Frenchy.

"Told me ten by six," said the Swede.

Frenchy took a break, leaning against the handle of his shovel and wiping his forehead. "That's awfully big for a grave."

"It's not a grave." The Swede flung another load of dirt. "Out here, you don't need one."

"Why not?"

"Nature handles the details." He looked up at his resting partner. "I'm not going to dig this thing by myself."

Frenchy huffed and put his shoulder back into it, constantly glancing around as he had from the start. "Are there really alligators out here?"

"Yes." The Swede hit some roots.

"Where are they?"

"All around. Now dig."

Frenchy put a foot on top of the shovel's blade. "So what is this we're digging anyway?"

The Swede was neck-deep down in the hole. "I don't think we're supposed to know."

A rustling in the swamp. Growing closer. The pair stopped and looked up.

"Think it's an alligator?"

"Frenchy? Swede?"

"Over here by the lantern."

"You're needed."

"What about the hole?"

"It'll still be there."

They began hacking their way back through tangled brush and cabbage palms. "We're definitely not in Chicago anymore."

Back at the lodge, more cars arrived. This time with a commotion.

Rumors shot through the building; people ran to the windows with glasses of bathtub gin. "Is it him?"

A deluxe Packard roadster pulled into a reserved space in front of the lodge. Armored doors, bulletproof glass, goons on running boards.

Someone rushed to open one of its back doors. Someone else threw a coat on the ground.

Out stepped an impeccably dressed man with a round face, the ends of a white scarf hanging over each lapel. And an unmistakable scar that nobody made the mistake of mentioning.

A movie star might as well have arrived. Partiers rushed to the porch, and the bodyguards cleared a path. Everyone excited, shaking his hand, heaping adoration.

Behind him, associates held the Packard's doors for two special guests from Illinois. The Santini brothers. Gino and Salvatore. They ran a dry cleaners on the south side, but they really ran whiskey down from Canada. Been doing so for years since the Eighteenth Amendment. They'd made Capone a nice bit of change. Now he was rewarding them with the finest time in his new Florida. All the best Miami restaurants. Gave them his Everglades Suite at the Biltmore in Coral Gables. But he'd saved the best for last: time to show off the crown jewel of the swamp.

Al put his arms around the brothers and led them to the bar, where a bald man in a tux filled a martini shaker. "Dominic, take care of my friends."

"Yes sir, Mr. Capone."

Then Al called over the girls.

Another pair of headlamps appeared up the Loop Road, but these approached much faster because the engine had been retooled with larger cylinders and a massive carb. The roadster arrived without slowing, racing around back and stopping with a controlled spin in the mud. Its doors and fenders had been specially fitted with a maze of concealed copper tubing.

Someone behind the lodge: "Crazy Murphy's here!"

Murphy was their best driver, Florida's predecessor to the Carolina's Junior Johnson. Ten drivers had the nickname "Crazy." Murphy defined it.

A platoon of men poured out the back screen door and filled jugs from a spigot concealed under the bumper.

White lightning from one of the largest stills deep in the glades.

PRESENT

The silence of shock filled room 21 at the Warm Mineral Springs Motel.

Serge slowly looked at Coleman, then at the boy. He opened his mouth, but nothing came out.

The boy was small and skinny for his age, untied sneakers, runny nose, both knees skinned, brown hair that Molly had been cutting with a bowl, dirty face like he'd been playing in a chimney. Ice blue eyes.

"Serge," said Coleman. "Are you okay?"

"I'm actually . . . a father?"

"Is that good?"

"Good?" said Serge. "It's great!"

"You sure he's yours?" said Coleman. "Molly's a piece of work."

The boy ran across the room and kicked Serge in the shin.

"Ow!" He hopped and rubbed his leg.

Coleman laughed. "He got you good . . . Ow!"

They both hopped and watched the boy sprinting as fast as he could in circles in the middle of the room. He made a sound with his mouth that jiggled as he ran.

". . . A-ya-ya-ya-ya-ya-ya-ya . . ."

Serge stopped hopping. "I'd say he's probably mine."

"What's he doing now?" asked Coleman.

"Sticking a fork in that electrical outlet." Serge bolted over and pulled a tiny arm back. The child punched him in the nuts. Serge doubled over.

Coleman giggled again. "He's pretty funny . . . Ow! Serge, he just stuck the fork in my arm!"

Serge got up and held his throbbing crotch. "He's definitely mine."

Coleman pulled the fork out. "I need Band-Aids."

"In my suitcase."

Coleman turned. "He's got a gun!"

Serge dove and snatched it away. He grabbed the tyke under the armpits and set him on the edge of a bed. Then he knelt in front of the child and held the weapon sideways in front of his face.

"That was very, very bad," said Serge. "You never point a gun at anyone unless you intend to shoot them. And always remember to check the chamber."

Serge ejected the clip and racked the slide to pop out the live round. "There." He handed the pistol back to the tot. "She's all yours."

"I'm impressed," said Coleman. "You have natural parenting skills."

"Sometimes I surprise myself."

The boy aimed the gun at the two men. "*Pow! Pow! Pow! Pow! Pow!* . . . You're dead. You're supposed to fall down."

Serge glanced at Coleman. "Fall down."

The pair hit the ground.

They faced each other, cheeks to the carpet, hearing little footsteps.

"What's he doing now?" asked Coleman.

In sequence, they each felt the gun barrel behind their left ear. *"Pow! Pow! . . . Pow! Pow!"*

"Those are double taps to the back of the head for certainty," said Serge. "Standard assassination procedure."

"Wonder where he learned that?"

"Probably in school. They grow up so much faster these days."

"Now he's going through our wallets."

Serge hopped to his feet. "All right, playtime's over." He reached for his billfold.

The boy pulled something from the back compartment. "A balloon."

"Serge," said Coleman. "He's got one of your condoms."

Serge took it away. The child extended his arm. "Balloon!"

"Okay," said Serge. "Since we just met, I'll give you a present to remember this day." He held up the small plastic package. "This is a special magic balloon. My gift to you. But don't open it now. You'll know when the time is right."

"Wow, thanks!" He stuffed it in his pocket.

Serge sat on the bed and hoisted the child onto his knee. "How old are you?"

He held up fingers. "Five and a half."

Serge smiled and looked over at Coleman. "Remember when you used to add halves to your age?"

"You don't anymore?"

Serge faced the boy again. "Your name really Serge?"

The child shook his head. "Mikey. But my mommy calls me Serge when she's mad at me . . . Is your first name Fucking?"

Serge's eyes popped. "What!"

"Mommy always calls you Fucking Serge."

Serge looked up at the ceiling and took a deep breath. "Okay, Mikey. I'm going to have to explain something to you. It's very complicated and you probably won't completely comprehend it until you're much older, but sometimes Mommy and Daddy can't live together anymore. They still love each other, but they have to get separate houses. Are you following me so far?"

Mikey nodded.

"Good," said Serge. "And this is the most important part: After Mommy and Daddy move away from each other, she is wrong about everything. Do you understand?"

Another nod.

"Great."

Mikey jumped down and went over to the cooler.

"Serge, he has a beer."

Serge took it away and wagged a finger. "Not for you. This is Stupid Juice."

"Serge," said Coleman, going through his backpack. "Have you seen my bag of weed?"

"Yes." He grabbed it from the child. "Here you go, Coleman. Try to be more careful."

"No problem. I'll just cram it way down the bottom and stick my lighter there, too—... Where's my lighter?" Coleman sniffed. "Do you smell something burning?"

"The curtains!"

Serge grabbed the bedspread and smothered the flames against the sliding-glass door. Coleman shook a can of beer and sprayed.

The fire was finally out. Coleman drank the rest of the can. "That was close."

Serge faced the child and placed stern hands on his hips. "That was naughty. Now give me the lighter. And the knife."

Mikey surrendered them. Then he ran in the bathroom and slammed the door.

"What's he up to now?" asked Coleman.

"Think he has to go potty."

Serge walked to the bathroom and tried the knob. He knocked. "Mikey, unlock the door."

Coleman came over. "Barricaded himself?"

More banging. "Come on, Mikey, open up!"

"I wouldn't worry." Coleman fired a joint. "Probably can't come to the door right now because he's pinching a loaf."

"Coleman! That's my son you're talking about!"

"Okay, pinching peanuts."

Their feet felt something. Serge looked down and saw water sheeting from under the door.

Coleman stepped out of the puddle. "I think he's bored."

"I got an idea." He banged again. "Mikey, come out and I promise we'll go to the toy store."

The door instantly opened.

"Can I get anything I want?"

"Within reason," said Serge. "Now lie facedown in the corner with your hands behind your back until we mop this up . . ."

Chapter Twenty-three

EVERGLADES 1929

The swamp night grew louder as people with rare access to spirits went a little overboard. Or a lot. That was the Santinis. The brothers staggered and slurred. Already made three trips each upstairs with the ladies—and won a bundle on roulette, because Al had told the operator of the rigged wheel to let them.

Then it was getting seriously late. But no slowing down for the Roaring Twenties. Piano tempo picked up. The Charleston.

Arms with meaty hands went around the brothers' shoulders again. "Having a good time?"

"Mr. Capone, this is the greatest," said Gino.

"Can't thank you enough," added Salvatore.

"I'm glad," said Scarface. "Nothing's too good for my best partners."

Capone turned the brothers around and walked them to the back of the lodge. "There's something extra special I'd like you to see."

"What is it?"

They stepped outside into dark desolation. Two other men emerged from the shadows.

Al removed his arms. "I'd like you to meet Frenchy and the Swede . . . Boys, show the Santinis our surprise."

"This way," said Frenchy, carrying an unlit lantern.

Gino, the older Santini, looked back. "Mr. Capone, aren't you coming with us?"

"I'll catch up. Just have to say good-bye to some people."

The swamp was rough going for the city boys. "What is this surprise?"

"You'll love it."

The trek became more impenetrable, branches tearing sleeves and cutting arms. Unaccustomed humidity stuck shirts to their backs. The brothers glanced around and wiped foreheads. "I can't even see the lodge anymore," said Salvatore. "How much farther?"

"Not too long."

Then they saw the freshly dug hole. Panic sliced through the gin, and they froze with big white eyes.

The Swede laughed. "It's not for you."

"Besides," said Frenchy, "you're Mr. Capone's favorites."

"Just a little farther," said the Swede.

It was more than "just a little," but they finally broke into a small clearing and stopped.

The brothers looked around. Salvatore slapped a mosquito on his neck. "So where's this surprise?"

Frenchy lit the kerosene lantern. "Mr. Capone said no trip down here is complete without seeing the real Florida." He held the light in front of them. "See that patch of water?"

"Mama mia! Are those real alligators?"

"The genuine article," said the Swede.

"That patch of water is what's known as a gator hole," said Frenchy.

"What's a gator hole?" asked Gino.

"Where the families live. Many more below, highly protective."

"That's the thing about the Everglades," said the Swede. "You can be walking along in ankle-deep water and without warning it drops off ten feet and you go down in one of these holes."

Gino was entranced. "Are we safe?"

"As long as we have guns."

The Swede and Frenchy produced pistols and aimed them toward the reptiles. "If they make a move, they won't make another. Go ahead, take a closer look."

The brothers inched forward. "They're amazing . . ."

". . . Look at the size."

"By the way," said Frenchy, "how's Bugs these days?"

The brothers spun around. "Who?"

"Moran," said the Swede. "Figured you'd met since you've been making extra deliveries to the North Side Gang."

"Isn't Al paying you enough?" asked Frenchy.

"Wait!" said Gino. The brothers raised their hands and began backing up at the sight of the guns now pointed at them. "We can explain."

Bang, bang, bang, bang.

The brothers took bullets in both feet. They rolled in the muck, clutching bloody shoes.

"Figlio di puttana!"

"What's he saying?" asked Frenchy.

"Your mom's a bitch," said the Swede.

"That's not polite."

Back in the lodge, guests heard the gunfire and stopped dancing.

Capone stood on the back porch, staring at a distant lantern that looked like a firefly. The bodyguard next to him lit a string of firecrackers and tossed it on the ground.

The crowd inside recognized the familiar Fourth of July noise, which only jump-started their frolic.

Out in the swamp, under a lantern's glow, the Santini brothers pushed themselves up from the ground and stumbled on wounded feet. "Just hold on a minute!" They retreated more. "We supplied Al with all he could take. But we still had a few cases left over. What's the harm?"

"Because Moran's gang is trying to kill him," said Frenchy.

"Listen, Mr. Capone still likes you," said the Swede. "Even after you double-crossed him."

Frenchy raised his pistol. "So he said no fatal shots."

Bang, bang.

The Santini brothers each took a slug in the gut like a boxer's punch. They hobbled backward from the force and splashed into the water.

The gunmen watched curiously. The surface of the gator hole remained quiet at first. Then the brothers surfaced and tried making it to the edge. Thrashing began. Their heads went back under. Then popped up again. The Santinis would have screamed, but were too busy getting a breath before going back down. It continued like this, more or less, for another minute. The water became still.

"Thought it would last longer," said Frenchy.

The Swede started back toward the lodge, lantern leading the way. "Told you we don't need no graves out here."

PRESENT

Toys "R" Them.

Serge walked down a bright, colorful aisle, holding a little boy by the hand. "What the hell is this stuff? All I see are galactic action figures and slimy eyeballs and video games to steal cars in the ghetto. Where are the toys?"

Coleman swung a plastic sword and broke something. "We better go to the next aisle."

They turned the corner.

"This isn't any better," said Serge. "Here's something called an X-Men Wolverine Claw." He took it out of the package and slipped it on his hand. Three giant talons extended from the glove.

"That doesn't look safe," said Coleman.

"No kidding. What are they selling to our children these days?" He resumed walking and looked down. "Mikey, see anything you like?... Mikey, did you hear me?"

Coleman nudged Serge. "I think he sees something he likes."

Serge looked up. A mother and daughter came toward them. The mother was a striking, statuesque blonde. The girl was Mikey's age. Serge leaned down. "You think she's cute?"

Mikey grinned and nodded.

Serge patted him on the shoulder: "Always remember, you can tell what a girl will eventually look like by checking out her mother. Hubba-hubba!"

Coleman put on his own claw hand and attacked an imaginary foe. "Take that! And that! . . . Serge, I don't remember boys being attracted to girls until much later."

Serge proudly thumped his own chest. "My son."

The parents grew closer. They exchanged smiles.

"Excuse me," said Serge. "Would you happen to know where the real toys are? They just have all these training instruments of torture and death, which he won't need for a while."

"I know what you mean," said the woman. "It's so hard to raise a child these days. All the bad influences—"

Behind them: "Ahhhh! My eye!" Coleman flung the X-Men glove off his hand and crashed into a bin of vaporizing plasma bazookas.

"Is he okay?" asked the mom.

"Not since 1973."

She extended a hand. "My name's Beth."

"Serge." He caught her briefly checking out his ringless ring finger. "Pleasure to meet."

Beth appraised Coleman and considered the potential gay factor, but then Coleman got the robot helmet stuck on his head. Nope, definitely not gay.

"So is your wife with you?"

"Single parent," said Serge.

"Really? Me, too."

Then small talk. But no mistaking the body language, leaning intimately toward him against her shopping cart. One shoe had come off and she twirled it on the ground with her toes. Serge had heard about the phenomenon: a small child by your side is a major babe magnet.

"So what do you do?" asked Serge.

"Librarian."

Serge gulped. Right in his wheelhouse. He'd given up the mating search since Molly, but this seemed too perfect to be true. What could go wrong?

Beth looked toward the side of the aisle and smiled. "They seem to be getting along."

Two children took turns punching each other in the arms.

"Mikey," said Serge. "What are you doing?"

"It's okay. We like it." Punch.

"Could you please try to be more of a gentleman?" said Serge.

The kids drifted behind their folks.

Mikey punched the girl. "You like surprises?"

She punched back. "I love surprises."

Mikey reached in his pocket. "Here, have a balloon."

Ten minutes later.

Coleman walked across the parking lot. "That was awkward."

"Gee, you think?" said Serge. "My son gives some kindergartner a rubber."

"Still, her mom got way too hysterical, scooping up her daughter and running over my feet with the shopping cart," said Coleman. "Like she's never seen a condom before in her life."

"At least not one being blown up in a store by her five-year-old daughter."

"Children do the darnedest things," said Coleman. "I remember when I was his age and saw some relatives I hadn't met before at this cookout. Didn't know one was missing a limb. Found the fake arm in the bedroom and got in the above-ground pool in a little boat and started paddling with the thing."

"Maybe it was the type of condom," said Serge. "Probably shouldn't have given Mikey one from my novelty collection. When I get back to the room, I'm throwing the rest away in case he gets into them."

"Novelty?"

"It had the head of Elvis." Serge pointed between his own legs. "If you're circumcised, that part at the end of your dick is Presley's pompadour."

"I noticed that when the little girl got it inflated."

"But did you have to laugh so hard?"

"It was funny."

"Then her mother became all huffy and swatted it out of her hand, and the thing goes flying through the air, zipping this way and that, and we're like: I wonder where it's going to land . . . Oooo, in that other mom's baby stroller. But how is that automatically *my* fault?"

"Then the manager told us to get out and never come back."

"I didn't care for his tone one bit," said Serge. "If you're going to act like that in public, you shouldn't be around kids."

Chapter Twenty-four

ONE HOUR LATER

An electric blue '69 Barracuda headed south on the Tamiami Trail.

"That's three toy stores now we've been eighty-sixed from," said Serge.

"No wonder retail is down."

"Coleman, you broke everything you touched."

"And you made all the children scream."

"Not my fault. It was that monster mask with the hatchet through the forehead," said Serge. "I was just taking a survey to see if it was an age-appropriate product. But after the first mom shrieked, I started running and forgot I still had it on."

"And carrying the toy chain saw."

"That didn't help," said Serge. "Where's Mikey?"

Coleman turned around. "Lying up on the ledge by the rear window."

"That takes me back," said Serge.

"That takes me back to last week."

"I'm hungry," said Mikey.

Serge looked in the rearview. "When was the last time you ate?"

"Breakfast."

"Coleman! My son hasn't eaten all day!"

"I have a taco left from last night."

"Where?"

"Back at the motel. Somewhere under the covers."

"There's a supermarket . . ."

Moments later, Mikey sat in the little child seat of a shopping cart. Serge had his feet up on the bar between the back wheels, zooming down the aisle. Coleman ran alongside.

"What do kids eat these days?" asked Serge.

"There's the beer," said Coleman. He grabbed two sixers.

"And here are the condoms," said Serge.

Soon the cart was half full.

Serge took a foot off the shopping cart's back bar for braking action to make a skidding U-turn at the end of the aisle. Then a quick push-start and off they went again, into the cereal section.

"Coleman," said Serge. "You and I have everything we need in the cart but still not a single thing yet for Mikey."

"Maybe you should ask another parent."

"Good thinking," said Serge. "Here comes one now."

Serge jumped down off the bar. Mikey climbed over the back of the safety seat and into the shopping cart's main bed.

"Uh-oh," said Serge. "She's one of those *new* moms, yapping away on a cell phone."

"What's wrong with that?"

"Cell phones are both a blessing and curse," said Serge. "They have their place, like, 'I'm locked in a truck and I think they just drove the car into a lake,' but this woman's only chatting away, ignoring her child and all rules of courtesy."

The carts approached until they were side by side.

"Excuse me, ma'am," said Serge. "I can tell that isn't an important call, so hang up and talk to me. I need to know what to feed my child . . . You're still on the phone. At that rate, the inattention to junior there will turn him into a scat-munching junkie, unless that's your goal . . ."

Mikey held up a six-pack and box of Trojans. "Stupid Juice . . . balloons."

The woman rushed off.

Serge turned to Coleman. "Now, what was *that* look?"

"Maybe we'll just have to figure out the food thing ourselves."

"They do say that parenting is on-the-job training." Serge scanned a wall of cereal boxes. "The key to being responsible is reading all the nutritional contents so you know what's going into your child."

"What are you supposed to give kids?" asked Coleman.

"I think lots of sugar. They put it in almost everything kids eat, so they must know what they're doing." He picked up a box of Wheaties and read the contents. "This can't be healthy." He set it back. "Where's the Quisp and Quake?"

"Remember Boo Berry?"

Serge kept working down the row. "All the best stuff is gone. Just fiber and nuts."

"Here's Frosted Flakes," said Coleman.

"Tony the Tiger!" said Serge. "Grab eight of those. I'll go look for the soda and candy bars. Then we'll load up on stuff from the toy section."

"Toys? But it's a supermarket."

"All supermarkets have a meager half-row toy section for kids to harass parents," said Serge. "And they're the best! Since parents are here for food, they're not going to spend much to shut their brats up, which forces stores to only stock the cheap classics: plastic handcuffs, paddleballs, bags of green army men, suction-cup dart guns and—I pray—Silly Putty, so I can press it on a newspaper to copy editorials about Federal Reserve policy . . ."

EVERGLADES 1929

"You've been skimming," said the Swede.

"No! I swear!" yelled the accountant.

Bang.

Splash.

"Feeding time," said Frenchy.

"Funny," said the Swede. "But this never seems to get old."

They trudged back to the lodge. Lively piano music. Another Friday night in full swing. And getting more popular, barely room to move. Corrupt judges smoked cigars by the fishpond. The beautiful people danced and downed martinis. Blackjack tables full. Roulette spinning.

A truck pulled around back. "Let's get some help out here!"

Frenchy and the Swede trotted down the steps. "Steamer trunks?"

"Just grab a handle."

"Damn, it's heavy," said the Swede. "What's inside?"

"Don't ask questions."

A phone rang inside the lodge.

One of Capone's top lieutenant's answered. He could barely hear above the clamor, and covered his other ear. "Could you repeat that? . . ." The call was Key Largo. ". . . Got it. Thanks." He rushed over and whispered in Al's ear. Capone nodded. That was all he needed to say. The lieutenant ran out the back screen door. "Frenchy! Swede!"

Another lieutenant directed steamer-trunk traffic. "They can't leave right now. I need them."

The first shook his head. "Straight from Al. Got to get them up Forty Mile Bend."

Everyone knew what that meant.

"Shit!" said the other lieutenant. "Move it! I'll watch the trunks."

The Swede and Frenchy ran to the front of the lodge and jumped in a pair of designated cars. They sped east on the Loop Road.

The lieutenant who had taken the phone call from their informant strolled over to the grand piano and told the musician to cool it.

"Everyone, may I have your attention, please?"

Liquor said no.

"Excuse me!" he shouted.

Noise dwindled. They looked toward that piano.

"Thank you," said the lieutenant. "There's nothing to worry about. We have everything under control and plenty of time, so please remain calm. We need you all to leave in an orderly fashion—"

"*Boooo!*"

"*I just got here!*"

"*What is this bullshit?*"

"Please, we need your cooperation," said the lieutenant. "The police are about to raid us."

So much for orderly.

A drunken stampede out all exits that left the floor of the lodge with shattered highball glasses, lost shoes and a broken necklace that sent pearls rolling under toppled chairs. Out front, a half-dozen cars sideswiped each other, snapping off mirrors and busting headlights.

Total contrast to the staff inside, boxing up everything with military precision.

Five miles east, the race was on.

The finish line: Forty Mile Bend, where the Loop Road joined the Tamiami Trail.

Two cars sped through the night, inches apart.

Junction ahead. *Come onnnnnnn . . .* The fork came into view. Cops not there. Yes!

The Loop's pavement was significantly lower, and both cars bounded up, back tires sliding. They straightened out and hit the gas.

The race hadn't been won by much.

Oncoming police lights up the Tamiami.

Frenchy hit the brakes, and the Swede whipped around on the left. He drove a quick hundred yards and made an expert 180-degree moonshiner's turn in the middle of the road. The drivers accelerated, then turned steering wheels at the last second for a slow-speed head-on crash designed to leave both cars sideways.

For insurance, Frenchy threw a match under a ruptured gas tank.

The police screeched up and jumped out. "Are you guys all right? . . ."

Much of the Tamiami Trail has no shoulders. And to this day, the mildest crash completely shuts down the highway for hours.

PRESENT

"Time to change motels," said Serge. "This one's gotten too hot for the tour."

"We're checking out?" asked Coleman.

"Car's already packed," said Serge. "Will you move it?"

"Just one more thing." Coleman set the motel room's alarm clock for three A.M. "I'm ready."

The '69 Barracuda cruised south on the Tamiami Trail and crossed the massive bridge over the Peace River at Port Charlotte.

A blob of Silly Putty hit the inside of the windshield and stuck.

"Mikey?" Serge looked in the rearview. "You good back there?"

Mikey nodded, munching a bowl of frosted cereal in the backseat.

Coleman sat content, toking his breakfast. He stopped and looked left and right. "What the fuck?"

"Don't swear in front of my child, you degenerate dick-wad!"

"Sorry, the joint flew out of my hand."

"Where is it now? Setting fire to the carpet?"

"I don't know—that's the weirdest thing," said Coleman. "If there's one area I'm dependable, it's hanging on to a joint."

"So what happened?"

"A sudden gust of wind. Like out of nowhere."

"You're roasted to the eyeballs."

"No, seriously."

Serge's dashboard notepad began fluttering and flew over his shoulder. "What the—?"

"Told you."

He checked the rearview. "Where's Mikey?"

Coleman turned around. "One of the back doors is open!"

Serge became unhinged. "My only son!"

Coleman knelt backward in his seat and reached down. "I got him." The child came back in, and the door slammed. Coleman sat back straight. "It's cool. He was just trying to pick something up off the road."

An hour later: Fort Myers.

The Barracuda sat in front of a Motel 3. Room 11.

Some kind of creaking, rhythmic sound from the other side of the door.

"Higher!" said Serge. "Go higher!"

Father and son jumped up and down on one of the beds. Coleman had been jumping on the other, but was thrown clear and knocked the cover off the air conditioner.

"Higher!" yelled Serge.

Coleman sat up and rubbed a knot on his forehead. "I thought we weren't supposed to jump on beds."

"That's what motel rooms are for." Serge sprang up again. "Everything you're not allowed to do at home."

"Don't the motel people mind?"

Boing, boing, boing . . .

"It's Motel 3. Everything in the room is manufactured to prison standards." Serge bounced up again, hair brushing the ceiling. "It's impossible to break anything."

Coleman tried fitting the a/c cover back on. "I think I just broke this."

Serge hopped down to the floor. "That's enough jumping pleasure . . . Mikey! Here! I'll catch you!"

The boy leaped into Serge's arms and they spun in the middle of the room. "Weeeeeeeeee! I'm a dad! . . . Mikey, let's do something else!"

Coleman was looking for another in a lifelong series of misplaced joints. "Wait, what's this? A bag of pills? I don't remember these. The last person in the room must have left them. Or maybe they're Serge's. He gets the *best* prescriptions from his psychiatrists." Coleman opened the sack and grabbed a bright orange capsule. "But he always refuses to take them, so it's not really stealing." His eyes shifted suspiciously to Serge on the other side of the room, playing with his son. Nope, they hadn't spotted him getting into the medicine. He turned the other way, popped the capsule in his mouth and chased it with beer. "Now, let's see what that bad boy does."

"I know!" said Serge. "We'll wrestle! Fathers are always supposed to wrestle with their kids!"

"Great memories," said Coleman, grabbing a chair and a bottle of whiskey. "I used to wrestle with my uncle. We'd roll on the floor and he'd act like I was stronger and let me crawl all over him and win every time."

"Please," said Serge. "That's amateur hour. If Mikey's going to succeed in life, I'll need to teach him the Pile Driver, Atomic Knee Drop, foreign objects, folding metal chairs and, of course, from the critically acclaimed movie *The Wrestler*, the one and only Ram-Jam! . . . Mikey, climb up on the dresser . . . Not high enough. Can you balance on top of the TV?"

The child nodded.

"Okay," said Serge, lying on the floor. "I'm the evil Ayatollah, and you've just knocked me into next week against the turnbuckle . . . The crowd's cheering you on! *Ram-Jam! Ram-Jam! Ram-Jam!* . . . Now raise your fists next to your ears and get ready for the headfirst dive to finish me off! . . . *Ram-Jam! Ram Jam!* . . . On three! . . . Ready? . . . One . . . two . . ."

Chapter Twenty-five

WARM MINERAL SPRINGS

A Crown Vic raced south on the Tamiami Trail.

"Motel secure?" asked White.

"Undercovers at all possible escape points," said Lowe. "Discreet like you said."

"Manager?"

"Held back maid service on the room. Sir, do we know if he's even still there?"

White shook his head. "But we have to assume so for the safety of civilians. That's why the under-covers."

"How exactly did we get the call?"

"Just like the state park. Retired couple with rheumatoid was down in the healing pool and recognized them from that TV show we did. Suspects were swimming with some bikers, acting weird."

"Weird?"

"One was doing cannonballs, and the other congratulated them on not being in a coffin."

Lowe pointed up the road. "There's the motel."

"Remember, we're going in ultra-quiet. Until we know his status—"

A motor coach passed them, blaring Ted Nugent.

White sighed and pulled up to the office.

The manager made another positive ID on the mug shots. He gave them the key.

"How many staying on that side of the motel?" asked White.

"Just three couples. Your guys slipped them away a half hour ago."

White led Lowe and Mahoney along the corridor, staying as close to the building as possible until they reached the door.

The trio braced against the outside wall, took deep breaths, then burst inside.

And froze.

Three sets of eyes processed the scene: burned curtains, flooded bathroom, marijuana, Frosted Flakes, Elvis condoms.

Mahoney wiggled a toothpick in his teeth. "Isn't it always the case?"

MEANWHILE . . .

"Serge, *Serge, Serge* . . . Are you okay, *okay, okay* . . ."

Serge sat up. "Where am I?"

"Motel 3," said Coleman

"What happened?"

"Mikey knocked you out."

"He did?"

"You've been gone for twenty minutes."

"Was it the Ram-Jam?"

"I don't know. He just jumped from the TV."

Serge beamed. "My son! . . ." He looked around. "Where is he?"

"Under the bed," said Coleman. "He grabbed a bunch of candy bars. I tried to get him out but he keeps biting."

Serge crouched down and pulled up the skirt of the bedspread. "Mikey, excellent Ram-Jam! I know what we can do next! Let's go to the playground, and I'll show you all the unapproved, alternate equipment usage. I saw a really cool one up the street."

Mikey crawled out.

Serge grabbed his keys. "This will be great! I can finally return to the playground without everyone staring because now I have a kid with me!"

Fifteen minutes later.

Everyone stared.

Mikey stood on the very top of the jungle gym, beating his chest.

Serge was at the bottom: "Now make roaring sounds and yell, 'I'm a silver-back gorilla, king of all I survey!' . . ."

They made the rounds of the rest of the equipment.

"No," said Serge. "Walk *on top* of the monkey bars."

Thanks to his new diet, Mikey was now even too hyper for Serge, and the tired new father let his son go free-range across the grounds.

Serge walked over and took a seat next to Coleman on a park bench. "I must be getting old." He leaned back and crossed his legs.

"Look at him go," said Coleman. "He's heading the wrong way up the slide."

"To the untrained eye." Serge grinned big. "This is a dream come true. I never thought it would happen, but it's like life is starting all over again . . . You know what I'm going to do?"

"What?" asked Coleman.

"I'm going to change. No more illegal stuff. Not even murder."

"You've got to be kidding."

"I have a child to think of now," said Serge. "Just watch. A whole new me."

Coleman put a hand over his stomach and made a queasy face.

"What's the matter?"

"I don't feel so good."

"Probably something you ate."

Probably that pill, thought Coleman. On the other hand, some of the best drugs make you nauseous at first—then, watch out! Coleman grimaced through the debut round of cramps and smiled about his future.

A young mom pushed over a baby carriage and sat at the end of their bench. She lifted the infant out. "Nice day."

"Fabulous!" said Serge.

She smiled. "Is that your son over there?"

Serge looked. "You mean the one beating the empty teeter-totter with a stick?"

The woman adjusted the baby on a blanket in her lap. "I think it's great what you're doing."

"You do?"

"Absolutely. Two men can raise a child just as well as anyone." She gave the infant a bottle. "There are so many children growing up with single parents or none at all . . . I don't understand all the hatred out there."

"Hate is bad," said Serge.

"Just wanted you to know that not everyone in this country is against you."

Coleman leaned. "Serge, what's she talking about?"

Serge shrugged and twirled a finger next to his head in the official "crazy" signal.

After a spell, the woman got up to leave. "Remember, there are a lot of us out there who are pulling for you."

"I'll make a note," said Serge.

"Who was that?" asked Coleman.

"Probably someone following my website."

The sun reached the hottest part of the day. The playground emptied, except for Mikey, who scampered impervious to the temperature.

Coleman shielded his eyes from the light and scanned the area. "Where'd he go?"

"What do you mean?"

"I don't see Mikey . . . Wait, there he is on the swing set."

"Jesus!" Serge grabbed his heart. "Don't do that to me."

"Who's the man sitting on the swing next to him?"

"Who *is* he?" said Serge.

"He's handing something to Mikey."

"It's . . . candy."

Serge and Coleman's heads simultaneously snapped toward each other. *"Stranger danger! Stranger danger! . . ."*

They jumped up and sprinted across the playground.

"Hey, you!" Serge said to the man. "What's the deal?"

Mikey smiled and held up his hand. "Look, Daddy. A lollipop!"

Serge smiled back. "And what do we say when a stranger wants to give us something?"

"Thank you?"

"No." Serge turned toward the man. "You're fucked."

"Now wait just a minute." The man began standing up from the swing. "I was only trying to be friendly."

Serge pushed him back down. "I like to be friendly, too. I'm going to teach you a friendly lesson so you'll think twice."

The man was bigger and younger than Serge. Bronzed, bushy hair, tank top from a local gym. "I'll do you a favor and forget about this misunderstanding. I haven't done anything. I'm going to stand up, and if you touch me again, I'll have you for assault. Right after I wipe the whole playground with your ass."

The stranger stood, sneering down four inches at Serge. He grinned lasciviously. "Besides, your wimpy son's a little too scrawny for my taste."

Coleman's eyes opened wide. "Uh-oh." He began slowly backing up.

The man looked over at Coleman. "What the hell's gotten into him?"

Even if the stranger hadn't been distracted, he wasn't fast enough to avoid the head butt in the mouth, then the nose, then Serge taking him to the ground, bashing away with fists that became skinned and bloody.

Coleman leaped on Serge's back. "Not here! We'll get caught!"

"Cool," said Mikey. "Can I play, too?"

Serge got up. "You weren't supposed to see that, at least not for a few more years."

"We have to get out of here," said Coleman.

"Not without our new friend." Serge reached in his pocket. "I'll back the car up. You distract Mikey."

Coleman was by the front bumper, sticking a hand under his shirt; Serge shoved his groggy guest into the trunk.

Mikey giggled. "Daddy, Coleman's making his armpits fart."

"Must have learned that at the job fair." Serge returned his gaze to the captive.

The man wiped blood from his eyes. "What's going on?"

"Let's go for a ride," said Serge. "I'm sure you're familiar with offering rides."

The trunk slammed shut.

Chapter Twenty-six

MOTEL 3

Coleman sat on the toilet. He smiled at the guest from the playground, tied up and lying in the bathtub next to him.

Serge knocked on the door. "How much longer are you going to be in there?"

"I don't know." He grunted. "Think this is a big one."

"Save the elegant details. Just how long?"

Another grunt. "You'll be the first to know."

Serge resumed pacing and mumbling to himself. He had put the hostage in the bathroom to spare Mikey, and he now had the double challenge of concocting signature punishment while keeping it from the boy. He reached the end of the room, turned and paced the other way. "What can I possibly do with that guy. Think! . . . Ow!"

Serge grabbed the side of his head, then turned to the bed, where Mikey sat with a cheap supermarket toy, removing the suction-cup tips from a plastic dart gun in order to put eyes out.

"That's my boy."

"Daddy, can we wrestle again?"

"Okay."

They rolled on the floor. Serge taught him the Spitting Cobra Strike, then writhed on his back as Mikey applied the Bangkok Claw of Death to his solar plexus.

The bathroom door flew open. Coleman ran out in excitement. "Serge! Come quick! You have to see this!"

"Mikey," said Serge. "Wait here and I'll show you the dreaded Nuclear Jellyfish." He got up and strolled to the bathroom door.

Coleman stared down into the toilet. "Check this out!"

"I am not looking again," said Serge. "Once will carry me for a lifetime."

"But this is different," said Coleman, getting on his knees for closer inspection. "It's something I've never seen before."

Serge cringed. "This is a sickening new low."

Coleman waved over his buddy without looking up. "You have to help me figure this out."

"Just flush already!"

"Not until you identify it. I think it's a miracle."

"You mean like how people look at a cinnamon roll and see the pope or Michael Jackson?"

"Just look."

"Then will you flush it?"

"I promise."

Serge threw up his arms. "I give and I give and . . ."—he caught a glimpse in the ceramic bowl—". . . Holy blessed Trinity!"

Now they were both kneeling side by side in front of the bowl. "How the hell did that get there?" asked Serge.

"That's why I wanted to show you. I think it's a sign from God."

Serge turned toward his pal. "Did you by any chance happen to eat a pill?"

"What? Me?" Coleman turned red with guilt. "Absolutely not! I wouldn't do that . . . Yeah, I did."

Serge jumped to his feet. "Coleman! You're a genius!"

"Every time you say that, I have no idea what's going on."

Serge glanced toward their guest in the tub. "I'd been rattling my brain for hours, but you just gave me the perfect idea! If they didn't think I was an artist yet."

"You're an artist?"

"My medium is irony." Serge knelt down and socked their guest in the jaw.

"What kind of idea did I give you?"

"I'll explain as we go." Serge reached into the tub. "Now help me prep the patient . . ."

THE NEXT DAY

Motel 3.

Police swarmed room 11.

A forensics team photographed every inch of the bathroom, swabbed the drains, peeled tape strips of latent prints.

Agent White ducked under the crime tape across the open door to the parking lot. "Who's in charge here?"

"I am," said Lieutenant Major. "You from the task force?"

White nodded. "How'd you find this?"

"Manager called after the guest in the next room reported that the alarm clock went off at three A.M. and didn't stop ringing." He reached out and knocked. "Thin walls."

Lowe and Mahoney joined them. "Think it's Serge?"

The lieutenant shrugged and looked back in the direction of the bathroom. "Good chance according to the all-points you sent out." He opened a file and checked a handwritten report, still in progress. "Victim had a rap sheet of inappropriate contact with children, recent probation issues of proximity to schools and playgrounds, but nothing proven." He closed the file. "Killed by some kind of elaborate and extreme method . . . we think."

"That's Serge," said Mahoney.

"What do you mean, you think?" asked White.

The lieutenant looked back again, where sealed evidence bags steadily flowed out of the bathroom and into cardboard boxes on the bed. "Haven't determined cause of death yet. Nobody's seen anything remotely like it."

"Wounds?"

The lieutenant shook his head. "Just a distended belly like he was about to give birth to quintuplets. Medical examiner's in there right now."

An evidence tech emerged with more sealed bags of rope and duct tape. White brushed past him on his way into the bathroom.

"I'm Agent White from the task force."

"Just give me a minute," said the examiner, kneeling over the tub with his back to the door. He wore blue latex gloves and shined a slender flashlight into the mouth cavity.

White looked over his shoulder at the swollen corpse. "Good Lord!"

The examiner opened the victim's mouth wider and got the light down the throat. "Unbelievable."

"What did you find?"

The examiner stood and snapped off the gloves. "Need to get him downtown for autopsy. If I tell you now and I'm wrong, you'll think I'm crazy . . ."

LEE COUNTY JUSTICE COMPLEX

If the sign didn't tell you it was the morgue, the smell would.

Agent White applied dabs of menthol Vaseline under each nostril.

Everyone circled a cold steel table with the naked, camel-shaped body. Except the hump was on the wrong side.

"Please back up and give me some elbow room," said the examiner.

Drama built as the autopsy continued through a checklist of the mundane. Combing the deceased for any exterior marks, taking hair and skin samples.

"So was your hunch correct?" asked White.

"Let me work," the examiner said through his face mask. "This has to be done in the correct order."

Finally, all the procedural details had been covered. Showtime.

The examiner grabbed a bone saw. "You might want to look away."

They did. The queasy, gnarling sound seemed to go on forever, then suddenly stopped.

The examiner reached for a tray of surgical instruments and picked up a spreader. "Look away again."

The suspense was killing them. "See anything yet?" asked White. He was out of line gabbing in the coroner's room, but everything was new.

"Hold your horses," said the examiner. "Almost there . . ."

He reached again for the tray and a long, razor-sharp knife, setting its edge along the base of the stomach. "Here we go . . . You all may want to step way back. This could get pretty— . . . just step back . . ."

No need to tell them twice. The audience retreated to the walls.

The blade made the initial puncture through the stomach. The examiner went much slower than usual, because of internal pressure. The incision was a third complete, contents expanding the stomach even more than anyone had anticipated. The mystery about to unravel.

But the pressure was too great. No delicate technique to complete the task. The examiner himself stepped back and, at arm's length, quickly finished the incision and leaped away.

"Holy mother!"

"Dear God in heaven!"

Someone covered his mouth and ran in the restroom.

They all stood silent, staring at something from a science-fiction movie.

In the middle of the room, the contents of the victim's stomach had emerged and mushroomed into something even larger than the already enormous belly.

Hardier souls tentatively stepped forward in awe to inspect the multi-colored bouquet of death that now bloomed atop the victim like a gory dinner centerpiece.

The examiner punched a fist in the air. "I was right!"

Chapter Twenty-seven

TWENTY-FOUR HOURS EARLIER

Motel 3. Room 11.

Two men went in the bathroom and knelt by the side of the tub.

"Coleman, remove the duct tape."

He ripped it off the man's mouth.

Serge bobbed with glee. "You're in for a real treat today!"

"What are you going to do to me?"

"It's like *Truth or Consequences*," said Serge. "Except I already know the truth, so for you it's all consequences. Sorry, my game, my rules."

The man stared up in terror.

Serge reached outside the tub and filled one hand from a plastic bag. His other hand went behind his back and pulled something from his waistband. He grinned and held two outstretched palms.

Terror turned to sobs.

Serge nodded at the contents of his left hand. "I want you to swallow these pills."

"I'm not swallowing those."

"Don't worry," said Serge. "They're non-toxic, child-safe—unlike you."

"I'm still not taking them." Louder sobs. "Fuck yourself!"

"Which brings us to the Consequence or Consequence portion of our program. You can swallow these capsules or . . ."—Serge's eyes went to his right hand— ". . . You can swallow this gun . . . But hurry and make your call: The game clock's running. Tick-tock, tick-tock, tick-tock . . . Wait! That's Serge's bonus buzzer! And everyone knows what the bonus buzzer means! You win a free escape clause! To make your decision easier, we'll leave the room right after your qualifying round and promise not to return. That way, if you take the pills and can free yourself to seek adequate medical attention in time, you win! . . . So the gun choice really doesn't make sense . . ." He produced a cell phone. "Or you can call a lifeline."

"I can?"

"No." Serge put the phone away. "I love to break tension with humor. But for some reason my guests never laugh." Serge scratched his own temple with the gun barrel. "Is it my delivery?"

The hostage gulped.

"Oh, I understand," said Serge. "Many people have a natural aversion to taking pills. Gag reflex and all . . . Coleman, be a good host and get this man a glass of water."

"Coming right up."

TEN MINUTES BEFORE THAT . . .

Room 11 of Motel 3.

Two men stared in the toilet.

"What do you make of it?" said Coleman. "It's not like any turd I've ever met."

"Me neither."

Coleman pointed. "There's the head. It looks like . . . an orange dinosaur."

"Because it *is* an orange dinosaur."

"God has chosen me for something."

"Yes, but not what you think. Come this way . . ." Serge left the bathroom and closed the door so the hostage couldn't hear.

"What is it?" asked Coleman.

"You know that pill you took?"

"The orange one?"

"It wasn't medicine. It was one of the things I bought for Mikey from that grocery store toy section. That orange dinosaur is a super-expanding sponge."

"I don't understand."

"Coleman, you must have seen them before," said Serge. "Didn't you read the label on the bag before you swallowed that pill?"

"I like to be surprised."

"It was full of brightly colored capsules. Children put them in a bowl of water, which dissolves the gel coating. Then the dry, compressed foam inside expands from the water until it blossoms. But what will it turn into? Some kind of prehistoric animal or spaceship? Then it finally takes shape at an amazing size, twenty or thirty times the volume of the original capsule. Kids love it!"

"What's the point?"

"To play."

"I get it."

"And so will our friend in there."

"Look," said Coleman. "Mikey's playing with matches."

"Mikey, that's dangerous!" said Serge. "Always close the cover before striking." He turned back to Coleman. "That should keep him occupied for the duration of our project, because we obviously can't have him seeing this. What kind of parent would I be?" He grabbed the bag of remaining capsules off the dresser. "Shall we dance?"

"After you."

They went in the bathroom, knelt at the tub and began rocking side to side with big smiles.

Serge: *"Everybody have fun tonight!"*

Coleman: *"Everybody Wang Chung tonight!"*

The hostage screamed under the duct tape.

PRESENT

Lee County Justice Complex.

The audience in the morgue overcame their squeamishness. And then some. They crowded around the steel table.

"I see a T. rex . . ."

"There's a stegosaurus . . ."

"And a pterodactyl," said Agent Lowe.

"This isn't a joke," said White.

"I remember playing with these as a kid," said Lowe. "Watching the bowl of water: Is it going to be a brontosaurus or a raptor or maybe a—"

"Lowe!"

"Sorry."

White turned another way. "Mahoney, tell me more about this Serge." He looked back at the autopsy table. "What the hell are we dealing with?"

Chapter Twenty-eight

CYBERSPACE

Serge's Blog. Star Date 583.739.

Today's topic: the Fugitive Parent.

The considerations of traveling with children are always important, but no more so than when you're a fugitive. Like proper nutrition and getting your cover stories straight.

In my case, being a fugitive parent is a recent development. Some children are delivered by doctors; in certain parts of Florida, they're delivered at gunpoint. Since I'm new at this, I thought we'd treat it like a reality show, and use this blog to track my journey of discovery as a father on the run.

First, you hear it a million times, but until you're at the party, you have no idea: *Never, ever* take your eyes off them. We're all human and can easily be distracted for the smallest fraction of a second, but you still feel like it's your fault. And if you have attention-deficit issues like me and it's a half hour, you really feel bad. We stopped at this water park, and you know how pet stores have those little clear balls you put hamsters in, and they roll around the house for lots of laughs? I found out they have great big ones for people to run across the surface of a pond or pool, and this water park was renting them. Mikey had two liters of Jolt cola for breakfast and was going Tasmanian Devil. Like any good parent, I thought it would be healthy to let him burn off some energy. So I put him in the ball, and he's zipping like crazy around the big pool. His legs are little, but the gear ratio with the ball's radius is multiplied, and he builds up ferocious momentum and hops the lip of the pool and now he's tearing across the pavilion, food scattering, other parents screaming and diving over benches. Then it got bad. Someone left a service gate open. And he gets out of the park! Now he's going cross-country, and we can barely keep up. And suddenly it hits me as I'm dodging cars and chasing a kid in a giant clear ball across the highway: No wonder parents are tired all the time . . . He finally got stuck in a ditch, and the ball was pretty scuffed from the pavement, so they made us buy it. Luckily, it breaks down in stackable curved panels for easy storage and reassembly. I tried it later myself, actually pretty fun. Except at first glance, I could have sworn the grocery aisle was wide enough. The ball's in our motel room now, and Coleman's sitting in it because it "really holds the pot smoke." . . . Then this afternoon I redeemed myself—learning from my mistake and becoming so vigilant I should get some kind of parent trophy. Wanted to teach Mikey history, so we stop by this field and I grab a shovel from the trunk because in my career you always keep one there, and we go out to re-create the Great Mining Collapse of 1896 and—you guessed it—I pulled him out just in time! I think I'm really getting the hang of this.

FORT MYERS BEACH

Serge hoisted his backpack off the bed. "Checkout time!"

"Again?" Coleman sat up in bed with mussed hair and grabbed a joint.

He felt a gun barrel at the back of his head. *"Freeze! Miami Vice!"*

Coleman dropped the joint and threw his hands in the air.

"Relax, it's unloaded," Serge called across the room. "I've been teaching Mikey while you were asleep. Figured if he's going to play with guns, he might as well do it right."

Coleman reached down for the jay. "Almost gave me a heart attack."

Serge grabbed his son by the hand. "The tour is picking up steam, so look alive!"

"Give me a minute." Coleman set the alarm clock for three A.M.

They left and locked the door. Serge turned to Coleman in the parking lot. "Watch Mikey while I return the key to the office."

"You got it."

Serge came back from the lobby, stood in an empty parking space and looked down at his shoes.

"Something the matter?" asked Coleman.

"Where's our car?"

"Maybe it was stolen."

Serge looked around in even greater distress. "Where's Mikey?"

"I don't know."

"You were supposed to watch him!"

"I thought he was with you."

"No! I said for you—"

"Serge! Over there!"

The '69 Barracuda came toward them and flew by.

"Look at me!" Mikey yelled out the window. "I'm driving! I'm driving!"

"How can his feet reach the pedals?" asked Coleman.

"I think he's standing up," said Serge, taking off in a sprint.

Coleman ran after him. "I don't think he's going to make the turn."

The Barracuda slowed at the end of the parking lot, but not before plowing into a row of shrubs.

Serge dashed the last yards and yanked the door open. He pulled the child from the car, clutching him to his chest. "Mikey! You okay?"

"I drove! I drove!"

"I'm both proud and angry," said Serge.

Coleman arrived panting. "Is he hurt?"

"No, just happy," said Serge. He handed the child to Coleman, then climbed into the car and reversed it back over the curb with a scratching of branches. "Everyone in."

They drove west through Cape Coral toward the Gulf of Mexico.

"Look at all the foreclosed homes," said Coleman.

"Area's been hit hard by financial twats." Serge eased up to a remote intersection.

Coleman looked oddly at the street sign. "Burnt Store Road?"

"Local pride is unpredictable."

They continued into undeveloped wilderness and crossed a small bridge to an appropriately small island. A village of tiny, colorful pastel cottages. Pink, yellow, lime. People in straw hats fished off a seawall.

"Dig the funky buildings," said Coleman. "Where are we?"

"Matlacha," said Serge. "Isolated enclave of art shops, family restaurants and hard-to-find motels. Perfect for the man on the run."

"We're staying here?"

"Got something even harder to find. The key to hiding out is crossing as many bodies of water as you can."

Another bridge, another island.

"Ow!" said Coleman. "Ow! . . . Ow! . . . Ow! . . ."

"Coleman, what's your problem?"

"Mikey keeps flicking me in the ear . . . Ow! . . ."

"So flick him back."

Coleman turned around in his seat.

"Ow!" said Mikey.

"Ow!" said Coleman. "Serge, why'd you flick me in the ear?"

"Because you flicked my son."

"But you told me to."

"Doesn't mean there aren't consequences."

"Ow! . . . He's still doing it."

"Okay, kids!" yelled Serge. "No more flicking. You want me to have a wreck?"

Coleman and Mikey glared at each other and stuck out tongues.

They hit Stringfellow Road and turned north. Coleman unscrewed a pint bottle. "Where are we now?"

"Pine Island." They passed several palm tree farms and a scattering of short residential streets named for fish. Mackerel, Trout, Sea Bass, Bonita. Country stores, screen-tented nurseries raising other tropical plants. Then even more isolated homes way back on dirt roads. "And in that direction, remnants of the ancient cross-island canal dug by the Calusas for their canoes. Lived here fifteen hundred years until the 1700s."

"What happened to them?"

"Europeans," said Serge. "It's how they're hard-wired: 'Hey, I see something really old and excellent! Let's wipe it out.'"

Coleman stared from the window as another grove of coconut palms went by. "I've never seen a Florida island like this. Where are all the condos and golf courses?"

"Over in douche-bag land." Serge took a left onto Pineland Road. "Fat cats haven't ruined this one yet because it's got a protected mangrove coast and almost no beach that is essential for assholes to sprout."

They reached the shore of Pine Island Sound and hugged the coast.

"You're slowing down," said Coleman.

"Because this is the place."

"We're staying at the Tarpon Lodge?"

"Just our jumping-off point."

They climbed from the Barracuda and into a blinding bright sun reflecting off the bay.

"Hold it, Mikey." Serge reached in his backpack. "I've got something for you."

The boy smiled and clapped. "What is it?"

Serge fitted a harness over the child's chest and shoulders, then hooked the end of a leash in the middle of his back. "There." He slipped his hand through the leash's other end. "That ought to thin out the drama."

Serge led them around to the docks. Or rather Mikey did, straining against the leash.

"Look at him pull," said Coleman.

Serge leaned back, digging in heels as they went. "It's like walking a pack of wolves."

A broad-shouldered man with a ruddy sportsman's complexion hosed out the stern of center-console whaler. He wore a mesh-back fisherman's vest, wide-brimmed sailing cap and dark, polarized sunglasses secured around his neck with a sky-blue lanyard.

"Captain Ron!"

The man looked up. "Serge!" He cut the hose and climbed onto the dock. Another big hug. "What have you been up to?"

"I'm on the run."

A belly laugh. "Same old Serge . . . But who's this little fella?"

"My son."

"I didn't know you had a son."

"Neither did I. Mom tracked me down and dropped him off at our motel."

"Whoops. One of those delayed surprises, eh?" The captain bent down and smiled at the boy. "What's his name?"

"Mikey."

Captain Ron extended a hand. "Pleasure to meet you . . . Ow, he kicked me in the shin."

"That's his way of shaking."

"He's definitely yours."

"Free for a run?" asked Serge.

"For you? Anytime."

"Let's do it . . ."

Chapter Twenty-nine

EVERGLADES 1929

Jazz piano drifted across the swamp.

Chandeliers twinkled through cypress and palmettos.

Another Friday night at Al's.

More and more cars arrived as word spread about the speakeasy in the middle of the Everglades that police couldn't touch.

Two pressure fronts had met earlier that afternoon over the gulf and moved inland, dropping a thick blanket of fog across the glades that made people think of Sherlock Holmes.

A string of headlamps approached, the only thing visible in the mist until the vintage cars took shape the last few yards.

Bartenders could barely keep up, and a roadster custom-fit with copper tubing in the doors had to make a high-risk, second run of the night. Crazy Murphy skidded around back. Capone's gang was already waiting with wooden-slat cases of thirsty, empty glass bottles.

Another group stood off to the side—way off, behind the cover of pines. Only four of them, making a final visual sweep for witnesses. When the quartet was satisfied, they formed a rectangle and began carrying something heavy across the swamp like pallbearers.

And faded into the mist . . .

. . . As one unnoticed bystander watched.

Crazy Murphy glanced back at the gang draining moonshine from his car. They wouldn't be done anytime soon.

He yelled back to them: "I'm going to take a leak."

"Why are you telling us?"

And Murphy slunk into the swamp.

Brush thickened, ground soggy. Murph was guided at first by the crinkling footsteps and faint voice up ahead—then by a lantern that came on in the distance. It usually provided just enough illumination for the work at hand, but now with the fog, there was a broader glow in the glades, sending eerie shafts that slowly swirled as they filtered through buttonwood and gumbo-limbo.

The curiosity was too much. Anyone with sense would have advised against continuing on, but Murphy was crazy.

PRESENT

Behind the Tarpon Lodge, four people climbed aboard a center-console whaler. Serge fastened a life preserver onto Mikey that practically swallowed the child. Then he cast off davit lines.

Captain Ron pushed the throttle forward. The boat idled away from the dock as gulls and pelicans took flight from the tops of pylons streaked with white poop. The whaler picked up speed through a tight channel of orange-and-green markers. Then open water. Ron gave it the fuel, bringing the boat up on the plane. Salt wind filled lungs and whipped hair.

A tiny arm poked out from under a puffy life vest. "Daddy, look!"

On both sides of the boat, dolphins leaped high in the air, over and over. They seemed to be looking right at them.

"Smile." Serge raised his camera. *Click, click, click.*

The captain banked the vessel to port. All around them in Pine Island Sound: uninhabited mangrove islands. Cove Key, Black Key, Rat Key, Bird Key. And a couple inhabited ones . . .

"I see some buildings," said Coleman. "What is that island?"

"Useppa, once a secret CIA training ground for Brigade 2506."

"Who were they?"

"Anti-Castro exiles recruited in Miami for the ill-fated Bay of Pigs invasion." Mikey's little feet left the deck, his upper body tipping over the gunwales. Serge jerked the leash, pulling him back on board. "Now a private club of luxury homes accessible only by boat."

Another hard bank starboard, and they skirted the southern shore. "That other island that just appeared ahead is our destination, Cabbage Key."

"The next fugitive stop?"

Serge nodded. "We've crossed enough bodies of water. Nobody could possibly find us there."

The dolphins jumped a final time and broke off to join a pod for a mullet run on the low tide. Captain Ron brought the boat around for dead reckoning on a shoal-guarded inlet that led to the freshly painted dock.

"Why does the island look so tall?" asked Coleman.

"Because it's got a thirty-eight-foot Indian shell mound. No cars or paved roads, just a nature trail, an old wooden water tower like you'd find at a whistle-stop in Flagstaff, and a rustic home atop the mound built in the 1930s by novelist and playwright Mary Roberts Rinehart, which is now a small inn with a breezy restaurant."

"What do you do there?"

"Nothing," said Serge. "That's the whole point. That's why I love Cabbage Key."

Coleman began to shake. "Nothing?"

"We can always hang out in the bar."

The shaking stopped. "Bar?"

"One of Florida's finest."

They eased to the dock, and Serge secured the lines. Then just as quickly, the passengers were all on the pier. Lines were off again. Ron gave a big wave. "Until next time . . ."

Serge watched the boat motor away into turquoise water. An impatient tug on his arm.

"Serge, can we go to the bar?" said Coleman. "Please?"

"Normally, I'd veto, but in this case, definitely."

Mikey pulled them along, climbing the mound and up the front steps.

Coleman stopped just inside the entrance and grabbed his chest. "This is heaven with stools." He ran and hopped on one. "Whiskey!"

Serge strolled over and grabbed his own seat. "Bottled water. And something with a lot of sugar for my son."

Coleman's eyes wandered around the deep-hued paneling and stuffed tarpon on the walls, competing with hundreds of patron-autographed dollar bills. Jimmy Buffett's dollar had its own frame.

Coleman killed his drink and raised a finger for a refill. "This reminds me of someplace."

"The No Name Pub in the Keys?"

"That's it."

"Makes sense, same vintage and values."

From behind: "Serge!"

He turned around.

"Rob! How've you been?"

"Can't complain. Wondering if you were dead."

"I know. It's been too long, but . . ." He waved around the interior. ". . . You've kept the flame burning."

"Who's this little guy?"

"My son, Mikey. Surprise."

Rob bent down to a small child chugging a can of soda with both hands. "Well, hello there . . ."

"He kicks," said Serge.

"Ow!"

"Coleman, I'd like you to meet Rob, the owner . . . Rob, my untrusty sidekick, Coleman."

"Pleasure," said Rob. They shook hands and he turned back to Serge. "So what brings you out?"

"I'm on the run."

"Who's after you this time?"

"Nobody," said Serge. "I'm fleeing unilaterally. You should try it."

Rob gave a laugh like the boat captain. Then he looked down. "What's Mikey doing now?"

"Trying to chew through his leash. Listen, we could use a room."

"Jeez, inn's full."

"Cottage?"

"Worth a shot. Check with the desk." Rob headed off. "I need to see the dockmaster about something, but we'll talk later. Great to see you again . . ."

It was an off-hour in the heat of the afternoon. Serge and Coleman had the bar to themselves. Almost. A single soul sat by himself on the last stool at the opposite end. Could be mistaken for a wrestler. Burly and muscular, shaved head like Mr. Clean. Hiking shorts, green-and-red Cartagena baseball jersey. Nursing a draft in a sweating mug.

People eventually began trickling in as the day cooled toward evening. A few occasionally approached the man with books to sign.

"Who's that guy?" asked Coleman.

"Randy Wayne White, the famous author," said Serge. "This is his turf, so don't do anything to embarrass me."

"Yo! Randy!" yelled Coleman. "Your books suck!"

Giggles.

"Thanks for sticking with the script," said Serge, then turned the other way. "Sorry about that, Mr. White. He ate paint chips as a child. And last week."

Randy just nodded and grinned, and returned to his beer.

Serge swung back to Coleman. "You're lucky he's a cool guy or he'd snap you in two."

"What's he doing here?"

"Being macho."

"But he's just sitting there."

"In his resting state, he's macho."

"What about sleeping?"

"Macho then, too." Serge gave a subconscious, parental tug on the leash. No resistance. "What the—?" He reeled it in until he came to the frayed end.

"Mikey chewed through?" said Coleman.

Serge dashed out the front door. "Mikey! . . . Mikey, where are you?"

Coleman tumbled down the steps and got up. "Mikey! . . ."

"Daddy! . . ."

"Did you hear that?" said Serge.

"Yeah, but where's it coming from?"

They frantically scanned the grounds. "Mikey!"

"Daddy! Look at me!"

They found the direction of the voice and gazed up. "He's on top of the water tower!"

"How'd he get up there?" said Coleman.

"It's got an observation deck and wooden staircase winding up inside the supports."

"Daddy! I can hang upside down!"

"Holy Jesus." Serge scrambled up the stairs and grabbed his son. He wagged a finger again in the child's face. "No tall structures."

Chapter Thirty

EVERGLADES 1929

Crazy Murphy crept forward in the night.

He tried to stay as silent as possible, except that was impossible with all the branches and unseen stuff below that crunched as he walked. But whatever noise he did make was drowned out by all the frogs and owls and insects and bursts of intoxication from back at the lodge.

As Murphy drew near, voices became louder. Just a step at a time, he told himself. Plant your foot first, then ease on the weight and carefully lift the previous leg. Soon he saw the first one. And a shovel. Then the other three, all silhouette, backlit by the kerosene lantern, laboring in shadow animation amid the fog.

What were they doing? He had to get closer.

Murphy slithered a few more yards and crouched. Practically under their noses. Normally, they would have spotted him except for the heavy, ground-level cloud seeping across the swamp. But that worked two ways: Murphy still couldn't see clearly. And he couldn't risk getting any closer.

Then he noticed a large cypress with a thick trunk for cover. Definitely near enough to the action. Only one problem: The tree stood across a brief open stretch of bright mist. It would only take a few seconds, but he'd be completely exposed.

Murphy got ready to spring five times. And pulled back five times. Heart pounding.

He closed his eyes, summoning will. When he opened them, all four men had their backs toward him.

He went for it.

A shovel stopped. "What was that?"

A second shovel stilled. "What?"

"I just heard something."

"There's all kinds of stuff out here." The shovel went back into the ground. "Probably a toad."

"No, it definitely wasn't a toad. Someone's out there."

"Your imagination's getting the best of you. Now get back to work. You want to be out here all night?"

Murphy was on his knees, peeking around the trunk. There was the lantern and jackets neatly hung from a tree, and shoulder holsters across perspiration-drenched shirts. His eyes went down to the ground.

"Oh my God!" He covered his mouth.

Murphy wasn't that crazy. He immediately realized what he saw carried a death sentence: I have to get out of here.

His brain raced: Just stay calm and reverse the process, and you'll be safe back at the car in no time. The first careful move was to turn around into a branch that broke off with a crack like a rifle shot.

All shovels stopped. "Don't tell me you didn't hear that."

"Shit," said Murphy. He took off with abandon.

A fog-encased figure ran across the clearing.

"There he is!"

"Get him!"

Shovels fell. Pistols flew from holsters.

Bang, bang, bang . . .

Back at the lodge, the crew filling bottles from Murphy's car stopped and looked toward the swamp. Funny they hadn't noticed any double-crossers being marched off to the gator holes.

Bang, bang, bang, bang . . .

Capone came out the back door. "What's all that shooting?" He grabbed a moth and ate it.

Murphy crashed through palmettos and thickets, mindless of noise, bullets whistling by his ears and slamming into trees. He could see the lodge. If he could only . . .

A bullet grazed his shoulder. He grabbed it on the run and looked at his hand. Blood.

Bang, bang, bang . . .

Another slug zipped through the fog without hitting anything in the woods. It shattered a bottle of hooch held by one of the guys at the car. They all hit the ground.

Murphy exploded out of the brush and dove onto the dirt near them.

"What's going on out there?" said the one still holding the neck of the broken bottle.

"I don't know," said Murphy. "I was just taking a whiz when suddenly all this shooting started."

"Your arm's bleeding."

"The gunfire made me jump. I scraped it on a tree."

Four men burst into the clearing behind the lodge. They looked toward the bottle-filling detail flat on the ground.

"See anyone come out of the woods?"

"Nobody . . . Just Murphy. He was taking a leak."

They turned toward the back steps, where Capone was now surrounded by bodyguards and two lieutenants.

"Someone's out there," said one of the foursome in soaked shirts. "I think they saw us."

A lieutenant stepped forward. "Did you finish?"

"No, we ran after him."

"Get back out there and finish!"

The other lieutenant opened the screen door and yelled orders into the lodge. More men came pouring down the steps. These had machine guns. They fanned out into the swamp.

Murphy got up. "Done unloading?"

The bottle guys nodded.

"Then I better be getting back."

He jumped in his car, and took off down the Loop Road.

PRESENT

Serge and Mikey climbed down the water tower.

"That was close," said Coleman.

Serge examined the short length of chewed-through strap attached to Mikey's back. He handed it to Coleman. "Hold this tight and don't let go for anything." Serge trotted off.

"Ow." Coleman rubbed his shin and called down from the shell mound: "What are you doing?"

"Checking with the dockmaster." Serge reached the pier. "Need some supplies."

Twenty minutes later, they were all down by the water. Serge screwed a steel clamp shut. "That should do it."

They headed back to the bar, Mikey leading the way again, this time on the end of a chain composed of thick, welded links with anti-corrosion coating used in marinas.

Coleman huffed up the shell mound. "Looks like one of the leashes people use to walk giant pit bulls."

"Except those don't have to be as strong."

They reclaimed their original stools. A new guest sat just to their left, wearing an ensemble of the most expensive yachting attire. Plowing through his third Johnnie Walker Black.

Serge nodded politely as he climbed back on his seat. "Evening."

An untanned, manicured hand extended his way. "Name's Hunter. Hunter Bleadoph."

They shook. "Serge. Serge Storms." Thinking: Where have I heard that name before?

"Great joint," said Hunter, snapping his fingers at the bartender and pointing down to an empty glass.

"So, Hunter," said Serge. "What brings you to these parts?"

"I'm hiding out."

Serge smiled at Coleman.

Hunter's refill came. "No bullshit. Who's going to find us here?"

"That's what I said." Serge ordered another bottle of water. "Trouble with the law?"

"You could put it that way."

"Who are you hiding from? Feds? State? Local heat?"

"Reporters." Hunter took a belt of scotch.

"Reporters?" said Serge.

"My company flew down from New York for a training seminar."

"What are you training for?"

"We're not." Hunter laughed. "That's just on paper for the government. I'm really here for a kick-ass vacation!"

"Bleadoph," said Serge. "Now I remember: You're the head of that troubled financial group, GUE. Got like seventy billion in bailout money."

"Eighty." Hunter smiled. "That's why we have to hide out and keep a low profile. The last couple of junkets, reporters swarmed all over the place, running stories on TV about our presidential suites, five-hundred-dollar-a-day room service, Dom Pérignon and ice-packed lobsters we had FedEx'd up from the Keys."

"You were persecuted," said Serge.

"Tell me about it." Hunter swirled his drink. "They all falsely reported that the taxpayers were springing for our luxury getaways, when nothing could be further from the truth."

"What is the truth?"

"The bailout money was kept completely separate, not a penny spent on lavish perks," said Hunter. "We made absolutely sure of that and scrupulously accounted for where every last tax dollar went."

"Where did it go?"

"Executive bonuses. And then the press had a problem with *that*."

"Don't they know anything?" said Serge.

"Exactly," said Hunter. "They're journalists, but *we're* the businessmen. And we know how to run a business."

"How *do* you run your business?"

"Move money from point A to point B."

"That's it?"

"Then move it back. You should see our homes."

"But how does that produce anything of value?"

"It doesn't." Hunter crunched a scotch-covered ice cube. "That's the whole idea. We finally perfected a business model that's pure profit."

"Amazing." Serge whistled. "How'd you come up with that?"

"Here's a crash course in the economy," said Hunter. "Americans get up each morning and go to factories and farms and fire stations and work their whole lives, creating actual products you can hold in your hands.

Or some service that benefits. I mean, what the fuck's that about?"

"Work isn't good?"

"It's the damn workers who crashed the economy."

"I thought it was you," said Serge.

"Don't be a comedian." Hunter started counting off on his fingers. "They lost their retirement accounts, their mortgages, their homes, even their jobs. Can't these assholes do anything right?"

"You on the other hand?"

"We ended up with all the cash. And then the people turned to the government and went, 'Holy shit! What happened to all our goddamn money? Do something!' So the government takes even more money from the workers and—this part is absolutely priceless—they give it all to us again! Now you tell me who's the success story."

"But what's so hard about accepting free money?"

"That's exactly what I was thinking when half the country screamed, 'I'll kick your fucking ass if you give me health care!'"

"Sounds too good for words," said Serge.

"It's good enough for one word," said Hunter. "Socialism."

Serge pounded the bar with his fist. "Fuck socialism."

"Don't say that!" Hunter took a swig. "I *love* socialism."

"You do?"

Hunter nodded hard. "Finest word in the English language. Just mention socialism, and everyone gets blinded by rage, takes their eyes off us and prints up T-shirts that insult the president." Bleadoph raised his hands toward the ceiling in exultation. "Thank God he was elected!"

"Forgive my ignorance," said Serge, "but weren't the bailouts socialism?"

Hunter shook his head. "It's only socialism if the money goes down, not up."

"A toast," said Serge. "To socialism!"

"To socialism!"

A glass of scotch tapped a plastic bottle.

"Enough about me," said Hunter. "What do you do?"

"Well, I work—"

"Hold a sec. *Work?*"

"Not to fear," said Serge. "I don't actually produce any goods or services."

"Whew! You had me worried."

"I just . . . move other people's money around."

"So we're kind of in the same line."

Coleman tapped Serge's shoulder. "Mikey's trying to get through the leash again."

"He'll stop when his teeth hurt."

"He found a hammer."

Bang, bang, bang.

Serge looked around the bar, then back at Hunter. "You mentioned a company retreat. Where's everyone else?"

"Oh, we're not staying here." He tilted his head south. "Booked this cushy place on Sanibel called – – – –" He looked down at his top-shelf drink. "I just came out here to put the taxpayers' money to work on a stimulus package."

"Serge," said Coleman. "I think he's about to break through."

Serge hopped down and grabbed the hammer.

Hunter stood up and drained his glass. "Have to catch the boat back to the mainland, but maybe we'll run into each other again sometime."

Serge shook his hand again and smiled. "I have a funny feeling that's definitely going to happen."

FORT MYERS

Three state agents sat around a table in a downtown diner. Outside, a gentle evening rain glistened under crime lights.

Plates with egg yolk had been pushed aside for a pair of maps. Lee County. One street, one nautical. Mahoney slowly slid his palms across them like a Ouija board. He stopped and tapped a spot.

Agent White slipped on reading glasses. "Sanibel? You mean the seashell place?"

"Boxcars." Mahoney's palms went back to the road map. He closed his eyes. Hands hovered ominously. He opened his eyes and tapped another spot. "Plus this flush."

"The Edison Museum?"

"Top-weight black pearl fix for the heritage fiend. We shadow-jockey for the deuce bank-shot."

"Who exactly cleared you for duty?" asked White.

"He likes to be around old stuff," said Mahoney. "We stake out the Edison in case he shows up. If he doesn't, it's on the way to Sanibel."

"How are you so sure you can predict his movements like this?" asked White.

"Loose chin?"

"Whatever. Any other places that look promising?"

Mahoney began sliding hands across the maps again. Fathom readings. Boat channels.

The hands began trembling and stopped on the nautical map over a small island with an Indian shell mound.

"Cabbage Key?" said Agent White. "Never heard of it."

Mahoney took his hands off the map and smugly flipped his Zippo.

Outside the diner, rain let up. A cast of people quietly watched the agents through the front windows. They sat in the parking lot in a variety of vehicles, including a black Beemer.

A hard knock on the driver's window. The man inside jumped.

Another knock.

An attorney named Brad Meltzer rolled down his electric window. "Oh, it's you." A hand over his forehead. "Gave me a start."

"Said I'd find you. We still have a deal?"

"I'm working on it now."

"It doesn't look that way. You're not thinking of running off with my grand?"

"Absolutely not," said Brad. "I know Serge's ultimate destination."

"Then what are you doing here?"

"It's a big place he's going. Got a couple clients who keep feeding me tips where he'll be next, because they want me to deliver a letter."

"You going to give him a letter?"

"No, he can't ever see the letter. It will ruin everything." Brad tried lighting a cigarette. "So I was hoping the detectives in there could help me narrow it a little."

"Your hands are shaking . . . Here, let me."

"Thanks."

"You're welcome. I'll contact you again in a day or so."

"I really am going to find Serge. I swear. You'll be the first to know."

"I believe you. Because you're too smart to even dream of fucking with me."

Chapter Thirty-one

THE NEXT DAY

Serge grabbed his backpack. "Thanks for the ride to Cabbage Key."

"Don't be a stranger," said Captain Ron, dropping the gang back on shore at the Tarpon Lodge.

The '69 Barracuda reached the mainland and parked at a strip mall in downtown Cape Coral.

"Why are we stopping here?" asked Coleman.

"Need to put together a gift basket."

Serge got out and went in the nearest door. Coleman followed him down an aisle. "What kind of gift basket do you get from a hardware store?"

Serge grabbed a bottle off a shelf. "Not the kind with sausages and biscotti."

A couple more aisles and they were done. Serge dumped his purchases at the cash register.

"They're all chemicals," said Coleman.

"That's right. Industrial cleansers, pest control, drain opener."

"Why do you need that stuff?"

"I don't," said Serge. "At least not for their intended purpose. But they won't sell me what I really need. So I'm forced to concoct my own recipe . . . Oh, and I'll also need one of these." He grabbed a construction worker's protective face mask with dual carbon breathing filters.

Next, a drugstore. Not as quick this time. Up and down aisles, squinting at shelves. A sprite young woman in an apron noticed. "Can I help you find something?"

"Actually, yes," said Serge. "Bath salts. They're alien to us."

She smiled. "For your wife?"

"No, socialists."

"Socialists?"

"They're so hard to buy for," said Serge. "They tend to re-gift."

She eyed him a moment, then: "You're almost there. Follow me." They went up the adjoining aisle, and the clerk pointed at the top row. "Anything in particular?"

"Something with almonds."

"I prefer jasmine myself."

"Almonds, trust me."

"Here's something. You think it's what you want?"

"Definitely. I'm sure it'll go over very big."

"Anything else?"

"Mixing bowls for baking. Gloves for cleaning toilets. Hair dryer for hair drying."

Once they were out of the store, Serge found the nearest garbage can and dumped out the salts.

"Now I'm really confused," said Coleman.

"Just needed the container." Serge headed for the car. "The key to gift giving is proper presentation."

They checked into a flophouse on 41. Serge grabbed a towel and scrubbed the sink and fixtures, then hit them with the hair dryer until they were bone dry.

"Why are you doing that?"

"Because there can be absolutely no moisture."

Various hardware-store purchases and mixing bowls lined the counter behind the sink. Serge slipped into thick gloves, then adjusted rubber straps behind his ears and rested the face mask atop his forehead.

"Serge," said Coleman. "Are you sure it's safe to work in this room with all that stuff?"

"Definitely." He pulled the face mask into place, muffling his voice. "These are meth lab motels. Against that, I'm Betty Crocker."

He dumped one container into the bowl, then flicked open a pocketknife and sliced through a half-dozen rodent bait traps.

Coleman bent toward the bowl. "What are you making? . . ." He stumbled backward. "Hey, what's the deal shoving me like that?"

"Are you crazy? You don't have a face mask."

"You said it was safe."

"I said the room was, not you."

Coleman walked to the far bed and clicked on the TV. "It's Nancy Grace."

"America's screech owl."

"Someone's missing again in Florida . . ."

Serge tuned him out. ". . . And another dash of this and some more of that, stir as needed, and that should just about do it!"

He uncapped the empty bath salts container and ever so carefully tapped the contents of the largest mixing bowl through its mouth.

Coleman clicked the remote to another cable show. "Florida again. Police are carrying out a garbage bag. They think the live-in boyfriend did it . . ."

Serge tossed his face mask on the bed. "Ready?"

Coleman looked up from the TV. "For what?"

Serge held out the decorative plastic container. "To deliver our gift."

"Thought it was supposed to be a basket?"

"Just remembered I hate gift baskets. You get one and go, holy fuck, look at all this great stuff! Then you rip it open in a glee-frenzy and go: What the hell? It's mostly cellophane and straw and a lousy cheese ball."

"Anything else?"

"Mini-jar of bullshit gooseberry jam. But this . . ." He held up the bathing product again. "You see the whole container and there's no false advertising."

"But it's still false advertising," said Coleman. "There are no salts inside."

"Oh, there are salts all right," said Serge. "Alkaline earth metal salts."

"You use them for bathing?"

"I personally wouldn't, but for the right gift recipient . . ."

The '69 Barracuda cruised south through Fort Myers on McGregor Boulevard—both sides of the street lined with old-growth palms that soared to the sky. Serge held a hand next to his face, preventing a view to the left.

"What are you doing?" asked Coleman.

Serge gritted his teeth. "The Thomas Edison Museum is coming up in a mile or so. Tell me when we've passed it."

"Why?"

"Because we don't have time to stop, but it won't be up to me if I get the slightest peek . . ."

A mile ahead: Three state agents left the Edison Museum and stood on the sidewalk by the entrance. Picture-taking tourists in shorts and sandals came across the street from the parking lot on the other side.

"No sign of Serge," said Agent White. He laced his fingers behind his head and stretched to get a kink out of his back. "Mahoney, where now? Cabbage Key?"

Mahoney shook his head. "Vibe cooled." He gazed in frustration back at the museum.

White patted him on the back. "Not all your hunches can be correct."

"Could have bet the farm." Mahoney fished a matchstick from his jacket. "The force is strong here."

"Let's just get going to Sanibel." White started across the street for the parking lot, but needed to wait for one last car to pass.

A '69 Barracuda went by, the driver holding a hand next to his head that blocked the view of his face.

Coleman looked out the back window of the Barricuda. "We just passed the museum."

Serge took his hand down from the side of his face. "That was close. Now we can make Sanibel before sunset."

Farther south, staying near the coast, they approached a tall new bridge. Serge stopped at the tollbooth.

"Jesus Christmas!" said Coleman. "Six bucks? That what it costs to pay for this bridge?"

"No, that's what it costs to keep riffraff like us out. Nice try."

"Keep us out of where?" Coleman lit a joint.

"The twin resort islands of Sanibel and Captiva."

He took a hit and giggled. "I know how to remember that: *Cannabis sativa*."

"You mnemonic rebel."

A pot cloud exhaled out the window. "Why do they want to keep us away?"

"So the people who tie sweaters around their waists can stroll unmolested along exquisite beaches in the seashell capital of America."

"Screw seashells."

"Shut yo mouth!"

"Just talkin' 'bout Shaft."

They faced each other, laughed and high-fived. "We still got it," said Coleman.

"Remember how to make the scream like that little fucker in Kool and the Gang?"

"*Yowwwwww!*"

Serge rocked in his seat. "Again!"

"*Yowwwwww!*"

From behind them: "*Yowwwww!*"

Serge and Coleman looked toward each other, then the backseat.

"It's Mikey!" said Coleman. "He's a natural."

"That's my boy," said Serge. "And not a single lesson."

"*Yowwwwww! . . .*"

Chapter Thirty-two

SANIBEL

A white Crown Vic sat in front of a packed resort. White slapped a mug shot onto the bar in at outdoor tiki hut.

"Seen this guy?" asked White.

"Nope."

A '69 Barracuda drove by.

People riding bikes, power-walking, looking healthy.

"Look at all the seashell shops," said Coleman. "They're everywhere."

"For the vicarious," said Serge. "True Floridians comb the beach on hands and knees."

"You're really not kidding about seashells."

"Once you get into them, they'll rock your world! You got whelks, cockles, scallops, tellins, murex, conchs, tritons, nautilus, and don't forget the chestnut turbans."

"I had no idea."

"Shells even decided wars in Florida."

"I am way too high," said Coleman. "I though you just said—"

"You heard me right." Serge began checking the side of the road for a particular resort. "Back in the nineteenth century, when federal troops battled the Indians across the Everglades and Florida Bay, it was almost impossible not to get lost among the countless, identical-looking mangrove islands. The military advantage fell to whoever knew the geography. And guess how the Indians did it?"

"Computers?"

"Fifty-nine varieties of the Liguus Tree Snail, each with its own distinctive color bands—and each hue exclusive to specific clusters of south Florida islands. The Indians knew them all, and that's how they navigated and won . . . Here's our stop." The Barracuda whipped into a parking lot with stone pavers for drainage.

The trio went inside and approached a front desk subtly framed by watercolors and potted island flowers. Behind them, the mandatory saltwater aquarium. A woman in a tropical shirt gave the greeting smile. "How are you doing today?"

"Seashells won the war," said Serge.

"The six dollars didn't work," said Coleman.

The greeting began to crack. "You have reservations?"

"No." Serge glanced around, leaned over the desk and lowered his voice. "We're not staying here. We're on the run and hiding out."

Her smile began a straight line. Call security or not?

Serge's eyes darted around again. "We're looking for someone else laying low. I'm a close personal friend of Hunter Bleadoph."

"*Ohhhh*, friends of Hunter." Back to good times. "You confused me at first about hiding out, but management briefed us on the media thing. Don't worry: We're on top of that."

"Could you ring his room?"

"My pleasure." She dialed and listened.

"Daddy!" yelled Mikey, holding up an arm. "Look! I caught a fish!"

"Mikey, put that back in the aquarium right now!"

Coleman pointed at the white bamboo floor. "It squirted out of his hand. I'll get it."

The woman behind the desk hung up. "I'm sorry. He doesn't seem to be answering."

Coleman hit the floor. "I got it! . . . Nope got away . . . Hold it. I got it . . . Too slippery. Wait, let me try again . . . Got it . . . No . . . *Ahhhhh!* Mikey jumped on my back! He's choking— . . ." (Cough).

Coleman reared up; a joint went flying from his pocket.

Serge reeled in the chain leash as Coleman resumed crawling by in the background. "Got it again . . . whoops . . ."

Serge managed a grin at the receptionist. "It's like I have two children . . . Know where Hunter hangs out around here?"

"Might try the spa. He's been getting a lot of massages."

"Did he pull a muscle or something here?"

"No, they just cost a lot."

"Thanks."

Serge scooped up a fish and tossed it back in the aquarium. "Let's go, kids."

They headed through a labyrinth of halls and reached an intersection. Ahead: the spa entrance. Left: bright sunlight through glass exit doors to the beach. Serge stopped and clenched his fists. The shakes started in his feet and rose to his throat.

"What is it?" asked Coleman.

"Damn! Come on!" Serge turned left and ran for the light.

Coleman took off after him. "But what about Hunter?"

"I'm a father now," said Serge, bursting outside through the doors. "I have responsibilities . . . Mikey! You'll love this! . . ."

An hour later, three people came back in the building. They made a left down the hallway and entered a pampering spa. People getting mud packs, cucumber slices on eyes, stationary bikes and treadmills with cardio-monitors and headphones. Someone with his back to them lay facedown on the massage table, taking a flurry of karate chops to the shoulders.

"Hunter?"

No answer. Serge walked around to the front. Not him. He looked at the masseuse, digging knuckles into neck tendons. "Seen Hunter?"

She angled her head toward the tanning salon on the other side of the room.

Serge walked over and bent down to a blue slit of ultraviolet light from the opening. "Hunter? You in there?"

"Who is it?"

"Serge, from Cabbage Key."

"Serge!"

The bed's cover flew up. Hunter swung his legs out in a skimpy Speedo. He removed protective goggles. "Great to see you. What are you doing here?"

"Thought I'd spend a little of the shareholders' money."

"That a boy! Couldn't have picked a better place." Something caught his eye. He paused and stared down curiously at Serge. Then Coleman and Mikey. "What's the deal with all your pants?"

The three looked at their shorts: pockets on hips ballooning to the max. Sand-covered knees.

"We went shelling," said Serge. "I'm now a responsible parent teaching my son: all Florida, all the time. Check it out . . ." He dug both hands deep in his pockets and produced twin piles of colorful sea treasures. "Angel wings, coquina, imperial venus, auger, cerith, angulate periwinkle . . ."

Mikey enthusiastically dug through his own pockets. "Shells!"

Coleman reached in his shorts and pulled out two fistfuls of seaweed.

Serge grinned. "He had a little trouble with the concept . . . So how've you been?"

"Feel like a billion." Hunter threw a towel over his shoulders and began walking. "I'd like you to meet the gang . . . The guy getting the shiatsu is Jessup."

The man in the massage chair looked over and waved.

"On the bike and isokinetics are Manfred and Addison. My top executives," said Hunter. "So what are you up to?"

"I was going to hit the hot tub by the pool. Incredibly relaxing, at least fifty water jets," said Serge. "Why don't you join us?"

"Is it free?"

"Yeah."

"Think I'll pass."

"But there's a bar out there. Drinks on my company."

"What are we waiting for?" Hunter turned. "Guys! free drinks."

Shift change at the reception desk.

The new clerk stared at a mug shot.

"Nope. But I just came on."

White looked at the other agents. "What do you think?"

Lowe stared into the aquarium, watching a joint float on the surface. "Doesn't seem like Serge's kind of place. It's too . . . nice."

White made a check mark on a chamber-of-commerce list. "Let's move. We got half a page left, and we're losing light . . ."

Behind the resort, the top half of a large reddish sun sat on the horizon of the Gulf of Mexico.

Hunter Bleadoph and his executive team had practically trampled each other running out of the spa. After changing in the cabanas, they reunited by the pool and climbed into the hot tub.

Serge and Coleman brought over the promised free drinks.

"Gracias," said Hunter, taking a Rémy Martin. "You were right about this tub. Jets are fabulous—couldn't be more relaxing."

"Yes it can," said Serge, walking around the deck in the cool sunset that produced a thick layer of steam from the water's surface. Perfect for his plan.

"Aren't you going to join us?" asked Hunter.

Serge pointed up at one of the top floors. "Forgot my swimsuit in the room. I'll get it in a minute." He smiled and surveyed the executives. "So what am I looking at here? A hundred million in taxpayer bonuses?"

Arrogant laughter from the tub.

Serge began laughing, too. He elbowed Coleman. Coleman began laughing.

Hunter stopped laughing and set his drink on the side. "You think too small."

"You're my heroes," said Serge.

"Don't worry, you'll get there," said Hunter. "Mark my words. I'm a great judge of character."

"You'd be surprised."

"No, really, you're destined for things."

"Appreciate it."

"I'd appreciate another drink."

Serge pointed his right hand like a pistol at Hunter. "You got it, big guy!"

Four drinks later:

"This is the life," said Hunter.

"That it is," said Serge, jerking the leash as Mikey strained to leap in the deep end of the adjacent pool.

"So when are you getting in here with us?"

Serge smacked his forehead. "I've gotten so caught up listening to your wisdom that I forgot to go back to the room."

Hunter became distracted. He turned: "Is there something I can help you with?" It wasn't friendly.

A family of four stood quiet and patient a few feet away. "We've been waiting to use the tub," said the father.

"Good for you," said Hunter. "Keep doing it."

The executives spread out to take up the tub's remaining capacity.

The dad gestured at a sign on a palm tree. "It says you're not supposed—"

Hunter turned. "I see it. Half-hour time limit for courtesy. So what?"

"You've been in there over an hour. I don't mean to be rude."

"You are being rude." Hunter's eyes went to the next person. "And what the hell are *you* looking at?"

The wife lowered her gaze. Her husband took her by the hand. "Come on, honey." They left abruptly with the children.

Hunter rested his head back and closed his eyes.

"I don't know," said Serge. "It is a rule."

Hunter, without opening his eyes: "Rules are for other people."

"But you never know when a rule could save your life."

"What's the matter with you?" said Hunter. "Thought we were on the same page."

"I'm sorry," said Serge. "It's just that there's so much to learn from you. Which reminds me—bathing suit. Oh, and I almost forgot something else . . . Coleman, take the leash. Mikey's going for the diving board."

Serge grabbed a bag off a rattan lounger. "I bought you a little something. Or rather my company did. Was going to get something else, but gift baskets are dead to me."

"What is it?" asked Hunter.

Serge pulled his hand out of the bag. "Bath salts."

"For my wife?"

"No, you guys," said Serge. "From Hong Kong. Outrageously expensive. Made from illegally smuggled endangered species . . ." He crouched down and dropped his voice like a co-conspirator. ". . . Asian aphrodisiac. Supposed to make your dick harder than a Polaris missile. Some of the staff here's pretty hot."

"Then I'll definitely have to try it," said Hunter, fingering his wedding band. "Leave it by our towels and I'll use it back in the room."

"Why not right here in the tub?" said Serge.

"I don't think you're supposed to put anything in this water."

"Rules are for other people."

"Ha!" said Hunter. "Hear that, guys? My star pupil! . . . Serge, dump it on in!"

Serge stood in silent thought.

"Well?" said Hunter. "What are you waiting for?"

"Just a last question," said Serge. "And it's an important one, because I want to study from your example how to make critical decisions in the future. Possibly the very near future."

"Fire away."

"How do you feel about seventy-year-olds with health problems who had to go back to work because their retirement nest eggs were depleted?"

"Fuck 'em," said Hunter. "Bad things happen to people all the time."

"So true. So very true." Serge unscrewed the lid, walked around to the upwind side of the tub and gently let his magic powder flutter down into the water. "My favorite part is the almond fragrance."

Serge recapped the bottle and pointed again at the upper floor. "Going to get my suit now." He began walking away.

"I smell almonds," said Hunter.

"That means it's working," said Serge. "I'll be right back."

"We're not going anywhere," said Hunter.

"I know," said Serge.

ONE HOUR LATER

A family of four returned to the pool deck behind one of Sanibel's finest resorts.

"Look at that," said the wife. "Those jerks are still in there."

"I can't believe it. They're sleeping," said the husband. He walked over to the tub. "Come on. You've been in there long enough . . . Wake up!"

No response.

"They're drunk," said the wife.

The husband crouched and shook Hunter's shoulder. He slumped forward, facedown in the water.

The woman's curdling scream filled the night and brought staff running from every part of the resort.

Chapter Thirty-three

NINE P.M.

A cell phone rang. "This is Lowe . . . What! . . . When? . . . Uh-huh . . . Uh-huh . . . That's strange . . . Where did this happen? . . . Thanks for letting us know." He clapped it shut and turned to White. "Sheriff's office. Got a report from one of the smaller local police departments. Four dead at a nearby resort."

White looked over from the driver's seat. "Homicide?"

"Don't know yet," said Lowe. "Scene still has them baffled. This family found all four bodies in a hot tub."

"What jurisdiction?"

"Sanibel."

"Sanibel!" White looked in his rearview at the bridge he had just crossed to Captiva. Brakes squealed. The steering wheel spun.

"Something else," said Lowe. "All four were corporate officers of GUE."

"That financial group that got the bailouts?" said White, straightening out the car and racing back toward the bridge.

Lowe nodded. "On some kind of secret retreat."

Mahoney nodded. "Serge."

"Wonderful," said White, hitting the gas. "The press is going to be all over this . . ."

THE TAMIAMI TRAIL

A '69 Barracuda sped south into the night.

"Is Mikey asleep?"

Coleman looked in the backseat. "Totally crashed. He looks so cute with your nunchucks."

Serge watched the roadside view go by. "When did all this development happen?"

"Where are we?" asked Coleman.

"Bonita Springs, just north of Naples. I used to love this part of the Tamiami, but scratch it from the A-tour." Serge cringed at the chain of chain stores out the windows. "This nightmare should clear by the next county."

"Been meaning to ask." Coleman mixed vodka with Dr Pepper. "What did you dump in that hot tub with those four guys? It wasn't actually something good for their dicks?"

Serge's head turned slowly with a sly grin.

"That's what I thought." Coleman chugged from a plastic tumbler. "Some kind of acid that burned them up?"

"Too pedestrian," said Serge. "Plus, they'd feel it coming on and jump out of the water. I take pride that my bath salts are very soothing, nothing but luxuriating pleasure . . . Here we go . . ." A sign at the Collier County line. Next: shopping centers, gated communities. "Damn, more development. At least there's refuge at our next stop . . ."

The Barracuda angled toward the shoulder of the road.

"Why are we parked?"

"To check the next stop." Serge pulled a small laptop from his backpack and opened it on his legs. "This one isn't just location but a sensitive time window." He tapped the keyboard. "Here's their website . . ."

"Then what was it?"

"What?"

"In the hot tub."

"I love chemistry." Serge scrolled down the screen. "The really fascinating thing is that normally stable compounds react vigorously upon innocent contact with air or water. Individually, the products from the hardware store wouldn't do that. And for some crazy reason, nobody will sell me a pre-mixed batch. So I had to put on my chef's hat in the motel . . ." He leaned toward the screen. "Oh, pleassssssse!"

"Found something?"

"This website says we might still have a day or so, unless misfortune strikes in the meantime." Serge handed Coleman the computer and pulled back onto the highway. "I've been waiting to see this my whole life! It's one of those things that should be on every true Floridian's Life List, like the elusive Flash of Green at sunset."

Coleman held the computer's screen to his face, then did a double take at Serge. "You're shitting me."

"About what?"

"This looks like something chicks would force us to do, much worse than guest towels."

"Coleman, Dendrophylax is a spiritual experience." A highway sign: EXIT III. Serge took Immokalee Road inland, passing under I-75 ten miles north of the toll-booth to Alligator Alley. "Sometimes you just have to stop and get in touch with your feminine side."

"You mean beat off?"

"Jesus! No!— . . . Well, actually we'll be in the presence of some pretty intense natural Florida beauty, so I can't guarantee it won't come to that."

"We'll have to take turns standing lookout."

The Barracuda left civilization and blazed across barren flatlands. "It's getting late. Let's put up someplace cheap and hit it in the morning."

Coleman chewed a peyote button. "What was the almond business back at the hot tub?"

"Still on that?"

"You never let me stay to see them croak."

"Like I said back at the resort, that sweet, nutty fragrance is my favorite part."

"Why's that?"

"Once you start smelling almonds, it's already too late."

SANIBEL

Hundreds of rubber-neckers lined the side of the road, pointing and gossiping.

Officers from multiple jurisdictions taped off the resort and held back the curious.

Distraught guests got free drink tickets.

And the press. Satellite trucks arriving nonstop. Some correspondents had already set up along police lines, going live under floodlights that turned night to day.

". . . Four confirmed dead . . ."

". . . Police releasing few details . . ."

". . . Unnamed source said all were top executives of embattled GUE . . ."

". . . Apparently attending a secret luxury retreat . . ."

One of the national cable channels was already taking an audience poll, overwhelmingly in favor of the day's events.

A Crown Vic rolled up. Agent White flashed a badge out the window, and an officer raised the crime tape for the car to pass.

More vehicles arrived.

". . . Reportedly found in a hot tub . . ."

". . . The seashell capital of the country . . ."

A commotion on the side of the road. A loud roar as a man with long yellow hair gunned a chopper.

TV people stampeded with cameras and microphones.

"Doberman! We'd like a word! . . ."

"Are you after the killers? . . ."

The bounty hunter climbed off the bike. "I'm after justice, American style."

The kickstand gave way and the bike fell on him.

Back behind the resort, three state detectives approached the hot tub. A crime scene in top gear. Photos, fingerprints. Two victims already bagged on gurneys.

The medical examiner swabbed foaming saliva from the mouth of the recently late Hunter Bleadoph. He dropped the sample in a clear bag, then tilted the victim's head back and pulled up eyelids.

"Excuse me . . ."

The examiner turned.

"I'm Agent White from the FDLE. These are Agents Lowe and Mahoney. I know you're busy but it's important for a case. Are we looking at homicide?"

"Give me another second." He opened the mouth cavity and shined a penlight, then up each nostril. Individual hairs carefully harvested to preserve follicles. A scraping of skin. He dipped a plastic bottle in the tub and capped it.

The examiner stood and handed the samples to an assistant. "The lab ASAP. Gas-chromatograph mass spectrometer." He turned. "Now how can I help you?"

"This is completely off-the-record because we don't need a panic, but we're tracking a fugitive who may be a serial killer." White looked down at the tub. "He could be involved here, if this wasn't an accident."

"It wasn't." The examiner snapped off his gloves. "We thought so at first, since no signs of trauma. Today it's a rarity, because manufacturers now isolate all the wiring, but some older tubs get a short circuit in the pump system and you've got electrocution."

"But it's not?"

The examiner shook his head. "Tip-off is musculature, quick acidic buildup in the fibers. This was something else. Won't know for sure until we get test results."

"But you have your suspicions?"

"Let's step aside." They walked behind the poolside bar. "What I'm going to tell you now is definitely off-the-record."

"Understood."

"When those spectrometer results come back, I'll bet my life we find spikes in heavy earth alkaline metals. I'm guessing compounds with barium or calcium."

"This is all Greek."

"If the compound also was mixed right, it would react aggressively with water, giving off a highly lethal hydrogen-cyanide gas."

"They didn't notice?"

"The tub's massage jets create turbulence and bubbles that would have masked the reaction in the water. And since it was cool last night, the rest was probably concealed in steam coming off the surface."

"Wouldn't it have stunk? That'd get me hopping out of the tub."

The examiner shook his head again. "Actually it's quite pleasant. The last thing they would have smelled was almonds . . . Now, if you'll excuse me."

White walked back to the other agents. "Mahoney, how's Serge with chemistry."

"Like falling off a log ringing a bell."

White exhaled hard and stared out at the sea. The Doberman crawled up the sand toward the resort like a stealth navy commando. Surrounded by TV camera lights that lit up the entire beach and drew a crowd of late-night strollers.

"We have to find Serge fast." White turned back around. "Any hunches in that gut, Mickey Spillane?"

Mahoney removed a matchstick. "Ghost rider."

Chapter Thirty-four

THE NEXT MORNING

Forty miles southeast of Fort Myers, at the upper edge of the Everglades, sits the scorched landscape of an outpost called Immokalee.

In the sticks.

Immokalee is a quiet agricultural community of migrants near the poverty line. It was originally named Gopher Ridge, but changed to an Indian word that translates "my home."

"Downtown" consists of a few small blocks that look like a place where you'd stop and ask directions to downtown. Cowboy hats, Spanish signs, taco stands, horseflies.

Our Lady of Guadalupe.

An inland pocket of Florida with no breeze. Stagnant heat that feels like it's pushing down on your shoulders. People sit on curbs and aimlessly walk streets in withering defeat. The chief source of entertainment is boredom.

The late Miami author Charles Willeford set a novel in Immokalee, where a farm boss locks the doors of a boardinghouse before each payday and fumigates the workers.

The Seminoles just put in a casino.

On the eastern side of town, across Lake Trafford, is a place even more remote where nobody farms. There is a parking lot but few cars. Today, a '69 Barracuda had its choice of empty spaces.

Three people got out. More windless heat, vicious humidity and the sizzling buzz of insects. Nothing but scrubland in all directions except a wooden building with visitor information, nature exhibits and a gift shop.

"We've arrived!" Serge pulled hard against a straining chain leash.

"Where?" asked Coleman.

"The Corkscrew Swamp Sanctuary. I love the Corkscrew!"

Coleman took a slug from a flask. "What's to do here?"

"Take sanctuary."

The flask went back in a pocket. "Still don't understand why you wanted to come here just to look at a single flower."

"Not just any flower," said Serge. "The ghost orchid. They attach themselves to trees in swamp forests."

"Ghost?"

"Most elusive orchid of all, immortalized by Susan Orlean in *The Orchid Thief.*" Mikey began pulling Serge toward the building like a sled dog. "Can only be found growing wild in the wetlands of southwest Florida and Cuba. The most rabid flower freak can live ten lifetimes without seeing one. And not for lack of trying. These people gladly march miles in hip-deep water just to stake out a tree at two A.M., waiting for a flower that blooms only one night a year. But the holy grail is the ghost orchid, whose sighting is so rare it makes the newspapers. And this is my big chance!"

"Hold it," said Coleman. "I can understand bird-watchers, but you're telling me there are people that just stand around watching a flower doing nothing?"

"And with a passion that eclipses the Frog Listening Network in Thonotosassa, who go out at night with tape recorders to cut CDs for easy listening in their cars."

They headed for the building. A deep motorized sound cut through the insect drone. Serge turned around. "Here they come now."

A giant air-conditioned tour bus pulled into the parking lot and stopped next to the building. Doors hissed open.

Off they poured, grouping together by the side of the bus. All white-haired seniors with uncharacteristic tans. All adhering to an unspoken dress code. Fanny packs, cargo shorts, straw hats, pith helmets, hiking boots, binoculars, long-range cameras and novelty T-shirts from their club chapter: I'D RATHER BE RESUPINATING, I BRAKE FOR EPIPHYTES and ORCHID LOVERS DO IT PERENNIALLY.

The driver opened the luggage bay.

Coleman scratched his head as the collection of enthusiasts reached into the compartment, unloading telescopes, tripods, video equipment, camera cases, collapsing sun canopies and folding canvas tailgating chairs with drink holders.

"This is a bonus," said Serge, getting out his wallet. "Seeing a ghost orchid *and* testing my next fugitive 'Out' technique."

"Flowers are an 'Out'?"

"All these clubs have lines of merchandise for fundraising. Watch and learn." He approached the gang. "Excuse me? Who's in charge of marketing? I'd like a whole bunch of your crap!"

"That's me," said a red-faced man with a British accent, knee-high socks and white nose cream. "What are you interested in?"

"Everything!"

The man pulled a styrene bin from the luggage compartment and opened the lid.

"Oooooooo!" said Serge. "I'll take three of each: T-shirts, tote bags, water bottles, laminated species guide, sun hats with roll-down neck protector, field glasses, can coozie for Coleman and that big souvenir button with a picture of a ghost orchid on a milk carton that says *Have you seen me?"*

"Our best customer," remarked the Brit, pocketing currency. The club went in the building for tickets.

Serge, Coleman and Mikey donned their new T-shirts and hats in the parking lot and followed the others inside.

They reached the ticket counter. "Two adults, one child."

"Here's a map," said the park employee. "You go out back here—"

Serge held up a hand for him to stop. "Don't need a map. Know the place by heart: two-and-a-quarter-mile, round-trip boardwalk through eleven-thousand-acre preserve of wet prairies, cypress marsh and pine flat woods." Serge reached. "I need a map for my files. How's our ghost orchid?"

"You're in luck. Just got a new bloom."

"Not the one I saw on the Internet?"

He shook his head. "The orchid they reported in the press fell off the tree a few days ago in the middle of the night. And wouldn't you know we got a ton of people the next day."

"Must have been a full-scale riot," said Serge. "Flower people torching the gift shop and tipping over police cars."

"No, they just left."

"What about this new bloom?"

"Sometimes when one drops from the tree, another takes it place. Sometimes not. That's why I said you're in luck."

"Where is it?"

"Take the boardwalk south." The man gestured out the back door. "It's way off the trail about fifty feet up the tree. You can't see it with the naked eye, so there's a photo and arrow attached to the railing showing where to point binoculars."

"Can I pretend to be Nicolas Cage?"

"What?"

"From the excellent Florida movie *Adaptation*, based on *The Orchid Thief*, which was inspired by true events at the nearby Fakahatchee Strand." Serge turned sideways. "Check my profile. People always say I look like Cage. Wait, I got that wrong. They always *don't* say it, but who's going to stop me?

Right? You look like someone I can trust. Do you have coffee?"

"You okay?"

"Super-duper! I totally rededicated my life in the parking lot: ghost orchids or death! . . . Mikey! Mush!" The child pulled Serge out the door.

They clomped down the winding boardwalk, bend after bend, until the bus people appeared.

Silent reverence. Cameras and binoculars. Others sat in their stadium chairs while a high-definition TV camera filmed from a tripod, and someone else held a directional boom microphone over the railing.

Serge and company quietly slipped behind. Coleman tugged his shirt. "There's way too many people to beat off. Maybe if we hang around until there's just a few left, and I can stand in front of you . . ."

"Coleman, I was being facetious."

"Is that where you put your finger up your ass?"

"Keep your voice down!"

Another tug. "I don't see it."

"The man said you need binoculars." Serge raised his. "Wow. It's incredible. It's awesome. It's taking my breath away."

He handed the binoculars to Coleman. "It's a flower."

Serge opened a book on the railing.

"What are you reading?" asked Coleman.

"River of Grass."

"What's that?"

Serge showed him the cover of a white heron gazing out over the landscape. "Groundbreaking preservation work by Marjory Stoneman Douglas, first published in 1947. A lone voice back when everyone else just saw dollar signs and a swamp that needed to be drained. But not Marjory! She single-handedly launched popular appreciation for one of our state's prized treasures, earning her the nickname 'Grande Dame of the Everglades.'"

"But what's the river part of the title?"

"Because the Everglades actually is a river. Except you wouldn't know it because it's fifty miles wide and the flow is too slow to notice since the land only slopes a couple inches per mile. Douglas was barely five feet tall and lived to be a hundred and eight, but even at the end she was, pound for pound, the deadliest political street fighter in the state. Even won the Presidential Medal of Freedom except, surprisingly, no action figures of her with eyes that shoot laser beams and a purse covered with poison-tipped spikes. Imagine what they'd be worth today in the original box with all the accessories."

Out front, the parking lot filled fast with a rush of vehicles led by a Crown Vic and trailed by a tour bus pounding Metallica.

"Sure hope you're right about this hunch," said White. "This was another long drive to nowhere."

Lowe wiped his forehead. "And hotter than hell."

Mahoney fanned himself with his hat. "Parlay lock. Flower hit the papers."

PART IV

The Last Frontier

Chapter Thirty-five

CORKSCREW SWAMP

Three state agents arrived at a ticket counter.

White continued his unending routine of holding up a badge and mug shots. "Seen these guys?"

"Not sure. We had a lot of people just come through." He put on reading glasses. "Maybe this one, but I could be wrong."

"Do you remember anything in particular?" asked White. "Think hard. A minor detail that might seem unimportant could be crucial to our case."

"Well, there was one thing, but it didn't make any sense."

"What was it?"

"He asked permission to be Nicolas Cage."

"Pay dirt," said Mahoney. *The Orchid Thief.*"

"What's that mean?"

"Tail me." He headed out the back door.

They reached the boardwalk, and Agent White unfolded his park map on the railing. "It's a big oval with no escape but a swamp full of gators . . . Mahoney, you go that way and Lowe and I will head the other. If he's out here, we can't miss him."

The trio split up . . .

A mile west on the boardwalk, a crowd of seniors watched with rapt attention. Serge's obsessive picture-taking blended in. Celebratory wine bottles sat empty on the planks. Some had cell phones out, texting fellow aficionados across the country.

Then, in silence, a flower silently fell off a tree and helicoptered down into the water.

Gasps

"*Son of a bitch! . . .*"

"*Motherfuck! . . .*"

"*Bullshit root structure! . . .*"

They angrily threw their gear together, preparing to hike back to the nature center.

"Perfect," said Serge. "Excellent chance to test my latest 'Out.'"

"You never told me what that was," said Coleman.

"Near the top of the fugitive's arsenal is camouflage." Serge pulled the brim of his hat down. "And the best camouflage is to hide in plain sight. Whenever there's a large, homogenous group all dressed alike, the human brain processes it as a single unit, not as individuals. And fugitive hunters are looking for an individual."

"But how are you going to test it?"

"See those two guys in white dress shirts coming toward us? Let's have fun and pretend they're state agents on our trail."

"Okay," said Coleman. "But I've been wondering. You've done a lot of stuff over the years. How do you know you're not really being tracked."

"The Law of Shit Happens: If you're worried about a specific problem like getting strangled in the food court, it never happens while you're thinking about it—only when you're daydreaming about sports cars or Totie Fields . . . Here they come. Keep your head down."

Two state agents approached an oncoming procession of surly orchid enthusiasts. White flipped open his cell and dialed. ". . . Mahoney? White here . . . Any sign of Serge?"

"Snake eyes."

"Mahoney, that doesn't put me any closer to a yes or no."

"No."

"Keep looking." He hung up and nodded politely at the passing visitors. "Where on earth can he be?"

"Up ahead," said Lowe. "It's the picture on the railing marking the ghost orchid site. But nobody's there."

"Maybe around the bend . . ."

Ten minutes later, Lowe saw movement through the cypress. "Look! Someone's coming on the boardwalk." He reached for a shoulder holster.

The person appeared.

White sagged. "It's just Mahoney. Let's call it a day and head back . . . Mahoney! We're going!"

Mahoney just gazing into murky water. A turtle surfaced.

"We covered the whole boardwalk from opposite directions," said White. "If he was here, you know we would have intercepted."

Mahoney continued gazing off the railing at the lettuce lakes and rubbed his two-day stubble. "Dizzy tiggle gashouse yegman biscuit-town."

White put a hand on his shoulder. "I have absolutely no idea what that means, but I want you to realize that despite my occasional annoyance, I sincerely appreciate your dedication . . . Now we all could use a little rest."

They made it back to the nature center and reached the doors to the parking lot.

"Oh, detectives?"

They turned around. The ticket man.

"That guy in the picture you showed me? Is this him?"

"Where?"

"On my security monitor. I rolled the tape back."

White ran over. "How long ago?"

"Fifteen minutes, tops." The man looked up. "Camera got him on the way out."

The trio raced around the desk for a view of the re-playing footage.

On the black-and-white screen, Serge and Coleman strolled away in the middle of a pack of seniors.

"I'll be damned," said White.

"Where'd he get the kid?" asked Lowe.

"We'll ask when we catch him."

They ran out the door.

White started up the Crown Vic and looked over his shoulder. "Mahoney, where to now?"

"The Big-H 29 shimmy-sham."

EVERGLADES

A '69 Barracuda sped south on Highway 29.

"Roadkill," said Coleman. "Armadillo."

"Got it." Serge swerved as vultures took off.

Mikey pasted his face to the window. "Squishy guts!"

"I think he's going to be a doctor," said Serge.

Kid Rock blared as they crested the overpass across Alligator Alley.

". . . *Singing 'Sweet Home Alabama' all summer long!* . . ."

"I didn't know you liked the Kid," said Coleman.

"I didn't," said Serge. "Or I was indifferent, until I heard he got in brawl at a Waffle House after a gig. Anyone with that kind of money who still goes to Waffle House, I'm down with." The song ended. Serge picked up his iPod and spun the click wheel. "This trip needs fugitive tunes or swamp music, and preferably both . . . Here we go . . ."

"Where are we going?"

"If you're a fan of studying maps and looking for the most remote dead ends at the edge of nowhere, you can't do better in Florida," said Serge. "I know a spot at the very bottom of the state where nobody but nobody will find us."

"Roadkill. Opossum."

The Barracuda slalomed around baked remains on the pavement.

Serge reached under his seat for a small shopping bag. He removed an item, peeled off the covering over its adhesive base and stuck it in the middle of the dashboard.

They passed a couple of places on the map called Jerome and Copeland, but what were actually just a few reclusive homes. Some had driveways off the highway, across dubious wooden bridges over a drainage canal.

Coleman stared at the dashboard. The head of a small plastic figurine wobbled to road vibrations. "Serge?"

"Yes, Tonto?"

"What's that?"

"You've never seen a dashboard bobble-head?"

"Many times. It looks like a baseball player."

"Used to be Derek Jeter."

"But you taped his legs together and painted his uniform into a dress. And glued cotton all over his helmet."

"Correct," said Serge. "I knew we were coming to the Everglades, and whenever they don't sell what I want, I have to make my own."

"Own what?"

"Marjory Stoneman Douglas bobble-head."

"Why did you paint her eyes red?"

"To shoot laser beams."

". . . *Amos Moses was a hell of a man . . .*"

"I remember this song," said Coleman. "Don't think I've heard it in thirty years."

"About a fugitive in the swamp," said Serge. "Good omen."

"Who sings it?"

"Another Sunshine State six-degrees-of-separation bonus: Jerry Reed."

"Roadkill. Unknown."

Another swerve. "Reed was in all three quintessential Florida fugitive films, the *Smokey and the Bandit* trilogy, starring none other than Florida favorite son Burt Reynolds. Filming locales included Jupiter, Indiantown, West Palm, Clearwater, Silver Springs and the Seaquarium, to name but a few."

"I dug the cop in those movies."

". . . *Gonna getcha Amos!* . . ."

"Sheriff Buford T. Justice, played by Jackie Gleason, who had moved his TV show to Miami Beach. Coincidence? I think we both know the answer."

"Remember Sally Field in those movies? She was hot back then."

"Still is," said Serge. "But I blanch at her new commercials. The heartbreak of the bandit's squeeze pimping bone-loss supplements . . . which reminds me, another degree of separation that brings us full circle." Serge grabbed his iPod and dialed another song, striking up a wicked fiddle. "One of our state anthems, 'The Orange Blossom Special,' was on the Smokey sound track."

". . . *Hey, look a yonder comin'* . . ."

Thirty miles back, a Crown Vic turned south on Highway 29. "Mahoney, you really think he came this way?" asked White.

"Hophead on the heritage pipe."

"Where do you think Serge is right now? . . ."

. . . Serge looked out Coleman's window as a side road went by. "We're getting close. That's the entrance to Fakahatchee Strand."

"I can't believe you're not stopping there. I mean, the book you mentioned at the sanctuary place. You always stop."

"Once you've seen a ghost orchid, the rest of your horticulture life is an ever-blackening downward spiral into lesser flowers. If I don't put a shit-stop to that right now, I'll find myself outside the nursing home in my power scooter with a watering can and strained-prune spit-up on my shirt."

"You're always planning ahead."

"Fuck that geranium nonsense."

They reached the intersection with the Tamiami Trail, one of the only traffic lights in the Everglades. Across the street, a police substation and tourist information center, where five wild boars sniffed the ground and people stood on top of cars taking pictures.

Serge pushed on.

Three miles later, the Barracuda cleared a bridge and cruised through the flat, open landscape of Everglades City.

"Over there," said Coleman. "That's the bank we stayed in during the hurricane."

"And here's the country church, Rod and Gun Club and Seafood Depot—in an actual railroad depot back when the trains ran wealthy northerners down a century ago." They entered a roundabout that circled a radio tower. "The museum's open!"

Brakes screeched.

Serge grabbed a thermos of coffee, chugged and tossed it to his buddy. "Wait here."

"Serge, you'll take forever," complained Coleman. "It's a museum."

"This is just a gift-shop blitz. I know the museum inside out, but they may have updated their product line. I check every time."

"Have they ever updated?"

"No."

He ran inside and lunged at the woman behind the counter. "New products? Hold nothing back! I already have everything! Maybe a scale model of the Walking Dredge that carved out the Tamiami. Or original blueprints and I'll build my own full-size job."

"Do you want to visit the museum?"

"No, this is a lightning strike. Always hit the gift shops first, in case some jerk gets the last Walking Dredge. Sometimes *only* hit the gift shop, like now if I've done the museum a dozen times. Check your old guest books: My visits are well documented. I'm the guy who needed several pages for the comment section, taking up slots for sixty other guests."

"You're the one who messed up our books?"

"I tried to write tiny, but so much needed to be said."

"You wrote nearly the whole history of the town. And a list of grievances to Congress."

"And asked for a new product line," said Serge. "What have you got?"

"Well, there's this plastic cup commemorating the eightieth anniversary of the Tamiami."

"Sold!" Serge began singing. "*There's a trail that's winding through the Everglades*' . . . That's from the 1926 song 'Tamiami Trail' on the Victor label. You have a vinyl copy in the museum."

"We know."

Serge turned and grinned wide. "I see . . . a guest book! . . ."

A Crown Vic crossed the bridge to Everglades City.

"Where should we start?" asked White.

Mahoney cut a deck of cards. "The museum."

Chapter Thirty-six

EVERGLADES CITY

A Crown Vic sat in front of a small museum.

Agent White approached the desk with a mug shot. Before he could get an answer:

"Just hoofed."

White turned and saw Mahoney with the guest book. "Let me see that . . ."

" 'Serge A. Storms, Tampa, FL. Gift-shop blitz: See attached comments.' "

White looked at the museum employee. "What are these tiny holes?"

"Said he was in a hurry." She held up typed pages. "And stapled these to the comment section."

"Let me see." He began reading. "Printouts from his website . . . and complaints to Congress?"

"He also left this," said the museum clerk. "To add to our product line."

Lowe squinted. "What happened to Derek Jeter?"

MEANWHILE . . .

"Another windy day in the Ten Thousand Islands. The number is not hyperbole. Many have become hopelessly lost in the maze of mangroves stretching from Marco Island below Naples all the way under the state to Florida Bay and Cape Sable. Not a few of the lost were law enforcement officers chasing locals running bales of pot—affectionately known as 'square grouper'—in shallow-drafting skiffs.

"The locals never got lost.

"But that was almost thirty years ago. The end came at 5:17 A.M. on the morning of July seventh, 1983, when two hundred federal agents blockaded Highway 29 and stormed the town in a massive dragnet.

"The *Miami Herald* dubbed Everglades City 'the town that dope built.' But today's another story and a cleaned-up community image. Nature lovers kayak down a well-marked route through the islands, sometimes pitching tents on elevated platforms in the water called chickees—at least until the first time they see a fourteen-foot gator lounging on top of one. There's a tiny airstrip on the south end of town with whispered ties to the contraband—and which now draws private planes of the ultra-rich who fly in just for lunch at the 'Stone Crab Capital of America.' But rumors still circulate about PVC pipes crammed with hundred-dollar bills that were buried under freshly poured concrete driveways to wait out the statute of limitations . . ."

"Serge," Coleman said from the passenger seat. "Talking to yourself."

"No I wasn't."

Coleman shrugged. "Don't make no difference here. You just asked me to tell you when you were doing it, so I did."

Serge turned around. "Mikey, was I talking?"

Mikey nodded, furiously jiggling the disconnected door handle.

"What was I saying?" Serge asked Coleman.

"The only part I caught was 'dope.'"

"That's right. We're in the most fugitive-rich part of the state, a national reputation as outlaw country and the perfect garnish for my Web presence. It's important to be relevant. I personally don't think so, but when store clerks ask me, 'How am I doing?' and I say I don't understand the appeal of that Sham-Wow guy or TV ads for medicine with a side effect of increased urges to gamble, well, that's the reaction I get . . . There goes the airport on the right. And here comes the famous Oyster House restaurant and observation tower, which means we're leaving Everglades City."

"I thought that's where we were staying in Everglades City."

"We are, but there's one more stop at the end of the line that's the most remote of all . . ." A '69 Barracuda headed across a long, winding causeway. Airboats zipped by, aggravating a flats skiff of fly casters. "Next stop: Chokoloskee, hanging off the bottom of Florida like a dingleberry. Before they built this causeway, it was an even more isolated frontier town, surrounded by water and built on another ancient Indian shell mound . . . I have to check in with Ben."

The Barracuda could go no farther. Because Florida didn't. Serge reached the southern shore of Chokoloskee at a bay by the same name and parked on a bed of pine needles.

Car doors opened. A stout breeze off the water cut into the ninety-eight-degree afternoon. Mikey pulled them toward the only structure in sight, a long wooden building atop sturdy stilts. Painted a dark, burnt red. The back deck overhung the water.

"What is this place?" asked Coleman.

"The beginning of time." Serge snapped a photo of a historical plaque. "Smallwood Store, named after Ted Smallwood, who built it in 1906. Indians would come in canoes to trade furs, and conch shells were blown to signal mailbags arriving by boat from Forts Myers."

"It's still standing?"

"Hard to believe since this location is total hurricane fodder, but the pioneers could teach today's developers a thing or two. Operated continuously until 1982, now a museum."

They went up the steps and through a patched screen door.

Oak barrels. Lanterns and kitchen pots hung from cluttered rafters. A Pan Am calendar over the postal window was frozen on July 1955.

"Ben!"

A man looked up from a newspaper. "Serge! We can't keep you out of this place, can we?"

"I'm required to stop in."

"Are we going to have to get a restraining order?"

"It's happened before."

"So whatcha been up to?"

"I'm on the run."

Mikey strained at the end of the leash for something large and breakable. Serge yanked the chain.

Ben leaned over the counter. "Who's the little guy?"

"My son."

"Life caught up with you?"

"Wife caught up with me."

"So what brings you around?"

"Need info. How's the Loop Road?"

"You're not seriously going out there."

"Might come to that. Capone's spirit is strong. Never seen his old place, or the Gator Hook. I know only the foundations are left, but . . ." He raised his camera and grinned.

"Don't shine me," said Ben. "You're chasing the myth."

"Never believed that garbage."

"A lot of people do. They've been digging all over the place out there for years."

"What's the word on the road?"

"Heard park service filled gaps from the wet season with marl. It's passable, but who knows how long?" said Ben. "Serge, I wouldn't go. I *live* here, and no place scares me like the Loop. I'm not ever going back."

"What happened?"

"Nothing. Just the hair on the back of your neck." He shook with the creeps. "This feeling that someone's watching you, like *Deliverance*."

"My favorite comedy," said Serge. "But it can't be that bad."

"Serge, everyone who lives around here has a story. Half the time it's just warning shots from the unseen woods. Other times, faces briefly appear in the brush, then dart off in a rustle of branches, like *The Hills Have Eyes*."

"Another great comedy," said Serge. "Speaking of movies, I brought you a present. Here . . ."

"A DVD?"

"Bootleg off the Internet from 1958: *Wind Across the Everglades*. Dubbed a second disc for you."

"Whoa! I've wanted this for years but could never find a copy."

"You'll love every minute. Way-ahead-of-its-time conservation movie filmed on location starring Burl Ives. It's set at the turn of the century when poachers decimated the glades bird population for their plumes, because chicks on Park Avenue used to wear those screwed-up hats. There's even a cameo by real-life swamp legend Totch Brown."

"Totch is in it?"

"But here's the part where you're going to crap: This Audubon guy takes the train down to Miami to fight the poachers. But because it was filmed in the fifties, Miami looked much different, so Everglades City was its stand-in."

"You're kidding."

"That's *still* not the best part," said Serge. "The guy checks into a hotel, and it's this place! I recognized it immediately from the way your counter slopes back underneath to accommodate hoop skirts, and the notches along the top for measuring pelts."

Serge pointed toward the watery view out the store's open back door. "Can you tell me where the spot is?"

"You ask every time, and I tell you every time."

"Because I have to get it exact for the record."

Coleman tipped over a jar and set it back up. "Didn't break. I'm not responsible . . . What spot?"

"The killing spot," said Serge. "On the beach next to this store. A fugitive named Edgar Watson was under suspicion for several murders, so he came down here and claimed a spread on Chatham Bend. Then more murders around here. Finally, Watson bought some bullets in this very store, saying he was going to kill someone else, and the town finally had enough. Practically everyone turned out to mow him down on the shore."

"It's all in the Peter Matthiessen books," said Ben. "Okay, twelve paces west from the third palm tree."

"Thanks! . . . Mikey! You'll love this!" They ran for the door. "We have to find a stick that looks like a rifle! . . ."

"Oh, Serge." Ben held up the DVD. "Don't know how to thank you."

"How 'bout you never saw me?"

―――――――

Chunky clouds blew in from Miami, casting patches of shade across the open panorama of the swamp. A few in the distance had dark shafts of rain angling down at palm hammocks.

A Crown Vic circled the few streets of Everglades City, where five hundred people live on a square mile of island. Past city hall and the sportsman's club, a grocery, fishing guide office, airboat ticket stand, up and down the neighborhood lanes of Copeland, Hibiscus, Gardenia. Small, tin-roofed homes and whitewashed bungalows with bent aluminum awnings dotted largely empty residential blocks that never had quite taken. Original palm trees ran high along roads like lamp-posts.

"Just missed him at the museum," said White. "How far could he have gone?"

"Maybe he left and went back," said Lowe.

"Nega-tory," said Mahoney in the backseat, making a cat's cradle with a yo-yo. "Serge is close, real close. Bumpin' brass tacks."

They swung east onto School Drive, winding along the docks at the edge of the Collier River. Stacks of encrusted crab traps and faded Styrofoam buoys, Johnson's Seafood, Island Seafood, City Seafood, Camellia Street Grill (seafood), back past the convenience store that sold three-pound bags of stone crabs for twenty dollars. Lowe looked out the rear window at their unshakable company of vehicles. The motorcade was long enough, and the city small enough, that as the detectives finished another surveillance loop, they almost caught up with the last vehicle following them.

"That's about all we can do for now," said White. "Three rounds. Covered every street in Everglades City."

"In Everglades City," said Mahoney.

"What's that supposed to mean?"

Mahoney's yo-yo walked the dog. "Chokoloskee."

"Choko-what?"

"I see it on the map," said Lowe. "Even smaller place, this little teardrop island below here down a dead-end causeway."

"With a museum," said Mahoney.

"There's a *second* museum?" said White. "Why didn't you tell me?"

He hit the gas and headed south.

Chapter Thirty-seven

CHOKOLOSKEE

"Shoot me!" said Serge.

Mikey and Coleman aimed sticks.

"Bang! Bang!"

"Arg!" Serge grabbed his heart and collapsed on the beach.

He jumped up. "Shoot me again! . . ."

On the other side of the Smallwood Store, a caravan led by a Crown Vic parked under pine trees.

Three agents ran up steps.

Ben smiled as the screen door creaked.

White rushed toward him with a mug shot. "This guy been in here."

Ben leaned and faked non-registration. "Nope, never seen him. Who is he?"

"Name's Serge. Take another look. It's very important, tant."

The other agents wandered the store for clues.

Lowe was overcome by how old everything was. To Mahoney, it was contemporary. He nodded at the 1955 Pan Am calendar. "The future."

"*. . . Shoot me! Shoot me again! . . .*"

"*Bang! Bang!*"

White turned from the counter. "What's all that yelling?"

"I'll check," said Lowe, walking out the rear door to the deck over the bay. He got an obscured view through the trees. "Nothing. Just some guy playing cowboys and Indians with his kid on the beach." He came back inside, and the three agents huddled.

"What do you suggest now?" asked White.

Mahoney picked up a jar of gum balls. "Serge ain't flashed marbles on the trifecta trip."

"And the translation?"

"Probably on his way here, so we should hang tight."

"Okay, you were on with the other museum," said White. "So we'll wait."

They walked around, entranced in the time capsule, even White.

"Mahoney," said Lowe. "I've been meaning to ask: Why do you talk like you do?"

"Dancing gums to slant the flimflam grease-lick jackaloo."

"That's what I thought . . ."

Outside, Mikey strained on his leash all the way back to their car.

"Another excellent re-enactment," said Serge.

Coleman opened the passenger door. "Look at all these other vehicles."

"History's catching on." Serge started the engine and grabbed his iPod. "Fugitive tunes!"

Whitecaps slammed the side of the causeway as the Barracuda sped north.

". . . *Go on, take the money and run!* . . ."

They reached the bottom of Everglades City and skidded into a parking lot.

"We're going to eat at the Oyster House?" asked Coleman.

"No, climb the observation tower." Serge pointed up at what looked like an old forestry service fire-watch platform. "I must climb all observation towers for the total picture."

Serge and Mikey reached the top. Coleman took a bit longer.

"Look at the bay! And Ten Thousand Islands! And the Everglades! . . ." Serge slowly pirouetted with his camera, taking another set of overlapping shots. ". . . And Chokoloskee! And the airstrip! And the big convoy of vehicles coming down the causeway! *I want to fly like an eagle!* . . ."

"What's up with all those cars?" asked Coleman.

Serge continued turning. *Click, click, click.* "The blackwalls on the sedan up front mean it's G-men, which means they're probably after some bad dude." *Click, click, click.* "Reminds me of Operation Everglades in 1983, when they arrested half the town."

"Reminds me of Orlando last week," said Coleman. "When they arrested Snapper-Head Willie."

The convoy passed and Serge lowered his camera. "I have the big picture. Now we can hit the bar."

"Bar?" said Coleman. He was the first down from the tower.

They walked next door to the convenience store. Motorcycles and pickups and an old Fleetwood. The store also served as a bait shop, liquor outlet and motel office for the nearby nest of cedar fishing cottages. On the south end of the building sat a large, open room. It was under the same roof but only screened in.

Serge opened the door, and Coleman ran for a stool. "Whiskey! Double."

"Bottle of water." Serge looked down. "Mikey, what would you like?"

The child pointed.

"Red Bull it is."

Jack Daniel's arrived. "What a cool bar," said Coleman.

"One of the coolest," said Serge. "The Rock Bottom—absolutely screams Everglades and lawlessness. The screens make it. Keeping out mosquitoes but letting in a bayou breeze. And I love the crusty regulars!"

Crusty regulars turned.

Serge spun on his stool and sat with his back to the bar, reliving fond memories from the interior: jukebox, pirate flag, ceiling fans, a single pool table under beer lamps, and an arcade game with a real punching bag.

Coleman waved for another bourbon and read signs behind the bar: CASH ONLY, LIVE COUNTRY BAND SATURDAY, PIT BULL PUPPIES FOR SALE and a warning that it's a federal crime to mess with someone else's crab traps. Where you'd expect a sink were two green buckets hand-labeled BLEACH WATER and RINSE WATER.

Mikey ran in circles and bit the chain.

"Think he needs to burn off some of that Storms family energy," said Serge. "Come on, Mikey!"

He led the boy across the bar, hoisted him up at the waist and let him go to town on the punching bag.

"Die! Die! Die you bastard! . . ."

"Mikey!" said Serge. "Where did you learn to talk like that?"

"It's what Mommy says when she stabs your pictures with knives."

The sun faded behind the mangroves. Neon flickered at the Captain's Table motel and the Seafood Depot. The Crown Vic returned from a run to the Tamiami, where White had checked in at the sheriff's substation, but no leads.

"Better find a place for the night." They rolled up to a large wooden building with yellow-striped canvas awnings.

White rang the bell at a reception desk with a mechanical cash register and antique rifles over mail slots. The cast from the rest of the vehicles formed a line behind him.

"What an old place," said Lowe. "And dark. Look at all the mahogany."

"It's the Rod and Gun Club," said White, filling out a registration card. "Built in the 1800s."

Mahoney and Lowe strolled the lobby, staring at walls covered with game trophies. Deer, hogs, pompano, cobia, barracuda, gator hides, turtle shells.

White held up a key. "Guys, let's go. We got another big day." He headed for the front door.

Lowe pointed back at the staircase. "Aren't we going up there? That's where the rooms are."

"No, got a cottage," said White. "They don't let anyone stay in the main building anymore."

"Why not?"

"Too historically valuable and too wooden. One forgotten cigarette, and the whole place goes up like a tinderbox."

They reached a cottage with an egret on the door and went inside.

Three detectives stared at two beds.

"Where's the sleeper sofa?" asked Lowe.

White opened his suitcase on a chair. "I love this job."

Night fell and Rock Bottom rocked. Music, dancing, spilled drinks.

"Serge," said Coleman. "Check it out! Naked babes!"

Serge came over, and they looked up at a roof beam with a row of framed black-and-white photos. Women posing in the swamp.

Serge covered Mikey's eyes. "I recognize these pictures. You can't mistake the style."

"Yeah, they're naked," said Coleman.

"No, I mean I know the photographer." Serge walked to the end of the row and the final picture: a husky, bearded man straddling a motorcycle, dressed all in black and topped with a black cowboy hat. The ultimate outlaw.

"I knew it!" said Serge. "This guy has hot babes from all over the world come down and pay him to photograph them nude out in the Everglades. He's Lucky."

"I should say so."

"No, that's his name, Lucky. Lucky Cole. And here's a phone number . . ." Serge went to the bar for a scrap of paper. "I need to get back in touch."

"He's a friend of yours?"

Serge nodded and headed with Mikey for the door.

"Where are you going?"

"We need to find a place to stay."

"But the sun just went down a minute ago. And I'm still drinking."

"You don't want to get stuck out here without a room." The screen door slammed behind them.

Coleman chugged. "Wait for me!"

Serge pulled into the parking lot.

"Look at all the cars," said Coleman.

"That's why I said we needed to get a room." He went inside and rang a bell. The manager appeared.

"Vacancy?"

"One cottage left." He grabbed a key off a hook.

"Man, this place is freakin' old!" said Coleman. "And dark!"

"It's the Rod and Gun," said Serge, filling out the registration card. "Teddy Roosevelt stayed here. And Nixon, so it's a wash."

Mikey led them across a lawn and up the steps of a cottage with a heron on the door. They went into the room as another door opened.

Three state agents stepped outside and stretched under a full sky of stars.

"This isn't half bad," said White, getting out a crick in his neck. "I could lose a lot of stress out here."

"I'm hungry," said Lowe.

White spotted a tiny neon sign up the street and began walking. "Let's get some fish at that depot place."

Back in the heron cottage: Serge unpacked socks and gadgets. Coleman lined up liquor miniatures atop the dresser. "Let's go out. I saw a tiki bar at the depot."

"Other plans."

"What other plans? It's only eight o'clock." Coleman unscrewed three bottles. "And we're out in the middle of nowhere."

"We have to hole up for website research." Serge ran cables from his laptop to the TV. "Let's watch *The Fugitive*. I got the complete first season boxed set."

"Serge!"

"Just one episode. Then maybe we'll do something."

"Okay, but only one." Coleman reluctantly sat on the edge of the bed next to Serge. "What are we watching?"

Serge enthusiastically rubbed his palms together. "Renegades on the road from town to town is a uniquely American TV genre. *Branded, Maverick, Kung Fu,*

Then Came Bronson, Route 66, The A-Team. But of all of them, *The Fugitive* is the only one that ever came to the Sunshine State: Episode 29, 'Storm Center,' first aired April fourteenth, 1964 . . ." Serge started the DVD.

"What happens in the series?"

"Same as my life. I come to a town, act nice to people, they're not nice back. Except Dr. Kimble doesn't visit hardware stores before leaving."

Coleman pointed at the TV. "There's a hurricane. He's holed up in Florida."

"Just like us! Isn't it great?" said Serge. "Mikey, another Red Bull?"

Wind howled, Kimble's double-crossed, a mystery revealed, the fugitive escapes. *"A Quinn-Martin Production."*

"That was pretty cool," said Coleman.

"And deeper than people think," said Serge. "Kimble is tracked doggedly by Lieutenant Gerard, who was patterned after the deliberately similar-sounding Inspector Javert from *Les Misérables.* Unlike other TV shows, Kimble and Gerard are complex characters who develop a mutual respect, to the point where Kimble saves Gerard's life a few times, and at other times the lieutenant intentionally lets the good doctor slip away."

"Kind of reminds me of someone."

"Me, too," said Serge. "But I just can't quite remember who . . . What's that sound?"

"Mikey's scratching at the door."

Serge stood. "Looks like I need to take him for a walk."

"I'll get my joint and miniatures."

Up the street, only a few bites of catfish left. Agent White threw his napkin on the plate. "I'm stuffed."

"Same here," said Lowe, tossing in his own napkin.

Mahoney didn't say anything. He had finished first and was reading a thick, dog-eared paperback.

"*Les Misérables?*" said White. "I didn't know you were into Hugo."

Mahoney turned a page. "Inspector Javert's aces."

White smiled and looked out the window into the dark street. "I notice a resemblance . . ."

Coming up the dark street: Coleman tossed a glowing roach in a puddle. "Mikey's really pulling hard."

"I think he has to pee," said Serge. "There's a place up ahead."

"The seafood restaurant?" Coleman uncapped a miniature. "Aren't the restrooms for customers only?"

"Most of the time," said Serge. "But who's heartless enough to deny a father with a boy on a chain."

They walked through the restaurant's waiting area and into the men's room as three detectives came around the corner for the register. "I got this," said White, pulling out a state-expense credit card.

Lowe stared at the giant, stuffed gator by the lobby bar. Mahoney grabbed a handful of toothpicks— "Need to squirt"—and headed into the men's room. He addressed a urinal, whistling the theme from *The Fugitive*.

In the closed stall behind him, Serge looked up with faint recognition at the tune, then shook his head and continued helping Mikey with his jammed zipper.

In the next stall. "Whoops, a little trouble here . . ." *Crash.*

Serge looked down at Coleman's face lying on the tiles under the stall's partition. "What the hell are you doing?"

"Gravity got me again." He pushed himself up.

Mahoney smirked as he finished his business. "Juicers." He rejoined the others in the lobby and headed back up the street for their cottage.

Two minutes later, the restaurant's door opened again. Serge, Coleman and Mikey began walking toward the Road and Gun. Far ahead: three silhouettes on the dim road.

Serge squinted at what looked like the outline of a fedora. "Naw, couldn't be."

Chapter Thirty-eight

2:59 A.M.

Everyone asleep at the Rod and Gun. Almost.

Detective Mahoney was a night owl. He sat up in bed reading Dashiell Hammett.

Next to him on the nightstand was a small transistor radio. In the wee hours, when there was less broadcast competition across the dial—and if weather conditions were perfect—he could pick up an atmospheric bounce from a powerful jazz signal out of New Orleans. It was an oldies station, playing nothing later than 1949. Vintage commercials continued the theme: Bromo-Seltzer, Barbasol, "Call for Philip Morris!" It was meant to make people reminisce about the past.

Mahoney was in the present. He turned a page . . .

Another cottage. Dark, silent.

3:00 A.M.

Beep! Beep! Beep! Beep! Beep! . . .

"What the fuck is that?" Serge threw off the sheets and hit a light switch.

Coleman sat up rubbing his eyes. "What's going on?"

Beep! Beep! Beep! Beep! Beep! . . .

Serge ran around the bed and smashed the Off button. "Forgot to unplug the clock. Some asshole set our alarm as a prank."

"Oh, that was me."

"Idiot!" said Serge. "If you're gong to be a jerk, at least wait till checkout."

"I got confused."

"Thanks. Now I'm totally awake." He slipped on shorts and sneakers.

"Where are you going?"

"For a walk." He opened the door with a heron.

At the other end of the Rod and Gun, Mahoney wore a red-and-white-striped nightcap. Cotton in his ears. Lowe snored. It was hard to miss the noise since they were crammed together in the same tiny bed. Agent White had pulled rank and gotten the other to himself.

But now Lowe's mouth was wide open, snoring like a buffalo. First Lowe had ruined Mahoney's radio listening, and now he couldn't even read. He traded in his nightcap for the fedora and decided to take a walk . . .

Serge strolled along the dock behind the club's main building. In the darkness, a small fish splashed, which meant a bigger fish behind it. Serge didn't see it because a rare Everglades fog had rolled in from Okeechobee.

Serge loved night fog.

He came around the back of the club and strolled up the street to the town circle. The few lights that were on cast a haunting glow, especially the blinking red one atop the radio tower. Fog thickened. Not a soul.

Serge was content.

He turned around at the old train depot and started back to the Rod and Gun . . .

Mahoney stood on the dock behind his cottage and struck a wooden match to see what was splashing in the water. Fog too dense. He blew it out and continued along the bank. Mahoney loved night fog because it put him in old movies, especially the climactic final confrontation with a nemesis. He formed a sinister smile, running classic flicks through his head as he came around the front of the Rod and Gun. *Farewell My Lovely, Notorious, The Big Sleep.*

On the other side of the club's grounds, a foggy shadow appeared, walking back to the cottages from the town circle.

Mahoney smiled wider to himself in the broken solitude. The other night figure completed the detective's movie fantasy: his adversary, squaring off for the big showdown . . .

Serge noticed the other night stroller. He stopped. So did the second man. Then the distant apparition tipped his hat toward Serge. Serge returned the salutation with a slight nod. The other man went back in his cottage, and Serge returned to his.

He closed the heron door and stretched with a yawn. He slipped back into sweatpants and under the covers.

He turned off the light and shut his eyes.

Silent and dark.

The light came back on.

Serge leaped from the bed. "Everyone up! Coleman! Mikey!"

Coleman lifted a groggy head. "Huh? What?"

Serge shook his shoulders. "We have to split! Now!"

Coleman sat the rest of the way up in bed, watching Serge throw stuff in his backpack. "What's going on?"

Serge snatched his toiletry bag. "Mahoney's here!"

"Mahoney? Are you sure?"

"Definitely." Serge zipped a compartment shut. "Just saw him outside. Took a few minutes for it to click because of the fog."

Coleman crawled out of bed. "Did he recognize you?"

"Don't think so. Maybe. Who knows?" He grabbed Mikey and hoisted the backpack. "But I'm not taking any chances."

"I thought you said nobody was after us—that we were just pretending to be on the run."

"Dreams come true." Serge opened the door and looked around. Coast is clear. He looked back. "Be super quiet and tiptoe to the car . . ."

Coleman stumbled over the threshold and crashed on the porch. A light came on somewhere. A tourist peeked out curtains. Dogs barked.

Serge dashed down the steps. "Run! . . ."

Coleman knocked over a garbage can.

Mahoney sat up in bed and turned on a lamp. What's all that racket?

He went to the window. A trunk slammed, then car doors.

"White! Lowe! Wake up!"

"What's with you?" said Lowe. "It's the middle of the night."

"I saw Serge!"

"Where?" said White, throwing his legs over the side.

"Right out there! He's getting away!"

"Have you been drinking?"

"No, I was copping a walk and got a visual."

"And you let him go?"

"Too much fog. Didn't register till just now when I glommed out the window." Mahoney grabbed his gun and hat. "Some number in another cottage blazed a porch light, and I nailed his mush hopping wheels."

White ran to the window. Red taillights from a Barracuda skirted the roundabout at the radio tower. High beams formed twin tubes of glowing fog that stretched fifty yards. The Barracuda made a skidding left at the depot and gunned it for the Tamiami Trail.

"Shit!" White jumped in his shoes.

The agents ran for the Crown Vic. More doors slammed.

Lights now came on in all the other cottages.

People poured out and scrambled for vehicles. Mayhem. They backed up, spun and jumped curbs to avoid crashing into each other and be the first to reach the driveway out of the club . . .

One mile ahead, Coleman faced backward in his seat.

"Anything?" said Serge.

"Just dark."

"Keep watching." Serge eyed the speedometer needle, wiggling at ninety. "I don't think our departure went unnoticed. Saw a lot of lights come on back there when we passed the depot."

"Still dark," said Coleman.

Ahead, a flashing traffic light.

"There's the Tamiami." Serge hit the brakes and watched the needle dip to forty-five.

"Why are you slowing down?"

"Sheriff's substation around the corner. Usually has a cruiser lying in wait for speeders."

"How do you know?"

"Everyone should keep a logbook like me."

Serge came to a full, slow stop at the light, then turned east and kept it under the limit. They passed the nose of a cruiser with parking lights on and a deputy sitting still.

"You were right," said Coleman.

Serge leaned over the wheel. "Now I just have to wait for a bend where the trees will put us out of radar . . . Here we go . . ."

The Barracuda made a sweeping turn, and Serge hit the gas. He opened his cell phone.

"Who are you calling?"

"Shhhh! It's ringing . . . Hello? Lucky?"

"Who the hell is this?"

"Serge! Your old pal! Bet you're thrilled to hear from me!"

"What time is it? . . . It's after three! In the morning!"

"Too early?" said Serge.

"You disappear for years! No contact whatsoever. Then out of nowhere you call in the dead of night and I'm supposed to celebrate?"

"I kind of have to ask a favor."

"Already figured that. What have you gotten yourself into this time?"

"I need you to open the gate . . ."

"And then close it real fast. I know the routine."

"Thanks."

"Damn it, Serge, it's good to hear your voice. But next time let's plan in advance for a cookout or something. During the day!"

"I swear."

"Don't, because it ain't gonna happen. Just call when you're near. I'll be waiting by the road . . ."

Two minutes back, a Crown Vic raced toward a flashing red light at the Tamiami junction. White pressed harder on the pedal. "Mahoney, which way would Serge go?"

"East."

"Is that left or right?"

"Right."

The Crown Vic made a skidding turn without stopping and accelerated toward Miami.

In the darkness, a deputy watched them blow by at ninety and lit up his rack.

Mahoney turned around. "Got local company."

"Lowe," said White. "Put on the bubble and let him know we're cops. And I'll see if we're indeed going the right way. " He grabbed the radio mike. "Collier sheriff, this is Agent White from the FDLE . . ."

A small, domed blue light began strobing from the Crown Vic's dash.

"This is Collier sheriff. . ."

"We're attempting a felony stop. Seen anyone come by?"

"Barracuda."

"How long?"

"Two minutes." The deputy noticed a string of headlights gaining on him from behind. *"You have friends?"*

White looked in his rearview. "Explain later. Can you get a roadblock?"

"Affirmative. I'll radio Miami-Dade—and the tribal police in case he tries to duck down Shark Valley."

They raced through Ochopee . . .

Ahead: "Still dark," said Coleman.

"How's Mikey?"

"Flicking my ears."

"Where is it?" said Serge, hunched over the wheel. "Come *onnnnnnn!*"

"What are you looking for?"

"There!"

Coleman saw a weather-beaten two-story clapboard building with boarded-up windows. "What is that place?"

"Monroe Station. Travelers' oasis back in the forties. Gas pumps long gone." Serge cut the wheel hard right. "It marks the beginning of the road."

The Barracuda barreled toward where no road seemed to be.

Coleman covered his eyes. "We're going to crash in those trees."

"No, we're not." Serge hit the high beams and a small gap appeared at the edge of the woods. "Watch your heads. It's going to get rough."

Into nothingness they went.

The Barracuda bounced wildly on the washboard dirt surface. Branches scraped both sides of the car as tires left the ground.

Serge constantly jerked the steering wheel back and forth to avoid crater-size potholes. "Anything?"

"Still dark," said Coleman. "Just lost a hubcap . . . How does anyone pass the other way on a road this narrow?"

Serge splashed through a washed-out patch of mud. "That's a problem . . ."

Behind on the Tamiami, a Crown Vic sped east.

Mahoney looked out the window at a broken-down building. "Stop! Pronto!"

White hit the brakes. The trailing deputy swung out into the oncoming lane to avoid a rear-ender.

"What is it?" asked White. "See Serge?"

"No, Monroe Station."

"You made me almost wreck for that?"

"Marks the beginning of the Loop Road."

"What's the Loop?"

Mahoney delayed his answer. He looked ahead up at the Tamiami, then south toward a small, desolate opening into the swamp. Decision time. "Sixty-forty Serge took the Loop. Hang a rico."

White knew there was no cushion for small talk. He stomped the gas, slinging through the gravel parking lot of the former filling station.

The radio crackled. It was the deputy. *"You not taking the Loop?"*

"Playing the odds." White accelerated and aimed his car at a tiny hole punched into the edge of the swamp.

The radio again: *"You sure you want to go down the Loop? At night?"*

"What's the matter?" asked White.

"I know some of the most fearless cops who won't . . . I mean, maybe I should go with you."

"No," said White. "I need you to keep heading up the Tamiami in case we're wrong."

"Ten-four."

The deputy accelerated east, and the Crown Vic disappeared . . .

Chapter Thirty-nine

THE LOOP ROAD

An electric blue Barracuda crashed through more branches and went high on a bank in a tight bend.

Serge snaked through the swamp as fast as he could, which was about thirty. Then over occasional creek bridges that seemed barely engineered for foot traffic. Wood storks and cranes and vultures flew off in the headlights.

They rode out the bone-jarring run in silence. A sharp right below the Monroe County line put them on a straightaway. A tight alley of trees perfectly lined up with a crescent moon rising from the east.

A half hour in, Coleman grabbed his queasy stomach. "How far do we have to go?"

"About twenty miles."

Another hubcap sailed.

"How far have we gone?"

"Eighteen . . . Alligator!" Serge slammed the brakes with both feet.

Coleman and Mikey watched breathlessly as the gator took its time, its nose into the brush on one side of the road before its tail had finished clearing the other.

Serge hit the gas.

"Lights," said Coleman.

"What?"

"I see some lights back there. A car's coming."

Serge swerved again. "Actual bulbs or just the ends of the beams?"

"Just beams hitting some branches way back there."

"Probably hasn't seen our taillights yet." He looked in the rearview. The beams behind him began straightening out, slowly swinging toward the rear of the Barracuda. "Damn!" Serge looked ahead. Still a good fifty yards to the next bend. He floored it.

The front wheels took flight, then violently slammed down, popping the back end up . . . They cleared the bend, just as the headlights behind them lit up the trees.

"I hate to do this," said Serge.

"Do what?" said Coleman.

Serge punched out his own lights.

"Jesus!" yelled Coleman. "I can't see anything. How can you drive?"

Serge sideswiped a cypress. "I'm using the moon."

"Will you be able to see if there's another gator?"

"No."

A hard left, then right, another left, another brief airborne adventure. Serge hit redial on his cell and cut left again. "Lucky? We're almost home. It's going to be tight—got someone crawling up my ass . . ."

"Gate's open. How far?"

"Couple hundred yards."

"I don't see your lights."

"Had to cut them."

"You what!"

Coleman tried holding his stomach down. "Lights back there again."

Serge, into the cell: "Almost there. But I can't see your place. Where are you?"

"I hear your engine. Get ready . . ."

"Don't see anything."

"You got company. Lights . . ."

"Still don't see anything."

"You'll have to trust me and turn blind," said Lucky. "I'll time it with the sound of your car . . ."

"Everyone hang on!" yelled Serge.

Lucky: "Three . . . two . . . one . . . turn!"

Serge cut the wheel, barely missing the left side of a solid, eight-foot-tall wooden stockade fence. But he was inside. Both feet on the brakes, the Barracuda sliding sideways. Behind them, bright lights and another engine sound.

An unseen man swung the gate shut. Then he hit the ground. They all held their breaths as the Crown Vic slowed. A search beam sent slits of light through fence panels, hitting bushes concealing the Barracuda.

The Vic sped back up. Everyone remained still inside the fence until the other vehicle's sound finally dissolved into a quiet rustling of trees.

Exhales.

Car doors opened. Serge got the customary bear hug that raised him off the ground. "You crazy bastard!"

"Good to see you, too, Lucky. You can put me down now."

"Who've you got with you?"

"Throwing up in your yard is my backup man, Coleman."

Lucky smiled. "Bumpy ride?"

"Yeah, but he does that anyway, so there's no baseline."

Coleman came over. "Sorry about the puke. Can I see nude women?"

Something darted behind them through the darkness. Lucky's head swung to the side. "What the hell was that?"

"Shit." Serge took off in a sprint. "Forgot the leash."

Lucky stepped next to Coleman, watching Serge's silhouette zigzag off into the night. "Did Serge bring some kind of wild animal in here with him?"

"Yes," said Coleman.

Two forms eventually returned across the lawn: One tall, the other . . .

"A child?" said Lucky.

"My son," said Serge. He looked down. "Meet Uncle Lucky."

"Well, hello, little fella . . . Ow!" Lucky rubbed his shin.

Serge jerked the end of the leash. "Just found out."

The left side of Lucky's mouth curled into a grin. "Wondering when you'd get to meet Mikey."

"What do you mean— . . . Wait, I didn't tell you his name."

"Molly, right?"

Another surprised look. "How do *you* know Molly?"

"Remember the old joke," said Lucky. " 'Have any naked pictures of your wife?' "

"Right," said Serge. "And the guy answers, 'No.' "

"And the punch line," said Lucky. " 'Want some?' "

Serge smacked himself in the forehead. "Don't tell me." Then a knowing smile. "You always had an eye for redheads."

A deep laugh. "That I do." He simultaneously slapped Serge and Coleman hard on the backs. "Why don't we go up and sit on the porch."

Chapter Forty

FIVE A.M.

The Tamiami Trail looked like some kind of chain-reaction traffic pileup, or hazardous materials disaster.

Scores of flashing red and blue lights. Countless police jurisdictions. Cars parked every which way at Forty Mile Bend.

Highway flares.

The command post.

All the brass were on the scene, poring over the same map spread across the hood of a Crown Vic. Agent White stretched his arms, touching a pair of spots on opposite sides. "Can we get a couple more roadblocks at each end of the Tamiami?"

"Shouldn't be a problem," said a Collier sergeant. "We'll put out a press release diverting incoming traffic to Alligator Alley. But I suggest moving the western checkpoint over here so we don't have to cover 29 . . ."

". . . Then it's down to just a few back roads into the swamp that have no way out," said a lieutenant from Miami-Dade. "We can get a chopper up at dawn and send prowler cars in for the sweep."

"Appreciate it," said White.

"One question," asked the lieutenant, looking up the road at a bunch of vehicles waiting on the side of the highway. "Who are all those people?"

White sighed. "Apparently this case has attracted a lot of attention."

In the background, Agent Mahoney stood next to a junior officer. "Brass knuckles?"

"No thanks."

THE LOOP ROAD

"Can I borrow a flashlight?" asked Coleman.

"What for?" said Serge, sitting in peaceful darkness.

Coleman walked around the porch. "He's got all these framed pictures of babes on the wall. But I can't see them too good."

"One on that table," said Lucky. "Knock yourself out."

The beam slowly moved over the photos. "Got a question," said Coleman. "How come the guys in that police car didn't knock on the gate or break it in. It's one of the first places we could have pulled off the road."

"But not the last," said Serge.

"It's the Loop," said Lucky. "Always been outlaw country. I remember back in the seventies, there were all these really bad guys—warrants, killers, anything—burrowed deep off the logging roads just east of here. The cops knew, but they didn't *want to know*, if you get my drift."

"It's calmed down since," said Serge. "Still, there's a handful of privacy fences like Lucky's, and some spooky driveways with KEEP OUT! and GO AWAY! signs."

"And they mean it," said Lucky.

Serge looked at the sky. "Starting to get light."

Lucky rubbed his knees and stood. "Better put that car under cover before the helicopters."

They drove the Barracuda under some trees and threw netting over it. Then a layer of branches and leaves. "That should do it," said Lucky.

Serge looked east. "Sun's coming up."

"Let me show you around . . ."

The growing daylight revealed the extent of Lucky Cole's private compound, the residue of decades of personality: several small wooden buildings and sheds and mobile homes with more makeshift wooden structures growing off the side. A screened Quonset hut for a pet goose and another with a prize apiary. Near the gate was a doghouse with a sign, VERY DEAD DOG, and what appeared to be such inside. A shack covered with license plates. A pole with arrows—NEW YORK, KEY WEST, CUBA. In the back, the shooting range, deluxe outhouse, open-air shower and, just beyond a small seawall holding off the swamp, a bathtub on a stilt platform out in the water, next to another sign, DO NOT FEED ALLIGATORS.

"I use the tub for model shoots," said Lucky. "Shower, too."

"This is my dream house," said Serge. "Like Citizen Kane's Xanadu, except the opposite." He looked toward one of the screened barns. "How are the hives?"

"Busy as ever. I'll get you a jar."

"Coleman," said Serge. "Lucky here makes some of the sweetest Florida honey you ever had. From his own secret strain of cross-bred bees."

"They do all the work," said Lucky. "I just get the credit."

"Did you see the Victor Nuñez film *Ulee's Gold*, shot up in Wewahitchka? Van Morrison sings 'Tupelo Honey' over the end titles."

"Possibly the greatest beekeeping movie of all time."

"Possibly the only," said Serge. "And Florida has it!"

"I have to pee," said Coleman.

"There's the outhouse," said Lucky. "Don't forget to sign the guest book."

Serge watched Coleman waddle off, then turned. "Listen, Lucky . . ."

"Here we go, another favor. What this time?"

"Why do you always think I'm going to ask a favor?"

"Because you always do."

"I do not."

Lucky folded his arms. "So what is it?"

"I need a favor."

"Fire away."

"I've got this Master Plan unfolding . . ." And Serge laid it out.

Lucky whistled. "That's a pretty big favor."

"Will you do it?"

"How can I ever say no to you?"

"Because I'll keep bugging you night and day?"

"Exactly," said Lucky. "But it sounds like we'll need help to pull it off."

"Know anyone? . . ."

Coleman finished his business and ran back to Serge. "You should see that outhouse!"

"I have, full of antiques."

"No, I mean more pictures of chicks all over the walls."

The photographer laughed again. "My passion."

Coleman stood in reverence. "You are the luckiest man alive."

"That's how I feel."

"It's like all my favorite magazines—"

"Coleman," said Serge. "It's *not* like your magazines. Those are skanky. You have to respect Lucky's art. He tastefully captures the female form in this exquisite natural setting, like Everglades versions of Lady Godiva . . ."

They heard a fast-approaching motorized whapping sound.

"Helicopter," said Lucky. "We should go back on the porch."

They climbed steps. Lucky took the stool in the corner. Pointy leather boots, black pants, black tropical shirt with palm trees, trademark black cowboy hat, trimmed white beard and clear blue eyes. Lucky always enjoyed the porch's effect on Serge, and now in daylight, he had the full dose, slowly walking around in the zone. Old cast-iron potbelly stove, old railroad safe, rack of antique rifles and shotguns, vintage Coca-Cola icebox, carved totem pole, female mannequin in sunglasses, kerosene lamps and on and on. And of course the photos, which is why Mikey's eyes were covered. The ones on the porch were somewhat clothed. Scant, but clothed.

"The mannequin's a redhead," said Lucky.

"I picked up on that," said Serge. He reached another wall, pulled up short and looked over at his host. "Molly?"

"She's quite a dish when she takes that librarian's bun down." Another smile. "What can I say?"

Serge returned to the wall. "This one's Molly, too. And this one. And this—. . . The whole row's Molly."

"One of my regulars who comes back every year, same time. You can set your calendar by her."

"They're getting younger," said Serge, moving along the wall. "This one's how she looked when we got married. And these are earlier." He turned around again. "How long have you known her?"

"Count the pictures."

"Fifteen years?"

"Sounds about right."

"Whew!" Serge stopped and rubbed his forehead. "Life's full of surprises."

"You have no idea."

"What's *that* mean?"

"Just idle chatter," said Lucky.

Serge reached the front of the porch. "You put up a menu board?"

"Sometimes I open the gate on weekends, set a sign by the street and open the 'store.' You should see the scared looks on faces as they slowly drive in."

"But who comes down the Loop Road?"

"Mainly bird-watchers who haven't heard the warnings. They shoot photos back up at Sweetwater Strand."

"I missed that in the dark."

"It's the Everglades. I've got the only trading post for miles in both directions."

Serge read the board: cigars, beer, ice, soda, hot showers ($7.50), motor oil, gas, aviation fuel . . .

"Get over here," said Lucky. He handed out three plastic spoons and unscrewed a mason jar that filtered a pure amber light. "Latest batch. Tell me what you think . . ."

They licked honey off spoons like lollipops. "Delish!" said Serge. "Your best yet! Flirtatious woody bouquet, daring balance, uncomplicated yet bellicose."

Coleman took the spoon out of his mouth. "Good."

Serge turned toward the front gate. "Do you think maybe . . ."

"Was wondering when you'd ask. The old places, right?"

Serge nodded.

"Then let's get in the truck."

TAMIAMI TRAIL

Monroe Station.

A half-dozen sheriff's cruisers and a Crown Vic sat in the gravel lot. Their occupants stood by fenders, comparing notes. Another map on the hood.

"Anything?" asked White.

A sergeant shook his head. "We covered all the back roads. I'm sending some boys again, but I wouldn't get my hopes up."

"Think he got away?"

"Not a chance with the roadblocks."

"Then where could he be?" asked White.

"I've seen this before," said the sergeant. "There are all kinds of trails and hermit camps. Someone could hold out for months, especially if he has local help."

"What do you suggest?"

The sergeant leaned over the hood and ran a finger along the map. "If I were you, I'd put all my chips between here and Forty Mile. Apply the pressure until he pops out. Airboats, infrared, search parties on foot checking even the smallest shack."

"Thanks," said White, turning. "Mahoney?"

Mahoney was staring at the narrow passage through the trees.

White looked with him. "That expression tells me you think he's still out there on the Loop Road."

A matchstick wiggled in teeth. "Bones."

"I'm not ready to go back in there." White arched his spine. "Back still hurts from last night. Why don't you take the Vic and I'll ride with the sheriffs."

"You're jake."

"Get out of here."

Mahoney jumped in the Ford . . .

Chapter Forty-one

THE LOOP ROAD

Lucky's truck headed west, bouncing through standing water. He was on his cell.

"Who are you calling?" asked Serge.

"Neighbors. Anyone will tell you not to stop on the Loop and poke around."

"But you live here."

"That's why I'm calling. I know this place. Don't want to be mistaken for a trespasser."

"Folks ask questions later?"

"That's the Loop."

The pickup continued vibrating down the uneven road.

"You do realize it's gone," said Lucky. "Just an over-grown foundation left."

"I'm all about over-grown foundations."

They drove another mile and stopped where there was nothing.

"Let's do it," said Lucky.

"I hear a car coming the other way," said Serge. "Better pull a little bit more off the shoulder."

They got out and crashed through thick vegetation, disappearing from the side of the road.

A Crown Vic drove by.

It was tough going on foot. No path, not even breaks in the trees, just dense swamp growth that had to be attacked and high-stepped. Something unseen splashed into nearby water.

"What was that?" asked Coleman.

"Better you not know."

Coleman stopped and unpocketed a flask with a shaking hand.

They hit a clearing. "Come on," Serge called back. "The foundation's waiting! . . . See? Mikey's not scared."

The chain leash was slack; Mikey walked up ahead holding Uncle Lucky's hand.

"There it is," said the big man.

"Cool!" Serge ran up and down the front steps, over and over, then walked to the approximate area of the dance floor that was now weeds. "Was the Gator Hook as rough as they said?"

"Rougher. First time I came here as a teenager, this real nasty dude was drinking by the door . . ." Lucky walked to a spot of dirt in front of Serge and looked down. ". . . He stops me and says, 'Son, you got a knife or gun on you?' And I'm shaking and say, 'No, sir,' and he says, 'Better get one.' I flew out of there. Took me a while to work up the nerve to come back, but once you got familiar with the place, it was like home. I remember the contests shooting dynamite."

"Dynamite?" said Coleman.

"Famous Saturday-night tradition," said Serge. "They'd stick dynamite up in a tree and shoot at it from the back porch. I was there once with my granddad—"

A loud sound above.

They looked up at the heavy covering of cypress and heard a helicopter swoop overhead.

"Are they going to do that all day?" said Serge.

"Must want you pretty bad."

"Some people can't let things go." Up and down the steps . . .

A few miles east, a Crown Vic sat still, just past Lucky's place up at an old gas station. Signs said it was established in 1920 and was currently closed because the owner had gone fishing, probably since 1975. Thick grass around twin rusty pumps said nobody had pulled up in a spell. Mahoney knew the turf, one of Florida's authentic ghost towns—still said *Pinecrest* on the maps, but might as well have been a misprint. It was a big logging community back in the twenties, before the Depression—and the hurricane of '47. Now just a handful of privacy types dug deep into the backcountry, and those tombstone gas pumps to mark the demise. Next door were a few limestone blocks in a circle where a fishpond had been.

Mahoney shook his head. Something not right. He started the car again and turned around . . .

Serge marched up and down the steps. "You knew Ervin Rouse?"

"Too well," said Lucky. "Lived just up the road from here. Even forty years later, he was still getting decent royalties for 'The Orange Blossom Special,' especially after Johnny Cash recorded it. Big check every three months, and Ervin would buy a new Cadillac, which of course he tore to pieces in no time on the Loop, and he blew the rest at the Gator Hook, where he'd drive each weekend to play, and by the end of the three months, he was walking to the Hook and running a tab. Then another check arrived."

"I heard he wrote it after watching the pride of the Pennsylvania Railroad pull into Jacksonville one night on its New York–Miami run," said Serge. "Finest bluegrass song of the twentieth century."

"That's the story," said Lucky. "A cantankerous son of a gun. If you annoyed him in the Gator Hook, he'd smack you in the head with his fiddle . . ."

They heard a car approach back at the road. As it was about to go by, the sound stopped. A door slammed. Then a crashing noise in the brush.

"Damn." Serge began retreating into the swamp. "How did they find me?"

The bustle in the hedgerow came closer until it was just about to break through the clearing. Serge stood ankle-deep in water, ready to bolt and take his chances with the wildlife. "Lucky, can you watch Mikey for me until I get back?"

"You're a scream," said Lucky. "No need to go anywhere."

"But someone's coming!"

"I brought a special guest."

The last branches parted and a younger man stepped into the clearing.

"*Charles?*"

"Serge!"

"I don't believe what I'm seeing."

Another big, backslapping hug.

"Man, Serge, when you want to make yourself scarce." Charles looked around at the steps and a few other broken pieces of foundation. "When Lucky called, I couldn't miss the chance to see you again."

"And the old place?"

"Bittersweet."

"Coleman! Mikey! I'd like you to meet Charles Knight. His father, Jack, owned the Gator Hook."

"He had to make a rule because of Serge," said Charles. "No children allowed to shoot at dynamite."

"Too dangerous?" asked Coleman.

Charles shook his head. "Winning all the beer."

Serge grinned. "I gave it away to the gang."

Charles turned to Lucky. "So what's this mysterious business you mentioned."

"Didn't want to say over the phone," said Lucky. "Serge and I need your help with a problem."

"What kind of problem?"

They filled him in.

Charles whistled. "That's some problem."

Lucky began walking back to the road. "Let's go scope out the place . . ."

A pickup pulled to the side of the road.

"The old gas pumps." Serge clicked a picture.

Lucky opened his door. "Welcome to Pinecrest."

They walked along the street, then turned through some weeds until they were standing before a circle of limestone blocks.

"The fishpond and those other stones are about all that's left," said Lucky. "Hard to imagine today, way out here in the boondocks, but what a scene this was eighty years ago."

Serge got down on his knees and rubbed the blocks. "Capone's old place. I never would have found it without you."

"Guess you'll want to take some pictures like usual," said Lucky.

"Just a couple."

"Couple hundred."

Everyone else waited back at the truck until Serge finished his photographic safari.

He returned with his camera. "I need to crash. Long night with the chase and everything—and what we have ahead. Plus Mikey's yawning."

"Me, too," said Coleman.

"Take my trailer," said Lucky.

They drove back to the compound. Fifty yards past the gate sat a yellow DeVille.

"Expecting anyone?" asked Lucky.

"It's that guy again," said Serge.

"Cop?"

Serge shook his head. "He's the mystery man."

As they approached, the DeVille turned around in the road and sped away.

Lucky drove through the gate. They went to the main trailer, and soon three people were dead asleep with their shoes on.

Chapter Forty-two

LUCKY'S PLACE

A helicopter whapped over the compound.

Serge sprang up in bed and ran to the window. The chopper kept going toward Miami. He looked around the inside of Lucky's trailer. Coleman and Mikey were still down for the count. Serge crept outside. "Lucky? . . ." He circled the outhouse and shower. "Lucky? . . ."

He came back around. "Luck—" He stopped. Up the driveway, the gate was open a crack. Lucky never left the gate open unless he was holding court on the porch. And nobody on the porch. This wasn't good. Serge tiptoed across the yard. He reached the gate and peeked through the opening. Still no Lucky.

Serge slowly pushed it open a foot and winced at the creaking of hinges. He poked his head outside.

"What the—"

Even from behind, it was a sight. Smack-dab in the middle of the Loop Road: legs in a wide stance, a statuesque redhead wearing nothing but ruby cowboy boots and a gunfighter's belt with a pair of .45-caliber Peacemaker revolvers on her hips. And just beyond was Lucky, crouched low behind a tripod, clicking away with a large-format Hasselblad camera.

Lucky stood. "Serge, you're awake."

The woman turned around.

"Serge," said Lucky, walking toward them. "I'd like you to meet Cynthia, my afternoon appointment."

The woman made no attempt to cover anything. "Hey there, Serge. You're kinda cute."

Lucky noticed Serge's eyes shift to the right. He turned around and saw a black Beemer slowly pull up and park on the side of the road fifty yards away.

"Cynthia," said Lucky. "We better go back inside and finish at the tub . . ."

They headed toward the porch.

Serge whispered. "It's time."

"Now?" said Lucky, glancing toward Cynthia climbing the tub's ladder.

"Everything set?"

"Final details wrapping up as we speak," said Lucky. "I set it in motion while you dozed."

"I'll go wake Coleman." Serge headed back to the trailer. "Can you babysit Mikey for me?"

Five minutes later, Lucky waved from the driveway, and Cynthia waved from the bathtub. A pickup truck rolled out of the compound.

Serge turned east. He looked in the rearview. A black Beemer started up and began following. Serge hit the gas and raced around a corner. At each bend, another glance in the mirrors. Beemer far behind but picking up speed.

A final turn. Serge saw the old Pinecrest gas pumps up the road. And a parked car.

"Look," said Coleman. "Someone's coming out of the woods . . . I recognize him."

"Charles Knight," said Serge. "Right on schedule."

Knight got in his car and drove off. Serge pulled up and parked in the just-vacated spot. They got out wearing rubber boots. "Don't look back," said Serge. "A Beemer should be just arriving . . ."

Coleman pointed. "There it is!"

"Thanks. Let's go."

They slipped through some trees and walked across a grassy clearing. Serge passed the remains of a fish-pond, then climbed the steps of the old Capone place. He reached the back of the foundation where the porch had been, leading Coleman down a slight, moist embankment.

Into the swamp.

The dry season had just ended. Water returning. Shallow at first . . .

Coleman's head kept swinging back and forth at every sound. "I'm getting the creeps again."

"Just stay close to me."

"What's that you're looking at?"

"A map." Serge held out his other hand: "And a GPS."

Clouds rolled in, adding to the already increasing darkness of the unchecked growth.

Serge pushed through branches and negotiated roots. Water bugs danced in puddles. The terrain sloped lower. Boots splashed. A python slithered down a trunk into the mud. Dragonflies and wasps. Coleman swatted in front of his face and bumped into Serge.

"Not that close."

"I hear something behind us."

"I know."

Reeds and more roots. An inch or two of water was now above their ankles. Serge tracked the changing digital number on his handheld unit. "Back up a few feet."

"Why?"

"We need to watch our step from here on. You can be walking along forever in shallow swamp, then suddenly go down over your head in a ten-foot gator hole."

"Gator hole!"

"If I go under, just stop where you are. I'll be right back. I can get out easily, but if we go in together, it'll be too interesting."

More splashes. A cottonmouth wiggled away in the water. Getting darker. Tree frogs, tree snails, algae, lily pads. A soft-shelled turtle on a rotting log.

Coleman looked back. "Serge, the sound's getting closer."

"Good." The ground sloped up. The GPS said another twenty feet. Serge trudged through saw grass to a small dry hammock of land with a cluster of hardwoods. He checked the number on the small screen and stopped.

So did the sound behind them.

Serge looked at his feet. "Here we are."

"Where?"

Serge squatted down and brushed away leaves and twigs. He began digging. But not for long. Six inches down, fingertips hit a flat surface. He ran his hands across the top until he found the edges of a large rectangle, then dug a trench around the sides. "Coleman, I need your help. There's a handle on that end."

"What is it?"

"Just lift."

Out it came. Coleman wiped his hands on his shirt. "Heavier than it looks."

Serge crouched in front of the old steamer trunk. He flipped a pair of latches. "It's unlocked. We're in luck."

"Luck just ran out!"

They turned around.

Someone with the wrong shoes for the job splashed toward them. Pointing a gun. "Step away from the trunk."

"Let me guess," said Serge. "You drive a Beemer."

"Smart guy." He waved them aside with the pistol. "But I'm smarter. I knew you'd lead me right to it."

"Serge," said Coleman, trembling. "Is he going to kill us?"

"Kill you?" The man walked sideways toward the trunk, keeping the gun aimed. "Don't be ridiculous. I'm a respectable attorney."

"Brad Meltzer," said Serge.

"So you know."

"I know you swindled my grandfather's old gang."

A devious smile. "Those were legitimate billable hours. But I deserved more. They knew about this chest but played dumb . . ." The smile dissolved to red-faced anger. "They owed me a cut! After all those years! Keeping them out of jail, setting up their measly estates! Now

I get it all!" He bent down in front of the steamer and took a deep breath. "No, I don't have to kill you because who are you going to tell? You got a million warrants and every cop in south Florida after you. If you're real nice, I'll give you a head start before I call a tip line that you were at Lucky's place." He reached for the latches.

"I wouldn't do that if I were you," said Serge.

"Oh, you wouldn't?"

"This was all a setup to get you out here," said Serge.

"You're only saying that now because I'm holding the gun."

"Think about it," said Serge. "Those letters. The confidential one you opened that mentioned me finding the map in my late grandfather's possessions. Bank account numbers and instructions to deposit. There never was a map."

"Really?" said Brad. "And yet you led me right to this old chest. I suppose that's an illusion, too."

Serge raised his palms. "People always think I'm lying when I'm telling the God's honest truth."

"Shut up!" said Brad, reaching again for the latches. "No more talk!"

Serge shook his head. "I wouldn't open that."

"I'm not you."

Serge whispered sideways to Coleman. "Start backing up . . ."

Chapter Forty-three

BEHIND CAPONE'S

The attorney smiled again. "It's *Geraldo* time!" He flipped the latches and raised the lid . . .

. . . Which triggered a quick aerosol burst of spray in his face and chest.

"My eyes!" He dropped the gun and began wiping. As he did, little bumping sensations from his waist to the top of his head.

Serge winked at Coleman. "I attached a little booby-trap string." Then he turned back to Brad. "Don't worry. It's non-acidic, won't hurt your vision—in the long run."

Brad blinked in blurriness. "What is this shit?"

"Just attracts them—and makes them aggressive, courtesy of Lucky."

"Makes who—. . . Ow!" The first sting of pain. Then dozens came in waves. The lawyer's vision began clearing, and he found his head in the middle of a swarm of honeybees. "Jesus! Mother!" Arms flailing, running in circles. More stings. "Get them off me!"

"Serge," said Coleman. "What's to stop them from attacking us next?"

Serge watched calmly with folded arms. "One thing that calms them down is smoke."

Coleman lit a joint.

Brad ran screaming, straight into a tree. He fell on his back.

Serge cupped his hands around his mouth. "In the water! Roll around in the water! It's only a foot deep."

Brad dove and rolled.

"Snake!" said Serge.

"Ow!"

"The bees are flying away," said Coleman.

"Because they're not Africanized killer bees. They only swarm to protect the hive." Serge walked over to the steamer trunk, where a few stragglers buzzed around a beekeeper's honey tray. He closed the lid.

Coleman strolled up, puffing his joint rapidly for added protection. He looked at Brad, panting at the base of a tree, scratching his body. "So the stings are going to kill him?"

"No," said Serge. "Just make him unattractive."

"His face," said Coleman. "Yuck. It's all covered with bumps."

"But he probably *is* going to die."

"Cool!" said Coleman. "You brought one of your really complicated death contraptions?"

"Yes."

Coleman looked left and right. "Where is it?"

"All around us."

"I don't see anything."

"It's the Everglades."

"The swamp?"

Serge spread his arms. "The glades are an infinitely complicated mechanism of life far more elaborate that anything I could rig together." He knelt and looked in Brad's eyes, swelling to slits. "The stings won't kill him, but he's going to get a fever and become pretty disoriented." Serge looked up. "And this far from the road, with that kind of tree cover, compass directions will be tricky for a city boy . . ." He leaned over Brad. "Tried to warn you. But I forgot: You're so smart. Now do you believe it's all a bullshit myth?"

Brad started to sob.

Serge leaned closer. He reached behind his back and pulled a large brown legal envelope from his waistband. "I just have a few documents for you to sign."

"Th-th-then will you let me go?"

"Absolutely." Serge held out papers and pen. "Just scribble next to the little stick-on arrows."

"I can barely see."

"Let me help you." Serge stuck the pen in his hand and positioned it at the appropriate spots. ". . . And sign here, and here, initial here . . . you're doing great, just a few more pages . . . and here, and here, more initials, one last baby here, *annnnnnd*—we're done! Now, that wasn't so hard, was it?"

"I—I—I can go now?"

Serge leaned even closer. "Boo!"

"Ahhhh!" The attorney jumped up and took off running.

"Wrong way," Serge told Coleman. "See what I mean?"

"He just bounced off another tree."

Brad spun around. "Where are you? I'll make a deal. Someone bribed me to help them find you. I'll tell you who it is if you get me out of here!"

"Who?" said Serge.

"It was—. . . Ahhhhh!" Brad took off running again.

"Some of the bees didn't leave," said Coleman.

Serge leaned against a tree for viewing pleasure. "If I was a betting man, I'd say he'll soon become more familiar with the Everglades than most of us will ever get the chance."

"I was hoping for something with a lot of sharp, rotating blades."

"Because you just watched that *Saw* movie," said Serge. "This is the thinking man's contraption."

"I like blades."

Screaming trailed off to the south.

"Brad sure is a nervous type," said Serge. "That isn't good for his blood pressure."

"I can barely hear his yelling anymore."

The attorney disappeared into a thrashing of cattails.

"Show's over."

They left.

Behind them, Brad continued plunging forward toward what he thought was the way back. He used his fingers to keep his eyelids pried open. "Yeah, my car should be right up here . . ."

Onward: wildlife hooting and cawing. Snapping sounds, plunks in the water. Brad's head swiveled around, getting jumpy and feverish, tripping and hitting more trees as vision continued to diminish. Another step . . .

Down he went, water over his head.

Bubbles.

Brad broke the surface with a gasp for breath. "Gator hole!"

He went under again, just his hands flapping above the water.

Then up again. "Help!"

Before going down the third time, Brad found a grip on something hard and pulled himself up. He stood shin-deep next to where he had just been splashing.

Thinking: That's weird. Maybe it's not a gator hole after all.

He got on his knees and felt under the water. Rows of old, rotten wood planks. His hands probed farther and discovered the hole in the boards where his legs had broken through. He easily pulled up one of the snapped pieces with bent nails on the end. When he did, something floated to the surface. He grabbed it with his left hand and propped an eye open with his right. "Holy shit!" He frantically ripped up more planks and splashed with both arms. More and more hundred-dollar bills floated up. He couldn't see it, but none were dated later than 1929.

Then, reckless exuberance. Brad broke off the rest of the wood, removed his shoes and slipped down inside, legs first, feeling around with his feet.

Toes detected something. Brad's head went under the water, and he came back up with a small gold bar in his fist.

"Yes! I found it! I actually found it!"

Lucky's pickup returned to the compound off the Loop Road.

"God loves me!" said Coleman. "Check the ass on that naked chick in the road!"

A killer redhead in a six-shooter belt. Lucky on the other side with his camera.

"That's Cynthia," said Serge. He stopped the pickup at the end of the driveway and got out. "Hey Cynthia!"

She turned around.

Serge jumped back. "Molly!"

Molly drew the revolvers and aimed them at Serge.

Serge raise his arms. "I— . . . We— . . . What are you doing out here?"

Lucky smiled from behind. "Molly had an appointment next week, so I bumped it up. Thought it would be a nice surprise getting you two back together." He raised the camera and resumed shooting. "I'm a hopeless romantic. I'm sure you guys can work something out . . ."

Molly cocked the hammers on both pistols. "You bastard!"

Lucky slid sideways. *Click, click, click* . . . "Molly, excellent action shots. Keep it up . . . Serge, could you step left. You're in the frame."

Serge kept his arms up. "I don't think she wants me to move."

Another rugged laugh from the photographer. "She's playing around. Those are just prop guns. They're not loaded."

Molly pointed guns at the sky and began firing away like the Frito Bandito.

Lucky lowered his camera. "Molly, where'd you get the bullets?"

She didn't answer. Just leveled the pistols again.

Serge took a slow step forward. "But baby . . ."

"Don't 'but baby' me. And don't come any closer!"

Serge froze. "I thought everything was mellow. I'm taking care of Mikey for us. We're having loads of fun!"

"I'll bet! I knew what dropping him on you would do to your life." She cocked the hammers again. "Doesn't mean I haven't forgotten everything you did to me. It's payback time!"

"But that's what you told me back at the motel," said Serge. "I thought the payback was Mikey."

"Just an appetizer." She stretched out both arms. "This is the main course."

Serge looked over her shoulder. "Thanks, Lucky."

"I thought this would go a little better . . . Uh, Molly?"

"Shut up!"

"Sweetie," said Serge. "How about we get away? I'll take you to this nice secluded place, very special, like a second honeymoon."

"So I can watch Coleman throw up all weekend?"

"Coleman can't come with us?"

Her arms stiffened. "You'll never change."

"Okay, no Coleman," said Serge. "How's that for change? A place on the ocean, just us—what do you say?"

"Then you'll ditch me in the room and run all over God knows where taking a million pictures, collecting brochures and bursting in at midnight to stash stuff in the toilet tank and tell me that if the police ask, you were with me all day."

"That's not good either?"

She stepped forward with dead aim. "This is farewell."

Serge winced and poised like a soccer goalie before a penalty shot—ready to anticipate the trigger pull. But which way should he jump?

Molly put her thumbs on the hammers and carefully set them back in the safe position.

Serge's muscles uncoiled. He slowly lowered his arms. "You're not going to kill me?"

"Just wanted you to go through that. Not much fun, eh?" She expertly twirled both guns on her fingers and re-holstered them. "Now you know how I felt while we were living together and I was trying to keep a clean house."

"Staring down gun barrels? Using guest towels? Call me insensitive, but I think there's a slight difference."

"That's exactly what I'm talking about! Your needs were always more important!"

Serge tilted his head and raised an eyebrow.

"What are you doing?" asked Molly.

He raised his other. A dreamy gaze with those piercing ice-blue eyes.

"Stop that!"

"Stop what?" said Serge, smiling warmly.

"You know precisely what you're doing!"

"I do?"

"Oh, Serge!" She clomped up the road in cowboy boots and slammed into him. "Take me! Now!"

She ripped open his pants, and they fell entangled to the ground. Serge pulled his shorts to his knees and began thrusting like a Roman centurion.

"*Oh yes!*" shrieked Molly. "*Oh yes!*"

Serge closed his eyes and thrust harder. "*. . . Nu Bamboo, Cedar Key, Myakka River, Snook Haven . . .*"

"*Don't stop! Oh, my God! Don't stop!*"

"*. . . Sanibel, seashells, Smallwood Store, Gator Hook Lodge, the Loop . . .*"

"Jesus!" said Coleman, glancing up and down the street for cars, then looking at Lucky. "They're doing it right in the middle of the road!"

"Come on." Lucky slapped Coleman on the shoulder. "Let's go back inside the gate. I think they want their privacy."

Coleman drank Lucky's beer on the porch and looked at photos. "How'd you get her to pose like *that?*"

"She wanted to."

"And this one with the boa?"

"Paid me."

"You're my hero."

An exhausted, sweaty couple walked up the dirt driveway.

Lucky got off his stool and leaned against a porch post. "Well, if it isn't the two lovebirds. Didn't I say you could work things out?"

"Let's not rush," said Molly, taking off the gun belt. She found her cutoff denim shorts and a biker tank top in the corner of the porch.

"Coleman!" said Serge. "Don't look at my wife while she's getting dressed."

Molly zipped up her tight, high-riding shorts and accepted a cold one from Lucky. They all melted into chairs in the sticky, late-afternoon heat.

Back on the Loop Road, a car quietly pulled up and stopped, hidden behind the stockade fence . . .

Molly took a long pull on the chilly Budweiser. "Where's Mikey?"

"Still asleep in the trailer," said Lucky.

Serge jumped up. "Can't tell you how much fun we've had! Okay, I'll tell you! We went to the super-market—"

"Serge, you're not the father."

"And then the hamster ball—... What do you mean?"

"You're not his dad."

"Of course I'm his dad."

Molly shook her head. "Needed a break." She took another big sip. "You have no idea what's it's like being a single parent these days."

"But he's just like me," said Serge. "Are you sure there isn't some mistake?"

"Positive." Molly drained the rest of her longneck and stood. "Now I need to leave him with his real father."

"But we were bonding so well," said Serge. "He was almost ready to go without the chain."

"It's not fair to you," said Molly.

Lucky got off his stool. "I'll go wake him."

"No, let him sleep." Molly set her empty bottle on the edge of the potbelly stove.

Lucky stopped at the trailer's door. "But you just said you were going to take him to his real father."

"No, I said *leave* him."

"I don't understand."

Molly looked at Serge and Lucky. Serge looked at Lucky and Molly. Lucky looked at both.

Coleman opened another beer. "I never know what's going on."

Serge walked over and put an arm around Lucky's shoulders. "I think what's going on is we have a new winner."

"But . . ." said Lucky. "How is that possible?"

Molly pointed at the middle of a row of framed photos. "Remember that one? It was taken right after I split with Serge and needed to book out of the Keys because those cops had some funny ideas."

Lucky put a hand over his eyes. "But it was just one time."

"You're a marksman." Molly trotted down the porch steps.

"Wait!" yelled Lucky.

Molly hopped in her turquoise T-Bird—"I'll call"— and she sped off.

Chapter Forty-four

Serge helped an unsteady Lucky sit back down. "You know, I've seen a lot in my life, but this has been quite a full day."

Lucky was still shaken. "I don't know how to be a father. What do I do?"

"My advice?" said Serge. "Put on a helmet and get in the game."

From behind: "Freeze! Don't move!"

Serge twirled around. "Mahoney? What are you doing here?"

The agent slowly climbed the porch steps with a drawn .38 Police Special. "You're under arrest."

"Wow!" said Serge. "What a day!"

Mahoney pulled a pair of handcuffs from his pocket and tossed them to Serge. "You know the drill. Make with the bracelets."

"Let's make a deal instead," said Serge.

"No dice," said the agent. "You're cognizant of our rules. I bagged you fair and square."

Serge shrugged. "Can't blame a guy for trying." He opened the first cuff.

Mahoney felt something hard and cold in the middle of his back. And a high-pitched voice.

"Freeze! Drop the gun!"

Mahoney seized up, then did as he was told.

The voice again. "Crockett, Miami Vice."

Serge jumped up. "Mikey! Excellent student!" He grabbed the agent's gun off the porch and motioned for Mahoney to take a seat.

"How'd Mikey get out?" asked Coleman.

"Must have popped a screen like I taught him," said Serge. "Lucky, I'd like you to meet my longtime nemesis, Agent Mahoney . . . Mahoney, Lucky . . ."

"You won't get away with this," said the agent. "Before the drop, I rattled teeth at a pair of badges I've been tooling with." He looked at his Mickey Mouse watch. "Should be crashing this party in a dime."

"I don't think so." Serge took his own seat and rested the gun hand on his knee. "You forget how well we know each other. You'd never radio the other cops until I was in your sole custody, or else some backup officer might nab me in the confusion of the takedown and get your collar—"

A screech of brakes from the Loop Road; another car came flying through the gate, slinging dirt.

Serge stood and prepared to dive over a porch railing. "Or maybe I'm wrong."

"No," said Mahoney. "That's not my boys."

A yellow Cadillac stopped in front of the porch. A diminutive man in a badly fitting suit got out.

"Who *is* that guy?" said Coleman.

"The Mystery Man," said Serge. "I've seen him all down the coast. But who does he work for?"

Mahoney used the opportunity to dive and grab the gun back. "You're under arrest!"

"No fair," said Serge. "The clock wasn't running. We were in a time-out."

"There are no time-outs in our rules. I'm taking you downtown."

Serge rolled his eyes. "Whatever . . ."

The man slowly approached the porch. "Any dogs around?"

Lucky shook his head.

"May I?"

"Join the club."

The man climbed the steps and handed out business cards. "Mort Wrigley, Sunshine Detective Agency."

Lucky looked at the card and tossed it in a cigar box. "What's your business?"

Mort turned. "Serge? Mahoney?"

The pair glanced at each other, then at the detective.

"Yeah?" said Serge.

"Yap," said Mahoney.

Wrigley removed an envelope from his pocket. "I have something for you."

"Why here?" said Serge. "I've seen you all over the state. You could have handed it to me a hundred times."

The agent shook his head. "I'm under strict instructions from my employer only to deliver this when both of you were together."

"Together?" said Mahoney.

"Who's your employer?" said Serge.

"Roy."

"Roy?"

"The Pawn King."

"How do you know Roy the Pawn King?" asked Serge. "Wait, why does your name sound so familiar?"

"They also call me the Undertaker."

"Mort . . . *the Undertaker*?" said Serge. "From my granddad's old gang? But you're too young."

"Junior."

Mahoney leaned. "Is he really an undertaker?"

"No, his dad ran a delicatessen. Inside joke."

"I can't divulge certain client information," said Mort, unfolding a page from the envelope. "But Roy was very specific. And emphatic."

tter. "Let me see that thing."

visiting   way down the page, he looked

of sick joke?"

erious."

l neared the end of the letter.

ky. "You're white as a ghost."

ription   newhere between shock and awe.

He listlessly passed the letter to

Lucky   t and looked at Serge, then at the

on the level?"

your

d the letter back. "So you're saying

ed a

. "In   said Mort.

from   can that be so?" asked Serge.

om Riviera Beach, right? Born at the same

nodded.

your ages are a couple of years apart?"

y nodded again.

did a lot of digging to confirm it for Roy and the

g. Didn't want to come out here and be wrong."

'I'm still not convinced," said Serge. "How did Roy

find out?"

Lucky offered a bottle. "Cold one?"

"Thanks." Mort took a seat. "They were all Chi-Chi when Mabel Mahoney—"

"My mother?" said the agent.

"Adoptive mother."

"I was adopted?"

"What a day!" said Serge.

Mahoney got the jitters. He pulled a presc bottle from his pocket . . .

"Mahoney! No!" said Serge.

The agent gobbled a few tablets and flagged for one of those tall boys.

"Serge," said Mort. "You probably know that mother had . . . mental issues."

"You can go ahead and say it." Serge snatch bottle of water from the antique Coca-Cola chest my book that's a positive thing. Probably got it Sergio and passed it to me."

"And your father the jai alai player was quite tense, too," said Mort. "But he could read the v ing. Come home from practice at the fronton, Mahoney would be outside in his diapers, trying start the lawn mower. He made a hard choice for w was best."

Serge looked at Mahoney. "I don't remember brother. This must have been early."

"It was," said the private eye. "He's two years older . . . And your granddad Sergio didn't know about the adoption until it was too late. He hit the roof, but confidentiality laws prevented the state from telling him where Mahoney went."

"Unbelievable," said Serge. "And me?"

"Your dad didn't know it at the time, but your mom was already pregnant again, and Sergio made him swear not to do anything without talking to him first." Mort sipped the longneck. "Then your dad had that *accident* in the jai alai game . . ."

"Right, he died," said Serge. "I'm over it."

"Your granddad figured where you'd end up once the state got the picture about your mother, so he stepped in and got you."

"I know that part," said Serge. "But how did his adoptive mother—?"

"Confidentiality wasn't as strict back then the other way around," said Mort. "Your family didn't know her, but she knew them. In fact, you two lived only five streets apart."

"That would put him on Twenty-seventh," said Serge.

"From what I understand, Mabel struggled with the decision to say something for years. She was finally going to tell your granddad, but found out he'd already passed. After that, she tried like crazy to track you down . . ."

"Good luck," said Serge.

". . . Earlier this month, she figured the rest of your granddad's old gang was getting up in years, and it might be her last hope for contact. She talked to Roy. And he talked to me, but they didn't have any money because some slimy lawyer—"

Serge smiled. "Brad."

"You know him?" asked Mort.

"Used to."

Mahoney stuck another pill between his lips. "But what's with all the cloak-and-dagger? Just like Serge, I've seen you all over the place. Why did we have to be together for you to break the news?"

Mort laughed. "Roy told me all about you two. Not the brothers part. The whole *Mad* magazine 'Spy vs. Spy' routine you guys have. He figured if I approached either one of you ex parte . . ."

"That means alone," Serge told Mahoney.

"I know what it means."

". . . That you'd think it was a trick the other was playing."

Serge and Mahoney in unison: "We would."

"Roy knew that, and here I am."

"This is too weird," said Serge. "It sounds right, but . . ."

"Genetics don't lie," said Mort. "Let me ask you this: Over the years of knowing each other, have you noticed any minor similarities of personality or habit? The least little thing?"

Serge looked at Mahoney. "What about great big similarities?"

"Royal flush," said Mahoney. "We're bro-hams."

"Tell us more," Serge asked Mort. "What else did Mabel say to Roy?"

"As I mentioned, you only lived streets apart. She'd often drive by your house on Thirty-second . . . Oh, and there was a playground at the end of your street."

"I remember," said Serge. "Playgrounds rock!"

"Sometimes she'd see you there and let Mahoney out."

"We *played* together as kids?" said Serge.

"While she sat with your mom and chatted," said the private eye. "She was dying to tell, but with your mom's condition, she didn't know how it might go. People are always contesting adoptions later. She didn't want to lose her son."

"I remember you now," said Mahoney. "When I was up in the air on the teeter-totter, you jumped off and made me crash."

"That's what teeter-totters are for," said Serge. "But what's with hitting me with that mud ball coming down the slide?"

"Slides are for ambush. Everyone knows that."

"What a day!" said Serge.

"Guys." Lucky grabbed his camera and aimed. "What are you waiting for? Give each other a hug."

The pair stood and awkwardly appraised their counterpart. Then all defenses crumbled at once and they grabbed each other in a sentimental embrace.

"I have a brother!"

"Me, too!"

Click, click, click. Lucky set his camera down. "I love a happy ending."

"It's quite a story," said the detective. "Separated after birth, flip sides of the same coin. One brother a cop, the other an outlaw. Moral decision whether to arrest."

"I feel like I'm in a Bruce Springsteen song," said Serge.

"Oh my God!" said Mahoney.

"What is it?"

The agent jumped up. "I wasn't bluffing. We have to hurry. Follow me."

Serge and Coleman ran down the steps after him.

"Mahoney," yelled Serge. "What weren't you bluffing about?"

"Calling the other agents on the radio." Mahoney reached his Crown Vic. "They could be here any minute." He stuck a key in the rear hood. "I'm surprised they aren't already."

Serge stared. "You don't seriously think I'm getting in that trunk. I know what that leads to. Trust me."

"Trust *me*," said Mahoney. "I'm your brother. The only trunks they're not checking at the roadblocks are cops'. There's no other way I can get you out of here."

"Then what if I just *stay*?"

Mahoney shook his head. "You'll be trapped. As we speak, they're forming swamp search parties with airboats and infrared. They think you're still, well, roughly where you are."

A roar.

Serge looked toward the road and the high-rpm sound of cars racing up behind the stockade fence.

Split-second call.

Serge threw Coleman in the trunk and dove behind him. Mahoney slammed the lid as five sheriff's cruisers whipped up the drive.

Two state agents jumped out, accompanied by a full detail of deputy backups. Hands on holsters.

"Where is he?" said White.

"Sorry I wasted your time," said Mahoney. "Could have sworn, but it was a false lead."

"You sure? What was it?"

Coleman began bumping around. Serge: "Shhh-hhh!" Mahoney coughed and hit himself in the chest.

"You okay?" asked White.

"Just swallowed some saliva." Mahoney noticed the back end of an electric blue Barracuda sticking out from some trees—the one he and the others had glimpsed hightailing it out of Everglades City. He began coughing and pounding his chest again.

"You sure you're all right?"

He nodded. "Let's go on the porch and I'll explain . . ."

The other agents wandered around the deck, entranced by photos. The desired reaction.

". . . And that's about it," said Mahoney. "I was canvassing the neighbors from Pinecrest back to here, and Lucky thought he remembered seeing some people matching the description, but they turned out to be bird-watchers."

"Uh, yeah, right . . ." Agents moved to another wall of photos.

The sky darkened. Wind began to blow.

Mahoney pointed back at the car. "So I guess I'll be going."

"Hold up," said White. "We'll all take the Crown Vic."

"No!" Mahoney's arms flew out. "I mean, no, I need it. Couple other long-shot leads. Probably won't pan out, and I don't want to drag you around and waste any more of your time than I already have. You should ride back with the sheriff."

"Positive?" said White. "I know we've had our differences, but I'm very impressed by all the hours you've been putting in. Let me lateral those leads to a couple of the deputies."

"Absolutely not." Mahoney shook his head. "I just need to be thorough and eliminate some things."

"Good man," said White. "You—... wait, what's different?"

"What do you mean?"

"You're not talking goofy."

"I . . . took some medicine."

"Glad to hear it." White trotted down the steps toward the deputies. "False alarm. Let's roll."

Mahoney heaved a sigh of relief and wiped his brow. The sky grew darker, wind gusting harder.

"Lowe," yelled White. "I'll be right with you." He began walking back.

"What is it?" asked Mahoney.

"Just remembered. I left my briefcase in the trunk . . . Toss me the keys."

Mahoney's heart almost blew. He began feeling his pockets with feigned futility.

"You didn't lose the keys, did you?" said White.

Mahoney opened his mouth, and it stayed open.

Lowe began walking up. "I got a spare set. Here, catch!"

Mahoney's eyes went wide as the keys seemed to arc through the air in slow motion.

When they were at the highest point, another loud, fast-approaching sound.

Everyone looked back toward the Loop Road.

". . . I . . . want to rock-and-roll all night! . . ."

A gleaming chopper smashed the middle of the stockade fence and tore across the compound, followed by a camera crew that ran on foot through the Doberman-shaped hole in the wooden barrier.

The gusting wind made the Doberman's American flag cape flap dramatically behind him, then whipped it around his face.

Everyone watched as the bounty hunter screamed and drove in blind circles before finally crashing into the beekeeper's shack.

The camera crew ran by, filming the Doberman as bees chased him in more screaming circles before finally diving off the seawall into the swamp.

Mahoney used the chaos to run to the back of Crown Vic and pop the trunk with his own key. Serge handed him a briefcase—"What a day!"—and Mahoney slammed the hood shut.

Agent White stood still, observing the TV crew pulling the bounty hunter out of the water. "Unbelievable."

Mahoney dashed over. "Here's your briefcase."

"What? Oh, thanks."

The agents and deputies drove off.

Mahoney stayed behind and waved back at the porch. "Don't know how to thank—"

"Just get out of here!" yelled Lucky.

Mahoney jumped in the Crown Vic, pulled out of the driveway and raced off down the Loop Road.

Epilogue

U.S. HIGHWAY 1

A Crown Vic headed south from the Everglades and reached the bottom of Florida City. Which meant the bottom of civilization on the mainland.

Mahoney stopped at a fork. "Preference?"

"Take the Card Sound Bridge."

That meant a left, where the bulk of the tourists were veering right.

A half hour later, on the far side of the bridge to Key Largo, the Crown Vic sat outside an infamous ramshackle roadhouse.

Three men sat on adjoining stools.

"Alabama Jack's," said Mahoney. "I should have known."

Serge raised his bottle of water for a toast. Mahoney and Coleman raised beer and whiskey. "To brothers."

"And me, too," said Coleman.

Drinks touched.

From the breezy doorway. "Serge!"

He turned around. "Skid Marks! Bacon Strips!"

Two more stools.

Serge pulled out a large brown envelope. "It's all there."

"What's all there?"

"The solution to your problem."

Skid Marks opened the packet and flipped through powers of attorney and other stamped documents with every caveat that put Brad's entire offshore portfolio completely in their control. He looked up from the last page. "But how'd you get him to sign all this?"

"You don't want to know." Serge took another pull of water and gazed out over the sparkling mangrove bay. "Can't make you accessories after the fact."

"Really appreciate it," said Bacon Strips.

Serge tossed another packet on the bar. "That's a bonus."

The bikers opened it and read Brad Meltzer's just-revised last will and testament. Skid Marks looked up. "It leaves everything to our families."

"But 'will'?" said Bacon Strips. "Doesn't that mean we have to wait until he dies?"

Serge just smiled.

Skid Marks closed his eyes. "You're right. We don't want to know."

Serge took another cold sip and turned to Mahoney. "So what now?"

"I'm retired."

"Retired? You can't do that?"

"Conflict of interest."

"That would be me?" said Serge.

"You have your rules—I have mine." Mahoney idly peeled his beer label. "Took an oath. One I can no longer faithfully execute. All that's left is turn in the papers and give 'em back the car."

"Promise to stop taking those stupid meds?" said Serge. "We've got a lot of catching up to do, and I want to have fun!"

"Any ideas?"

"Enjoy fishing?" said Serge.

"Got a place in mind?"

"That I do."

Mahoney nodded. "Bogie Channel."

"I hear the bonefish are biting."

"Let's roll."

Mahoney threw cash on the bar, and they went back out to the Crown Vic.

Serge grabbed the handle on the passenger door. "Sorry about the teeter-totter."

"Just don't do it again."

THE LOOP ROAD

Splashing in the swamp.

A few hundred yards behind the old Capone place.

Greed was the hallmark of a Miami attorney named Brad Meltzer. Overruled all other human instincts. Eating, sleeping, survival.

With night on the way, and eyelids swollen big, Brad remained hard at work. The broken boards would be several feet underwater during the rest of the year, but right now they still remained in reach.

Brad dove down again and came up with fistfuls of soggy currency, which he carefully unfolded and added to the growing damp stacks at the base of a tree. Next to a small pyramid of gold bars.

He returned to the hole and jumped back in. Then up again with more wadded bills. Before he climbed out, another splashing sound to the north.

His head swung. "Who's there?"

A blurry form approached.

Brad pulled his right eyelid up.

"Oh, it's you. I was just about to call. I found Serge." No reply.

Brad climbed out of the underground wooden box. "I thought you'd be happy. You didn't actually think I'd steal your thousand dollars. I— . . . What's the gun for?"

Silence.

"Oh, I get it. You want a cut of *this*." He dumped more cash next to the tree. "I was going to tell you about that, too. It was a freak discovery—just happened. My cell phone got wet, but I was going to call as soon as I got out of here. I swear."

Nothing.

Brad's chest heaved. "Since we're practically partners now, it's only right you should get, say . . . twenty-five percent. No need thank me."

Quiet.

Brad bit his lip. "Okay, half."

Just crickets.

"Please, put the gun down," said Brad. "You're scaring me."

A drilling stare.

Desperation. He finally nodded to himself. "Fine. You can have it all."

The gun came closer.

Brad's hands went up. "Wait! No! Molly!"

Bang.

THE NEW LUXURY IN READING

We hope you enjoyed reading
our new, comfortable print size and found it
an experience you would like to repeat.

Well — you're in luck!

HarperLuxe offers the finest in fiction and
nonfiction books in this same larger print size and
paperback format. Light and easy to read, HarperLuxe
paperbacks are for book lovers who want to see
what they are reading without the strain.

For a full listing of titles and
new releases to come, please visit our website:

www.HarperLuxe.com

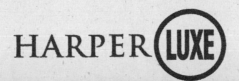